Shark attack!

Ben was suspended in a clear black void beneath a thick, murky ceiling of greenish brown—the underside of the surface layer through which he had just penetrated. Below his slow, pedaling fins, the lake looked bottomless. His entire world became his kick and his breathing.

Then something brushed hard against his legs. He righted himself and sensed something else near him. No mistaking that. It was something big, moving fast. And very close to him. He turned his light on it and the instantaneous glare revealed a seething mass of sharks behind him, around him, everywhere—big sharks with thick, bronze bodies and razor fins, knifing back and forth, all in a frenzy. . . .

SHARK LAKE

John McKinna

AN ONYX BOOK

ONYX
Published by New American Library, a division of
Penguin Putnam Inc., 375 Hudson Street,
New York, New York 10014, U.S.A.
Penguin Books Ltd, 27 Wrights Lane,
London W8 5TZ, England
Penguin Books Australia Ltd, Ringwood,
Victoria, Australia
Penguin Books Canada Ltd, 10 Alcorn Avenue,
Toronto, Ontario, Canada M4V 3B2
Penguin Books (N.Z.) Ltd, 182–190 Wairau Road,
Auckland 10, New Zealand

Penguin Books Ltd, Registered Offices:
Harmondsworth, Middlesex, England

First published by Onyx, an imprint of New American Library,
a division of Penguin Putnam Inc.

First Printing, September 2001
10 9 8 7 6 5 4 3 2 1

PUBLISHER'S NOTE
This is a work of fiction. Names, characters, places, and incidents either are
the product of the author's imagination or are used fictitiously, and any
resemblance to actual persons, living or dead, business establishments,
events, or locales is entirely coincidental.

For my wife, Teresa, as always.

PROLOGUE

He'd been here before.

Caught in the black embrace of a midnight sea.

The perpetual chill of the deep ocean sharp on the sliver of exposed skin between his wetsuit collar and the neck-dam of his heavy commercial dive helmet. Sediment and sea lice whirling out of the darkness, illuminated by the glare of his helmet-mounted light as he struggled forward, the taste of heliox breathing gas cold and metallic on his tongue.

Overhead and all around, a silent cathedral of ruined steel: massive tubular support members crumpled and twisted into fantastic shapes, extending off into the shadows at bizarre angles. The hurricane-wrecked oil platform now little more than another in a long line of rusting monuments to the sea's utter disregard for the works of man.

Ben paused, panting, as an eerie, grinding shriek echoed through the black water. Metal against metal—something heavy shifting somewhere, deep in the tangle of collapsed I-beams and support members. He could feel the vibration through the immense steel platform leg he'd been following.

The sound faded gradually, and he resumed mak-

ing his way into the center of the wreckage, hauling
the heavy cables of the burning torch behind him.
Looking back to check the lay of his dive hose, his helmet light illuminating the murky water behind him, he
caught the faint outline of a large shark drifting along
at the edge of visibility, some twenty feet away. It disappeared unhurriedly into the surrounding darkness.

Sand tiger, Ben thought. *Big, ugly, and harmless.* He
redoubled his efforts to pull the burning cables along
the collapsed platform leg. Another dozen yards and
he'd be at the well, on top of its sheared conductor
pipe. *At least*, he told himself, muscles straining, *I'd
rather think it's a sand tiger. . . .*

He reached up and twisted open the free-flow valve
on the front of his helmet, the sudden jet of gas from
the diffuser bar along the top edge of his faceplate
clearing the condensation from the glass. An involun-
tary shiver ran up his spine. It was cold on the bottom
tonight, even for the northern Gulf of Mexico at 310
feet in late November. And the fact that his body's core
temperature decreased with each exhalation of the
heat-conducting heliox mix he was breathing didn't
help matters.

Another grinding shriek indicated more shifting of
heavy steel somewhere in the darkness. The vibration
shook the fallen leg he was straddling and once again
he froze in place, looking around in every direction,
casting the pale glow of his helmet light over the tangled maze of broken pipes and beams surrounding
him. Whatever was moving, he couldn't see it. The
harsh sound died away.

He clawed his way forward another ten feet and got

his left glove on the edge of a gaping fracture, where the forty-eight-inch-diameter tubular steel leg had buckled and split like a beer can under the terrible force of the hurricane. Hauling up some slack in the burning cables, he looked down. According to the previous diver, the well and its collapsed conductor were fifteen feet directly below this leg break. He strained his eyes, but could see only empty black gloom beneath him, lightly dusted with sediment particles.

But the well had to be there. Pulling up another twenty feet of dive hose, holding the coils of burning cable in the crook of one elbow, he slipped off the platform leg and drifted rapidly downward, feetfirst, searching for the bottom.

The pale, tubular shape of a conductor pipe loomed up out of the darkness. Ben got a boot on it, but was too far to one side. He fell past the pipe another four feet, sinking to his knees in the cold muck of the seafloor. A cloud of mud billowed up around him, glowing a milky gray in the harsh glare of his light, and began to drift off sideways in the slight current.

He felt around the base of the conductor, orienting himself. The thirty-six-inch-diameter steel tube emerged from the mud at a steep angle for approximately five feet, at which point it had buckled completely and fallen like an axed tree. The greater part of its length stretched off horizontally along the bottom, through a jumble of broken support members, and vanished into the enveloping darkness.

"I'm on the well," Ben heard himself saying.

His ear speakers crackled with static. "Roger that," came the disembodied reply from the topside radio operator, sitting in the central dive shack of the oil-field work boat hundreds of feet above him. "Fifteen minutes of bottom time left. Get cuttin', Gannon."

"Stand by," Ben said. He drew an ultrathermic burning rod from the pouch on his hip and inserted it into the head of the oxyelectric underwater torch. Clamping the cutting rig's ground cable to a rusty pad-eye protruding from the side of the conductor, he flipped the darkened UV-protective eye shield hinged above his faceplate into the down position and squeezed the torch head's O_2 trigger, simultaneously scratching the rod tip against the conductor wall. "Make it hot."

In the dive shack far overhead, the radio operator closed a large knife switch with a high-voltage *snap*. The tip of Ben's burning rod ignited instantly in a sizzling blue-white flash, accompanied by a burst of smoky bubbles. Smoothly, rapidly, he began to cut through the inch-thick steel of the conductor, moving downward vertically in a straight line, the metal wall offering no more resistance than if it had been made of wax.

The idea was to burn out a two-foot-by-three-foot rectangular window in the outermost conductor pipe, then do the same with the four internal annuli, exposing each in turn. The fifth and narrowest pipe, in the exact center of the conductor assembly, was the downhole tube for the well. It was to be cut completely through in two places at least one foot apart, the section removed, and wire-line gear fed into it from the back deck of the work boat. Using a robotic tool on the end of the wire-line, the damaged well could then be sealed off permanently hundreds of feet below the seabed, preventing a possible uncontrolled eruption of oil and subsequent environmental disaster.

The two-foot-by-three-foot section of curved plate steel sagged slightly as Ben finished cutting out the first window. Draping the torch over his shoulder, he got his gloved fingers under the still-warm edges of the plate and heaved it out of the opening, letting it tumble into the soft mud at his feet. Wasting none of his precious remaining bottom time, he locked a fresh rod into the torch head and fired it up on the next annulus with a blast of O_2 gas.

The second window went more quickly than the first, the wall thickness of the inner pipe only half that of the external conductor. Ben pulled the burned plate out of the way, working fast, and reached inward to strike an arc on the next exposed annulus, his right arm inside the external conductor up to the shoulder.

Without warning, the first internal annulus slipped downward more than two feet, catching his biceps in a shearing pinch. The pain of it drove the breath from his lungs in a hoarse gasp. Instinctively, he yanked backward, which only served to saw the ragged, burned edges of the two windows deeper through the thick neoprene of his wetsuit and into his skin. The two huge pipes, one sliding inside the other, weighed tons. A downward slip of another six inches, and his right arm would be scissored off just below the armpit.

With a grinding metallic moan, the inner pipe shifted slightly. Ben yelled in agony. A bright red billow of his own blood erupted across his faceplate. *That's it*, he thought dimly, *the arm's going*. He could hear the frantic sounds of the topside crew shouting at him over the radio, shouting at each other . . . hear the distant roar of compressors and the whine of winches as his support team scrambled to jump the standby diver.

Too much pain. His brain began to overload, shut down.

"Hold on, Ben!" The radio operator's voice crackled in his ears. "Nick's comin' down! Hold on, boy!"

Nick, Ben thought dreamily. *Nick Fenzi's the standby. Good man, Nick . . .*

There was another eerie metallic shriek, which Ben Gannon recognized—with terrible calm and equally terrible certainty—as the sound of his right arm being sliced off.

Suffocating.

Smothering.

Darkness filled with flashing pinpricks of hot light . . .

Ben came clawing up out of the nightmare in a cold sweat, the drenched bedsheets twisted around his legs and hips, his chest heaving as he sucked in air in great, ragged gasps. Arms propped behind him, he let his head fall back and blinked thickly at the moonlight flooding in through the skylight above the berth.

Nick Fenzi's familiar dark, seamed, grizzly-bearded face was hanging in empty air, looking at him. Not smiling, not frowning—just looking down expectantly. Ben blinked again, letting his breathing slow and the panic ebb away. As it did, Nick's face seemed to do a slow fade, his expression never changing, until it disappeared completely into the shafting pale light of the quarter moon.

Beside him on the double sea berth, Sasha Wojeck stirred and rolled over, her long blond hair tangled and unruly, hiding her face. She made a little sighing sound before resuming the steady, rhythmic breathing of deep sleep. Ben looked down at her, her hand curled up against her hair and cheek like a little girl—and kept on looking. The sight of Sass made the pulsing echoes of the nightmare fade faster.

Whew.

Been years since he'd had *that* one.

He lay back against the pillow, breathing almost normally now, and raised his right arm. The ugly white scar encircling his biceps had faded considerably over the past fourteen years, but was still plainly visible against his workingman's tan. He ran the fingertips of his left hand along it. As usual, the scar tissue felt hard, knobbly, and insensate, as if it did not really belong on his body.

Sass was fond of pointing out, only half-jokingly, that the arm wound and the jagged keloid on his left shoulder blade—the result of an underwater blowback explosion—represented two of his nine lives as a commercial oil-field diver. Seven to go, buddy, she'd chide him. Ben rubbed his scarred upper arm and stared through the open skylight at the star-shot black heavens. After being caught in the deadly pincer grip of the conductor and annulus, the fact that he'd had even *one* life left to live had been due solely to the fast, sure actions of Nick Fenzi.

He tried not to think any more about it, tried to

close his eyes and go back to sleep, but it was pointless. The more he struggled to push the old images
from his mind, the faster his brain worked, until he
was bolt awake, lying beside Sass on damp sheets and
looking at the insides of his eyelids. The long-ago accident was going to replay itself in his head, in its entirety, and that was that.

Carefully, so as not to wake Sass, he slipped his legs
out of the sea berth one at a time and padded across
the gently rocking cabin sole to the companionway
ladder, clad only in his boxer shorts. The varnished
wooden steps creaked softly under his bare feet as he
climbed up and out into the steering cockpit.

A warm, light wind was breathing out of the vast
expanses of the Indian Ocean to the southeast, across
the Gulf of Aden, driving little rills across the midnight black water that lapped against the *Teresa Ann*'s
stout teak sides as she rode at anchor. Less than four
hundred yards off the starboard stern quarter of the
forty-four-foot bluewater sailing ketch, the lights and
cooking fires of the ancient city of Al-Mukkala glittered along the low, barren coast of Yemen. The smell
of burning dried camel dung and crisping goat meat
wafted in and out on the breeze. The desert tribesmen
would often stay up all night: talking, eating, and indulging in their favorite diversion—chewing *qat*.

A half mile farther to seaward, Ben could pick out
the lumpy black toadstool shape of the supertanker oil
transfer station he'd been contracted to help install, sil-
houetted against the luminous starlight glow emanating from the ocean's surface. Its navigation lights
winked on and off in lazy rhythm, warning away any

near-shore shipping traffic. Three more days of hard diving, flanging, and welding, and the job would be done, with a fat paycheck from AdenOil—the Arab conglomerate financing the installations in Yemen—waiting in the Al-Mukkala office.

Settling himself on the *Teresa Ann*'s hefty cockpit coaming, Ben stared down through the stainless-steel tubing of his vessel's safety rail and into the black water . . . past the shimmering surface pocked with the blurry reflections of stars . . . and far into the depths where he—and the relatively few men in the world like him—had spent a lifetime working. . . .

He had been nearly unconscious with pain and blood loss when Nick Fenzi reached him, the more senior diver taking less than a minute and a half to swim downward three hundred and ten feet, starting from the back deck of the work boat. His arm had seemed gone, nerveless, as if it was hanging from his shoulder by a mere thread of flesh or sinew. Slipping as he was into a bottomless black hole from which there would be no return, he knew; the most welcome sensation he'd ever felt in his life was Nick's big gloved hand on his shoulder, squeezing reassuringly.

Nick had taken a fast look at the situation, then rammed the short crowbar he was carrying across the cut annuli, jamming them so they couldn't slide any farther. Taking up the dropped torch, he'd struck an arc with a new burning rod and skillfully cut a semicircular divot out of the upper pipe, freeing Ben's arm. As they'd begun their rapid emergency ascent through the murky black water, Ben recalled, the tenders above reeling them in by their dive hoses, he'd been vaguely aware of Nick swatting with a chipping hammer at the ugly, ragged-toothed head of a huge sand tiger shark that had come sniffing in too close, drawn by the scent of fresh blood. With his other hand he'd locked onto the chest webbing of Ben's harness, keeping him near. As he'd said later, grinning wearily past a Marlboro Light, he hadn't gone to all that trouble to swim down and cut Ben free only to lose him on the way up.

Ben had been medevacked to an onshore hospital by helicopter, locked in a tiny portable decompression chamber with a pressure bandage bound around his arm. One hundred and fourteen stitches and two reconstructed tendons later (not to mention four months of lost work time), he'd been as good as new. Well, nearly.

He flexed his right arm and stretched it behind his head. Though he hardly noticed it at all now, he'd never completely regained the range of motion he'd had prior to the accident. On the other hand, he didn't often find it necessary to force his arm back between his shoulder blades like a human pretzel. The one legacy of the accident that he occasionally had to deal with was an alarming niggle deep in his scarred biceps muscle that tended to appear whenever he had to work at substantial depth on an extended deco table. He usually took care of it by requesting an extra ten minutes of oxygen in the decompression chamber.

With a skittering splash, a two-foot-long needlefish burst clear of the black water alongside the *Teresa Ann* and tail-walked over the shimmering surface for a hundred yards toward the lights of Al-Mukkala; its slender wake dusted with tiny green sparks of phosphorescence. Ben blinked and came back to reality.

He sighed and looked around. Reality was *good*. He was at home on the *Teresa Ann*. Sass, the best lady who'd ever been turned out of the female mold, was down below in their berth, sleeping contentedly. He was at the end of a satisfying and successful diving contract, with money in the bank and another fat chunk soon to come. He gazed up at his vessel's sturdy mainmast and stainless bluewater rigging, then back at the mizzen and the clear stars winking overhead in the black-velvet sky. The weather had been fair, not too hot, not too humid—unusual on the southern tip of the Arabian Peninsula—and was expected to remain that way through the month . . .

Who could complain? And what *if* a nearly forgotten nightmare had come squirming up out of the depths of his memory? You lived your life, you grew older, and as you did, all kinds of things happened to you along the way, good and bad. Some left permanent marks on your psyche, just as the conductor accident had left a permanent mark on his arm. Battle scars from the journey of Life, mental and physical. Badges of honor of a life fully *lived*—the days not squandered in fearful immobility and formless anxiety.

Ben got to his feet, smiling to himself. No, the odd nightmare was a small price to pay for the life he'd led, the life he was leading *now*. He could feel the desire to lie down beside Sass and drift back off to sleep returning.

Strange, though, how vivid that same nightmare had been, replaying itself after all these years. And how near Nick Fenzi's familiar face had seemed, hanging there in the moonlight . . .

CHAPTER 1

Sass drained the last of her coffee and set the skidproof mug down on the cockpit steering bench, brushing the breeze-ruffled strands of tawny blond hair out of her eyes.

"Ahhhh," she intoned. "*Very* good. Mocha, huh? And that's supposed to be around here somewhere?"

Ben nodded, sipping at his own mug, his blue-jeaned legs stretched out comfortably along one of the *Teresa Ann*'s lazaret seats. "That's right. The word *mocha* comes from the port city of Mocha, farther up on the Yemeni coast. So much of this high-grade Arabian coffee was traded through there over the centuries that eventually it took on the city's name. Same with a really fine variety of Arabian glove leather."

"Wow," Sass said. "I'm kinda impressed over here, Doctor." She dug at him with a bare toe, her teeth grinning white in her tanned face.

Ben caught the foot in a firm grip, making her yelp. With his other hand he set down the coffee mug and picked up a thin paperback book lying on the seat beside him. "*Peabody's Guide to Modern Yemen*," he stated, waving it at her. "Have a look sometime, kiddo, it'll expand your mind."

Sass giggled mischievously. "Why, *shucks*," she drawled, doing her imitation of a fluff-brained Southern belle, "Ah don' needa read no *boooks*, honey—not when Ah got me mah ver' own Shugah-Daddee . . ." She wiggled her toes in his hand.

Ben laughed and turned her loose. "Seriously, have a look at it," he said. "Lots of useful information in there."

She recovered her foot and sat up, tossing her hair off her forehead. "I'll check it out when we get back this evening. You ready?"

"Ready as you can be for a fifteen-hour workday." He stood up, his heavy leather safety boots thumping on the teak grating of the cockpit, and stretched his lower back, kneading his fists into it through his gray T-shirt. "Aaaarrgh. I think I'm getting old."

Sass grinned at him, collecting the two empty coffee mugs. "Forty-one ain't old, Methuselah."

Ben smacked her on the butt as she elbowed her way past him, laughing. "Thirty-seven is, though—for a *girl*."

"Chauvinist pig," she called cheerfully over her shoulder, and disappeared down the main companionway. A few seconds later the muted clattering sound of dishes being washed in the galley sink resonated back up through the open hatch.

Ben leaned down over one of the aft cleats and unwrapped the painter of the small inflatable Zodiac dinghy that was floating off the stern. Pulling the boat in, he led it around to the *Teresa Ann*'s lee side, opposite the forward end of the cockpit. He sat back on the roof of the main cabin, waiting for Sass, and glanced at his watch. Five-thirty, local time. The forty-dollar black-plastic Casio G-Shock he'd had since 1989 beeped the half hour as he looked at it. He smiled, thinking of the multitude of casual sport divers he'd known who gloried in flashing their two-thousand-dollar, gold-and-platinum Swiss diving watches, believing that the expensive little wrist ornaments marked them as "authentic divers." In actual fact, nothing could have been farther from the truth. Real blue-collar commercial oil-field divers favored the inexpensive and reliable G-Shocks. They were accurate, leakproof to hundreds of feet, and their plastic bands would rip clear of a man's wrist if accidentally caught in moving cable or rigging. Only yuppie scuba divers with too much money wore Rolex Submariners.

The sun was not quite above the lip of the eastern horizon, the sky glowing a rich blue in anticipation of desert daylight's brilliance, when Sass climbed back up through the companionway and slid the hatch closed behind her. She put a hand on Ben's back to steady herself and stepped out of the cockpit onto the deck.

"Let's go," she said. "I want first crack at those merchants in the *souk* today. I paid too much for that cardamom tea last week and I want revenge."

Ben laughed, holding the Zodiac close to the *Teresa Ann*'s side, as Sass climbed lithely over the safety rail and down. "You—a well-mannered blond American female of the tourist persuasion—you're going to outbargain a mob of Yemeni shopkeepers who speak only Arabic, in their own *souk* in the middle of Al-Mukkala, by communicating in English words of one syllable—plus grunts, groans, and charades . . . Correct?"

Sass grinned up at him as she settled into the bow of the inflatable. "Yup, that's about it. Except that I'm not as well-mannered as I used to be."

Ben climbed over the safety rail and stepped down into the dinghy, gathering the painter as he did so. "Good luck. Just be sure you wear *purdah*, okay?"

Sass tugged at the gauzy, voluminous scarf around her neck. "Got it. Head covering, veil." She pointed at the leg of her khaki trousers. "Long pants. Long sleeves. No skin at all." She shook her head. "Hotter than hell. You just *know* this custom was invented by a man."

"Islamic law," Ben said. "It's their way. You walk around in shorts and a tank top like a sorority sister on spring break in Fort Lauderdale and these people get *highly* offended. Like I said, it's their way. If you get a little hot and itchy under that veil, just think how you'd feel if some Yemeni man visiting the Florida Panhandle came into the restaurant back at Wojeck's Marina and started spitting *qat* juice on the floor."

"Right." Sass nodded, pulling the scarf up over her blond mane and started to tie it in place. "When in Rome . . ."

"Exactly."

Ben sat down in the stern of the Zodiac, twisted the throttle handle of the dinghy's fifteen-horse Johnson outboard, and yanked the starting rope. The little motor roared into life immediately, belching a cloud of blue smoke. Ben revved it in neutral for a few seconds, then shifted into forward and spun the inflatable around in the direction of Al-Mukkala. They were up on plane almost immediately, skimming over the dark dawn water toward the bleached stone towers of the ancient city, the ornate tops of which were just being lit by the first rays of the rising sun.

Ben strode through the narrow, medieval-looking streets of Al-Mukkala, his boots scuffing on the hard-packed, stony dirt. On either side of him, the fantastic architecture characteristic of many old Yemeni cities rose into the burning blue sky, shadowing the close throughways and keeping out much of the direct heat. Probably the world's first skyscrapers, the ornate brick-and-stone buildings—many of them seven to nine hundred years old—had been built by long-dead Yemeni masons to heights of eight, ten, and twelve stories. Some were higher still, and all were decorated with intricate patterns of whitewashed or brown-washed brick. Many exhibited colorful stained-glass windows, particularly on their *mafraj*—or upper—floors, through which the hard white light of the desert sun beamed and was, in turn, cooled into kaleidoscopes of red, blue, and green.

Though it was early, the narrow streets were full of people, hurrying to run errands and attend to business before the intense heat of the afternoon forced nearly every Yemeni into a state of lethargy—a lethargy exacerbated by the national obsession with chewing *qat*. Terrible, according to some modern Western observers: an entire nation virtually addicted to a mildly narcotic plant, quite content to let productivity shut down halfway through the working day. But Western observers were not Yemenis, who had evolved a pace of living consistent with the dictates of their harsh, hot land, and who were by and large happy with the routine of their lives.

Ben was accustomed, by now, to the eyes lingering on him as he walked past—a tall, relatively fair American in a country of short-statured, dark-haired, swarthy Yemenis. Here and there women shuffled by, some carrying baskets or bags of food. They were swaddled from head to toe in loose black, gray, or white cloaks, the odd flash of brilliantly patterned cloth adorning their outfits. Only their black, expressive eyes were visible between their *purdah* head wraps and veils, following him with a mixture of curiosity and wariness.

The men—some standing, some squatting on their haunches at the side of the street with their backs to the buildings—looked him up and down as he passed. Most were smoking acrid-smelling cigarettes. Far from being uniform, the clothing of the Yemeni man was wildly varied. Nearly all wore the basic *lungi*, a full, skirtlike piece of material like a loose kilt, in addition to a variety of belts, scarves, and sashes. Closed-toe sandals were common footwear. But from that point on the stylistic choices seemed unlimited. Inexpensive Western shirts and jackets were common, as were T-shirts, pullover cottons and silks, and Turkish-looking body wraps, all in vividly contrasting colors. Headgear ranged from small, finely embroidered skullcaps to large, colorful turbans.

Virtually omnipresent in the Yemeni man's idiosyncratic ensemble was the *jambiya*, the traditional Arab dagger worn in the belt or sash, over the stomach. Often objects of great beauty, they were custom-made for the bearer by master cutlers who labored for many hours over each wickedly curved blade, engraving and inlaying hilt, handle, and scabbard with leather, silver, and brass.

Many men carried guns openly, the favored weapon being the Russian-made Kalashnikov automatic rifle, or AK-47. But like the *jambiya*, their presence was more a statement of masculine individuality than a threat. Rarely, Ben had been relieved to learn, were they fired with deadly intent.

Approaching a low, narrow archway that constricted the street, he stepped courteously aside as a Yemeni man and his twin sons—who could not have been more than six years of age—marched through the cramped opening in the opposite direction. All three were dressed for some formal occasion, the sons miniature reproductions of their father, clad in jade blue European suit jackets, khaki-colored *lungi* pants, and red-and-white-checked *burnooses* . . . their matching ensembles complete with full-sized *jambiya* daggers and Kalashnikov rifles. The man, clearly a tribal leader of some sort, stared directly at Ben as he passed, his lean, dark-mustachioed face unsmiling in the customary macho Yemeni manner. Taking their cue from their father, the two little boys glared up at Ben as well, each radiating all the ferocity an overdressed, overheated six-year-old lugging a heavy machine gun longer than he was could muster.

Ben frowned back gravely, trying not to crack a smile, which could have been perceived as mockery.

As for stepping aside and letting the family pass—it was their country, not his, and years of working in exotic locations around the world had taught him that a little strategically applied deference went a long way. People everywhere had their pride. Being an Ugly American, he knew, not only interfered with your ability to get anything constructive done, but in certain parts of the world could be downright hazardous to your health. Yemen, by recent estimates, was a country of seventeen million people—people who were traditionally sensitive about personal honor—and fifty million guns.

As the Yemeni father strode out of sight around a bend in the street, flanked by his two little sons, their short legs scurrying to keep up and the stocks of their rifles bumping along on the stony dirt, Ben turned and ducked through the archway. Hopping over the little gutter of filthy water, cigarette butts, and discarded *qat* leaves that ran down the middle of the street, he continued along another hundred yards or so until he came to the doorway of a particularly aged-looking building. The crumbling brick of the geriatric structure had been coated with pale gypsum in an effort to inhibit further weathering, incidentally obscuring whitewashing patterns that were probably hundreds of years old.

Crossing a stone threshold so old and worn that it could have been scuffed by both the mailed shoes of Richard the Lionhearted's more wayward Crusaders and the Mocha leather boots of Saladin's elite cavalrymen, Ben passed from the medieval atmosphere of the street into the marginally cooler, blandly modern interior of AdenOil's Al-Mukkala branch office. Hastily erected Sheetrock had concealed the old building's internal walls—effectively eliminating the character it certainly would have had—in favor of the sterile white boxiness of the Western corporate environment.

Accustomed to the shady, muted tones of the street, he waited for his eyes to adjust to the harsh glare of the fluorescent lights chained to the cheap drop ceiling overhead. One of the long bulbs was flickering steadily, throwing an irritating, eye-straining luminous pulse over the entire room. For the hundred thousandth time, Ben silently reaffirmed his lifelong commitment *never* to let himself get stuck having to make his living in a human hamster cage like this.

A pudgy Pakistani with a round, jowly face, small, pursed lips, immense black bags under his eyes, thinning hair smeared back over his bald spot, a complexion the color of volcanic ash, and an expression of incalculable sadness was sitting behind a cheap particle-board desk, one of the legs of which had broken off and been replaced by two stacked bundles of computer paper. He was the only person in the room. A cigarette was smoldering in a brass ashtray set on top of a pile of ledgers, and empty Styrofoam coffee cups overflowed the plastic trash can beside the desk, littering the gray commercial-grade linoleum floor with their conical white corpses.

"Hi, Prakash," Ben said pleasantly. "Keepin' busy?"

Prakash Poohram looked up at him forlornly. "Most definitely, yes. Oh, yes, definitely I am." The Pakistani accent was strong. "Always much to do here, Mr. Gannon. Many calculations, yes." His fingers fluttered compulsively across the keys of the calculator beneath his hand.

Ben nodded, looking him up and down. Prakash was wearing at least half a cup of coffee and a substantial amount of cigarette ash on the front of his rumpled white dress shirt, which was wet under the arms with perspiration. He looked absolutely miserable, uncomfortable and disorganized; but Ben knew that the exact opposite was true. Here in this cluttered little office, Prakash, a genius with numbers, was utterly in his element. The AdenOil supertanker transfer station installation off Al-Mukkala had been, from its outset, one of the most cost-effective projects in the conglomerate's history—thanks in no small part to the airtight accounting of Prakash Poohram. He appeared to need the stale odors, bad lighting, poor diet, caffeine, and nicotine of the office the way Ben needed fresh air and the open sea. He positively *flourished* on it.

"Came in this morning to see about my checks, Prakash," Ben said. "They going to be ready by Thursday? We'll be done on time out there, unless one of those freighters gets careless and runs into the transfer platform in the next day or two."

The little Pakistani looked immensely pained. "Oh, my goodness, Mr. Gannon, *please!*" he opined, shaking both his hands in the air. "Please let us not even think about such a possibility! Such trouble! Such expense! *Ooooooooh . . .*"

Ben grinned and sat on the edge of the desk, which trembled ominously under his weight. "I'm kidding," he said. "The platform's well marked with nav lights. And most of the Red Sea traffic stays well offshore. We can see the ships passing by from our anchorage at any time of night, and they're almost always miles away."

Prakash shook his jowly head. "And what of the Russian tanker that came so precipitously close to colliding with the station only last month? Such distressing irresponsibility, yes? That fool of a captain ran his vessel aground only ten miles east of Al-Mukkala. Thank heaven the bunkers were empty or there would have been the most profound spillage of oil, yes? *Oooooooh* . . ." He waved his hands again.

"The guy was drunk," Ben said, "and so were all his bridge officers. Not the usual situation on a ship running from Djibouti to Bombay. The chances of that happening again anytime soon are very slim."

"I am wishing most extravagantly that you are right, Mr. Gannon," Prakash replied, looking like he was about to cry. "Most extravagantly I am." He dropped his eyes and began to rummage around on the desk. "Hmm. Hmm. Before I forget . . . there was a special delivery letter for you not an hour ago. Knowing as I did that you would be coming in to the office this morning, I instructed the carrier to leave it with me. Hmm. Hmm . . ." He shuffled paper energetically. "Ah. Here it is."

Ben took the crumpled brown business envelope the little man held out. "Thanks." He examined it briefly, noting the point of origin, and frowned. "*Addis Ababa?*" He glanced at Prakash. "Isn't that in Ethiopia?"

"Oh, yes, Mr. Gannon." The little man nodded rapidly. "Most definitely, yes, it is. The capital city, I can in fact assure you."

Ben smiled. "Well, that's highly Selassie of you, Prakash. I appreciate it."

The jowly head tilted sideways in confusion "Haile Selassie?"

"Right." Ben waved a hand dismissively. "It's an old joke, my friend. A silly American joke. Never mind." He folded the envelope in half and slid it into the hip pocket of his jeans. "I'll read it later. Probably an old oil-field buddy of mine on a job somewhere in North Africa, wanting to get together for a beer."

"Indubitably, indubitably," Prakash enthused, bobbing his head. "Now then . . ." He paused to slip an Egyptian cigarette into his mouth and light it. "Your checks." More paper shuffling. "Hmm. Ah, here it is." He scanned a single-page corporate memo and then beamed up at Ben, his smile trickling smoke. "I am most pleased to inform you, Mr. Gannon, that due to the excellent service you have rendered to AdenOil over the course of this project, you have qualified for the full amount of the performance bonus agreed upon when we negotiated your contract eight weeks ago. I am instructed to remit the full amount of said bonus to you immediately, with the entire balance of your contract fee to be paid three days from now, upon completion of the last few underwater linkages on the transfer platform. Will this be satisfactory?"

Ben nodded. "Sure. And thank you. Glad it went as well as it did. I had some good topside hands out there. Makes a lot of difference."

"Oh, most definitely, yes."

"What I'd like you to do, Prakash," Ben continued, "is cut me a check for ten percent of the bonus amount that I can cash for local currency while I'm in Yemen. Sass will be stopping by sometime this afternoon; you can give the check to her. The other ninety percent I'd like wire-transferred into my overseas work account in Geneva. Credit-Suisse is the bank, remember? You have my account number. Three days from now, we'll do the same with the rest of the contract fee, okay?"

"Oh, yes," Prakash said. "It most absolutely will be no problem."

Ben glanced at his watch and got to his feet. "I'll confirm the deposits by telephone in the next couple of days—then we'll be all squared up, eh?" He held out his hand. "Thanks for everything. It's been a pleasure working with you for the past two months."

The little Pakistani rose awkwardly out of his chair and clasped Ben's hand. "Most assuredly for myself as well, Mr. Gannon. A distinct pleasure." His eyes swiveled over Ben's shoulder toward the door. "Ah. And here is Naji to escort you to the work-boat docks this morning. I asked that he provide conveyance for you aboard his motorcycle after our meeting today, in order to save you the usual hot walk."

Ben turned. Standing in the doorway of the office was the familiar figure of Naji al-Tahl, the lean tribesman from the northern Hadhramaut—a vast area of barren desert and badlands—who, along with a dozen of his relatives, provided local security for AdenOil's employees and their foreign contractors. Nearly as tall as Ben, he wore a plain black Bedouin-style turban and cloak, *lungi* pants and sandals, and carried an old .303 caliber Lee-Enfield British military rifle casually in the crook of one arm. An ammunition bandolier ran diagonally across his chest over the black, robelike outer garment, gleaming with brass rifle cartridges. Two knives were visible in the rich blue sash that encircled his midsection: the omnipresent *jambiya*, and the longer *yataghan*, a bayonet-like short saber with a double-curved blade and no cross guard on its haft. A pair of sharp, intelligent eyes—startlingly blue—glared out of Naji's lean, hawk-nosed face below the voluminous turban, lending him an unnerving, predatory appearance.

And then he grinned, strong white teeth flashing against his dark skin and black goatee, and his fierce demeanor dissolved in a welter of crow's feet and laugh lines.

"Ah, *Ben-Ya-Min!*" he declared, spinning out the long form of Ben's name with distinctly Arabic modifications. "You are in the process of separating this Punjabi money changer from some of his filthy lucre, is it not so? Surely you will have a little *baksheesh* for your poor old friend Naji, will you not?" He grinned like a hyena and rubbed his thumb and forefinger together, "The generosity of Allah falls most regularly upon the generous."

Ben turned the palms of his hands toward the ceiling in a gesture of mock helplessness and shrugged. "What can I do, Naji?" he mourned, playing along. "They pay me pennies and I keep a wife who spends dollars."

The tribesman roared with laughter. "Ah, was it ever so! Obviously, you do not beat her often enough; thus, she has become willful and uncontrollable. Praise Allah that your barbarous culture does not per-

mit you more than one wife at a time, lest an over-
abundance of such females compound your losses!"
He bellowed with laughter again and spat a long
stream of *qat* juice on the floor.

Prakash stared tragically at the puddle of leafy spittle glistening on his already soiled linoleum and rolled
his eyes back in his head in a display of long-suffering
patience. Ben chuckled, nodded a final goodbye to the
little Pakistani and moved toward the door. Naji was
far too visceral a man for Prakash; the mercenary
tribesman and the cloistered accountant occupied opposite ends of the male spectrum.

"Something you need to know about American females, Naji," Ben said, as they stepped over coffee cup
after coffee cup, "they don't take well to *beatings*. Most
of them would run to a lawyer, and a lot of 'em would
simply beat the hell out of you right back. The one I've
got, if I laid a hand on her the wrong way—she'd do
both. You see?"

The lean Yemeni shook his swarthy head. "Alas,
what you describe is a recipe for sustained misery. A
man unwilling to discipline his wife? My sympathies
to you, and I will pray for Allah the Compassionate
and Merciful to deliver you from your unworkable situation."

"Well, thanks," Ben acknowledged. "I appreciate
it." He smiled to himself. The irony-laden verbal joust-
ing could have gone on for hours. To Naji, who had in
fact met Sass numerous times and truly liked and respected her, such sustained gibing was a form of entertainment; expressive wordplay a high art. That the
half-Bedouin, Arabic-speaking tribesman was able to

converse so eloquently in English—a second language learned as a teenager from a British Red Cross doctor and teacher who had run a charity health clinic in the remote northern Hadhramaut—was a constant source of amazement to Ben. Often, over the past several months, he'd wished for a fraction of the fluency in Arabic that Naji possessed in English—regardless of how convoluted with formality the Yemeni's phrases sometimes came out.

Ben and Naji had first met at the security gate of the AdenOil work-boat docks. They'd liked each other immediately—the American commercial diver and the Arabian desert tribesman—two men born half a world apart, into cultures as different as night and day. Over the past two months, they had come to know each other well, Naji guiding Ben—and often Sass—through the richly social environment of Al-Mukkala and the surrounding countryside.

They'd found few personal barriers between them. As always, Ben had noted, cultural variations in appearances and customs were interesting, mentally stimulating . . . but ultimately superficial. Under the skin, the world over, people were all the same. Either you clicked with someone—respected and liked him—or you didn't.

"You get the sidecar on that old motorbike fixed yet?" Ben asked over his shoulder, stepping out into the street. "Last time I was in it I thought it was going to rattle right off and dump me in the ditch."

He failed to get Naji's answer. Hearing was suddenly made difficult by the hard steel muzzle of an AK-47 being shoved into his left ear.

CHAPTER 2

Ben stumbled to his right, flinching away from the pressure boring into the side of his head. Rough hands shoved him sideways even farther, and he lost his footing on the stone threshold, falling heavily on his hip against the crumbling brick wall of the building. The loose cloth of a desert garment flapped in front of his eyes . . . a brown-skinned forearm and hand clawed at his face. Someone with a high-pitched voice was shouting excitedly in Arabic.

Then he was lying on one elbow on the hard ground, blinking and coughing out dust, *lungi*-clad legs milling around him. He swiped at his eyes, rubbing them clear, and pushed himself up to a sitting position. A sandal planted itself in the center of his chest and drove him back heavily against the wall, knocking the wind out of him.

"Stay out of the way, *Amreekehnee*," an Arabic-accented voice rasped. "This is not your concern."

Despite the fury that was boiling up inside him at having been blindsided into the dirt, Ben was forced to sag back and let the spasm gripping his lungs pass. It gave him a few seconds to let his temper cool and take in the situation.

Three Yemenis were standing in front of him, clad in loose desert half shawls and *lungi* kilts. Two more were on the other side of the narrow street, scowling and flexing their fingers on the stocks of their AK-47s. All five of them had shaved heads and wore identical skullcaps of black, red, and white yarn. Their attention was riveted on a sixth man, also wearing the skullcap, who stood in the center of the street facing the doorway of the AdenOil office. It was he who possessed the agitated, high-pitched voice. With it, he was directing a torrent of rapid-fire Arabic at Naji, who was standing calmly in the doorway, his rifle still cradled loosely in the crook of his arm.

Like his compatriots, the man was carrying an AK-47, one hand on the grips. With the other he was gesturing wildly in the air, visually accentuating his shrill barrage of words. His shaved head, beaklike nose, and emaciated features, supported on a long, stringy neck that jutted forward out of his voluminous gray cloak, gave him a decidedly vulturous appearance. Ben cocked his head, still waiting for his lungs to inflate properly. Although he couldn't make much sense of the staccato Arabic, every fourth or fifth word seemed to be a curse.

He glanced over at Naji. The lean tribesman appeared to be totally unaffected by the storm of abuse washing over him, a look of vague amusement playing across his dark, hawklike face. Once, his uncannily blue eyes flashed over in Ben's direction, checking to see if he had been injured, then returned to settle on the nearly apoplectic man in the center of the street.

The rant continued as Naji stepped off the threshold

and moved forward, looking around pointedly at the other five Yemenis. They shifted nervously as he advanced, skirting him, fingering their automatic rifles. Ben got his first good breath, his chest throbbing, as Naji stalked around into a patch of sunlight, turned, and gazed calmly at his abuser, his arms still folded around his old Lee-Enfield.

The vulturelike man paused in his tirade to lick the foam from his lips and, abruptly, Naji cut in. "By the Prophet, Sahdman," he remarked in English, "must you babble your grievance against me in such offensive tones? Are you a man or a washerwoman?"

Crooked teeth showed in Sahdman's emaciated face as the skin drew back tight in a snarl. "Curse you, Naji al-Tahl," he hissed, responding in fractured English of his own, "you and all your bastard clansmen are thieves and deceivers. Your women are all—"

"Have a care, baldhead," Naji interrupted, his blue eyes glittering. "It is not the women of *my* tribe who are known far and wide to turn the occasional coin with their dirty favors."

Sahdman's dark face blanched. His eyes narrowed to slits, and his sneer deepened, pulling his lips even farther back from his teeth. Shaking with rage, hyperventilating, he walked into the patch of sunlight next to Naji, stopped, and very deliberately spat on the lean tribesman's shadow.

"Son of a brothel woman," he began, "you—"

There was a sudden ringing sound of steel sliding on leather as Naji's *yataghan* came out of its scabbard in a blur, so fast that Sahdman's five companions could not even begin to bring their weapons to bear.

By the time they did, in a *clack-clack-clacking* of Kalashnikov actions, the razor-sharp edge of the long, curved knife was across Sahdman's protruding Adam's apple, Naji holding it at arm's length.

Delicately, he twisted the blade so that its tip dug into the soft spot just below the junction of Sahdman's jaw and ear, lifting him up on his toes. The skinny man's eyes bugged.

"Higher," Naji said softly, manipulating the *yataghan* with surgical skill. "Good. Now step in closer to me."

Sahdman teetered forward on his tiptoes; his arms spread downward, the AK pointing at the ground. Naji brought him in on the tip of the knife until they were virtually nose-to-nose. The five tribesmen on the periphery began to shuffle closer, their rifles trained on Naji's head. He appeared to pay them no notice whatsoever.

"Tell your curs to move back against the buildings, baldhead," Naji said quietly. He smiled. "Or your tongue will be hanging from the new mouth I will give you beneath your chin." He turned the razor-edged blade on Sahdman's throat slightly, shaving a few coarse hairs from the skin. "*Now.*"

Sahdman stared at him, his face twitching, for several long seconds . . . then waved a jittery hand at his companions. They hesitated, glancing at each other. Then, muttering, they began to back away slowly, their AKs sagging downward. Behind them, Ben rose to his feet, breathing hard. He looked around. The street, which had previously been full of pedestrians, was completely deserted. The average Yemeni, it seemed, was quick to recognize a confrontation stemming from a tribal feud—and get well clear.

Ben retreated silently into the narrow doorway of the spice shop just behind him as the five gunmen backed up under the little establishment's sun awning. A heavy wood-and-fabric affair, the awning was hinged to the exterior wall overhead and supported by a single block-and-tackle arrangement, the weight-bearing rope made fast to a cleat on the doorframe. Intent on Naji and his long knife, Sahdman's cohorts had apparently forgotten all about the American diver they'd manhandled into the dirt just moments before.

A small noise made Ben glance down. Behind a dozen large brass bowls heaped with ochre-red and curry brown powdered spices, a Yemeni woman was crouching, hugging her daughter between her knees. Above the *purdah* veil, her eyes glared up at him with a mixture of fear and suspicion. The little girl, her face uncovered, simply gave him a moppet's smile. He smiled in return, putting a finger to his lips. Very quietly, the woman began to herd the child toward a curtained doorway at the rear of the shop, and Ben turned his attention back to the two men in the center of the street.

"You appear to have made a mistake," Naji was saying, just loud enough for the five gunmen to hear his every word. "Without meaning to, I am *certain*, you have spat upon my shadow. Ordinarily—" He paused to lift the point of the *yataghan* a quarter inch or so as Sahdman momentarily became restless balancing on his tiptoes, the veins standing out on his forehead and neck. The thin man in the skullcap arched upward and went rigid again, emitting a brief gurgle—and Naji continued: "Ordinarily, I would consider this an unforgivable insult, but since we have known each other for so long, and bearing in mind that you have clearly dribbled upon that which you should have not *unintentionally*, I propose a solution." He grinned like a Cheshire cat. "We will stand here as the sun passes overhead, and when my shadow has moved beyond your little puddle of slime, we will simply pretend that your misdirected expectoration *never occurred*. Is this not fair, my friend?" He tweaked the knife under Sahdman's jaw upward just a hair. "Hmm?"

Sahdman managed the neat trick of nodding without moving his head up and down—thereby avoiding impalement on the *yataghan*'s point. Unlike Naji, who wore a full black *burnoose* turban, his scalp and face were exposed to the direct heat of the morning sun—already intense though it was still relatively early in the day. Sweat poured down his bony temples and drawn cheeks as he stood there on the tip of the lean tribesman's knife, head cocked back, eyes blinking and bulging.

For the next five minutes Naji and Sahdman occupied the center of the street in silence—the one relaxed and immobile in his dark desert robes, his arm flexed upward to hold his *yataghan* in place; the other teetering shakily on the balls of his feet, his arms spread out at his sides, one hand still gripping his Kalashnikov, his half shawl drenched in sweat. Ben watched the little drama play on from behind the doorframe of the spice shop, his eyes flickering here and there, trying to envision what would happen next. And what he might be able to do about it.

The sun burned down on the two men, moving overhead with agonizing slowness, until at last the trailing edge of Naji's shadow cleared the rapidly drying puddle of saliva. Sahdman's eyes were practically rolling up white in his head as Naji maneuvered him around with the knife until he had been repositioned in a direct line between the desert tribesman and his own five cohorts.

"Your gun, I think," Naji said. He transferred his Lee-Enfield from the crook of his elbow to his shoulder in one smooth motion, hanging it from its strap, and reached down for Sahdman's AK-47. The knife he kept pressed to his opponent's throat. "Pass it to me—*gently*, my friend—and we will see about backing slowly away from here, you and I, while your men stay put and . . . shop for spices. Agreed?" A flick of the knife. An acquiescent gurgle. "Ah, you see? We are getting along splendidly."

His arm shaking, Sahdman brought the machine gun slowly up, moving it in toward Naji's hand. With his entire head slick with perspiration, his eyelids fluttering, he appeared to be on his last legs . . . or *toes*. But as Naji's fingers touched the AK's stock, Sahdman jerked the weapon slightly and dropped it.

It wasn't much, but it was enough. As the blue-eyed tribesman grasped for the falling gun out of reflex, he eased the pressure of the *yataghan*'s edge on Sahdman's throat. The emaciated man threw himself backward, away from the blade, and landed flailing in the dirt.

He rolled to his knees, one hand clasping the side of his neck, and let out an odd sound: *"Eueugghh . . ."* Blood began to appear between his fingers. He stared at Naji for a few seconds, his eyes wild in his skull-like face, and then shrieked, *"Kill him!"*

Naji was already moving as the words left Sahd-man's lips. But the street was relatively open and there were no doorways nearby through which he could bolt. And the five AK-47s in front of the spice shop were coming up very quickly.

In one quick motion, Ben released the awning's support rope from its cleat. The heavy wood-and-fabric shroud dropped instantly, swinging inward on its hinges, and collided with the five gunmen like a giant flyswatter. With muffled shrieks, they were slammed to the ground in a cloud of dust at the shop's entrance. One of the AKs went off with an earsplitting chatter, punching holes of daylight in the fallen awning.

Chaos ensued in the darkened shop. Ben seized a large brass bowl of ground hot pepper that he'd spotted earlier, held his breath, and flung the contents across the five Yemenis floundering at his feet. Then, quickly, he ducked out into the street between the awning frame and the building's wall. Choking screams rang out inside the spice shop as hot pepper granules encountered unprotected eyeballs. The awning slatted and bulged in sync with the frantic thrashing of the men on its interior side. More screams of agony.

"Yalla! Bisura, Ben-Ya-Min!" Naji was laughing with delight as he beckoned. "This way, my friend! Hurry, before those fools locate their own heads again!" He

paused to gaze down at Sahdman as Ben sprinted across the street to join him. "Bring more of your ridiculous kinsmen next time, baldhead; perhaps you will have better luck."

"*Eueueugghh . . .*" gurgled the skull-faced man, staring up at Naji, the hand pressed to his neck slick with blood.

"It is unfortunate that you attempted to cut your own throat on the blade of my knife," Naji continued, thoroughly enjoying himself. He began to back away rapidly, Ben now at his side. "I suggest you apply oil of frankincense to that little scratch—and try to be more careful in future." He grinned at Sahdman with great relish, then spun on his heel and ran with Ben down the narrow, twisting street.

"*Ya salem!*" Naji chortled in amazement, as they dodged into a narrow alley. "By the Beard of the Prophet, my friend, that was nicely done!" He was practically beside himself with glee. "Five of those motherless jackals downed all at once—and yourself unarmed! Heh-heh-heh-heh! A memory I shall treasure forever, *inshallah!*"

"Don't give me too much credit," Ben panted, just behind his shoulder. "If that awning hadn't been handy, you'd have had more holes in you than a sea sponge. And I wasn't even really thinking about what I was doing. . . ."

"Aha! Even better!" Naji enthused. "Is not the best fighting always a matter of instinct? The man who just saved my life is being too modest, *azun!* I am in your debt, *Ben-Ya-Min*, my good friend." He reached back and tapped Ben's arm. "This way, through here."

They ducked under a clothesline sagging with wet laundry and trotted off down a hidden alley so narrow that Ben's shoulders scraped both walls. Naji led the way, looking like a tall black ghost in his loose desert robes. The air in the alley was still and redolent with the smell of dog dung . . . it was a relief to emerge into the hot, bright sunlight at its far end. There they paused for breath beside the dilapidated old motorcycle and sidecar that was Naji's primary form of transport in and around Al-Mukkala.

"By the way," Ben said, sucking in air, "didn't you tell me once that Yemenis don't like to use the guns they carry in any actual disputes? Your exact words, I believe."

"Ah. Yes." Naji nodded seriously. "This is not always so."

Ben waited for him to elaborate, but evidently the lean tribesman considered his brief explanation adequate. Ben shook his head slightly. This wasn't the first time he'd found himself confronted by a contradiction in the Arab world, but no matter how many times it happened, he never quite got used to it.

"Come, my friend," Naji urged, throwing a *lungi*-clad leg over the seat of the motorcycle. "We must go. We fled in a roundabout way, back to this infernal machine, and the AdenOil offices are just through that other passageway." He indicated a dark opening between the nearby buildings. "Sahdman and the other baldheads may come looking in this direction, and I heartily believe that we have ruined their sense of humor!" He kickstarted the ancient motorcycle as Ben climbed into the sidecar, then threw his head back and bellowed with laughter. "*Inshallah!* Is it not so?"

Dirt and stones sprayed out from beneath the rear tire as he popped the clutch, and the battered bike lurched forward with a sickly *BLAAAAAAT*, spewing blue smoke. In a cloud of dust, they careened off down the narrow street toward the oil-company docks on the Al-Mukkala waterfront.

Naji utilized only one speed when operating his motorcycle—breakneck. The cackling Arab, black robes flying out behind him, and the American diver, hanging on grimly to the frame of the jouncing sidecar, raced pell-mell through the very heart of the ancient city, scattering pedestrians before them. Only the fact that the ill-tuned bike's stuttering roar sounded advance warning of their approach prevented them—it seemed to Ben—from racking up a couple of victims every hundred yards or so.

"By the way," Ben shouted, squinting into the slipstream, "what was that all about back there?"

Naji grinned. "Sahdman? It is nothing—a mere trifle. His tribe has nurtured a minor grievance against mine for some time now. A matter of honor."

"What's the beef?" Ben asked.

"Eh?" Naji glanced over at him, one eyebrow raised.

"What's the argument about?" Ben rephrased.

"Ah. A woman." Naji leaned hard to the left as he gunned the motorcycle through a hairpin turn in a spray of gravel and dust. "Was it ever so? Are not women the ultimate source of virtually all conflict that plagues men in this life?" He laughed. *"Inshallah!* But we must have them, must we not?

"A woman of Sahdman's tribe was betrothed to one of his relatives. But she did not desire him since, like all his kin, he was bald and ugly and possessed of a rank and offensive body odor—I suspect due to a failure to habitually wash his private parts. A relative of *mine* who had admired her from afar, learned of her dilemma and—appreciating as he did her succulent curves and lively mind—resolved to kidnap her into our tribe and make her his first wife. As he was, like all *my* kin, tall and handsome and scrupulous in his personal hygiene, she was not averse to the abduction and did not resist. In fact, on the appointed evening, she slipped a sleeping elixir into her betrothed's drink, took his best rifle, stole his camel, rode to the edge of her tribe's settlement, and was sitting beneath the stars waiting to be kidnapped—carrying all her personal possessions—when my relative arrived on the scene."

"Sounds like he had to drag her away kicking and screaming," Ben remarked.

"Does it not?" Naji chuckled. "She signaled her beloved with a shielded candle-lantern so that he could locate her in the dark hills—two double flashes followed by a single flash. This episode has come to be known in my tribe's history as the Affair of the Five Flashes. Nothing more than a simple tale of True Love triumphant. Regardless, Sahdman and his people bear a grudge against me and my kin because of this—and a few other minor events—to this day."

Ben looked over at him. "It wasn't you who kidnapped her, was it?"

Naji shook his head. "No. My great-great-grand-father. At the time of the opening of the famous canal called Suez."

Ben thought for a moment, mentally reviewing some of the local history he'd been reading since cross-ing the Arabian Sea—and bracing himself as the bike skidded around yet another tight corner. Then his memory regurgitated the details and he glanced at Naji again: "The opening of the Suez Canal? That's 1869!" he said incredulously. "Sahdman's tribe has been feuding with yours over one woman who didn't want to get married for more than *one hundred and thirty years*?"

"Sadly, yes," Naji replied. "They could not see the humor in it, apparently, choosing instead to make it an issue of honor. Sahdman's great-great-grandfather was the unfortunate man who lost his tribe's one great beauty to my ancestor." The blue-eyed tribesman shrugged. "If he had been less ugly, and less revolting in his personal habits, he might have kept her. But it was not to be. *Inshallah*. Allah willed it so."

One final wrench of the handlebars and the rattling motorcycle shot out from between two whitewashed brick buildings and into the open lot at the gated en-trance to the AdenOil boat docks. It slid to a halt with a half spin, throwing up a spray of crushed gravel. As Ben climbed out, a bit shakily, Naji clapped him on the shoulder.

"I will come for you, my friend, when you are done with your underwater work today, lest Sahdman and his baldheads seek a little misplaced vengeance." He chuckled, gunning the bike's throttle. "By the Beard of the Prophet! Five of the unwashed rascals with one blow! Allah is good, is he not, *Ben-Ya-Min*?"

He roared off, scattering gravel, in a cloud of blue smoke.

CHAPTER 3

The lionfish were beautiful—living works of art—but they were also a problem. Common in the warm waters off Al-Mukkala, they grew to nearly two feet in length, their basslike bodies festooned with elongated fins and poisonous spines. Wildly colorful, trailing fleshy pennants of yellow, orange, red, and brown from their natural armament, they were also highly territorial, becoming bad-tempered and aggressive when anything—regardless of its size—encroached on their chosen piece of underwater real estate.

Three large specimens had taken up residence in and around the last unmated pipeline flange on the oil transfer platform. Standing on the white-sand bottom in ninety feet of gin-clear water at the platform's base, Ben struggled to line up the facing flange of the massive flex-hose that would eventually be used to pump Yemeni crude into the holds of oil-thirsty supertankers—the last of ten such hoses he'd been contracted to install. At the same time, he was continually prodding one or more of the agitated lionfish away from the work area with the socket end of a large hydraulic impact wrench. The feisty creatures kept charging in toward his gloved hands, fins and poison-tipped spines splayed out, trying to both bite and impale him.

"Dammit," Ben muttered into his dive hat's oral-nasal mask, jerking his fingers away from another on-rushing set of spines. The two flange faces slipped out of alignment by a couple of inches, and he cursed a second time under his breath. He jabbed at the offending lionfish with the impact wrench, which sent it fleeing around to the far side of the pipeline assembly. As annoying as they were, he didn't have the heart to injure the beautiful little animals. On the other hand, he didn't need a couple of fingers blown up like overripe plums from toxic puncture wounds, either.

Heaving the hose flange back into position with his shoulder, he quickly inserted the half dozen nine-inch retaining bolts through their respective holes and nutted them—all the while eyeing the hovering lionfish, trying to determine which one would be the next to lunge in and attempt to cripple him.

A trickle of sweat ran down his brow and into his left eye, stinging it. Blinking, he cracked his dive hat's free-flow valve and rested for a moment, letting the none-too-cool compressed air pumping down from the surface through his umbilical hose blast across his face. He'd always found the shallow waters of the Persian Gulf and Arabian Sea oil fields too warm for comfort when doing heavy work. Ninety-degree surface temperatures were not uncommon, and it often felt as though that soupy heat extended all the way to the bottom.

Ben shut off his free-flow valve. *Fatal heat stroke under fifteen fathoms of seawater*, he mused. *What a way to go. No insurance company would believe it.* He hefted the bulky impact wrench up to shoulder height, manipulating its stiff, awkward hydraulic hoses out of the way, and slipped the drive socket over the head of the first retaining bolt. When he pulled the trigger, the staccato metallic vibration sent the lurking lionfish bolting for the far side of the platform.

He had the flange buttoned up in less than five minutes, thereby fulfilling his contract obligations to Aden-Oil two days ahead of schedule. He went over the bolts with the impact once more, ensuring that they were torqued down to engineering spec, then stepped back across the ocean floor to survey eight weeks' worth of hard work. A glittering school of silver bar jacks cruised past the ten pipeline-to-transfer-hose flange assemblies he'd first fabricated topside in the welding shack of the field boat, then installed on the pipeline risers that emerged from the seafloor at the platform's base.

It was a good job, Ben decided. Quality product for the fee charged.

"Abdul," he said into his hat's tiny mouth-speaker.

"*Ay-wa?*" came the reply from the topside radio operator, a sharp Yemeni roustabout whom Ben had dragooned into service to keep an eye on his air pressures while he was working underwater. Though he spoke very little English, the man had been a quick study, absorbing Ben's crash-course training and turning into a competent radioman, compressor tech, and decompression chamber operator in less than a week. That the transfer of such relatively complicated information had been achieved largely through hands-on demonstration and charadelike gesturing was still a source of amazement to Ben. Had their roles been reversed, he doubted if he'd have done as well as Abdul. The more he traveled the world, the more impressed he was with its various inhabitants—no matter what their race, religion, relative wealth or poverty.

"*Gib-lee foh,* " Ben instructed in his awkward Arabic. "Bring me up."

"*Tay-ib,*" Abdul replied smartly. "All right."

With very little delay, Ben's umbilical hose began to move upward, a second Yemeni tender on the boat deck reeling it in hand over hand. When the slack was nearly gone, he laid hold of the nearest bottom-to-surface riser and began to climb, habitually keeping himself to the safe Sur-D O_2 ascent rate of twenty-five feet per minute.

He looked down one last time at the gleaming new flange assemblies—and couldn't help breaking into a smile. You had to admire tenacity. Already, the lionfish were back.

It was hot in the decompression chamber, baking as it was under the burning afternoon sun on the back deck of the field boat. Weeks earlier, Ben had rigged an awning over the ten-foot-by-four-foot pressurized steel cylinder, and tied a hose at one end so that seawater continually ran over the top of it. It helped a little, but not much.

He lay on his back in the narrow metal tube of the inner air lock—which was blown down to the atmospheric equivalent of forty feet—a towel around his hips and an oxygen mask strapped to his face, sweating all over the thin vinyl mat beneath him. Through the tiny, two-inch-thick Lexan porthole, Abdul peered in at him regularly, checking that he was not exhibiting any signs of decompression sickness or oxygen toxicity. The roar of the two diesel-powered 120 cfm diving compressors, muted by the chamber's thick steel walls, reverberated faintly through the lock's interior.

Ben held up the special delivery letter that Prakash had given him that morning and read it for the fifth time. It was from Maggie Fenzi, Nick Fenzi's wife:

Dear Ben,

Nick's in trouble. Bad trouble. I don't know what to do. He always told me that the one guy he knew he could count on for help when he really needed it was you. Call me at the Hotel Tafari in Addis Ababa, Ethiopia, as soon as you can. The international number is 251/1/518401. Bart Grissom, the operations manager at Subsea Oilfield Services in Houston, told me he'd heard you were working a contract for AdenOil in Yemen. That's how I found you. I'll be here until you call, or I run out of money.

Please, Ben. It's Nick. And I have nowhere else to turn.

Love,
Maggie

He gazed at the hasty ballpoint scrawl, holding the creased Hotel Tafari letterhead between two fingers to avoid soaking it with sweat, and trying to imagine what Nick could have gotten himself into that would have generated such a note from his wife. The Maggie Fenzi he knew was not given to panic. She was dry-humored, tough, and street-smart—much like her husband. Something of a hard case. Coming from her, this letter was practically a scream of hysteria. It was damned disturbing.

Almost as disturbing as wondering why, less than twelve hours previously, he'd seen Nick's disembodied face staring down at him as he awoke from an inexplicable recurrence of a long-ago nightmare.

He stuck the page up between the air valves of the inner lock—where he couldn't sweat all over it—and looked at his wristwatch. Ten more minutes of sucking O_2 in this miniature Turkish bath, then a two-minute pressure bleed to break the hatch and escape into the clean air and sunshine.

An additional half hour to secure the gear and the job site, plus a twenty-minute run in to the AdenOil boat docks. Ben readjusted the uncomfortable black-rubber mask over his nose and mouth and breathed in deeply, the oxygen hissing through the unit's regulator.

And a few minutes more to locate a phone in the dock compound that could handle international calls.

Ben had never heard Maggie Fenzi sound so lost and frightened.

"Things were slow in the Gulf of Mexico last year, Ben, remember?" she was saying. "Oil prices sagged, so there were no big summer contracts put up for bid. Offshore Underwater Services had to lay off about twenty percent of their divers, but Nick didn't expect to be one of them. He'd been there for twelve years, for God's sake. But they dropped him like he was a new tender fresh out of dive school."

"I didn't hear about that," Ben said sympathetically.

"You know I was in the South Pacific for a few months last year."

"Yes, I do." Maggie sniffled, as if still pulling herself together from a bout of crying. "Anyway, he got angry and stormed out of the ops manager's office . . ."

"Nothing wrong with that," Ben interjected. "Being laid off is tough, but it's usually temporary. Divers are always getting into pissing contests with management about their scheduling."

"Yes, but they don't always upend an oak desk on the guy sitting behind it before they make their exit."

"Oh, jeez," Ben said. "He didn't."

"He did." There was a pause. "It was more than he could take. Over a decade with O.U.S.—and they ignore his seniority, drop him, and keep on thirty other divers half his age with only three or four years of company time in. He's made millions for them with his offshore labor and leadership since the late 1980s. He's been busting his ass diving in the oil field for thirty-three years, and now that he's fifty-seven—and the discs in his neck are bulging from wearing heavy dive hats, and his lung capacity is two-thirds of what it used to be from breathing weird gases, and every joint in his body hurts from taking a bad bends hit at one time or another—the company uses a little downturn in oil prices to junk him out like an old compressor. Just get him off the books before he turns into a liability—before they have to compensate him for the physical beating he's taken or pay him large retirement benefits."

Ben was silent as Maggie drew another breath.

"Nick knew exactly what they were doing to him,

Ben. He's proud. He wasn't going to take it lying down. He blew, trashed the ops manager's office, and O.U.S. banned him from the property. They also blacklisted him to a lot of the other operations people on the Gulf Coast—so he wasn't getting much work.

"He'd been talking about opening a little jewelry store—you know we both like gemstones. Really get into the trade in a small way, and forget about life offshore. All he needed was one more good season to be able to fund a little place, buy some startup inventory . . ." A tiny sob escaped her throat. "It was so . . . *unfair.*"

Ben found himself at a loss. "Life often is," he said, and regretted it instantly. *Lame.*

Maggie coughed, then pulled herself together. "Tell me about it," she replied bitterly. "Anyway, he started calling around overseas and got in contact with Berndt Olssen—do you know him?"

"Sure. Old Norwegian diver who used to work the North Sea out of Stavanger. I did a job with him off the coast of Scotland about seven years ago."

"Right. Well, he started his own small diving company, doing a lot of exploration support work in North Africa—Morocco, Nigeria, those kinds of places. He told Nick that he'd landed a contract for the government of Bisotho. You know it, right? I remember Nick telling me that you'd worked there a few years back."

Ben's recollection of the place was clearer than he would have preferred. A hot, steamy little fifth-rate country right on the equator at the southern end of Somalia, bisected by a single large river that snaked one hundred miles from a vast inland lake to the Indian

Ocean. Virtually undeveloped except for its small capital city, a set of aging locks—built by the British and then rarely used—that bypassed a 250-foot cataract in the river about fifteen miles from the lake, and a few oil platforms pumping low-grade crude in the coastal delta area. A history of internal ethnic warfare and despotic, corrupt governments. During the short time Ben had been in Bisotho, the country had seemed on the verge of erupting into a killing ground of inter-tribal hatreds. He'd worked his platform installation contract for British Petroleum, packed his gear, and gotten the hell out of there on the first ramshackle flight to neighboring Kuballa—a well-run nation of similar size that was as peaceful and stable as Bisotho was tumultuous.

"Yeah, Maggie," he said. "I know the place."

"Olssen had put together a mixed crew of British, Norwegian, and French divers. Nick was the only American. The job was to provide underwater support for exploratory drilling in that one big inland lake the river flows out of. Bottom surveys, sampling—that kind of thing. They were working off a medium-sized jackup rig that had been brought upriver a month earlier.

"Then—" Maggie's voice broke, and Ben could hear her fighting to get control of herself. "Then, the lid on that . . . that . . . *fucking excuse for a country* . . . blew off. There was a coup. Some maniac tribal leader—who calls himself 'King Billy,' for God's sake—overthrew the government in a matter of hours, and one half of Bisotho started killing the other. The *Malmoq* tribe against the *Quori* tribe. Haven't you heard about this?

It's been all over the international news for three weeks."

Unconsciously, Ben shook his head. "No. To tell the truth, I've been so wrapped up in what I've been doing that I haven't read a newspaper or listened to any sort of broadcast in more than a month."

"It's genocide down there," Maggie said. "A human-rights nightmare. The *Nimitz* was on training exercises north of Madagascar near the Seychelles and had to send a Marine helicopter to the capital to evacuate the staff of the U.S. consulate. They barely got them out alive."

"What happened to Olssen's crew?" Ben asked quietly.

There was a choking sound over the phone. "They heard what was happening over single-sideband radio and abandoned the jackup rig. When they got to the shore of the lake they went looking for a vehicle that could carry all of them along the mountain road and through that main pass to the Kuballan border. They were far enough inland that the violence spreading out from the capital city hadn't really reached them yet. They found an old Land Rover and got going. And they made it. But halfway there, Nick . . . Nick . . ." Her voice crumbled in despair. "Oh . . . *God* . . ."

"Hey, hey," Ben said helplessly into the phone. "Easy, now. What about Nick?"

"They stopped so Nick could get water for the radiator from a stream and this band of nigger soldiers with guns and machetes grabbed him and took him awa-a-a-y-y . . ."

Her words tumbled out, ending in an anguished wail. Ben stood stunned, holding the phone. Hearing

Maggie sound so unlike herself, from the ugly racist epithet to the complete despair in her voice, was almost as shocking as learning what had happened to Nick. He listened in silence as the floodgates opened and her words came thick and fast.

"The soldiers were yelling and firing at the Land Rover as Olssen and the rest of the crew drove off. How could they just leave Nick there like that? When they got to Kuballa they reported what had happened, but no one could do anything. Olssen called me at home in Louisiana and broke the news. He said he thought that the men who'd grabbed Nick were called Leopard Soldiers—supposedly the shock troops of this king, or tribal leader, or whatever the hell you call an insane nigger who's in the process of murdering half of his own countrymen."

Twice now with the nigger thing. Ben felt the corners of his mouth tighten. If it had been some ignorant redneck talking, he wouldn't have given it a second thought. Coming from Maggie Fenzi, it was vaguely sickening.

"Did you report Nick's kidnapping to the State Department?" he asked.

"Of course! It was the first thing I did. Olssen had already done it, by the way—called them and told them they had a U.S. citizen being held illegally in Bisotho. When I spoke to them they said they already knew about it, and that they were, quote, *taking steps to look into the matter*, unquote. I flew from New Orleans to Washington and got in to see one of the senior State Department officials, and he assured me that they were, quote, *pressing the issue very hard*, unquote, and that I should stay in contact for more information. I got a hotel, went back the next morning, and was told that, quote, *the U.S. State Department is working all available channels to effect a resolution to the problem*, un-fucking-quote! I stayed in Washington for a week before I realized that all I was ever going to get was goddamned *quotes!"*

Ben cut in as gently as he could. "There's nothing at stake for the U.S. Bisotho has no real trading relationship with us, no oil to speak of—although the government's looking for larger reserves inland—and no valuable mineral resources. A few alluvial diamonds are hand-dredged out of the upper reaches of the river; that's all. Not enough to constitute a real industry. Remember the Persian Gulf War? We only get mad about people chopping up women and children if it's going to threaten our national security or cost us another dollar a gallon for gasoline. Were there any other Americans reported missing? Any other foreign nationals at all?"

"No," Maggie whispered. "Nobody else."

"Then they're not going to do anything. The Marines aren't going to be landing in waves in some tiny little African country just to find one misplaced oil-field diver. The State Department is stringing you along."

"I know."

"You could try the news media. Newspapers, television. Draw attention to Nick's kidnapping and put pressure on the State Department that way."

"By the time anything happened," Maggie said,

"I'd be old and gray, and Nick would probably be dead."

A few beats passed while Ben considered. "If he's not dead already," he said finally. There was silence on the other end of the phone. "Mag?"

A little cough—followed by the sound of a cigarette being lit with a metallic lighter. "He's not dead," she said. "I know where he is."

"You do? Where?"

"In an old prison on an island at the south end of the big lake."

Ben's brow furrowed. "How do you know that?"

"Uplink satellite e-mail. He had one of those new handheld units with him. They're no bigger than a Zippo lighter—microtechnology, you know?—and somehow he managed to keep it. Maybe he slipped it into his boot. I got five short messages from him, the last only three days ago. Then, I guess, either they found the unit or the batteries gave out." She paused. "He's there, Ben, stuck in a hole somewhere on that rock. He must be able to see the sky or the uplink wouldn't have worked, but they've got him and they're not letting him go. God knows what they're doing to him . . . or have done already." Maggie's tone was dry now, as if she was all cried out.

"Can't you tell *that* to the State Department?" Ben asked. "It's proof that he's there."

"They don't want to hear it," Maggie said.

Ben blew a long breath out. "And you think I can help?"

"Yes," she replied. "I came right from Washington to Addis Ababa just to get into the same general part of the world as you . . . because I knew you could and would help us."

"How?"

"There's a way to get Nick out of that prison and off the island," she said, "by approaching underwater. He told me how in his last e-mail. The island itself is considered escape-proof because of the lake. You might remember. It's called Tib . . . Tibura . . . Tib—"

"Tiburi Kunga," Ben said. "It just came back to me."

"Do you remember what it means?" Maggie asked.

"Yes," Ben replied. " 'Shark Lake.' "

It was well after sunset when he finally made it to the gate of the AdenOil compound, lugging his dive hat and two heavy gearbags. He'd been on the phone for nearly four hours. Naji was waiting for him, chatting in Arabic with the guard in the security booth.

"A long day," the lean tribesman observed. "But productive, hopefully?"

Ben hoisted his gearbags into the sidecar, then placed his dive helmet on top of them. "Not bad," he replied with a weary smile, "considering it started with a street fight."

Naji grinned. "I was just recounting your exploits to Manat, here; particularly the disabling of Sahdman's five associates with a single stroke. He agrees with me that it was a most sublime maneuver. In addition, he agrees that since we have undoubtedly renewed the baldheads' sense of insult, it would be judicious of us *not* to be seen in and around Al-Mukkala for the next few days . . . perhaps longer."

"That shouldn't be a problem," Ben said, climbing

into the sidecar on top of his gearbags. He propped his booted legs up on the frame of the little windscreen and stretched, yawning. "I'm done with the job as of today . . . and something else has come up. I'll be sailing out of here tomorrow."

Naji made a farewell gesture to the guard and mounted the motorcycle. "Ah. It saddens me to hear that, my friend." He kickstarted the old machine and revved the engine a couple of times. "There is still much we could have seen and done together. This is a vast and ancient land; it holds many mysteries yet to be unraveled. But a man must be what he is. You have found more work beneath the sea?"

Ben rubbed his eyes. "Not exactly. What I've found is more like a boatload of trouble." He waved his hand. "Never mind. It's not your problem, Naji."

The blue eyes flashed, and the lean tribesman straightened in his seat. "Trouble? But you must tell me about this, *Ben-Ya-Min*, my brother. You must let me help."

Sighing, Ben shook his head. "You can't really help with this, Naji. It's a long way from here, and it involves many things that are outside your experience—no offense intended. And the situation could be—no, *will* be—highly dangerous. I may be wrong even to consider what I'm thinking about doing."

Naji was so alert he looked electrified. "Dangerous? Wrong? Surely you will explain these things to me, my brother."

Ben looked at him. There was no point in trying to put Naji off once he was on the scent of something that intrigued him. He'd learned *that* much about the lean Yemeni over the preceding two months.

"A small country in Africa, to the south of here, has fallen into civil war. A very bad situation. An old friend of mine is caught in the middle of it. His wife has asked me to try to get him out of there." Ben rubbed his eyes again. "Somehow."

"Ah," Naji said, nodding. "I see." He looked at Ben directly and smiled. "I will be going with you."

"No," Ben replied firmly. "No, you won't. This is nothing to do with you, Naji. This is about repaying a debt I owe because of something that happened a long time ago. It's something *I* have to do. You understand?"

The Yemeni's shrewd eyes narrowed. "Ahhh. This friend saved your life once, and now you cannot abandon him to his fate, is it not so?"

"Something like that, I guess."

"I can tell by the look upon your face that it is *exactly* like that. So, a man whose life has been saved by another owes him a life in return? This is what you believe?"

"Evidently," Ben said. "Or I wouldn't be doing what I'm about to do."

"Ah." Naji slapped a hand on his chest, looking triumphant. "That is why I am going with you. Did *you* not save *my* life only this morning, my brother?"

"That wasn't—" Ben protested.

"Did you or did you not smite the baldheads before they could shoot me down in the street?"

"Yes, but—"

"Would you have me owe you a life and yet refuse

me the opportunity to repay you? Would you have me carry the burden of such a debt for the rest of my days?"

Ben had no answer for that.

"It would not be charitable of you, *Ben-Ya-Min*, to treat your brother Naji in such a way."

The lean tribesman smiled slowly at Ben's continued silence.

"*Inshallah*," he said. "Allah wills it so."

He slipped the motorcycle into gear, and for once, started down the road at a leisurely pace, barely above an idle. It was dark, the sun long gone below the western horizon, and the stars pinprick sharp in the blue-black sky overhead.

Sitting on the gearbags with his arms crossed, a faint smile played across Ben's face as he considered how deftly he'd just been outmaneuvered.

CHAPTER 4

On the morning of the *Teresa Ann*'s third day out of Al-Mukkala, the sun rose like a fiery copper ball from a restless, whitecap-frosted eastern sea. The heavy oceangoing ketch was galloping along under full sail on a beam reach, her leeward rail buried more often than not; rising and falling, surging through the dark crests and troughs of a strongly running eight-foot swell. Contrary to her captain's usual habit, not a single reef had been taken for the night. The *Teresa Ann* was a vessel in a hurry.

Sass had drawn the midnight-to-four watch, but stayed in the cockpit until five-thirty to give Ben an extra hour and a half of sleep. Now they were both huddled together at the steering station, sipping strong coffee, Ben's bare foot on the lower arc of the wheel, keeping the boat on course. The *Teresa Ann*'s windward forward quarter smacked into the foaming crest of a swell—sturdy teak meeting a ton of moving water with a shuddering *thump*—and the two of them ducked simultaneously as a sheet of wind-whipped salt spray flew across the cockpit, the hard droplets stinging like birdshot where they encountered bare skin.

"Ow," Sass said with a grin, rubbing her wet forearm. "That's been happening all night. You know, if we fell off a couple of degrees, we'd be on more of a broad reach and wouldn't take so much spray." She looked at Ben expectantly.

"Yeah," he said, sipping coffee, "and in about two hours our bow would be crunching into a reef somewhere off the coast of Somalia." He glanced at the compass. "We'll stay on a course of two-two-zero degrees at least until we pass Mogadishu. After that, the coastline turns more to the west as it continues on down toward Kuballa and Bisotho. We can fall off the wind a little more then." He raised an eyebrow at her, a trace of a smile playing on his lips. "That okay by you, Admiral?"

Sass lifted an eyebrow right back at him. "If you say so, Captain Bligh." She grinned and took another slug of coffee.

The upper hatch of the main companionway slid back with a thud and Naji appeared, bareheaded, the wind ruffling his mane of curly black hair. He was wearing a loose white pullover shirt and *lungi* kilt, a small rug rolled up and tucked beneath his arm. Stretching his neck, he gazed up at the straining sails and took a deep breath of ocean air.

"Aaaaaahh! A good day to be alive, is it not?" He bowed slightly to Sass. "*Sabah il-kheyr, ya madehm,*" he said, then grinned at Ben. "And good morning to you, my brother! Allah surrounds us with beauty in this life, does he not?"

Ben looked out over the azure seascape, up at the

silver-blue dawn sky, and finally at Sass. "That he does," he agreed.

The lean Yemeni stepped up out of the hatchway and climbed onto the low roof of the *Teresa Ann*'s main cabin. He glanced first to the east, then to the west, and inquired, "Which way is Mecca this morning?"

Ben glanced at the compass and twisted around in his seat. "'Bout like that," he said, chopping his hand northward at a ten-degree angle off the starboard stern.

"Thank you, my brother." As he did five times a day, without fail, Naji unrolled the small, embroidered mat he carried, knelt on it in the direction Ben had indicated, and began the preliminary ablutions that preceded his daily prayers. He appeared not to notice the heaving of the vessel or the random gusts of spray that peppered water droplets onto his back, but touched his forehead repeatedly to the roof of the cabin and recited his verses in low, rapid tones, his eyes closed.

Ben and Sass kept a respectful silence until he had finished, absorbing some of the spirit if not the letter of the ancient Islamic prayers. Whatever name he went by—Allah, Jehovah, Yahweh, or any one of a hundred others—it was easy to believe in God on the open sea. More often than not, He was the only help you had.

Naji rolled up his prayer rug and slid down into the cockpit. "Are we close yet, *Ben Ya-Min*? This is the third day, is it not?"

"Right," Ben affirmed. "We left Al-Mukkala at dawn forty-eight hours ago. With this wind, our taffrail log indicates an average speed of fourteen point one knots—which is damn fast for a boat of this size and design, by the way—and GPS confirms it. It's eight hundred and forty nautical miles from Al-Mukkala to Krumake, the port capital on the Kuballan coast. If the wind holds, at our speed we'll make the entire run in three-and-a-half days."

Naji nodded seriously. "Indeed. Indeed." There was a somewhat blank look on his face. "So . . . We are close, then?"

Sass leaned in. "The answer you're after, Naji," she said, "is 'yes.' " She patted Ben's arm with affectionate patience. "He does that now and then. Ask him what time it is and he'll tell you how to build a Swiss watch."

Ben smiled and lifted an eyebrow in her direction. "Was I doing that again?"

"Yup," Sass said. "Kinda cute, if somewhat boring."

"Truly my brother possesses a vast knowledge of ships and the sea," Naji weighed in diplomatically, trying not to grin. "A fact which gives me great comfort, since I am presently sitting atop both."

"There, you see?" Ben remarked, digging a knuckle into Sass's ribs. She twisted away, laughing. "A man who appreciates skill and experience. No more comments from the peanut gallery."

Sass stuck a finger in her mouth and made a gagging sound as she got to her feet. "That's *Admiral* to you, bucko. And with that, I am retiring to my berth. I'm exhausted. Good night, Naji."

"*Tisbah a-la-kheyr*, Sasha," the tribesman replied, courteously using her full name, as he always did. He waited until she'd descended through the main companionway and slid the hatch shut before commenting: "A good one, that, my brother."

"She's a pistol," Ben acknowledged. "Carries her own weight."

"Indeed."

Naji sat in silence for a long moment, surveying the gusty seas around the bucketing ketch. "You hide your worry well, *Ben-Ya-Min*," he said finally.

"Do I?" Ben leaned easily to his left as the *Teresa Ann* rolled into a trough and laid her starboard rail down. "Glad I gave you that impression. But hiding it doesn't make it go away, unfortunately."

"Of course not. You do not yet have enough information to effectively plan your friend's escape."

Ben nodded. "That's part of it, all right. From what his wife told me, there's a way to sneak Nick out of the prison he's in without drawing any attention from the people who are keeping him there. But the prison's on an island in a big lake in the middle of Bisotho. I don't know how we're even supposed to enter the country, much less get close to it.

"The whole place is one big slaughterhouse. Everyone with any sense has gone either to Kenya in the south or Kuballa to the north. When we meet Nick's wife in Krumake tomorrow, I hope she fills in a few more of the 'how-tos' and 'what-ifs,' because I'm not about to get myself or anyone else killed trying to pull off something that can't possibly work. If we can put together a plan that seems feasible, then I owe it to Nick to give it a shot. But I'm not going in there like John Wayne charging up Mount Suribachi. This isn't

Sands of Iwo Jima. I'm no commando, I'm an oil-field worker, and I'm not interested in committing suicide."

Naji grinned, nodding. "Ah, yes. *Yohn-Wayne*. A formidable fighter. The Large Duke is much loved and respected by the men of my tribe."

"Eh?" Ben looked at him. "You know about John Wayne?"

"Certainly. A great warrior and leader of men."

"He's a *movie actor*."

Naji lifted a finger. "In his movies, he demonstrates himself to be a fine example of a proper man. He is courageous, he is compassionate, he is just, he is merciful. He is swift to punish the evildoer, but slow to condemn the good man gone astray. In battle, he is terrible to behold, leaving his slain enemies strewn about the landscape, so that their wives may wail and lament over their bodies and the vultures pick and tear at their livers and eyes and—"

"I get the picture," Ben interrupted quickly. "Naji, I thought you couldn't get those kinds of American movies in your country. Where do you go to see them? I thought the *Imams* frowned on anything like that."

The tribesman leaned over with a conspiratorial smile. "Well, confidentially, my brother, we do not always listen to every little thing the *Imams* say. Like Sahdman and his baldheads, some of them are woefully without humor. Who can live under the influence of such people without some small respite? Fortunately, the *sheik* in my clan's area of the Hadhramaut is a man of great practicality and munificent character. He has provided a movie house in his own compound for the use of his friends and dependents. It was there

that I first learned of the great warrior *Yohn-Wayne*."
He nodded happily.

"Huh!" Ben grunted. "What's your favorite John
Wayne movie?"

"Ah!" Naji enthused. "Undoubtedly, *The Con-
queror*."

Ben frowned. "I don't think I remem—" He stopped
in mid-sentence. "You mean that ridiculous flick
where he played Attila the Hun or Ghengis Khan or
something?"

"He was a great *khan*, yes, who led a mighty hoard
of riders armed with swords and spears. The suffering
he inflicted upon his opponents was most inspiring."

Ben grinned at his feet. "What others have you
seen? *The Searchers? True Grit? Red River?*"

"These are not familiar to me," Naji said, "but I
have seen many of the Large Duke's finest movies. The
titles are imprinted upon my memory: I have seen
*Randy Rides Alone; The Star Packer; Pals of the Saddle;
Ride Him, Cowboy*—"

"All the good stuff."

"Truly, my brother."

Ben chuckled and nudged the wheel, correcting the
Teresa Ann's course slightly.

"'The Large Duke,'" he repeated, looking out
across the rolling swells. "God bless him, I get the feeling that, in a few days, it'd sure be handy to have him
around."

The wind gained strength throughout the day, until
at dusk the anemometer was showing a steady thirty
knots. Ben took the eight-to-twelve watch, then turned

the wheel over to Naji just after midnight. When he crawled into the sea berth in the main cabin, Sass was awake.

"What are you going to do when we reach Kuballa, Ben?"

She'd been asking variations on that question for three days, her apprehension growing hour by hour. Given the bleak, uncertain scenario thus far, he could hardly blame her. Jamming pillows around his body to brace himself against the *Teresa Ann*'s roll, he lay back and blew out a long breath.

"Talk to Maggie, and look at what kind of plan she's got for springing Nick. Other than that, I don't really know, babe." He brushed her hair aside and tugged gently at her earlobe. "This is improvisation all the way."

She put the point of her chin on his chest and fixed her blue eyes on his. "Ben."

"Uh-huh?"

"Promise me you won't improvise your way into an early grave."

He half smiled. "Not me, kiddo. I love life too much."

"I know you. You'll get within arm's reach of Nick, and then because you think you owe him you'll stay five seconds too long when the shit hits the fan instead of cutting and running—like you *should*."

"You're giving me too much credit," Ben insisted. "I'm a coward at heart."

She thumped his chest. "*Ben*."

"Okay, look. The way Maggie explained it to me, I don't have to do anything violent or heroic. It'll work because it's basically a diving job—except that I'm liberating a man from a hole in the rock instead of liberating oil from the ocean floor. And she says there's a way to get me in, and both of us the hell *out*, very quickly."

"But *how*?"

Ben passed a hand over his eyes. "That's the thing. She didn't give me any details over the phone. Just said she was flying from Ethiopia back to Kuballa on the next flight, and she'd be waiting for us in Krumake with more information." He sighed. "I couldn't turn her down, Sass. You should have heard her. She sounded like she was coming apart at the seams. I've never heard her talk the way she did. And you *know* what I—we—owe Nick Fenzi."

Sass laid her head over on his chest. "Yeah." She was silent for a moment. "Maggie said she was flying *back* to Kuballa?"

"Uh-huh."

"But just before we left Al-Mukkala I thought *you* said that *she* said she'd come directly from Washington to Addis Ababa, looking for you."

Ben looked at her. "That's right. She did." His brows knitted in puzzlement. "That's odd. She didn't tell me she'd gone to Kuballa first. Maybe she just misspoke. She was pretty stressed out."

"Hm. I guess."

They lay together quietly for a few minutes, listening to the myriad sounds that were ever-present in a wooden vessel under sail—the surging rush of water along the hull; the muffled creaking of mahogany, oak, and teak in constant flexion; the noisy patter of salt spray hitting the glass of the overhead skylight; the high moan of the wind in the rigging. As always, it was like being in the belly of a living thing.

Ben gazed up at the captain's compass mounted upside down directly over his head. It never varied more than two degrees east or west of two-twenty—and then only for a moment. Sass watched it with him.

"Naji steers well," she said. "How can he do that?"

"Do what?"

"Take to the sea so easily when he's spent all of his life in the desert."

Ben smiled. "I asked him that. He says the desert and the sea are very much the same. Remember the Rub Al-Khali, the Empty Quarter of southern Saudi Arabia? He calls it 'The Ocean of Sand.' It shifts and flows constantly, just like the sea, and if you fall off your vessel when you're crossing it—in this case, a camel—you're pretty much dead meat."

"That's poetic, but it still doesn't explain how he steers so well."

"I was getting to that. Naji's been around. One of the things he did when he was younger was make his first pilgrimage to Mecca aboard a trading *dhow*. He liked it so much that he worked on her for two years, making runs up and down the Red Sea from Djibouti to the Suez. Became one of the best helmsmen on that trade route." Ben chuckled. "Our desert tribesman is an old sailing hand. You think I'd let him sit a watch up there by himself if he hadn't already proven he knows what he's doing?"

"I have to admit: I've been wondering about that for two days now," Sass murmured. "Now I don't have to wonder anymore." Her voice was slurring. "Time to catch some *zeeeees . . .*"

Ben cradled her head in the hollow of his shoulder and watched the 220-degree mark of the compass card dance steadily along the lubber line, until his eyelids went heavy and he, too, drifted off to sleep.

By midafternoon of their fourth day at sea, the wind had fallen to half its former strength. It was still quite adequate for moving the *Teresa Ann* along, but her speed had dropped to nine knots. Her leeward rail now high and dry, she rode easily through much-diminished swells, flying a large balloon jib Ben had set in addition to her usual full suit of sails.

At precisely 3:24 P.M. local time, she foamed past the bouncing seabuoy—a rust-streaked, nine-foot-tall white can—that marked the entrance to the Krumake ship channel, and headed down the fairway on a dead run, her sails wing-and-wing. Four miles distant, the lushly vegetated coastline of Kuballa sat atop glittering emerald green shallows, accented here and there by the low white buildings of the port capital. A large school of stingrays, their brown bodies contrasting vividly with the aquamarine blue of the deep channel water, darted out from beneath the *Teresa Ann*'s driving bow, their winglike fins flapping furiously just below the surface.

The ship channel was a slender, zigzagging pathway through an otherwise-impenetrable series of coral reefs that guarded the approach waters off Krumake. On either side of the ketch, the telltale yellowish brown color of shoaling coral clearly demarcated the line between clear sailing and a sudden, catastrophic stop. Standing with one leg hooked around the railing of the bow pulpit, Ben surveyed the various channel markers ahead through a pair of high-powered Zeiss binoculars. According to the chart, there were no less than three doglegs between the seabuoy and the harbor. He picked out the first one, some three hundred yards ahead, then went aft to the cockpit and started the *Teresa Ann*'s auxiliary diesel engine.

As they slid into the first dogleg, Ben rounded the ketch up into the wind, taking advantage of the tiny bit of extra sea room the turn afforded, and held her in position with the engine while Sass and Naji dropped the sails, working from bow to stern. The air filled with the buffeting racket of loose canvas being flogged by a stiff breeze.

When the sails had been furled and lashed down, Ben swung the *Teresa Ann* off the wind and down the starboard side of the fairway, revving the diesel up to three-quarter speed. As he did so, two shallow-draft outrigger canoes came scudding off the coral flats, unmindful of the jagged rock just beneath their keelless hulls, and into the channel, their patchwork lateen sails pulling hard. They approached the big American ketch to either side, heading seaward. Each canoe held sheaves of fishing net dotted with red, green, and yellow ball floats, a half dozen buckets of longline, and four ebony-black Kuballan fishermen, three of whom stood on the windward gunwale of their small craft, counterbalancing it. The helmsman sat on the canoe's overhanging stern, steering with a lashed paddle.

As they zipped past, port and starboard, all eight

men waved energetically, strong teeth grinning
sharply white in dark faces, and let out shouts of welcome—the words unintelligible but the meaning clear.
Waving back from the top of the *Teresa Ann*'s cabin,
Sass could clearly see intricate patterns of scarification
on the blue-black skin of each man's face, chest, and
arms. Then, in seconds, the fishing canoes were astern,
leaving twin wakes of sizzling white foam sketched
across the turquoise water.

"Moving out!" Ben said, spinning the wheel. "Impressive. I bet they're doing sixteen knots."

"They looked like a pair of four-man windsurfers,"
Sass agreed. "They're so *narrow*. What happens if they
catch more fish than they can hold?"

Ben shrugged. "Split the haul between both boats
and then let the rest go, I guess."

The second dogleg was coming up, marked by a
green spar buoy that was barely afloat. Ben glanced at
the screen of the compact fishfinder mounted on the
cockpit steering pedestal, checking the channel's
depth and bottom profile, and maneuvered the *Teresa
Ann* through the turn onto the new heading. "A little
maintenance needed, I believe," he said, eyeing the
damaged marker. "That looks like it's been hit recently."

"If so, it was a poor helmsman indeed who let the
vessel under his hand wander so close to the reef,"
Naji sniffed with a professional's disdain.

The low buildings of Krumake were much larger
now, standing out chalky white against the surrounding tropical foliage. A dozen miles behind them, above
the coastal plain, the mist-wreathed mountains that

formed the border with Bisotho squatted along the lower edge of the sky like dark gray sentinels. Ben raised the binoculars to his eyes. The waterfront of the small harbor was lined with wooden cargo docks: a quarter of them relatively new, the other three-quarters rotting off their sagging pilings. Multicolored fishing canoes and dories bobbed everywhere, and one rust-bucket tramp freighter, listing badly, was tied up in front of what looked like a loading silo for bauxite or some other unrefined mineral. Ben lowered the glasses. It was a fairly typical small third-world port.

"All right," he said. "When we get in there, we'll take a quick tour around the harbor to find the best anchorage. Sass, put this up on the main spreader halyard, will you?" He handed her a small yellow flag he'd taken from beneath the helmsman's seat. "Hopefully, customs and immigration in Kuballa isn't run by the local mafia."

He sat down behind the wheel, letting out a long breath. "And thennnn—with any luck—we'll find Maggie Fenzi waiting for us at her hotel . . . with a *lot* more information than we have right now."

CHAPTER 5

The customs official's name was Mr. Kikkononikakka, and he was the only person Ben had ever met whose head appeared to be twice the size horizontally that it was vertically. This jarring physical aspect was further enhanced by a pair of tiny eyes that were set less than an inch apart; a broad nose that had evidently been squashed flat at one time or another; and a huge mouth equipped with lips that resembled a pair of jumbo franks. In addition, he was prodigiously fat in the upper body and as bald as an egg. Little beads of sweat glistened like minute diamonds all over the blue-black skin of his scalp and neck.

Watching him over Ben's shoulder, Sass was reminded of a celestial navigation text that described the shape of the earth as an "oblate spheroid"; or flattened ball. That was Mr. Kikkononikakka's head, in the extreme. He looked like an equatorial African version of Jabba the Hutt.

He was also one of the friendliest customs officials either Ben or Sass had ever encountered, jovial and informative. He became positively rapturous upon discovering the crisp new American hundred-dollar bill that Ben had placed inside the first of the two passports he'd handed him. Whisking it into the breast pocket of his white uniform shirt—which was adorned with green-and-black epaulets approximately the size of small roofing shingles—he stamped the two U.S. passports with barely a glance and returned them to Ben, grinning like the man in the moon.

"Ho-ho, by Jove!" he said. "Necessary checking of documents moving along smartly, don't you know? And now, please, quick looking at travel papers of this gentleman over here, good heavens and by thunder!" He indicated Naji, continuing to grin all over his incredible face.

Clad once again in black desert half shawl and headgear, Naji was in macho Arab mode, leaning against the forward bulkhead of the *Teresa Ann*'s main cabin with his arms crossed, dignified and aloof. He produced Yemeni papers from beneath his robe and silently handed them to Sass, who passed them on to Mr. Kikkononikakka. Spreading them out on the galley table at which he and Ben were sitting, the customs official surveyed the Arabic script—with which he was obviously unfamiliar—for a few seconds, then began energetically stamping everything in sight. When all of Naji's papers seemed sufficiently covered in official green Kuballan ink, he ceased his pounding, grunted in approval, and handed the bundle back to Sass.

"All in order, all in order!" he informed them. "Welcoming you to Kuballa, great Scott and goodness gracious! Always happy to receive visitors from America—hurray for George Bush and Abraham Lincoln! Hurray for Coca-Cola, by thunder!" He looked over at Naji. "And visitor from Yemen, too, of course, of course—hurray for Yasser Arafat! Hurray for Saddam Hussein!" He nodded amicably, grinning like a gigantic cherub, apparently certain that he had chosen a string of references flattering to everyone.

"Thank you," Ben and Sass replied in unison, smiling and nodding back. Naji nodded once, imperceptibly, his face blank. Mr. Kikkononikakka stood up, rising to his full height of six feet plus—for all the bulbous weight in his upper body, his legs were long and slender—placed a couple of gaudy visitor-orientation pamphlets on the table, and snapped shut the catches of his leather briefcase. Ben and Sass got to their feet as well.

They climbed the companionway ladder to the cockpit, where the customs official paused and indicated the wooden dock alongside which the *Teresa Ann* was tied. "You moving boat down into government yard, along customs pier," he suggested. "Not leaving nice boat here, no-no, by Jove! No danger, but thievings of ropes and pulleys and buckets and silver spoons when you away, tut-tut! Very annoying and just not cricket, old boy! Moving boat to customs pier, my sons keep close watch, you bet your boots! Ten dollars American each day, okay? Very fair price for security, don't you seeing and agreeing? Sons of Kikkononikakka first-class chaps, all temps in local constabulary, most dependable, I say! Absolutely safe for boat, yahoo and tallyho!"

"I appreciate that, Mr. Kikkononikakka," Ben said, catching on quickly. He reached into the pocket of his shorts, retrieved a small roll of bills, and peeled off another hundred. "For ten days, in advance." He placed it in the customs official's hand. "And if there have been no problems with the vessel by the time we leave, I like to pay a bonus as a gesture of appreciation—as long as that's all right with *you*, of course, sir."

"By Jove, absolutely and don't you know it, old chap!" Mr. Kikkononikakka enthused. "Boat policed carefully night and day, you bet! No creepings and skulduggery from dishonest persons, blast and confound it!" He nodded emphatically.

"Thank you," Ben said. He pointed down the ways. "Over there, by the green warehouse? That's the dock?"

"Absolutely, by thunder! You slipping boat down there, lickety-split! Plenty of deep water for happy and gay floating! No problem!"

And with that, he stepped off the *Teresa Ann* and proceeded down the dock toward the government warehouse, pausing once to beam at them and indicate again, with elaborate gestures, exactly where they should reposition the big ketch.

Krumake proved to be relatively clean and well laid out, with cobblestone streets and whitewashed buildings, many of which were of older European design. The orientation pamphlets Mr. Kikkononikakka had left were quite informative. Founded in 1802 by the British, and named—with singular lack of imagination—Port Royal (Ben had observed, in the course of his travels, that there seemed to be at least one British "Port Royal" for every degree of habitable latitude on Earth), the settlement had been constructed around a central hub, or town square, with streets radiating out

from it like the spokes of a wheel. A short, wide boule-
vard connected the square to the waterfront, where in
colonial times everything from slaves to spices to bales
of exotic bird feathers—destined for the hats and
headdresses of wealthy European women—had been
loaded onto square-rigged merchantmen for export to
the West.

Early on during the interminable nationalistic
squabbling that preoccupied much of Europe throughout the nineteenth century, the British lost their small
trading settlement to the French, who renamed it Port
Royale—thereby demonstrating that they had no more
imagination than the Englishmen from whom they'd
taken it. The French then promptly lost it to the Ger-
mans, who had been casting about for a little colonial
respectability in Africa for some time. When every
blond-haired, blue-eyed Aryan in the garrison died of
either sunstroke or dengue fever within a year, a
sheepish German government quietly gave the
town—which they'd renamed Koniglich Hafen (Royal
Port)—back to the British . . . who by that time were so
busy killing Russians in the Crimea that they couldn't
even be bothered to rerename it, much less post a garrison there.

The succeeding one hundred years saw the British
relinquish control over their East African Protectorate,
pull out of Kenya, and go through a series of political
contortions as colonial white Rhodesia became modern black Zimbabwe. With the fate of major ports such
as Mombassa, Zanzibar, and Dar-Es-Salaam hanging
in the balance on a semiregular basis, scarcely anyone
noticed when, in 1932, the British suddenly aban-

doned what had come to be known as Krumake—in so doing endowing it with the distinction of being the only African port ever to be discarded by a European power in the twentieth century due to lack of interest.

Fortunately for Krumake, the enlightened leadership of a succession of visionary black African intellectuals, all members of the regionally dominant *Kubal* ethnic group, resulted in the creation of the small independent state of Kuballa during the late 1950s. Adherence to democratic principles, ethnic harmony, and geographic isolation from its troubled neighbor, Bisotho, to the south, had enabled Kuballa to remain peaceful and relatively prosperous—in spite of the political and ethnic conflicts that periodically flared up just outside its borders. Currently, according to what Mr. Kikkononikakka had said, the problem was refugees. The Kuballan military was fully deployed along the mountain passes, intercepting continuous streams of terrified people fleeing savage fighting in Bisotho, and redirecting them to Red Cross–supported internment camps.

In Krumake, however, there seemed to be little indication of the strain the country was under. The streets were moderately crowded but clean, and the faces of its inhabitants reflected no concerns beyond those of everyday living. As Ben, Sass, and Naji made their way around the west side of the town square, they were acknowledged time and time again with friendly nods and smiles from the almost universally handsome, ebony-skinned Kuballans. Sass felt an odd tug in her chest when she got a good look at the memorial monument to Kuballan independence that occupied the center of the square. According to Mr. Kikkononikakka's pamphlets, it was a bronze likeness of the country's first president, frozen in the act of breaking the door of a slave cage off its hinges.

The Hotel Excelsior, just a few hundred yards north of the square, looked exactly like what it was—an immense, ornate, whitewashed anachronism—a remnant of Britain's imperialistic past, dating back to the days when empire-builders like Cecil Rhodes constructed grand hotels and society clubhouses from which the white ruling class could rob the continent blind in luxurious comfort. Now, though it had lost much of its grandeur and was showing its age, the Kuballan government routinely subsidized its maintenance and required that the standard of service be kept high, recognizing that foreign investment was difficult enough to attract without the additional burden of having to put up visiting corporate executives, in from abroad for a first impression of Kuballa, in fly-ridden flophouses. The Excelsior was still, by far, the best hotel in Krumake.

Ben trotted up the broad stone stairs of the main entrance and through a beautifully carved mahogany-and-glass revolving door, which looked old enough to be original. Sass and Naji followed him into the main lobby; a thoroughly Victorian affair boasting a twenty-foot-high ceiling, heavy wooden crown moldings, and several Greek Revival–style fluted columns. The British imperial effect had been toned down somewhat by the placement of brightly colored African tapestries on every possible wall space. Rattan paddlewheel fans rotated slowly above armchairs and sofas upholstered with imitation zebra, cheetah, and leopard skins, and a massive front desk of polished ironwood occupied most of one wall near the revolving door.

"Ben! Sass!"

At the sound of the sharp female voice, they both turned to see Maggie Fenzi rise from an armchair beside one of the columns and start toward them, her high heels clicking loudly on the marble floor. A tall brunette with a hard, muscular leanness that Ben—in spite of liking her as the wife of a friend—had always found slightly unfeminine, she was wearing a no-nonsense business suit of charcoal gray, the skirt hemmed high enough above the knee to show off the well-turned dancer's legs she still possessed at age forty-nine. Her face, attractive enough but perpetually lined from a diet of lettuce leaves, Fresca, and menthol cigarettes, seemed even more pale than usual, the skin typing-paper white behind the black mascara and maroon lipstick she favored. Her jewelry was conspicuous enough to distract from her overall look rather than accentuate it; she wore a sapphire-and-emerald broach, an amethyst necklace, and diamond stud earrings. Multiple rings festooned her fingers.

"I can't tell you how much it means to me to see you," she said to Ben. She gave Sass a hug. "Hi, honey. I wasn't sure you'd be coming, but I'm glad you did."

"Where he goes, I go," Sass remarked. "Most of the time, anyway."

"Yeah, that's usually been the case, hasn't it?" Maggie smiled and looked at Naji. "Hello."

Ben touched her arm. "This is Naji, Mag, a friend of ours from Yemen. He's here to help, if need be."

The lean desert tribesman bowed slightly from the waist. "A pleasure, *ya madehm*," he said.

Maggie looked a little uncertain as she took in the hawk-nosed, blue-eyed face and the black Bedouin garb, but renewed her smile anyway. "Nice to meet you, Naji."

She gestured toward the elevator. "Why don't we go up to my room? We can talk in private there. The hotel bar stays open late, and it's kinda nice. We can always come down for a drink later if we need it."

Sass lifted an eyebrow. "If we *need* it?"

Maggie looked at her. "Honey, you never know. I've needed a half dozen drinks every night for the past three weeks."

Ben frowned. "I thought you and Nick were both charter members of AA, Mag."

Something resembling desperation flitted across Maggie Fenzi's face.

"Not anymore," she said.

The room lacked the musty colonial elegance of the lobby, having a sterile modern decor typical of any American highway motel chain. A few of the ubiquitous polished-wood carvings of elongated heads that were common throughout Africa stood on top of generic hotel furniture, and the walls were decorated with mass-produced, sloppily impressionistic paintings of tropical foliage and flowers, rendered in lurid purple and red acrylics. The mounted head of a small warthog adorned one wall, looking rather moth-eaten and out of place.

"That thing's damned ugly even for a warthog," Ben commented, gazing at it.

"It's all the company I've got in here," Maggie said. "That and these wooden heads." She waved her maroon nails at the impassive carvings. "The other night I had about eight too many bourbon and waters, passed out, and woke up at three o'clock in the morning with the goddamned things talking to me. When I screamed I think I shook some plaster off the ceiling." She glanced at Sass, sitting opposite her on the bed, and suddenly her face cracked and she began to cry.

"Aw, baby . . ." Instinctively, Sass pushed aside the map spread out between them on the bedspread and slid over next to her, enfolding her in her arms. "Shh . . . shhhh . . ."

Ben caught Sass's eye, exchanged a slight nod with her, and got up from his chair. Walking around the bed, he picked up the map, moved to the far end of the room, and spread it out on top of a chest of drawers. Then he turned to Naji, who was leaning against the wall with his arms crossed. "Come have a look at this, Naji."

The tribesman moved up beside him. "What have you, *Ben-Ya-Min*?"

Ben tapped a finger on the large blue blot in the center of the map. "According to what Maggie told me four days ago, this is where I have to go. It's called Tiburi Kunga—Shark Lake."

Naji looked at him. "I do not like the name, my brother."

"Uh-huh. Anyway, as I explained back in Al-Mukkala, my friend Nick is being held on a small island at the lake's southern end. In an old prison or fort or something. I've got to get him out, and when Maggie gets a grip on herself again"——he glanced over at the two figures huddled together on the bed—"she'll tell us exactly *how* I'm supposed to do that. I hope."

Naji regarded the sobbing woman. "Indeed," he muttered sympathetically.

Sass was stroking Maggie's dark hair back from her temples, one arm around her shoulders, talking to her softly. Ben and Naji studied the map in silence, familiarizing themselves with details of the lakeshore's contours and the topography of the surrounding countryside. Outside, the sun was dipping below Krumake's higher rooftops, beaming misty orange rays through the window as the hot afternoon faded into sultry evening.

Finally, Maggie blew her nose and sat up, looking pale and disheveled but otherwise in control of herself. Plucking a brush off the bedside table, she ran it through her hair a dozen times, wiped the mascara runs from beneath her eyes with a tissue, and cleared her throat.

"I'm sorry," she said, her voice hoarse. "I've been doing that a lot. It comes over me without any warning, I'm afraid."

"Don't worry about it, hon," Sass chided gently. "You've got good reason."

"Yeah, Mag, really," Ben added. He picked up the map, came across the room, and spread it out on the floor near the bed. Pulling up a chair, he sat down next to her. "Do you feel like telling us what it is you think we can do to help Nick?"

She shook a menthol slim out of the pack on the bedside table and lit it with an expensive Dunhill lighter. "All right," she said, exhaling a stream of smoke and flicking her maroon thumbnail repeatedly against the cigarette's filter end, "here's the idea."

They crowded around as Maggie leaned over the map and touched a nail to a small dot at the extreme southern end of the lake. "This is where Nick is," she said. "On this island. I got all the info I could about the place from the small English-language section of the library here in Krumake. During the 1870s, the French took possession of what's now called Bisotho—particularly the area around this lake and the river that flows out of it to the Indian Ocean. Called it 'French East Africa' or some damn thing. They lasted here just over two years before the Sultan of Zanzibar kicked them out. Anyway, during that time, the French Foreign Legion built a fort on this island, not far from the entrance to the river.

"Bisotho had been pretty peaceful for about three years before things blew up just last month, so I was able to get some fairly recent information on the fort. Some archaeologists from a Kenyan university had been investigating it and published a few articles, complete with drawings."

She reached down and withdrew a file folder from the lower shelf of the bedside table. Sticking her cigarette in the corner of her mouth, squinting against the smoke curling up around her eyes, she undid the string that held the flap shut and pulled out three or four photocopied diagrams, originally done in a draftsman's hand on grid paper. She passed the first one to Ben.

"These are to scale. Basically, the place hasn't changed since the Foreign Legion built it a hundred and thirty years ago."

Ben gazed at the drawing. "Looks a lot like some of those old Civil War–era forts you see back in the States. Plenty of archways, tunnels, and underground vaults." He pointed at the bottom of the page. "These little rooms down here might be cells, don't you think?"

"They're cells, all right," Maggie said. "Dungeons. Apparently the French were big on dungeons. According to what I read, the Legionnaires called it *Le Bastille d'Afrique.*"

" 'The African Bastille,' " Sass said.

"Right. Sounds like a cozy place, huh?"

Sass licked her lips. "Not really."

"You think Nick's in one of these cells?" Ben asked.

Maggie shook her head. "No. Like I told you over the phone when you called from Al-Mukkala, he has to be able to see the sky for the little uplink unit to work. It can't acquire a passing satellite otherwise. So he can't be in any of these cells—they're nothing but holes in the rock without windows. He wouldn't be able to send any e-mails. And besides, the Kenyan scientists noted that nearly all of them had collapsed.

"One of his messages said 'in well.' I didn't understand what it meant until I saw the drawings of the fort." She pointed at a diagram of the structure's small inner quadrangle. "See that? That's where the drinking water used to come from. It's an old well the French dug, originally to give the garrison a water source within the fortifications. It ended up being used as a prison pit after two other wells were put in. Whenever they had more prisoners than cells, they just stuck them in the bottom of the big well. There was a grating over the top of it—not that anybody would have been able to climb out."

"Nice," Sass commented.

"Uh-huh. Anyway, the Kenyan archaeology papers say that the soldiers dug down through the limestone the island's made of for about thirty feet—and then punched through the roof of a big flooded void full of clear, fresh water; right at lake level. The lake itself is quite murky, except close to the island. The farther away you get, the murkier it is, so the archaeologists figure that a large freshwater spring eroded out a dome or cavern system right under the fort, and clear water flows outward from the island's perimeter."

"Odd," Ben said. "A hollow island. At least below lake level."

"That's what they think," Maggie went on. "But check this out. There are written records of French Legionnaires catching *'les requins'* up to ten feet long . . . *right out of the well.*"

Ben was silent for a moment. "Huh," he muttered. "How about that."

Naji pulled at his goatee. "What is *'les requins,'* my brother?"

"It's French," Ben said. "It means 'sharks.'"

"Wonderful," Sass grumbled. "And ten feet long, no less."

"See this drawing?" Maggie produced another photocopied sheet from the folder. "It's a schematic of the
well. You can see what the soldiers did—they dug
down through the soft limestone for—what?—exactly
twenty-nine feet, making a cylindrical hole ten feet
wide, and then broke away about a third of the bottom
to get through the roof of the flooded dome. So there's
a landing down there—about ten feet long by seven
feet wide, and a flooded opening to the dome or cavern below about half that size."

"And the dome is infested with sharks," Sass said.

"Well," Maggie replied blandly, "there were some in
there when the Legionnaires dug through the roof
over a hundred years ago. And I guess there still are.
Nick's last e-mail included the phrase 'sharks in well.'
Every so often, a small one noses up in the pool at the
bottom of the pit. That's what gave him the idea that
there just might be a way out underwater."

"What are sharks doing in a freshwater lake?" Sass
inquired. "And in freshwater caves, too? They live in
the ocean."

Ben cleared his throat. "Well, most of them do. But
there are certain sharks that can make the transition
from salt to fresh water, or just live in fresh water all
the time. Back home in the States, bull sharks have
been caught in the Mississippi River as far up as Vicks-
burg. In Central America, in Lake Nicaragua, there are
freshwater sharks that have actually attacked native
fishermen over the years. And there are underwater
sea caves along the coast of the Yucatán in Mexico with
freshwater springs in them. Saltwater reef sharks
swim into them and hang out, breathing in the fresh

water like some kind of drug. It anesthetizes them. Pretty weird."

"I remember you telling me about those Yucatán sharks now," Sass said. "They call them 'The Sleeping Sharks.'"

Maggie cut in again. "Here in Africa, they've got Zambezi sharks, which are apparently just another subspecies of bull shark, that swim upriver from the ocean and bite people's feet off in shallow water now and again, miles inland. So it's not unusual to find a freshwater shark in Africa. They're around. And that's how Shark Lake got its name, by the way. They're in there, even in the hollow dome under the island."

She looked straight at Ben and took a long drag on her cigarette. "Do you see why this is interesting?" she asked.

"Yeah," Ben replied. "If there are ten-foot sharks in that underground dome, it can't just be a go-nowhere hollow eroded out by the spring. Sharks need to feed—they can't live in a dark, flooded hole in the ground. And how would they get in there in the first place? There must be a connecting underwater passageway—probably several—from the dome to the lake. And if a ten-foot shark can swim through it . . ."

". . . so can a man," Sass finished.

Maggie stubbed out her cigarette in the ashtray on the bedside table and reached for her pack of menthols. "Here's the whole plan, in a nutshell: I've found a guy with a floatplane who's willing to fly into Bisotho at night and land on the lake, pretty close to the island. No one will be able to see the plane in the dark with its lights off, and the pilot says there's usually a night fog hanging on the surface. You slip in, Ben, in diving gear, and swim for the fort, underwater. He takes off again. You find your way to Nick through the underground waterway, bring him out, and rendezvous with the plane two hours later. Simple."

Sass was white-faced. "He's not doing that," she said. "That's the craziest thing I've ever heard."

"He can do it," Maggie said. "I know he can."

"But that's idiotic!" Sass exploded. "He's supposed to find his way into an unknown underwater cavern system in the dark, with sharks and God-knows-what-else for company, and figure out exactly which way to go before he uses up all his air? Have you ever been on a cave dive? Those limestone caverns can go on forever!"

"The island's only a few hundred yards across," Maggie argued. She lit another cigarette. "The dome under it can't be all that big. And the water should be crystal clear, so he'll be able to see okay with a light."

"Wait, *wait!*" Sass went on. "There's so much wrong with this it isn't even amusing. How do you know Nick's still in the well? When was the last time you uplinked to him?"

"Not *to* him—*from* him. I was never able to send e-mails back to him. I could only receive his." Maggie paused to draw on her cigarette. "Nearly a week ago, now." She blew out a cloud of smoke. "I don't know for sure if he's still in there, but I think so. And every hour that goes by—"

"Increases the chances that they'll move him, if they haven't already," Ben finished. He thought a moment.

"I'll need the right gear," he said. "I have some on the boat. But there are a few things—"

"What about the soldiers in the fort?" Sass demanded. "Those are the ones responsible for the genocide going on in Bisotho right now, aren't they? Who do you think you are—the Terminator? You're going to get your head blown off!"

Ben considered. "I don't think so. I'll be underwater, out of sight, the whole time. If Nick's down in that well, I hardly think anybody will be watching him. All he has to do is slip into the water with me, breathe off my octopus regulator, and swim back out to the plane. No soldiers. No shooting."

"*Ben*, " Sass pleaded. "You aren't seriously considering this . . ."

"A substantial risk, my brother," Naji weighed in. "A man should think twice before burrowing into a hornet's nest."

"Oh?" Ben replied, looking him in the eye. "Like I did when I took out Sahdman's five gunmen back in Al-Mukkala?" He turned to Sass. "Like Nick Fenzi did seventeen years ago when he swam down three hundred feet into a pile of tangled steel to cut me free before my arm could be sliced off?"

There was dead silence in the room. A subtle expression of triumph crept over Maggie Fenzi's pale face.

"If we're going to do this, then the sooner the better," Ben said. "I need to go back to the boat to organize the gear I'll need. Mag, you say this pilot's ready to fly?"

"Yes."

"So tomorrow night's okay?"

"Yes. But I'll check with him and make sure."

"Good," Ben said. He rose to his feet. "Do you have a vehicle?"

"The pilot does," Maggie replied. "I can use it."

"All right. Drive down to the boat tomorrow, sometime after noon. I'll have equipment to transfer to the plane." He paused. "And by the way . . . this guy can fly half-decently, right?"

Maggie nodded. "As far as I know. He's been bush-hopping in Africa for a while."

"Glad to hear it," Ben said, "because if he turns out to be some kind of drunk with a junker plane who's going to crash us into Shark Lake at night in a fog, I'm going to change my mind about going."

CHAPTER 6

It was just before six the following evening when the borrowed Land Rover swung off the main road leading out of Krumake and onto the tiny dirt airstrip at the edge of town, Maggie Fenzi at the wheel. Gear shifted and air tanks rang together as the vehicle jounced over pothole after pothole, loose gravel peppering the underside of the chassis. In the passenger seats, Ben, Sass, and Naji braced themselves against the violent motion.

"Sorry," Maggie called over the grinding of gears, slowing down. "Forgot about those damn divots."

The airstrip was little more than a fifty-foot-wide slash through the surrounding jungle, approximately the length of a football field, which had been cleared and leveled by a bulldozer. At its far end was a small Quonset hut, its corrugated metal sides brown with rust. A faded wind sock flopped limply at the top of a short flagpole near its front entrance.

A very large delta-wing hang glider was sitting on the runway in front of the hut, canted over with one wingtip in the dirt. Some unrecognizable machinery was strewn around it. There was no sign of a conventional aircraft.

Ben frowned as the Land Rover pulled up beside the hut. "Where's the plane?" he asked.

Maggie braked the vehicle in a cloud of dust and looked over at him. "That's it," she said, turning off the ignition.

Ben blinked through the windshield as the dust drifted away. "You're kidding."

"Don't judge too quickly," Maggie cautioned. "All these bits and pieces assemble into a really neat ultra-light floatplane. It's big, too—a four-seater." She pointed at a couple of narrow aluminum-skinned hulls lying in the weeds. "Those are the pontoons."

They climbed out of the Land Rover, stretching their cramped limbs, and surveyed the junkyardlike surroundings. Things didn't look any more promising upon closer inspection.

Ben blinked again. "*This* is the plane?"

Without warning, an ear-shattering roar split the evening air, accompanied by an eruption of blue smoke from behind the Quonset hut. Everyone jumped, and Sass clapped her hands over her ears. The savage noise rose and fell in pitch as someone manipulated the throttle of what sounded like a seriously diseased outboard engine.

Ben looked at Naji and Sass, then everyone looked at Maggie. She was shrugging and trying to say something, her lips moving, but her words were completely drowned out by the racketing noise.

As quickly as it had begun, the roaring stopped. There was a final flatulent discharge—*PLOOF*—and a single large smoke ring blew out horizontally from behind the hut, turned gracefully onto its side, and drifted upward through the still air.

A few seconds later, a man stepped into view, wiping his hands on an oily rag. He stood with his head back, mouth open, watching the big zero of smoke disintegrate against the sky. It appeared to take a few seconds for him to become aware that there were four people standing in front of the Quonset hut.

When the information finally sank in, he did a physical double take and started toward them, his mouth still hanging open. Ben ran his eyes over him. About five-ten, slender and gangly. Khaki bush shorts, sleeveless blue-denim shirt, and Kuballan open-toe sandals of twisted river reed. Shoulder-length blond hair, very straight, streaky from exposure to the sun and held in place with a leather headband. Maybe thirty-one or thirty-two years of age . . . not exactly weak-looking, but with very little in the way of muscle tone. His tanned face seemed fixed in something of a happy hangdog expression, amplified by sleepy blue eyes and the habitually open mouth.

"Maggie-babe!" he drawled, shambling up to her with his arms wide. He planted a hand on her left buttock, drawing her in, and smeared a long, loose kiss on her carefully painted lips. She went slightly rigid but didn't actively resist, placing her hands on his elbows in one of the standard female neutral-defensive positions. The occasional bubbling sound suggested that she was having trouble getting air. Ben, Sass, and Naji waited in silence.

When at last he was done mauling her, the blond-haired man straightened up, set Maggie back on her feet, and flashed an openmouthed grin. "Salutations, buds. Jefferson Deadhead Jones, here."

Maggie straightened her skirt and brushed a fallen lock of dark hair back from her temple. "Uh—Jeff's . . . Jeff's the pilot. Jeff, meet Ben Gannon."

Ben's face displayed the pleasant, noncommittal expression he utilized when dealing with unknown corporate executives and oil-field bosses. He extended his hand. "Hi," he said evenly. "Pleased to meet—"

"Call me 'Head,' dude," Jefferson Deadhead Jones interrupted, clasping Ben's hand in an oil-slippery grip and wringing it. "Everybody does."

Sass was regarding Maggie with a withering look, somewhere between *I don't believe you actually did it with this guy* and *you're out of your mind if you think Ben's flying off into an African revolution with "Jefferson Deadhead Jones"*—a.k.a. *"Head."*

"All right, 'Head,' " Ben said. "This is Sass, and—"

"Far out, man!" Head was staring at Naji. "Check out the threads on this bad boy!"

"His name is—"

"Waaayyy cool, dude," Head cut in again. He stuck a hand out toward Naji. "I'm Head. Or 'The Head,' if you prefer."

"I am Naji," Naji said quietly.

Head guffawed, slapping his knee. "You are *wild*, man! You look like an extra from *Lawrence of Arabia*. You got that whole Rudy Valentino thing going, don't you?" He turned to Ben. "Where'd you get this guy? The whole Arab-retro thing, I really dig it!" He looked back at Naji. "It's really blowin' my mind, man!"

Not smiling, Naji dropped a hand to the hilt of his

yataghan. "Perhaps your mind would be less 'blown,' "
he growled, "if I were to trim a few of the protuber-
ances from your impudent carcass."

"Whoa." Head backpedaled hurriedly, glancing at
Ben. "I'm sensing a little hostility here, dude."

Ben's smile was thin.

"Aaahhh—Jeff," Maggie interceded, pulling the
pilot toward her by his belt loop, "why don't we get
right down to business, hmm?" She grazed a finger-
nail down the top half of his breastbone, her lower lip
sticking out in a cross pout, and batted her long black
eyelashes at him. "I'm not very happy with you, I'm
afraid. You *promised* me you'd have the plane ready to
go at sundown." The pout deepened.

Sass thought she was going to be ill. Ben looked on
with his trademark bemusement, and Naji's face was
like stone.

Head's loose grin spread from ear to ear. "Hey,
babe, no problem! Another twenty minutes and she'll
be all back together. I was just settin' the timing on the
engine." He turned to Ben and Naji. "C'mon, dudes!
She's back here. Check her out!"

He set off with his shambling gait toward the rear of
the Quonset hut. Ben lifted a skeptical eyebrow in
Naji's direction and motioned with his head that they
should follow. As they began to trail after Jefferson
Deadhead Jones, Sass caught Maggie's elbow, holding
her back.

"What the hell d'you think you're doing?" she
hissed.

The cross-sexy pout was gone from Maggie's face.
In its place was the hard, streetwise, slightly desperate

expression she'd worn in the lobby of the Hotel Excelsior. "What do *you* think I'm doing, Sass?" she said, her tone edgy.

"I think you're throwing your stuff in this hippie-boy's face and leading him around by the nose, that's what I think."

"How observant." Maggie dug a menthol slim out of her jacket pocket and stuck it between her lips.

Sass felt her temper flare. "What is this shit? I thought we were friends. We came here to help you."

"We are. You are. And I'm damned grateful." The pricey Dunhill lighter flicked and a little cone of blue flame crisped the end of Maggie's cigarette.

"Then what's the idea of hooking Ben up with a guy named 'Head'—who talks as if he never grew one of his own—and his ridiculous kite?"

"Look." Maggie blew out a stream of smoke, one arm folded across her chest. Her free hand was poised upward, a thumbnail snapping repeatedly against the cigarette's filter. "Jeff has been—"

"You mean 'Head.'"

"If you like. Head isn't as brain-dead as he looks, in spite of his middle name. He's some kind of trust-fund kid who's over here in Africa trying to save the wildlife. He's actually got a contract from one of the big nature conservancies to count and monitor game-animal populations in this area—using his ultralight floatplane as an observation platform. The thing really flies, and Jeff—*Head*—has literally thousands of hours in the air at the controls. He knows what he's doing. I asked around in Krumake."

Ben and Naji had disappeared around the corner of

the Quonset hut after the pilot. The ringing sound of metal being tapped on metal became audible, along with the rise and fall of male voices.

"So," Maggie went on, "to answer the sixty-four-thousand-dollar question—yes, I slept with the guy. The day after I got to Kuballa, as a matter of fact. I needed to find someone with a floatplane, and he was it. I had to be ready for you, didn't I?"

Sass winced. "Couldn't you just pay him, for the lovagod?"

"Nope. He wasn't interested in money. He's got enough of his own. I had to find some other way to convince the boy, and there wasn't time to fiddle-fart around. So I fucked him. That got his attention." Maggie sucked disinterestedly on her cigarette. "Works every time."

"Not how I'd have handled it," Sass remarked.

"Yes, well, that's easy for you to say, isn't it?" Maggie retorted. She finger-snapped the butt of her cigarette onto the hard ground in a little shower of sparks. "Your guy's free and healthy. Nick's stuck in a hole in the ground with a bunch of gun-crazy niggers hovering around him . . . if he isn't dead already." She looked hard at Sass. "I want him out, and I'll do what I have to do to *get* him out." She blinked. "Ask yourself if you wouldn't do the same for Ben, and be *real* honest about your answer."

She stalked off toward the rear of the Quonset hut. "C'mon. Let's see what they're doing."

Sass ground her teeth, but decided to reserve further comment. As she started after Maggie, the sputtering roar of the engine once again filled the air.

Ben, Naji, and Head were standing next to what looked like a large homemade dune buggy without any doors or side panels. A high, elongated cage of aluminum tubing sat on four small rubber tires, housing two pairs of molded fiberglass seats, one row set behind the other. The entire back end of the contraption was engine—a fiendish-looking apparatus that resembled a giant lawn mower gutted and turned on its side. A large metallic pusher propeller was mounted on a short shaft at the rear of the power plant.

The cage was shaking mightily on its wheels as the motor coughed and spat at a rough, fast idle. Even at low revs, the noise was deafening. Head half slid into the pilot's seat, grabbed the stick controls, and grinned over at Ben.

"Watch this, dude!" he yelled.

He squeezed something, moved a foot on a pedal, and there was a loud *ka-THUNK* as a drive clutch engaged. The contraption leaped violently two feet to the right. The propeller rotated once, slowly, then spun into a transparent silver disc. A ferocious windblast flattened the dry grasses behind the engine, scattering small stones and kicking up a storm of reddish dust.

The machine lurched forward—only to be stopped short by the tethering cable that extended back from beneath the chassis to the corner foundation of the Quonset hut. It bucked and skidded from side to side like a pit bull snarling against a leash as Head revved the engine up to several thousand rpm. The racket was incredible. Sass was sure she could feel her back teeth shaking loose.

Head was laughing like a maniac as he disengaged

the clutch and cut the engine. In a repeat of its earlier performance, the power plant backfired out a single large smoke ring—*PLOOF*—as it died. Finally inanimate, the machine sat on the hard dirt emitting little bubbling and steaming noises, waves of heat shimmering above the engine cowling.

"Whoooaaa! How's that for power, dudes?" Head blurted, grinning like a jack-o'-lantern. "You could fly over Mount Everest with that much stroke!" He shambled around the forward end of the cage. "Now look here, all we needa do is push this baby around front, bolt on those two pontoons, attach the wing, and we're ready to rock 'n' roll. It don't take ten minutes—'specially if I got a couple of extra hands." He beamed at Ben and Naji. "Then we load up your gear and take off."

"What kind of range does this thing have?" Ben asked, putting his hands on the frame and starting to push. Naji did the same, leaning into the cage near the rear seats.

"Four hours of flying time," Head replied. "See those big fat tanks twinned up on either side of the engine? Lotsa fuel. I had that done to give me more roamin' room, you *comprende*?" He pointed off toward the southwest as they trundled the cage along the side of the Quonset hut. "We buzz over to a little airstrip at the foot of those mountains, refuel, then hop over to Bisotho and set down in Shark Lake . . . Tiburi Kunga, y'know?"

"Yeah," Ben said. "I know."

"We scoop up your buddy and beat feet outta there. Simple."

Ben looked at him. "Uh-huh. Simple."

As the fiery African sunset glimmered behind the low hills to the west, suffusing the tiny airstrip and its surroundings with a powdery red-gold light, Naji pulled an embroidered cloth bag from the Land Rover and slipped its wide strap over his head. He adjusted it diagonally from shoulder to hip, on top of the ammunition bandoliers that already crisscrossed his chest, then retrieved his old Lee-Enfield rifle from a gun rack above the Rover's rear seat. Settling it into the crook of his elbow, he patted the breech and walked toward the now fully assembled ultralight floatplane, which was sitting in front of the Quonset hut with Ben's dive gear strapped into one of its rear seats. As he did so, he glanced toward the two figures standing beneath the spike-laden limbs of a nearby marblewood tree.

Ben and Sass had been arguing quietly under the thorny canopy for more than ten minutes.

"Look," Ben was saying, trying to keep the exasperation out of his voice, "I've made up my mind. I have to go, and that's that. It's Nick, kiddo. Don't tell me you don't understand, because I know you do." He put his hand on her shoulder, squeezing gently.

"Get—your—hand—*off*—me," Sass enunciated between her teeth, shrugging free. "You're not listening, Ben. I'm telling you, something's not right with Maggie. She was always a hard case, but she gave up her old life and turned herself into someone a normal person could stand to be around. Office management isn't glamorous, but at least it's honest work. Now she's acting like a cross between Mata Hari and the Bride of Frankenstein. You don't see it?"

"Yeah, but she's upset," Ben replied. "She wants Nick back, and I owe it to him to try and get him out of there."

Sass rolled her eyes in frustration. "You sound like a broken record. Will you *please* listen to me? I'm telling you, something isn't right. Sure, she'd like Nick back—but it's not that simple. I don't think that's all she wants . . ."

"All right, *what*?" Ben demanded, his patience shredding. "*What* is it she wants? Lay it out for me."

Sass shook her head helplessly. "I can't. It's just a bad vibe I'm getting. I can't put my finger on it. It's everything. She's drinking again, she's screwing this weirdo, when she talks it's 'nigger' this and 'nigger' that—she's like someone we don't even know."

"Ah, jeezus." Ben paused for a moment, then gently set the knuckle of his forefinger under Sass's chin and looked into her eyes, close. "You know I always listen to you. Always. But if you can't give me any reason not to go other than 'I've got a bad vibe,' then I have to give this a shot." He smiled. "You know I can't do anything else."

Sass gave up. She put her forehead on his collarbone and breathed out a long sigh. "How about this. Jefferson Deadhead Jones will probably fly you into a mountain in the middle of the night and get you killed in a fiery goddamned explosion."

"Hm. Probably won't happen. But Naji and I will keep an eye on him, in case he has some kind of acid flashback or something. Hopefully not at three or four thousand feet." She looked up at him, not happy. "Hey. Just kidding."

"You really think he can fly that thing in the dark?" Sass muttered.

Ben nodded. "I get the feeling he can. I watched him set it up. He knows the rig like the back of his hand. I think he can fly it well enough for this one-shot deal."

She twined her fingers into the longish hair at the back of his neck and tugged. "You willing to bet your life on it?"

He smiled down at her and folded his arms around her narrow waist. In the gathering dusk, the ultra-light's engine coughed and sputtered into life once more.

"Apparently so," he said. He took her hand and began to walk toward the aircraft. "Hey. Sit tight, and monitor the satellite uplink unit and the VHF radio. I'll be back in a few hours."

CHAPTER 7

With Head and Ben belted into the front seats and Naji
sitting in the rear next to the diving equipment, the
ultralight floatplane rattled and roared down the dim
runway, gathering speed. It took three high wobbling
bounces, and on the fourth clawed its way into the air.
Head banked it around immediately, overflying the
Quonset hut and Land Rover, and leveled off on a vec-
tor toward the dark mountains to the southwest. Ben
could barely make out Sass and Maggie standing near
the wind sock pole, waving. He raised an arm—and
then the ultralight was moving rapidly over dense
black jungle, the darkness pierced here and there by
the occasional glint of water.

Ben turned in his seat and glanced back at Naji. The
lean Yemeni tribesman was sitting with his arms
crossed over his chest, his face composed, calmly
chewing a mouthful of *qat*. The slipstream goggles he
wore made an odd contrast with his billowing black
robes and *burnoose*, as did the insulated muffs that pro-
tected his ears from the noise of the engine. He caught
Ben's eye, nodded, and smiled.

Ben smiled back and faced forward in his seat
again. Naji was a steady one, and no mistake. Being

condemned to passenger status in Head's rattletrap ultralight was a bona fide nerve-frazzler.

Another in what was apparently to be a never-ending tattoo of faltering skips in the engine's rhythm sent Ben's heart into his mouth, his hand clamping down on the aluminum tubing of the ultralight's cockpit framework. The entire airframe shuddered, and the floatplane lost several feet of altitude. As the power plant's throaty whine evened out once more, Ben found himself wishing that he *felt* half as relaxed as Naji *looked*.

A hand tapped his knee, and he glanced over to see Head pointing down and to the left. Below, the jungle had given way to a wide riverbed, its low banks and sandbars gleaming palely in the moonlight. A line of bulky shapes was clearly visible against the shimmering silver water—a herd of elephants, fording the shallows in single file. As the ultralight whined overhead the lead animal shied sideways, flaring its ears and raising its trunk.

They flew on, following the river as it meandered lazily across the plain toward the mountains, now all but invisible against the blue-black sky to the south and southwest. Every half mile or so their approach would send a flock of waterfowl—flamingos, herons, storks—spooking across a sandbar in a synchronized panic, and here and there the slithery shape of a crocodile would suddenly explode into motion and come writhing down the mudbank to splash into the placid waters.

After nearly an hour and thirty minutes in the air, a small cluster of lights appeared dead ahead, hazy in the evening mist. As the ultralight dropped toward them, Ben could make out a single line of blue landing lamps. Try as he might, however, he could not see the ground—a fact that became more and more alarming as the little plane lost altitude. Unlike the light-reflective riverbed, the dry, vegetated terrain of Kuballa's upland plain revealed little detail from the air at night.

The finicky engine stuttered as Head reduced the rpm and manipulated the cable-controlled flaps of the tail assembly. The ultralight fell sharply, the blue lamps rising through the darkness ahead to line up just to the right side of the aircraft's nose. Ben squeezed the frame of the cockpit until he was sure his fingerprints were cold-pressed into the aluminum. The slipstream and engine noise howled around his earmuffs, and the blue landing lamps rose to eye level. There was still no sign of the ground.

With an impact that nearly herniated every disc in his spine, the ultralight set down hard. Immediately, it was airborne again, Head racing the engine and manipulating the stick controls and foot pedals furiously. The machine dropped once more, bounced, and caught a pothole with its left front wheel. With a tooth-jarring wallop, the ultralight heeled over on its right-side wheels, its starboard wingtip dipping to within six inches of the ground. Ben closed his eyes and hung on, grimacing as the plane careened through an invisible cloud of shadflies. The tiny insect bodies smacked into his face like wet BBs.

Head wrenched the ultralight to the starboard, forcing the left-side wheels to drop back to the ground. There was a loud *POP* as the machine ran over one of the blue landing lamps, blowing it out—and then they were trundling to a halt in a choking cloud of dust and engine exhaust, streamers of night mist swirling around the aircraft like gossamer wraiths. A hazy, glaring illumination emanated from spotlights on the outside of three small shacks, a scant fifty feet ahead, at the end of the row of blue lamps.

As his heart attempted to batter its way out through his breastbone, Ben turned slowly, breathing hard, and fixed Head with an icy stare. In the rear seat, Naji calmly spat a long stream of *qat* juice onto the ground and removed his earmuffs. He waited until Head and Ben had followed suit before commenting,

"Next time, I will take a camel and leave two days earlier."

Head removed his leather headband and ran his fingers back through his lank blond hair. "Oh, wow, man," he said. "Heavy landing." He grinned, gapemouthed, at no one in particular. "Faaaar out."

Resisting the urge to throttle him, Ben began to say something but was cut off by a shout from the direction of the shacks.

"*A-what-a-you, mon???*" A dark figure was running toward them, arms waving and haystack hair flying. "*Break my lights, to Ras, an' tear de place up! One rude white boy, you!*"

Head looked up, unperturbed. "Cecil, what's happenin'? Good to see ya. Whoa—you're lookin' uptight, my main man." The loose grin renewed itself on the pilot's mooncalf face. "You gots to chill, bro. Cool runnin's, *seen*?"

"*To bloodclot wi'you!*" the figure yelled, stopping in

front of the plane's nose. He was a black man of about Ben's height, dressed in a dirty gray mechanic's cover-all, barefoot, with an immense mane of dreadlocks that fell past his shoulders. His complexion, while dark, was lighter than that of an ebony-skinned native Kuballan, and his face more narrow, with a straight nose and high cheekbones. He was so mad he was lit-erally stamping his feet.

Head cut the engine, and as it died, turned to Ben, and said, "This is Cecil. He hails from Jamaica—real live Rastafarian. He decided to come back to the old country, get in touch with his roots. He used to do maintenance on the tourist jets in Montego Bay for Air Jamaica, an' now he runs this little strip." Head beamed at Ben. "There's more bush-pilot and safari traffic out here than you might think. Keeps him goin'." The engine punctuated his remarks with its signature backfire, the smoke ring ejecting into the night mist.

Head climbed out. "So, my main man, you have fuel for me? Top me up? I got a little gig to do here."

Cecil glowered at him. "You pay for my *bloodclot* light first, Head-mon. *Den* we talk about fuel, *seen*?"

"*Seen*," the gangly pilot said, nodding. "Sounds fair to me." He dug into the pocket of his baggy shorts and came up with a fistful of Kuballan bank notes. "Here, dude."

He handed over the entire wad to Cecil, who jammed the bills into his own pocket without counting them. As Ben and Naji unbuckled their seat belts and stepped out of the plane, the barefoot mechanic sucked his teeth in annoyance and waved a hand at the ultralight. "You pay me more for gas."

"Aww, man," Head protested, looking very hangdog, "what I just gave you is more'n enough for a new landin' light *and* forty gallons of gas."

Cecil held out his hand. "Charges include light, gas . . . plus aggravation, irritation, and safety violation fine. Two hundred *kubals* more."

Head shrugged and dug out another wad of crushed bills from his opposite pocket. "You're holdin' me up, man," he said, grinning. "Thievin' me blind."

"*Ras*," Cecil snorted. "You got plenty a' money. You see me? I-an'-I got problems, Head-mon. Trouble over in Bisotho comin' *my* way these days. *Bloodclot!* Two days ago me an' my woman wake up to hear ref-u-gees breakin' into storehouse. Me go out wi' my shotgun an' stop de banditry. Den dem folk dey try to steal my gas truck, *seen*? Dem hungry and afoot, Jah know! But me haffa run dem off wi' shots in de middle of de night, or dey take everyt'ing." He shook his dreadlocked head. "Ninth time in t'ree weeks."

Ben folded his arms. "I thought the military was handling the refugees as they came over the border."

"Huh!" Disgust twisted Cecil's features. "Army? Dey stop one, let two go around. Not enough soldiers to deal wi' so many scared an' hungry people, *seen*? An' hungry people gonna steal before dey starve." He turned and began to walk back toward the shacks, waving his arms in the air. "Bad business in Bisotho, *to Ras! Malmoq* peoples killin' *Quori* peoples." He sucked his teeth angrily. "You wait—lemme get gas truck."

"Sure thing." Head looked at Ben. "Guess there's a lot of people comin' through the pass these days."

"Which pass would that be?" Ben inquired.

Head pointed off to the south toward the nearby mountains; black shapes looming up against the night sky. "The one we're goin' to fly through to get into Bisotho. It's over there, about five miles away."

Ben squinted into the misty darkness. "I see a few more lights."

"Kuballan army units, probably, dude. Camped out at the pass to keep the refugees from just pourin' in from Bisotho."

"I heard they were moving them into internment camps. That's rough."

Head shrugged. "I guess it beats gettin' shot . . . or chopped up with machetes."

A pair of mismatched headlight beams swung out from behind the airstrip shacks, and a dilapidated Ford pickup of early 1950s vintage began to putter down the runway toward them, wobbling on tires of different sizes. As it approached, Ben saw that the rear bed was packed full of fifty-five-gallon fuel drums, multicolored and running with rust. Cecil pulled the ancient vehicle in beside the ultralight, braked, and climbed up out of the doorless cab onto the nearest drum.

"Yes, a bad business, *to Ras*," he said, uncoiling the hose of the hand-cranked fuel transfer pump. "Much misery, much killin' over in Bisotho." He shook his black-maned head. "An abomination in Jah's eyes. Bredren peoples should not treat each other so. He who kills his own brudder shall wear de mark of Cain, so Almighty Jah say."

"*Selah*, " Naji intoned, his voice low.

Cecil looked up sharply as he fed the fuel hose into the ultralight's starboard tank. "Oho. A mon who reads 'im scripture." He smiled at Naji and turned back to his work. "*Selah* . . . A long time since me did hear a mon speak dat holy word."

Head pulled vacantly at a strand of his long hair. "Cool. What's it mean, dude? Kinda like 'here's to ya' or somethin'?"

"*Cho-Ras!*" Cecil sucked his teeth in irritation, cranking the handle of the fuel transfer pump. "Backward white boy—no trouble me, mon!" He scowled and bore down on the pump handle.

Head reeled slightly. "Whoaaa. More hostility. Looks like The Head ain't ridin' the same vibe as the rest of the boys tonight. Bummer."

Naji caught Cecil's eye, then opened his mouth and spoke. "*Selah* is a very old word. A mysterious and magical word. It often means 'so be it.' Or perhaps, 'it is true.' Or it can be a blessing. But it is the best kind of word—because it can also mean whatever the speaker *wishes* it to mean."

"Well spoken, mon," Cecil muttered. He paused in his cranking to reposition the fuel hose in the ultralight's second tank.

Head's eyes had gone glassy. "Cool," he said.

Cecil pumped in silence for another two minutes before there was a gurgling burp and fuel ran down the side of the tank. Pulling the hose out and capping the fill, he frowned over at the gangly pilot. "Where you flyin' tonight, Head-mon? You can't count de animals after dark."

The loose grin returned to Head's face. "Pickin' a dude up, bro. Taxi service."

"Where?" Cecil persisted, coiling up the fuel hose.

Head waved off into the darkness. "South. In Bisotho."

"*Bisotho?*" Cecil flopped the hose up onto the fuel drums and regarded Head directly. "You crazy, white boy? You no hear what me say jus' now? A madhouse, dat place."

"Nah," Head replied. "We're in and out. No problem."

Cecil looked at Naji, taking in his stern features and the ammunition bandoliers crisscrossing his chest, then over at Ben, standing quietly beside the aircraft's tail with his arms folded, tall and fit. A bemused smile spread over his dark face.

"Maybe so, Head-mon. Maybe so." He climbed into the cab of the truck. "Get off my airstrip, now mon! An' don't break no more lights, *to Ras!*"

There was a sickly chugging noise as he turned the engine over. After a dozen labored revolutions it caught, and he pulled away from the little plane, the truck wobbling on its mismatched tires. Wheeling around through the mist in a wide arc, headlights glaring, the expatriate Rastafarian headed off once more toward the trio of shacks.

Ben removed his jacket and began to shed his shirt as Head walked around the ultralight, rechecking the fuel caps and pontoon clamps. On the opposite side of the plane, Naji repositioned the dive gear, making sure it was secure, yet easy to access from the front and rear passenger seats.

"Is this where you change into Superman, dude?" Head inquired.

Ben finished stripping down and pulled a light thermal diving suit of layered black Lycra from one of the gearbags. "Yeah. Something like that."

"Faaaar out, man."

Ben cleared his throat as he smoothed the diving suit up over his legs. "Head. Let me ask you a question, okay?" He glanced at Naji as the lean Yemeni climbed into his seat and sat down, his swarthy face registering a distinct lack of amusement.

"Shoot, man."

"You're around thirty, right? Born about 1970?"

Head grinned sloppily. "Close. Seventy-one, dude."

Ben worked his arms into the suit. "Right—1971. You probably didn't even get laid until the late eighties." He took a moment to lean toward the pilot. "So why do you keep acting like a Haight-Ashbury hippie? I gotta tell you, it's fucking irritating. The sixties are over, my friend . . . and you weren't even there in the first place."

Far from being insulted, Head looked cognizant for the first time all evening. "Ohhhhhh, I get it. You don't dig my retro demeanor. Dude, it ain't an act. It's my old man's fault."

Ben zipped up the front of the tight-fitting suit. "How's that?"

"You've heard of the Grateful Dead? Jefferson Airplane?"

"Sure."

"My old man was a roadie for both of 'em. You're right. Haight-Ashbury—the whole San Francisco flower-power thing. My mom, she was the original flower child, dude. Petals in her head insteada gray matter. The night I was born she dropped acid and never came back, just stayed high. The boys in the white suits had to drag her off to the loony bin. So it was just me and my old man from then on.

"He formed his own band the month after I showed up. Remember The Ultimate Spinach? The Flamin' Groovies? The Strawberry Alarm Clock?"

"Yeah," Ben said. "I remember all that nonsense."

"Record companies were throwin' contracts around right and left, man, tryin' to get in on the rock 'n' roll action. My old man said, hey, if they can do it, I can do it—so he formed a band called The Raging Asparagus. You heard of them, right, dude?"

"No," Ben said.

Head shrugged. "Okay. Anyhow, this is what happened. The Raging Asparagus had the right name and the right look—my old man and his buddies looked like Frank Zappa and the Mothers, times ten—so that was cool. Problem was, none of 'em could play a note. My old man, I think Jerry Garcia taught him three chords once, but he forgot them. The drummer was so stoned all the time they had to duct-tape him onto his stool." Head paused to grin. "Serious wackos, man. They make me look like G. Gordon Liddy."

Ben was getting weary. "Uh-huh. And then . . . ?"

"They signed a two-album deal with one of the monster record companies, but they never got slotted into the studio. My old man, he wasn't much of a musician, but he sure understood contract law. Like some kinda natural hippie legal genius or somethin'. He took 'em to court for nonperformance and got like a million bucks in punitive damages. Then he turned it into fifty million by buying into a little company called Apple Computers. Ain't that far out, dude?"

"Yup," Ben said slowly. "I have to admit it is."

"So I got money," Head said. "An' that's why I talk the way I talk. But at least I come by it honestly, man."

Ben walked around the ultralight and climbed into the front passenger seat. "Where's your father now?" he asked.

"Oh. Dead, dude."

"Really? Sorry about that." Ben softened his expression a bit. "What happened?"

"Cop shot him."

"He did? Why?"

Head grinned his openmouthed grin and stepped up into the pilot's seat. "Let's just say that that when you're drivin' through Georgia at midnight in a big ol' Lincoln Town Car, loaded down with cash, coke, and sensimilla, and you look like Frank Zappa's evil cousin, and an armed Georgia state trooper pulls you over and says, 'Sir, your eyes are bloodshot. Have you been drinking?' . . . the correct answer is not 'No, oinker-boy, I haven't—but *your* eyes are glazed. Have you been eating doughnuts?' "

The lanky pilot laughed, swept a few fallen strands of blond hair out of his eyes, and fired up the ultralight's engine. Two minutes later, they were airborne.

CHAPTER 8

Head took the little floatplane up to fifteen hundred feet as they entered the pass, the black mountains on either side of them rising at least twice that high. Where the pass opened onto the Kuballan plain, Ben could see a curved line of military transports bottle-necking the valley's mouth. Several light tanks were interspersed among the trucks, and fires and generator-driven lights glowed near each vehicle. Tents had been pitched behind the motorized barricade, and dozens of soldiers were clearly visible, milling around like ants.

Two huge wire enclosures had been erected behind the Kuballan military line, in the open scrub just to the east. Both were illuminated by electric pole lights, their fences topped with coils of razor wire. Armed guards patrolled the outer perimeters. The grounds within were crowded with makeshift lean-tos, posses-sions, garbage—and people. Two great masses of people crammed in shoulder to shoulder.

As the ultralight flew on, a narrow road became dis-tinguishable on the valley floor. Along it glittered a chain of small campfires, and around them huddled thousands of *Quori* refugees, unable to move forward by reason of the presence of the Kuballan military blockade. Climbing above the road to escape the crush would have been out of the question. The broken talus slopes and vertical cliffs that lined the pass were all but impossible to traverse.

The little plane banked smoothly through a bend in the valley, soaring to within two hundred feet of a sheer rock wall. Ben glanced up past the delta wing. Overhead, the sky looked as hard and black as a dome of obsidian, its surface encrusted with stars. The rising half-moon hung between two dark summits to the southeast, washing the valley's upper crags with a pale, eerie light.

He turned in his seat, gazing back and down. Already, the flickering refugee campfires were fading in the distance. In less than a minute they had been swallowed completely by the dark gloom of the valley floor.

Head gained another five hundred feet of altitude as they approached the narrow middle section of the pass. The ultralight began to shake as it encountered updrafts and side gusts spinning off the nearby peaks, and everyone had a bad moment when the little plane suddenly plummeted at least fifty feet while negotiating a particularly nasty patch of turbulence. Gunning the engine, Head wrestled them back onto an even keel . . . and then they were past the high central point of the mountain range, in much cleaner air, and starting their descent toward the far end of the valley.

Ten minutes later, the dense interior jungle of Bisotho lay spread out before them; a thick black carpet shrouded by drifting banks of steam and mist. Unlike the upland plain of Kuballa, which was quite dry, the corresponding region of Bisotho consisted entirely of a single immense watershed with poor drainage—a vast, flooded basin riddled with twisting streams, creeks, and bayous, and dominated by the central large lake, Tiburi Kunga.

As Head took the ultralight lower, Ben began to notice a scorched smell in the air—an acrid combination of woodsmoke, petroleum fumes, and charred paint. It intensified with their decreasing altitude until, at about three hundred feet above treetop level, they were flying through a semivisible pall of suspended soot, their eyes, throats, and sinuses itching and burning.

A dim red glow appeared through the treetops just ahead . . . and then the ultralight emerged over a large clearing occupied by fifteen or twenty clapboard shacks. Every one of them was on fire. Flame, smoke, and sparks whirled up toward the little plane, borne on a palpable wave of heat.

Ben blinked the stinging smoke out of his eyes and refocused. Lying on the ground between the burning shacks, clearly illuminated, were dozens of human bodies—men, women, and children—contorted into positions that suggested flight, agony, or both. Trotting among them were numerous heavily armed soldiers wearing forage caps, spotted camouflage clothing, and full field gear. In addition to an automatic rifle, every man appeared to be carrying a long machete.

A gust of black smoke momentarily blotted out the scene below, then blew away in the slipstream. His eyes watering, Ben coughed twice, spat, and stared downward again.

A thin figure in a patterned native dress was running between two of the burning shacks—a young girl, perhaps twelve years of age. Two of the camouflage-clad soldiers were in hot pursuit, machetes waving. As Ben watched, a third soldier stepped out in front of her from behind a tree, grabbed her arm, and swung at her with his long blade.

Chop. The first blow took her in the side of the head. *Chop.* The second, between the neck and shoulder. The girl wilted like a poleaxed calf in the soldier's grip. As she fell to her knees, the machete continued to hack downward, over and over. *Chop. Chop. Chop. Chop.* The two pursuing soldiers stepped in close, their own machetes raised . . .

And then the ultralight shot out over black jungle again, the flame-lit horror of the doomed *Quori* village vanishing in an instant. Ben felt numb, a sick bile rising in his throat. Swallowing, he looked over at Naji. The hawk-faced Yemeni stared back at him, shaking his head, his mouth a grim line.

Head reached over and tapped him on the knee, pointing dead ahead. Ben squinted through the sooty lenses of his flight goggles. Far off in the distance, barely visible above the steaming jungle canopy, was the shimmering surface of a large body of water. He glanced back at Head, and the pilot mouthed the words "Shark Lake."

More fires were burning off to the east, little islands of hot light flickering in a dark sea of trees. To the southwest, Ben thought he could make out a column of military trucks parked along a narrow roadway, headlamps off, but it was impossible to be sure.

The lake was coming up fast, moonlight reflecting off it in a long, silver-cobbled path. The leaf canopy thinned, revealing the drowned, swampy land beneath, and then the last few trees lining the shore swept under the pontoons and the ultralight soared out over the black waters of Shark Lake.

Only a few minutes later, they encountered a dense fogbank. Head pulled back on the controls, increased the rpm and lifted the floatplane up a few hundred feet into clearer air. Punching the illumination button of the little GPS unit that was clamped to the airframe next to his shoulder, he checked his position, peered down at the mist in apparent confusion, then nodded and grinned to himself. Beside him, Ben observed his performance with a mixture of stoicism and apprehension. Whatever Head was about to get them into, there was little he or Naji could do about it now.

The fog was very thick in the central part of the lake, but as they flew to the southeast it became less dense; the drifting banks more intermittent. Ben estimated that they had covered more than twenty miles over the water when suddenly the curtains of mist parted to reveal a small island, still some distance away, dead on the ultralight's nose. A mere stub of rock, it was crowned by a man-made structure—high-walled, square, and black in silhouette. Several pinpoints of light glowed along its rampartlike upper edges.

The hair prickled on the back of Ben's neck, and he smiled inwardly, amused at his own reaction. It was like something out of a bad movie. A regular Dracula's castle.

Head cut the rpm back and the ultralight began to descend. At about 150 feet above the water the fog closed in again, and the island disappeared from view. The slipstream turned damp and chilly on Ben's face, and streamers of moisture condensed on his flight goggles, obscuring his vision. Not that there was anything to see—they were flying inside what was essentially a low-level cloud, in gray-out conditions.

Ben looked down past the pontoon. Somewhere beneath them, the black surface of Shark Lake was coming up very fast. But all he could see was one continuous wall of shadowy, tumbling mist.

He glanced over at Head. The long-haired pilot was chewing his lip—his mouth not hanging slack, for once—and trying to concentrate. The mental effort appeared to be giving him considerable pain. Fleetingly, Ben hoped he could set the ultralight down before his temporal lobes ruptured.

Head was doing a fair job of keeping the pontoon tips high under minimal rpm. The little floatplane continued to descend through the fogbank in a controlled fall, its glide ratio very steep. The engine noise had dropped to a mere mutter.

It felt wrong. The descent was too fast for such a completely blind landing. Ben was about to yell at Head to bump up the rpm when the ultralight hit the water.

The impact was far worse than that of the previous smackdown on Cecil's backcountry landing strip. Sheets of spray exploded out to either side of the pontoons and up against the light aluminum floor of the cockpit. A tremendous jolt shook the airframe, rattling

Ben's teeth in his head. Simultaneously, there was a loud *CRACK* and the entire fuselage sagged to the left, nearly throwing Naji out into the darkness. Only his seat belt saved him.

"*Shiiiiiiiiiiiiiiit!*" Head shrieked, hunched like a gargoyle over the wildly shaking controls. A horrific vibration set up throughout the aircraft as it hurtled across the water, enveloped in mist, damaged and off-balance.

The plane skidded first one way then the other, its port wingtip only inches from catching on the lake's surface. As it slowed, the propeller whirled up a cloud of spray, drenching and half-smothering everyone in the cockpit. The clattering vibration lessened, then ceased entirely. Creaking, canted badly to port, its overheated engine growling and steaming, the ultra-light drifted slowly to a halt on the windless black water, shrouded in mist as dense as cotton batting.

Head cut the engine. It wheezed and died with its characteristic smoke-ring backfire—*PLOOF!* Then, quite suddenly, all was silent but for the dripping of water and the creaking of overstressed metal.

"Oh, wow," Head mumbled, slumping back in his seat and staring out through the droplet-covered lenses of his flight goggles. He pulled down his earmuffs so that they hung around his neck like a dog collar. "Oh, wow."

Stripping off his own goggles and muffs, Ben looked back at Naji. "You all right?"

The lean Yemeni already had his headgear off and was wiping the moisture out of his goatee with a fold of his *burnoose.* "I believe so, my brother." He looked toward heaven. "*Inshallah*. It was not my time, nor yours—no thanks to this inept miscreant!" Leaning forward, he jabbed a hard finger into the back of Head's shoulder. "Rot you and your incompetence! You are a one-man plague of vexations! May Allah the Compassionate and Merciful rip the entrails from your body and strangle you with them in the slowest possible manner!"

Head, who had turned in his seat, went pale. "Whoooa. Hostile imagery, dude."

"I will kill him now," Naji said to Ben, his hand going beneath his robe.

"Wait, wait," Ben replied hurriedly. "Hold on, Naji . . . please." He scowled at Head in exasperation. "Why the hell'd you come in so steep, goddammit? You nearly pancaked us back there!"

Head grinned and shrugged helplessly. "A slight miscalculation, dude. I usually feel my way around fine when I fly after dark, but there's an evil vibe in the fog tonight. It was playin' havoc with my ability to commune with the Zen ethers."

Naji offered Ben the hilt of his *yataghan*. "Perhaps you would like to kill him," he suggested.

Ben held up his hand. "I'll pass," he said, shaking his head. "For now." He rubbed his eyes. "*Zen ethers?* Why the fuck didn't you just watch the altimeter, Head?"

"Well, it's kinda busted, dude. It don't work below one hundred feet."

"Christ." Ben blew out a long sigh. Then he set a foot down on the starboard pontoon, shifted his weight onto it gingerly, and attempted to peer under the tilted fuselage toward the port side. "What happened over there? Looks like the front strut supporting the pontoon gave way."

Naji leaned over carefully, his head and shoulders only inches above the water. "You are right, *Ben-Ya-Min*. The front strut is broken. The rear strut is somewhat bent, but still intact."

"Shit, really?" Head exclaimed, bending down to look. His weight overbalanced the listing ultralight and for one heart-stopping moment Ben was sure they were going over. Throwing his weight outboard, clinging to the leading edge of the delta wing, he managed to prevent the aircraft from flipping. Head leaned back hurriedly over the passenger seat. Naji, who had been dunked from the top of his *burnoose* to his waist, pulled himself inboard seconds later, puffing and blowing.

"Oops. Sorry, Naji-dude," Head said. "We're a little tippier than I thought."

Naji wrung water out of his loose sleeves. "You are *Shaitan* incarnate." He was so angry he was calm, which was truly frightening. "If I do not find occasion to dismember you and bury the pieces far apart before this affair is done, it will be because I am dead."

Head blinked at him, then turned to Ben. "Dude, I don't really think I can hang with this guy. The vibes just ain't happenin', you dig?"

Ben swung himself inboard onto the pontoon. "You can't 'hang,' huh? Head, just exactly where do you think you're going to go?" He sat down in the front passenger seat again, next to the pilot. "Look . . . we're here, like it or not. And we're not wasting the trip, understand? So get with the program. The only way we're going to be able to fly out of this place is if we get that broken strut jury-rigged. That'll be up to you and Naji, because I'm going after Nick, just the way we planned."

Ben reached under his seat and came up with a small laminated chart of the lake, about five inches wide by ten long, a narrow grease pencil clipped to its edge. Glancing at the GPS unit mounted beside Head's shoulder, he drew a small *X* at the lake's southern end.

"That's where we are right now," he said, "according to the GPS. About three-quarters of a mile from the shoreline, and"—he penciled in a small dot just west of the *X*—"about half a mile from the island. Here's what we're going to do. I'm getting geared up and swimming for that rock over there. You guys motor this plane over to shore with the little two-horse outboard and try to fix the pontoon strut."

Ben glanced at his watch. "We'll meet back here in . . . two hours. This is a good distance from the island—even if the fog clears, the plane probably won't be spotted at night. I've got my waterproof GPS; you've got that one." He pointed to the unit on the airframe. "I synchroed them before we took off. The positions they give should be identical and repeatable within about twenty feet. Pass me the little yellow box in that first gearbag, will you, Naji?"

The Yemeni leaned down, rummaged, and handed Ben a yellow impact-resistant container about the size of a large cellular phone.

"Thanks." Ben opened it and extracted a second GPS unit, this one encased in hard black rubber. Flipping up its stubby antennae, he punched a couple of waterproof buttons. "Give it a second or two to acquire a few satellites."

"You will be able to find your way to the island?" Naji asked. "A compass course underwater, perhaps?"

"You could do it that way," Ben said, "if you plotted the course on a chart and then got the correct bearing from the compass rose. That's the old way—just keep your eyes on your wrist compass and swim until you bump your head on your target. Trouble used to be, if you got into a crosscurrent in zero visibility, you could swim a perfect course and still get pushed off to the side of the target without knowing it. Or you could just be a little erratic in your swimming and miss."

He held up the rubber-encased GPS. "This is better. I can punch a waypoint into this thing and it'll tell me which direction I have to move in—right or left—in order to stay headed for the target. It doesn't matter if I veer off by mistake or get pushed by a current—the satellites track me every few seconds and update my course information. See this little screen?" Ben pointed at the small liquid-crystal display at the top of the GPS. "This floating arrow tells me which direction to turn. These numbers tell me how far off course I am, how far it is to the target, and how far I've already come."

"I have heard of them, but never seen one up close," Naji said. "I recall you using something similar aboard the *Teresa Ann* during our voyage here. A remarkable instrument, my brother."

Ben smiled. "Remarkable, yes. Unusual, no. Fifteen years ago this was top-secret military technology. Now every Boy Scout in the local troop has one of these to go hiking in the park. Times change.

"I already entered the waypoint of the island from the chart back in Krumake. Also, I entered a secondary waypoint on the shore opposite the island—in both your unit and mine—as an alternative rendezvous location, in case we miss each other." He paused as the little GPS beeped three times and flashed its reddish screen. "There. It's acquired enough satellites. It knows where I am. The last thing we'll do after I get geared up and drop in will be to punch in the same present-position waypoint simultaneously. That way, two hours from now, we'll both come back to exactly the same spot in the middle of the lake—here—and you can pick me, and hopefully Nick, up." He forced a can-do grin onto his face. "Got all that?"

Naji nodded. "Absolutely, *Ben-Ya-Min*."

There was no doubt in Ben's mind that the sharp, capable Naji had. It was a comforting thought. Then he regarded Head.

"Understand the plan, Head?" he asked.

"Huh? Oh, sure, man—no problem, whatever works." The pilot nodded happily, looking somewhat distracted, as usual.

Ben's eyes narrowed. "Hey. You're not communing with the fucking Zen ethers again, are you? Listen up. You're the one who's got to reprogram that GPS if it goes down for some reason. I don't want to be swimming around out here in the dark by myself two hours from now. You'll be back at the drop-in location exactly *two hours* from the time I splash, right?"

"You got it, dude," Head said. "Me and the Naji-man are on the case. Guaranteed." He gave Ben a thumbs-up.

"Okay," Ben said. "Pass that set of tanks around and give me the regulator in that little black bag. Let's get this show on the road before we die of old age."

Ten minutes later, Ben was perched on the edge of his seat, fully suited up. Two eighty-cubic-foot air cylinders were harnessed to his back with a Poseidon Cyklon regulator attached to the yoke manifold connecting them. Two second-stage hoses with breathing mouthpieces hung by his side, as did a third hose that terminated in an instrument console containing air and depth gauges and a compass. A high-volume, weight-integrated buoyancy compensation vest covered his torso, and extremely long, high-propulsion fins were strapped to his feet. On his face he wore a wide-angle mask with reflective lenses that hid his eyes and enhanced his vision, an underwater penlight taped to its strap. A SOG Navy SEAL knife was strapped to one leg, and he held the compact GPS unit in one gloved hand, its short leash clipped to a D-ring on his harness. A large nine-volt underwater searchlight hung from a second D-ring, and a compact caving reel loaded with high-strength Dacron twine was attached to a third. A spare mask and a pair of short fins were duct-taped securely between his air cylinders. All the gear, from the tanks to the buoyancy compensator to the mask and fins, was jet-black.

"Ready, Head?" Ben inquired. He held up the GPS and pushed the waypoint input button. The unit beeped as it instantly recorded the position of the ul-tralight and its occupants. A second later, Head did the same with his.

"Done, dude," he said. "Got her."

"Beautiful," Ben acknowledged. "See you here in two hours. If I'm not here on time, wait half an hour. Then go to the secondary GPS waypoint on the shore. Maybe I'll show up there. If not—don't hang around in daylight. Take off before sunup and get back over the border to Kuballa."

He clamped the mouthpiece of the Cyklon regula-tor's second stage in his teeth and stepped off the pon-toon into the surrounding fog. There was a splash, and he was gone.

CHAPTER 9

The ripples from Ben's entry lapped against the pontoon, and then the black water was still once more, tendrils of fog drifting lazily above it.

"The dude's got *cojones*," Head commented. "You wouldn't get me in that water for all the hash in Lebanon. They don't call this Shark Lake because it's full of guppies."

"My brother *Ben-Ya-Min* has swum with sharks many times, all over the world," Naji said. "He knows what he is doing."

"No doubt." Head nodded. "But it ain't just the sharks. There are some nasty-ass crocodiles in here, too." He pointed off into the fog. "Mostly, they hang out along the shore over there. Where we're going."

Naji eyed him and patted the stock of his old Lee-Enfield rifle. "We shall be watchful."

Head guffawed. " 'Watchful.' Dude, these critters ain't vegetarians. They make their living by sneakin' up on big juicy animals like you and me and snatchin' 'em into the water without warning."

"Then it would be best to work quickly and quietly," Naji said. "Let us get under way. We must not be late for the rendezvous with *Ben-Ya-Min*."

"Right, right," Head replied. "We just need to get that little outboard—" He turned to find a gold-and-green eye the size of a quarter staring at him from less than a foot away. "*Yaaaagh!*"

He shrank back violently. The eye merely blinked at him. The huge, long-necked water stork that had floated silently in out of the fog was utterly unperturbed by his flailing reaction. Four feet tall from the waterline to the top of its sharp-billed head, it was covered in sleek white feathers. The leathery, knubbled skin around its brilliant eyes was black with the odd fleck of crimson.

Naji chuckled evilly. "Another beast for you to fret about. Tell me—do you think this one will swallow you whole? Or merely peck your eyes out?"

"Not funny, dude," Head muttered, looking injured. He flung a hand toward the stork. "Beat it, bird." The animal merely turned its head and regarded him coldly with its opposite eye.

"All right, enough," Naji said. "We must go. Is this the engine?" He tapped the cowling of a tiny outboard clamped on the edge of a cutaway in the aluminum floor just behind the two rear passenger seats.

"Yeah," Head replied. "Just unbuckle the tie-down strap, tilt the shaft down into the water, and plug in that fuel line. See the little tank under your seat? That's the gas. Three gallons of two-cycle mix just for puttin' around with."

Naji lowered the engine and connected the gas line. Then he squeezed the primer bulb several times, pulled out the choke, and yanked the starter cord.

"You've done this before," Head said. "I didn't know they had outboard motors in the desert."

Naji looked up at him sideways. "I have actually shaved with an electric razor and ridden in a *real* automobile as well. It is hard to believe, is it not?" He yanked the starter cord again and the outboard sputtered into life. Manipulating the choke, Naji slipped the engine into gear and throttled up. Slowly, the floatplane began to move through the water, the noise it emitted little more than a high-pitched purr. "Come, fool, watch the compass," he growled at Head. "Direct me."

"Sure thing, man." Head looked at his compact control console. "Swing around to the right some."

A splash close to the ultralight caught his attention. "Hey, hold on." Naji throttled down and slipped the engine into neutral. "What was that? Maybe the Bendude's come back."

"Do you see him?" Naji asked, peering into the dark mist.

Head shrugged. "No. But I heard a splash . . . Hey, where's that bird?"

"How in the name of the Prophet should I know?" Naji looked at him in disgust. "Obviously, it has taken to the air and that is what you heard."

"Maybe." As Head watched, several dozen large white feathers drifted past the starboard pontoon. "Maybe not."

Naji put the engine back into gear. "Enough time wasted. We go."

*　　　*　　　*

As soon as Ben hit the water, the small amount of ambient moonlight that had been present in the fog vanished. The upper layer of the lake was choked with brown algae, which reduced visibility to two feet or less. Ben could barely see his hand at arm's length, even with the aid of the slender underwater flashlight taped to his mask strap. Dropping down through the first fifteen feet was like swimming in pea soup, the water was thick to the touch and uncomfortably warm. Not wanting to ingest any of it, he clamped his lips more firmly around the mouthpiece of his regulator.

At sixteen feet he encountered a thermocline. The amount of temperature differential surprised him— the lower layer felt a good fifteen degrees cooler. Also surprising was the sudden increase in visibility. The water below sixteen feet was virtually sediment-and-algae-free. He switched on his flashlight again.

He was suspended in a clear black void beneath a thick, murky ceiling of greenish brown—the underside of the surface layer through which he had just penetrated. Below his slowly pedaling fins no bottom was visible. He reached an arm up into the murk over his head. It was like dipping a hand into a stew pot. The temperature of the surface layer had to be in excess of ninety degrees—that of the layer below it, less than seventy-five.

Twenty feet was as good a depth as any at which to approach the island. Switching off his flashlight to save its batteries, he brought both the luminous depth gauge on his instrument console and the backlit GPS up to his faceplate. Orienting himself and spinning to face the correct direction, he began to swim strongly through the utter darkness, his eyes locked on the two instruments.

The island was less than half a mile away—four-tenths of a mile, according to the GPS—but a fully equipped diver, even one fit and experienced, was doing well to make one mile per hour underwater. It looked to be a twenty-five-minute swim, at least. Ben settled into his kick—a powerful, rhythmic snap—not too fast—that used the whipping elasticity of his long fins to maximum advantage.

His entire world became his kick, his breathing, and the position of the directional arrow at the top of the tiny red-glowing GPS screen. Staying near a depth of twenty feet was easy. As soon as he drifted up more than three or four feet, the algal murk of the surface layer obscured his vision, and his head felt as though it was being parboiled. Reading the depth gauge was merely a backup check.

He had been powering along doggedly for nearly fifteen minutes when he felt a strange sensation on the side of his face and neck—a sudden pressure wave, as if someone had just kicked a fin close to his head. He slowed his swimming for a few seconds, glancing around at the empty blackness, then set his mind back on the GPS. The little red screen's distance-to-waypoint number read .08 miles—eight-one-hundredths of a mile.

He was pleased—he'd really made time, and he wasn't all that tired. To distract himself from the physical effort of kicking, he converted the decimal mile reading into feet in his head. Four hundred and twenty-two . . . and about a half . . . feet. The island was only a stone's throw in front of him.

Nick. Nick was in there. Somewhere.

Or maybe he wasn't.

An ambush attack of uncertainty began to well up inside him. He was completely alone, floating in an empty black void in unfamiliar territory in the middle of the night. He had no idea what the submerged rock of the island looked like. How the hell was he going to find—

Something brushed hard against his legs, interrupting his kick and rolling him off-balance. He righted himself and another pressure wave from an unseen source surged against his face. No mistaking that. It was something big. Moving fast. And very close to him.

He hadn't wanted to use the large searchlight so close to the fort, but the urge to see what was threatening him was overwhelming. Breathing hard, he swung it up and squeezed the on/off trigger.

The instantaneous glare revealed a seething mass of sharks behind him, around him, everywhere—big sharks, some more than ten feet long, with thick bronze bodies and scythelike fins, knifing back and forth over top of each other in a near frenzy. The powerful light flashed off their white bellies as they twisted and turned, darting off to both sides, up into the soupy murk just overhead, and down into the empty darkness below. Ben hardly had time to recognize them, with their broad heads and heavy-shouldered builds, as huge specimens of the dangerous Zambezi—or bull—shark, when one of the animals charged the light, tooth-studded mouth gaping.

Out of sheer instinct he punched back with the sturdy housing, striking the shark on the nose and deflecting the charge. The impact nearly broke his wrist. Another shark rammed him from behind, hitting him high in the back between his neck and shoulder. The force of the blindside rush tumbled him over in a complete somersault, knocking his mask ajar and flooding it.

He pressed it to his face and cleared it of water with a blast of air. Sharks swarmed everywhere, excited by the motion, by the light, by his presence . . .

This is no place for Mrs. Gannon's little boy.

He flashed the searchlight toward the bottom.

Nothing.

He spun in the water column, light pointing out and down, looking for—

Rocks!

He punched another charging bull shark in the gills, inverted himself, and swam for the sunken outcrop with all the strength in his legs.

On the upper catwalk behind the ramparts of the old fort, the lone Leopard Soldier assigned to sentry duty paused in his slow patrol and peered down at the misty surface of the lake. There it was again. A faint flash some two hundred feet out from shore that momentarily turned the black water a glowing brown.

Thoughtfully, he drew on his herb spliff and waited to see if the strange light would reappear. It did not.

The lake below was as dark and placid as a vat of crude oil.

He exhaled, the familiar warm burn of marijuana spreading throughout his chest, and continued his leisurely stroll around the ramparts, his heavy jungle boots scuffing on the worn stone of the catwalk. There were many strange and inexplicable things to be seen in the trackless swamps and jungles of Bisotho. A brief flash of light emanating from the depths of Tiburi Kunga at night was just one more oddity to be noted, then quickly forgotten. It might be a new world, but the old gods—some of them malevolent—were still around, lurking, ready to make mischief.

He drew on his spliff again. It was not wise for a man to look too deeply into the unknown. Things could be disturbed that were best left alone.

Still, there were standing orders from Colonel Klegg that any unusual sightings around the fort were to be reported immediately. And if the sentry knew one thing for certain, it was that failure to follow the White Colonel's orders was not only unwise—it was often *fatal*. He fingered the compact walkie-talkie clipped to his breast pocket.

A man also didn't want to be made a fool of. Or waste the White Colonel's time. The Leopard Soldier drew on his spliff and regarded its dull red ember. There was enough herb left to savor through one more slow circuit around the rampart catwalk. He would keep a sharp eye out for more lights, and then decide whether or not to report what he had seen when the last of the good smoke was gone.

*   *   *

As Ben got a hand on top of the nearest boulder, one of the sharks tracking him from behind in the darkness snapped its jaws shut on the blade of his right fin. In an explosion of ferocious energy, the unseen animal shook him like a terrier shakes a rat, nearly dislocating his leg from his hip. Before he could twist around to kick at its head with his free leg, it bit clean through the fin's carbon fiber-reinforced rubber, tearing off half the blade. The violent shaking stopped, and Ben clawed his way across the rock, looking for—

A crevice! It was narrow, almost too narrow to accommodate a fully dressed diver. But it was shelter. Tanks clanging on the walls of the cleft, his arms and shoulders scraping against protrusions of rock, he forced his way down into the opening.

He got in about a body length before the crevice bottlenecked to less than a foot, and he could go no deeper. Flattened out between the two rock walls, he managed to scramble and squeeze around until he was more or less upright, wedged in so tightly he could barely inflate his lungs.

He directed the searchlight upward. Just overhead, outside the cleft, a mass of pale bellies swarmed, as thick as leeches. A great bronze head twisted down at him, biting at the light, the eye rolling back white and dead. He punched upward with the housing, fending the shark off. The fin of another animal swiped across his arm, its edge like a rasp, tearing open the fabric of his Lycra suit.

Time and time again, for what seemed like an eternity, Ben punched, shoved, and gouged at shark after shark with his one available arm, praying that the searchlight would not go out and leave him in total darkness, blind. The penlight taped to his mask had been scraped off during his desperate rush into the crevice.

The bull sharks were relentless. Frighteningly powerful and aggressive, only the thickness of their huge wedge-shaped heads kept them from penetrating far enough into the cleft to clamp down fully on Ben's head or shoulders. But they would not stop attacking. Shark after shark charged in, writhing and snapping, as if trying to batter its way through the solid rock to get to him.

His arm was going numb, the fingers holding the searchlight losing their grip, when suddenly—as if cued by a silent signal—the bull sharks disappeared. Completely. The tumbling mass of bronze bodies and pale bellies lifted away into the darkness, leaving only empty black water.

Ben sagged in the crevice, gasping air into his lungs through his regulator. He turned the searchlight this way . . . that way . . . The only thing above him was the column of silvery bubbles from his own exhalations.

Not a shark in sight.

He inched upward until his head and shoulders cleared the crevice's top edge, and aimed the light around the lake bottom. Nothing but muck and a few protruding rock outcrops like the one in which he'd taken shelter. No sharks. Not even a minnow.

Emerging completely from the crevice and checking his compass, he began to follow the contour of the rock southward. A glance at the GPS confirmed that the island was directly in front of him, a matter of yards away. Expecting to be hit from behind at any moment, the back of his neck prickling, he pulled and kicked his way along the jagged spur, the reverse pressure in his ears making him conscious of the fact that it was sloping steadily upward.

He checked his air-pressure gauge. Just over 3200 psi remaining. The special high-pressure twin tanks on his back had contained 4800 at the start of the dive. *Damn*. He'd used a lot of air, and hadn't even found the entrance to the underwater dome yet.

He flashed the searchlight ahead and around. Something unusual was happening. As he moved forward, the water was becoming clearer and cooler, even though he was ascending. Then he remembered—it had to be the zone of outflowing springwater that encircled the island.

A sudden thought occurred to him and he switched the light off. Since he was now in clear water—in all likelihood without a murky top layer—any illumination he used would be visible from the surface, regardless of his depth. The fluorescent face of his depth gauge read fifty-one feet. Relatively shallow—and he was going to have to move higher up the island's sunken rock buttresses in order to search for some kind of cave entrance.

He lay on the rock in total darkness for several minutes, breathing very slowly, considering. He had to move along the island's perimeter—probably at about thirty feet—and use the searchlight to illuminate the cracks and gaps in the rock face. It was the only way he was going to find the entrance.

Maybe they hadn't thought the whole thing through, hadn't planned well enough. Maybe it was all just a dangerous wild-goose chase . . .

He shook himself in irritation. Too late for that kind of pointless thinking. This was here and now. *Get on with it*.

Pushing off, he began to swim along the nearly vertical rock wall, lighting it up with the beam of the searchlight. He felt exposed, vulnerable. Anyone looking down from the fort would have to be blind to miss the light. And there was always the chance that the sharks would return, swarming out of the surrounding darkness to attack once again.

The rock wall was craggy and irregular, lined with deep vertical cracks and fissures. Any one of them had the potential to be an opening to a hidden cavern. As he kicked onward, the uneven strain caused by the torn fin beginning to cramp his leg, a real sense of futility began to well up inside him. It was *so* dark . . . there were *so many* nooks and crannies . . . and try as he might to breathe conservatively, his air was being used up—

Shark. Ben froze, hanging motionless in open water, neutrally buoyant, tracking the big animal with the searchlight. It glided by less than fifteen feet away, bronze hide gleaming against the black void, its sharp heterocercal tail undulating slowly. The soulless eye swiveled in its socket, reflecting the glare of the light like an empty glass.

Another movement, ten feet lower. Ben trained the light downward. A second shark, larger than the first, was swimming in the same direction—outward, away from the island—at the same unhurried pace. Neither animal made any move toward him.

He flicked his fins and drifted in to the rock wall. Grasping a thin ledge, he hung there quietly in the darkness, probing the surrounding water with the searchlight beam. A large mass of torn fishing net was draped across a nearby limestone spur, several deteriorating Styrofoam floats still attached to it.

There were at least a dozen sharks visible, some moving in toward the rock face, some moving away. All were swimming with an almost trancelike slowness—in contrast to the frenzied, aggressive behavior that others of their kind—or perhaps these—had just exhibited only a few hundred yards away.

Moving cautiously, Ben pulled himself around a column of rock and peered into the darkness along the beam of the searchlight.

A great vertical crack, at least eight feet wide, bisected the rock face just ahead of him, stretching up toward the surface and down into the gloom below as far as he could see. Swimming in and out of it, at varying depths, were twenty, thirty—perhaps more—bull sharks, gliding along in calm, orderly fashion, as if their behavior had somehow been synchronized.

Ben watched them for a moment, silent killers drifting through the cool black void. There was no change in swimming patterns—no indication that they were aware of him at all. He glanced at his air-pressure gauge—2950 psi.

Heart pounding, he pushed away from the rock face and began to swim toward the dark, gaping fissure.

CHAPTER 10

The Leopard Soldier sergeant rapped smartly twice on the thick wooden door and waited. When there was no response after a full minute, he knocked again, harder. This time there was a muffled curse, a thump, and a shriek followed by what sounded like a despairing wail. The sergeant, a big man with scarification tattoos decorating his pitch-black face, shifted uncomfortably on his feet, hands clasped behind his back in the at-ease position. Then the door opened and he found himself eye-to-eye with the White Colonel.

Afrikaner Amon Klegg was stripped to the waist, the mat of white hair covering his hard, bony chest damp with sweat. What was left of the prematurely white hair on his head was worn in a crew cut. His khaki jungle trousers were tucked into the high tops of his custom-made leather bush boots, and a small automatic pistol rode in a black full-flap holster on his right hip. Under his left arm, in a headlock, he held a young native girl not more than fourteen or fifteen years of age. She was completely naked, her ebony skin shining with sweat, and breathing with obvious difficulty. But she bore the distinctive scarification patterns on her shoulders and upper arms that marked her as a

member of the hated *Quori* tribe, so the sergeant could-
n't have cared less if the White Colonel had broken her
neck then and there. He was a *Malmoq*—like all Leopard Soldiers—and sworn to rid Bisotho of every last
Quori, by any means at his disposal.

Klegg stepped forward into the doorway, with the
girl—bent over at the waist—following helplessly. A
little moan escaped her lips, and the wiry South
African jerked her head roughly in the crook of his
elbow.

"Keep still, you black bitch," he snapped. He spoke
in English—one of several command languages and
dialects he used—but it was heavily *Afrikaans*-ac-
cented—*Kip steel, you bleck beetch*. The girl sagged in
his grip and fell silent. Klegg raised his eyes to the
sergeant's. "Well?"

The sergeant of Leopard Soldiers swallowed. Amon
Klegg had one of the most unnerving faces into which
he'd ever had to look. All his features—eyes, nose,
mouth—were small, narrow, and set too close together. And the lines of his face were permanently
twisted somehow, as if a large screw had been embedded directly between his brows and given one complete turn. He looked mean, bitter—and perpetually
on the verge of rage. His eyes were the most frightening thing of all. They were pale gray—almost the same
color as his parchment-paper skin—and hooded like a
viper's.

"Sentry atop rampart, *sah!*" the sergeant barked, his
own English barely decipherable. "He see lights in
watuh, *sah!*"

"What lights?"

"*Sah?*"

"What bloody kind of lights, eh? Eh?" Klegg had an abrupt, pinched way of speaking that kept anyone conversing with him badly off-balance. It was quite unnerving. The sergeant grimaced and swallowed hastily again.

"Sentry not say, *sah*! Not boat or aircraft lights, though. Lights *deep in watuh*, near to island, *sah*!"

"What the bloody hell . . ." Klegg snarled. He spun around, yanking the girl with him. She let out a little shriek, her hands going to the whipcord forearm around her neck. The sergeant's eyes automatically dropped to her firm young buttocks and thighs. Her smooth black skin was striped with welts, some of them leaking blood. The sight simultaneously attracted and repelled him. She was well shaped and pretty, despite being a *Quori* bitch. Perhaps the colonel would toss this one into the barracks, reasonably undamaged, to provide the men with a little entertainment. He hoped so.

Klegg marched the stumbling girl across the room toward a narrow window that overlooked the lake, throwing her onto a roughly constructed bed in passing. She flopped over, cracked her temple against the crude headboard, and lay still, curled up and whimpering. The White Colonel didn't give her a second glance as he unlatched the rusty iron grille that barred the window, pulled it back, and leaned out.

He craned his neck this way and that, scanning the waterline below the walls of the fort, then withdrew into the room. "Not a light anywhere," he muttered.

He stalked back to the doorway, scowling at the big sergeant.

"When I'm interrupted in my quarters by a sentry report," he snarled, "I expect it to contain specific details, eh? Not the paranoid mumblings of some incompetent fool smoking herb on guard duty, eh? Eh?" He jammed a hard finger into the sergeant's sternum and leaned in close. *"See that it doesn't happen again."*

"*Sah!*" The sergeant got his heels together quickly and saluted. "I understand, *sah!*"

"Good. Get out of here."

"*Sah!*" The big man wheeled and marched off down the dank stone corridor, relieved that the exchange was over.

Amon Klegg watched him go, then shut the door and turned back toward the *Quori* girl trembling on the bed.

"Fucking *kaffirs*," he said under his breath.

Forty-one feet below the lake's surface, almost directly beneath the window of the White Colonel's quarters, Ben swam slowly toward the crack in the rock wall, reducing the glare of his searchlight by shielding the lens with his free hand. The grayed-down torpedo shapes of the bull sharks drifted by in the subdued light, now barely visible. Ben paused at the edge of the crevice to let a ten-foot-plus specimen, less than arm's length away, glide out into open water. Then, with a flick of his fins, he propelled himself into the black gap.

Immediately, he was aware of a mild current—not strong, probably less than an eighth of a knot—flowing out of the fissure. The water was now very cool and sweet to the taste, unlike the turbid upper layer of the open lake. He waited until he had penetrated a good fifteen feet, then took his hand away from the searchlight lens.

The powerful light illuminated a fantastic vertical corridor of limestone, varying in width from six to ten feet, slightly slanted, with a jagged ceiling twenty feet overhead and no visible bottom. The walls on either side had been carved by untold centuries of water flow into abstract friezes of incredible beauty, the pale stone opulent with lush contours and rippling rugosities.

Through this elegant sunken channel, suspended in the crystal-clear water like great living ornaments, swam dozens of bull sharks. Some were moving toward him, others were headed deeper into the island's drowned interior. All exhibited the same oddly trance-like behavior—mouths gaping wider than normal, gills pumping, crescent-shaped tails undulating with exaggerated slowness.

Ben hung there for a moment, completely still, marveling at the superb natural spectacle illuminated by his searchlight. A particularly large bull shark was coming straight for him out of the gloomy recesses of the channel. As the animal drew to within five feet, he exhaled completely, emptying his lungs of air, and sank slowly beneath it. The pale belly passed overhead, the pectoral fins spread like aircraft wings. The shark's swimming rhythm never changed.

Upon inhaling, Ben's neutral buoyancy returned and he found himself on the tail of another shark that had just passed beneath him, heading deeper into the crevice. He unclipped the snap hook at the end of the spool of caving line attached to his harness, took a quick wrap around a nearby spur of rock, reclipped the line onto itself, and began to follow the animal into the dark vaults ahead.

After traveling a mere hundred feet, the crevice narrowed and took a forty-five-degree turn to the left. The more restricted space did not seem to affect the sharks . . . above and below him, they continued to cruise in both directions, the tips of their pectoral fins nearly touching both walls in some of the tighter spots.

There was a slight rumbling—more a vibration than an actual noise—and Ben looked back in time to see a whitish cloud of limestone dust, shards, and larger chunks falling through the water about twenty feet behind him. He trained the light upward, realizing instantly what had happened. The rising bubbles from his own exhalations had disturbed delicate rock formations on the crevice's ceiling, causing a minor cave-in.

Alarmed, he shot a glance directly overhead, then swam on after the shark, paying out line from the caving spool as he went. If his bubbles were going to cause the previously untouched ceiling to shed chunks of rock, it was best not to linger too long in one place. What he'd seen fall had looked relatively lightweight. He wondered briefly if his exhalations could cause something really heavy to come down. *Hell, why not?*

The shark he'd been following was about thirty feet ahead, fading into the gloom. He kicked after it, trying to keep his movements smooth, natural. The great predators drifting through the underwater corridor had been tolerant of his presence so far. He didn't

want to provide them any stimulus—such as thrashing—that might change their behavior.

The pressure on his ears was increasing slightly. He
cleared them and checked his depth gauge—forty-
eight feet. His guide shark was planing lower as it
swam forward. A quick look overhead confirmed that
the ceiling was much closer than it had been . . . the
crevice was sloping downward at a shallow angle.
Something else to worry about. If he got much deeper
and had to stay there for any significant amount of
time, he was going to run into decompression problems—assuming he didn't run out of air first.

He glanced at his air-pressure gauge—2645 psi. The
twin tanks on his back were big, but their capacity was
not infinite. And he was going to need as much air to
get back out of the crevice as he'd used getting in . . .
more, if Nick was with him and breathing from the
same supply through the octopus regulator.

The shark's slowly sweeping tail was only five or
six feet in front of him now. He could feel the pressure
waves generated by its movement wafting past his
face. The animal was swimming at constant depth
again, right around fifty-two feet, according to the
depth gauge. The ceiling of the channel had come
down to within a body length of Ben's head, and the
walls on either side had gradually encroached until
they were barely four feet apart. He flashed the searchlight downward. Below him, the sharks were stacked
more closely now—undulating languidly over the top
of each other in both directions, without touching, like
a slow-motion swarm of giant tadpoles.

He sensed a slight vibration again, and looked back

in time to see a small dust cloud of limestone falling through the water ten feet behind him, a few silver-dollar-sized shards spinning downward more rapidly past the slender thread of his caving line. At that moment, for no apparent reason, his searchlight flickered. The little hesitancy in the comforting glare sent a cold chill through his chest. If the light failed, he was going to have a devil of a time getting out of the sunken passageway, even with the caving line to follow. And if the line cut over a sharp edge as he was groping along in total darkness, that would be *it*. He'd be dead meat . . . and so would Nick, if he happened to be there.

The relatively new searchlight had never leaked, never let him down. *For the love of God, don't start now . . .*

Ben ran his fingers over the line spool on his harness. About three-quarters gone. It held two hundred yards, so he'd penetrated in excess of 450 feet. On dry land, a healthy man could run that distance in less than twenty seconds. Underwater, alone, in an unknown cave system, on limited air, with a touchy light—not to mention bull sharks for company—450 feet was a *very* long way.

Abruptly, the passageway took a sharp right turn—so sharp that when the beam of Ben's light first reached the back wall, he thought for one horrible moment that the crevice had dead-ended. But the guide shark flexed its sinuous body, dropped a pectoral fin, and curved around the right-hand wall without hesitation, momentarily disappearing from view. Casting another wary glance down at the numerous sharks just below him, Ben kicked to follow.

As he swam through the turn, the rock walls on either side of him suddenly began to open outward, then vanished altogether. All at once he found himself floating in empty water, as if back in the middle of the lake, with no visible boundaries or points of reference. It disoriented him momentarily, and a wave of vertigo surged behind his eyes.

Pedaling his fins, he spun in place and directed the searchlight back the way he had come, looking for a structure on which to focus. There was the crack, much narrower than at its lake end, vertically splitting the pale limestone rock face. And there were the sharks, emerging from and cruising back into the opening at various depths—on down into the gloom beneath him. With his sense of balance restored, the dizzy, sickening feeling passed as quickly as it had come.

He turned slowly, breathing easily, and set his thumb beside a button on the searchlight that would switch its function from narrow-beam spot to high-power diffuser. It consumed more battery juice, but the sacrifice was necessary—it would provide a few precious seconds of broad illumination and enable him to get an overall look at his new surroundings. He tilted the searchlight upward slightly and pushed the button.

A great sunken cathedral appeared before his eyes, a massive natural chamber of shadowy limestone arches and thick pillars. It looked to be roughly circular, about two hundred feet in diameter, with innumerable ledges, protrusions, and small fractures lining its pale walls. Through this huge, silent gallery, like miniature zeppelins floating through a cloudless sky, drifted dozens of bull sharks, eyes implacable and mouths gaping.

Ben switched his light back to narrow beam and directed it at the nearest ledges. Incredibly, lying on them were more bull sharks, grouped in twos and threes, motionless but for the pumping of their gills. Much like the free-swimming animals, they appeared to be in a state of torpor, oblivious to his presence.

He caught a movement out of the corner of his eye and turned to find the wedge-shaped head of a huge shark looming out of the darkness on his left shoulder. Maneuvering sideways, he let it bypass him with less than a foot of clearance. On impulse, he reached out and dragged a gloved finger along its sandpapery side. The shark did not react.

As it had in Maggie Fenzi's room in the Hotel Excelsior, Ben's memory flashed on the "sleeping" sharks he'd encountered in the coastal caves of Mexico's Yucatán Peninsula. Those had been ocean-dwelling sharks seemingly anaesthetized by the presence of fresh springwater. Although the Tiburi Kunga bulls were permanently adapted to life in a nonmarine environment, something similar was going on here. Their behavior within the confines of the island's passageways and caverns more or less paralleled that of the Yucatán sharks. Ben wondered what could cause such extreme lethargy in animals designed to live out their lives in ceaseless motion. A higher oxygen level in the pristine springwater, perhaps . . . or some unknown dissolved mineral component.

It occurred to him, as he swam deeper into the great cavern, that it didn't really matter *what* was keeping the sharks from acting as aggressively as they had out in the open waters of the lake, as long as it kept working for the next hour or so. With Nick or without him, he'd have to be clear of this underwater maze by then. His air was nearly half-gone.

He drifted up as he swam along, rising toward the cavern ceiling. It made sense that the opening in the bottom of the prison pit would be at or near the highest point in the overhead rock. He flashed the searchlight along it; swimming on his back, straining his eyes to look into every crack, gap, or void that could permit the passage of a man's body. There were too many to count.

Something tugged at his harness. It was the caving spool, out of line. Frustrated, he flashed the light up at the convoluted ceiling. Two-thirds of it had yet to be searched. But he was quite literally at the end of his tether.

Making a quick decision, Ben dropped down through twenty feet of open water to a nearby pillar formation. Unclipping the caving spool and line from his harness, he secured them to the thickest pillar with a wrap and a couple of half hitches. Then he reached into the pocket of his buoyancy compensator and drew out a five-inch-long Cyalume lightstick. Bending the hollow plastic tube, he snapped the internal glass ampule that separated its active chemicals and quickly shook it. The combined liquid began to fluoresce immediately, emitting a ghostly green-white glow. He clipped the lightstick's plastic eyelet to the retaining strap of the spool, then kicked back toward the ceiling.

Veering around a couple of cruising sharks, he turned over on his back and began to swim rapidly along the cavern ceiling, probing here and there with his light. Things were getting critical. If he didn't find the pit opening in the next few minutes, he was going to have to leave or get caught without enough air. Just behind his pedaling fins, a few fragments of limestone tumbled downward, dislodged by his exhalations.

Where the hell is it?

A dark recess, like a sloping chimney, appeared to his left. He maneuvered beneath it, breathing hard with the increased exertion, and paused. His bubbles cascaded upward, disappearing into the narrow void. Aiming the searchlight directly overhead, he peered up into the shadows.

The light glinted off the roiling silver billows of his exhalations as they broke through a shimmering water/air interface about ten feet up the limestone chimney. A thrill ran through him as he drifted up into the gap. The surface area looked to be about five by three feet . . .

This has to be it.

A thought occurred to him and he looked back the way he had come, shining the searchlight down toward the limestone buttress where he'd tied off the caving line. Picking the formation out of the gloom with the light's narrow beam, he flicked the trigger off and on. In the momentary darkness, the Cyalume lightstick had not been visible.

He took a compass bearing on the buttress and set

the bezel—087 degrees. *Remember that. It might end up being the most important number of your life.*

He switched off the searchlight as he ascended, very slowly, through the chimney, placing his gloved hands on the opposing walls. The shimmering surface above him quieted and settled, although it still refracted a miniscule amount of illumination—perhaps moonlight—which rendered it just barely visible. Ben wondered at its calm for a couple of seconds before realizing that at some point during the short ascent he had stopped breathing, his lungs only half-full of air. No exhaust—no agitation.

He paused, his scalp less than six inches below the surface, and removed the regulator from his mouth, letting it dangle by his side. Then, placing his hands on the rock near the waterline, he raised his head noiselessly into the air.

With his lips just clear of the water, he exhaled and took in a quiet, controlled breath. Then another, and another, until the pounding in his chest lessened and the choking feeling of oxygen debt left him. Then, gingerly, he pushed his face mask up onto his forehead and tried to focus in the near-total darkness.

It took a good fifteen seconds for his eyes to adjust, but eventually he could make out a circular area, directly overhead, where the unrelenting blackness was slightly less . . . *black*. Another ten seconds and he was able to see a few faint pinpricks of light: stars. It dawned on him that he was looking up at the sky from the bottom of a deep shaft, perhaps ten feet in diameter. In the darkness, it was hard to say *how* deep . . .

maybe thirty, forty feet. Exactly as Maggie had described the prison pit.

The rocky floor of the shaft was about a foot above the waterline. Ben slipped his fins off and hung them on his wrists. Then he got the ball of his right foot on a decent edge, the sole of his left back against the rear wall, and lifted himself halfway out of the water. He braced there, dripping, his eyes probing the darkness.

Something stirred against the far wall of the pit, an indistinct form about six feet long. Ben squinted, trying to see. Then there was a single hoarse cough, and he was sure.

"Nick," he said quietly, "it's Ben. Ben Gannon. You want to go home?"

CHAPTER 11

Sass took another sip of her martini-on-the-rocks and stared at the minute hand of the polished wood clock hanging behind the bar of the Hotel Excelsior. Slowly, it moved onto the three. A quarter past midnight. It had been over four hours since the ultralight carrying Ben, Naji, and Head had taken off from the little dirt airstrip outside Krumake.

She grimaced as she swallowed the watery gin. The ice had long since melted and the drink was luke-warm. She didn't want it anyway; it was something to hold in your hand when you couldn't sleep.

The short drive back to the hotel from the airstrip had been suffused with awkward silences. Maggie, at the wheel of the Land Rover, hadn't met Sass's eye once; she was responding to her pointed questions with a string of bland generalities. By the time they'd reached the hotel, Sass's temper had been close to boiling over. Maggie had headed directly for her room, saying that she was feeling sick, had a migraine, and was going to knock herself out for a few hours with a sleeping pill.

Sass scowled into her rocks glass. She'd been tempted to offer *Mrs*. Fenzi the opportunity to save her medication.

She glanced up at the clock again. Ben had said to be back at the airstrip by 5 A.M., and also to stand by the VHF radio—if they were forced to set down somewhere in the Kuballan bush, they were going to have to be picked up by Land Rover. But, he'd added, it was unlikely that they'd be back across the Bisotho/Kuballa border before four in the morning, even if everything went without a hitch. And they were to keep checking the satellite uplink unit. She and Maggie would have one, he'd have Maggie's spare.

Sass looked gloomily at the two small electronic devices on the bar next to her elbow. Both were silent, their active LEDs dark. *Not so much as a peep.*

Knowing full well that it was the worst possible thing she could do, she stared at the second hand as it ticked around the clock face. Its movement was excruciatingly slow. Overhead, the rotating fans gave off a barely audible hum as they circulated air past Sass and the dozing, black-jacketed Kuballan bartender—the only two people in the room.

There was a creaking of brass hinges and the heavy teak-and-cut-glass door to the main lobby opened. Sass glanced around disinterestedly as a tall European with graying sandy hair and a matching beard, dressed in travel-rumpled khakis, walked up to the far end of the bar, dropped a large duffel bag to the floor, and set a boot on the foot rail. Wearily, he leaned on the polished thornwood of the counter and rapped on it loudly to awaken the bartender: "Vodka on the rocks, a double. Finlandia, if you have it."

At the sound of the Scandinavian-accented voice, Sass straightened on her stool. She peered over at the newcomer intently. "Berndt?" The man looked around. "Berndt Olssen?"

"*Ya*. I'm Olssen. And you are . . . ?"

"Berndt, it's Sass Wojeck. You remember, we met in Stavanger after the Elf Aquitaine project back in '93 . . . at the corporate dinner celebrating the successful installation of those three huge North Sea oil platforms. I was with Ben Gannon."

"Ah! Yes!" The man took his drink from the bartender and moved toward her. "Of course—I know Ben. The freelancer from the Gulf of Mexico. An excellent underwater welder, as I recall." He slid onto the stool beside her, paused for a moment, then smiled. "And now I remember you too. *Sasha*, no? You must forgive me"—he rapped his knuckles lightly against his temple—"forty years of breathing unnatural gases while deepwater diving has not done good things for my memory."

"That's what Ben says," Sass said, smiling back, "unless he forgets."

"Ha-ha! *Ya*, " Olssen chuckled. "Just like that, exactly." He tipped the glass up and banged back half the vodka in a single swallow. "Ahhhh. Nectar of Odin. May I buy you one?"

Sass shook her head and raised the dregs of her martini. "No, thanks. I'm good." She touched his glass with hers. "But nice to see you, Berndt."

"Likewise, Sasha." They both sipped.

"So," Sass said. "What brings you to this cozy part of the world? A fondness for stultifying humidity?"

"I was about to ask you the same question."

"I beat you to it," Sass countered.

"Fair enough." Olssen signaled to the bartender for a refill. "Actually, I'd much rather not have to be here. I've had a bit of a financial disaster with my last diving project. It may put me out of business. I'm only here to sniff around and see if there's any way I might be able to salvage the situation—even partially."

"What happened?"

Olssen sighed. "I was running a small exploratory drilling operation in the large central lake of Bisotho, the country just south of here. We were taking core samples and doing bottom-survey dives for the Bisothoan government—the *former* Bisothoan government, that is. Now there's some kind of maniac in charge down there, killing people right and left."

"I heard," Sass said.

"*Ya*. Anyway, I had a team of experienced oil-field divers—international boys, very good at their jobs—and a few drillers, all working for me off a mid-sized jackup rig that I'd leased from TransArctic Oil. It had been sitting idle at a mothball dock in Bahrain for nearly two years, so I was able to negotiate a good price for its use. I had it towed from the Persian Gulf to Bisotho, then up the Tiburi River to the lake, through the old British locks that bypass the Tiburi Cataract. We started work immediately, and things were going fine until the bloody country—excuse my language—blew up in revolution." He took a long sip of vodka.

Sass's eyes were wide. "Wait a minute, wait a minute. *You* were running a drilling rig in Shark Lake just a few weeks ago? That was *you*?"

"Shark Lake—Tiburi Kunga—yes, I was. But we

had to abandon the rig and run for our lives. It was a judgment call on my part. I had to get the men out. There were reports of armed marauders—Leopard Soldiers, they're called—attacking people at random and cutting them to bits with machetes. Particularly the indigenous *Quoris*. A terrible thing. We just barely made it across the border to Kuballa, through the main mountain pass, in a truck we'd commandeered.

"So we escaped. But for me, there remains the financial problem of the leased jackup rig. In order to get such good terms on the rental rates I was forced to accept one hundred percent liability for any damage to it. So I had to buy short-term maritime insurance to cover the vessel for the duration of the project. In order to be able to afford the *insurance* rates, I had to accept a policy with a very large deductible. I rolled the dice, gambling that we were unlikely to sustain any significant damage to the rig while engaged in this quiet inland coring and surveying job. But now, TransArctic's jackup rig has technically been lost. The last I saw of it, it was sitting abandoned at the extreme southern end of Tiburi Kunga in the middle of a country that was busy destroying itself.

"Now, TransArctic Oil—not known for their altruism or patience—wants their rig back . . . or at least the money they claim it is worth. They're taking advantage of the situation to turn an aging drilling vessel into an insurance windfall—but even if the insurer pays, I—via my little company—am responsible for the deductible. It's tied to the total the insurance company ends up paying out. If they pay one hundred percent of the insured value—which is quite inflated—I have to pay one hundred percent of the deductible amount."

"And how much is that?" Sass asked.

"Two point four million dollars." Olssen smiled bitterly, raising his glass to his lips. "You don't happen to have a winning lottery ticket you could spare, by any chance?"

Sass shook her head, her expression rueful. "No. Sorry, Berndt."

"Ah, well. Such is life." Olssen swallowed another mouthful of vodka.

There was a short silence. Then Sass leaned forward. "Why don't I tell you what *I'm* doing here?"

"Hm, yes." The old Norwegian diver nodded. "I apologize. My head is so occupied with my own troubles that I'm forgetting my manners. Go ahead."

"I'm waiting for Ben," Sass said.

"And where is he?"

"Right about now, he should be diving in Shark Lake, trying to rescue Nick Fenzi from an old prison fortress on an island at its southern end."

The vodka glass slipped from Olssen's hand and clattered on the bar top. "*What?*"

Sass repeated it, word for word. The Norwegian's lean face turned purple. "Nick Fenzi?" he said incredulously. "He's after *Nick Fenzi*?"

"That's right. He was working with you, wasn't he, Berndt?"

"Yes, but how did you know that?"

"I didn't." Sass waved a finger at the bartender. "Another martini, please."

"Put it on my tab," Olssen instructed him. "As you were saying . . ."

"I was saying I *didn't* know," Sass continued. "All Ben told me was that Nick had been working on a jackup in Bisotho and been captured by so-called Leopard Soldiers. He didn't specifically mention that it was you who'd been running the job. There wasn't any reason for him to. I just put two and two together."

"But what is this about Fenzi?"

"We're pretty sure he's being held in a prison pit in an old fort on an island. There may be a way to swim up into the pit through an underwater cavern. Ben's gone in by floatplane to try and bring Nick out."

Olssen sat back, goggling. "No. He's risking his life for that bastard Fenzi?" This time, the Norwegian was too taken aback to apologize for his language.

"Pretty much." Sass frowned at him. "Why 'that bastard Fenzi'? You don't like Nick?"

"*Like* him?" Olssen rolled his eyes. "I *did*—until he stole the truck that was carrying the whole crew safely out of Bisotho and abandoned us all in the jungle while we were collecting fresh water at a stream."

It was Sass's turn to be astonished. "He did *what*?"

"Stole our escape truck and abandoned us all in the jungle, about twenty miles from the Kuballan border. It was only by sheer good fortune that we found another operable vehicle before we encountered any Leopard Soldiers or *Malmoq* paramilitary units. There's a good chance we all would have been hacked to pieces, otherwise."

Sass blinked at him. "So Leopard Soldiers didn't

grab him and haul him off? He just drove away and left you there?"

"That's right."

"Where did he go?"

Olssen's face hardened. "I don't know," he said, "and frankly, I really don't care. But I suspect it has something to do"—he reached into his shirt pocket—"with *this*."

He set a small brown object about the size and shape of an unshelled peanut on the bar. One end of it appeared to have been sliced off, exposing a glassy interior.

"What's that?" Sass asked, studying it.

Olssen raised his vodka glass to his lips. "A diamond," he replied. "A very high-quality alluvial diamond."

In his quarters in the old fort on Shark Lake, Amon Klegg settled into the wooden chair at his command desk and sipped from a mug of tea, letting the heat generated by his bizarre sexual exertions evaporate from his body. He'd dragged the *Quori* girl out into the passageway, half-dead, and thrust her into the arms of the big sergeant, much to the man's delight. A bone for the troops to gnaw on—before they buried it.

His eyes ran over the magnetic map of Bisotho on the wall above the desk. Things were going well. The Leopard Soldiers he'd been hired to train and deploy were blanketing the country with coordinated mayhem, wiping out any remnants of the former government's military forces and simultaneously conducting a campaign of terror against the *Quoris*. He smiled over the rim of his tea mug. Once properly initiated, operations like this were self-perpetuating, rolling across the landscape under their own momentum, the field soldiers feeding off their own adrenaline and bloodlust. All he had to do was monitor radio reports by his unit commanders and update their map positions from time to time.

It was beautiful. His own little *Blitzkrieg*. He'd always thought that Hitler's Nazi generals had adopted the right approach when they'd rolled their Panzer tanks into Poland in 1939. Hard war, fast war, no mercy. Just like the ongoing overthrow of Bisotho.

He shifted in his seat. He'd provided absolutely first-class mercenary command services to King Billy and his supporters, and the results so far had been excellent. But in hindsight, although the fee he'd negotiated was generous, he should have held out for more. Another problem—only half of the money had been paid into his Swiss bank account prior to the operation—and it was unlikely, now that Bisotho was under King Billy's control, that he would ever see the other fifty percent.

Not that he hadn't expected such a development all along. His Royal Highness and Maximum-Ruler-For-Life King William Napoleon Shaka Mogambo was only a shifty little *kaffir*, after all—despite his grandiose title and name. His supporters—*ministers*, he called them—were no better: a vile assortment of scheming black thieves with just enough white-European schooling to make them annoyingly pretentious and unaware of their own inferiority. Klegg's hatred of them all was so ingrained it was almost casual.

King Billy might have been blood heir to the tribal leadership of Bisotho's *Malmoqs*, but to Amon Klegg he was little more than a semideranged megalomaniac—a veritable mental case rumored to be suffering from terminal syphilis. This opinion had been reinforced on several occasions since the beginning of the coup. Klegg could recall vividly the morning he'd witnessed the pompous little tyrant issue a decree that henceforth, on the first day of each week, between sunup and sundown, all citizens of the country would be required to walk backward—and only backward—everywhere they went, as a gesture of respect for their new king. Failure to comply would be evidence of disloyalty to the new regime, punishable by summary execution.

Only a few days later, His Royal Highness and Maximum-Ruler-For-Life had followed up this enlightened piece of legislation with a novel means of engineering consensus within his administration. When a senior advisor suggested to King Billy that one of his more homicidal decrees might benefit from a slight rephrasing, he had the man staked out and the original version tattooed repeatedly over every inch of his body—until the now *ex*-advisor died of heart failure.

Klegg understood the shock value of creative sadism in the initial stages of building a cult of personality—he'd studied Hitler and Stalin—but one didn't have to be ham-handed about it. That was the trouble with his current employer, he decided. He lacked subtlety. But then, what could you expect from a syphilitic *kaffir*?

The very *last* thing he expected was that the man

would pay his debts—such as the other half of Klegg's fee. Which was why the little brown pebble sitting on the edge of the desk was so interesting. Klegg had spent several years as a backcountry security chief for one of South Africa's largest gemstone producers. He knew a raw diamond when he saw one.

Exactly *where* the American currently residing in the prison pit had gotten it was, literally, the million-dollar question. Only slightly less interesting was why the man had been skulking around the crocodile-infested shores of Tiburi Kunga in the middle of a bloody revolution, when he clearly should have been running—like every other foreign national in Bisotho—for the safety of Kenya or Kuballa. He'd tried to pitch the diamond when the Leopard Soldiers had captured him, but a sharp-eyed corporal had noticed it.

The military coup had been in its preliminary stages when the American—one Nicholas Fenzi, according to his wallet—had been grabbed, and at the time Klegg had been very busy. In hindsight, he supposed, he could have had the man tied to a chair and ordered one of the Leopard Soldiers to peel his genitals for him with a straight razor, until he was only too glad to spit out everything he knew about the diamond. But that would have been so like King Billy, so . . . *unsubtle*.

Now that the military operation was proceeding under its own momentum, and there were only peri-odic radio reports from the field to monitor, he could take his time in dealing with this Nicholas Fenzi. Un-doubtedly, ten or eleven consecutive days of isolation in the prison pit, with only the occasional bowl of cornmeal mush for sustenance, had already softened him up a bit. Their first meeting—in which Klegg had personally pistol-whipped him just to take the edge off his insufferably lowbrow American arrogance—had been a brief enough affair. He was looking forward to renewing their acquaintance at length.

Klegg finished his tea, picked up the little brown stone, and began to roll it between his fingers, feeling its weight.

Where there was one, there were usually more.

CHAPTER 12

It had taken Naji and Head only fifteen minutes to motor the ultralight through the fog to the shore of the lake, but another ten to locate a spot where they could pull in without tearing the fabric of the delta wing on a gnarly profusion of overhanging branches. Finally, they'd been able to start nosing up against the exposed tree roots at the waterline, Naji cursing the delay with his usual eloquence.

"Shaitan's beard, man, can you not see the limb rubbing against the front of the left pontoon? Kick it away, will you?" Frustrated, the Arab revved the little outboard, attempting to bull past the obstruction.

"Dude, I'm tryin'," Head replied, his hands already full of overhanging foliage. "*Yaaghh.* Mosquitoes like B-52s."

"Never mind the—ah! There!" The limb gave way, scraping past the pontoon's side, and the ultralight slid into the gap in the trees. The twin floats crunched lightly into the interlocking roots lining the shore, and Naji shut down the motor.

"We will not be late to pick up *Ben-Ya-Min*," he stated. "Look now. How best to repair this damage?"

He knelt between the seats and leaned over the port side, running his hand along the broken pontoon strut.

Head clambered past him, rocking the ultralight, and squatted on the forward section of the float. "Oh, wow. Bummer. It's really fubar, dude. We're gonna have to replace that strut with something."

Naji looked up. "*Fubar?* What is fubar, exactly?"

"Oh, sorry. It's something my old man used to say," Head explained, grinning gape-mouthed. "F-U-B-A-R. Foo-bar. It stands for 'Fucked Up Beyond All Recognition.' It's official American military terminology, he told me."

"Indeed," Naji remarked. "How sophisticated."

"Really, dude." Head swiveled on the pontoon, his sandals making a squeaking noise on the wet aluminum, and peered off into the tangled, dripping branches surrounding them. "Man, it's foggy. And *damp.*" He slapped his bare arm. "Shit. We're gonna get eaten alive in here."

"All the more reason to commence the repair," Naji said curtly. "There is no more time to waste. What can we use to replace this broken support?"

"Huh." Head stared at it for a moment. "I dunno."

"Think, fool, think!"

The long-haired pilot looked out into the tree branches again. "Gimme a minute, okay?" He fell silent, his mouth hanging open, and stared into the fog. Naji ground his teeth and leaned over to inspect the break again.

"Well, you know what, dude," Head said finally. "This tree over here is called a marblewood. Nearly as hard and dense as lignum vitae. See that branch with

the bend in it? If we could cut it off a foot or so on either side, we'd have something about the same shape
as that busted strut. A little thicker than the aluminum,
but just as strong."

Naji gazed at the branch. "Exactly like a planked
ship's knee," he agreed. "This is a strong wood, you
say?"

"To the extreme, my man. They used to make machine bearings out of it."

The lean Yemeni got to his feet. "One foot on either
side of the bend, you're sure?"

"Yeah," Head responded. "Trouble is, we don't
have anything that'll cut marblewood. That stuff's like
iron, dude. I've seen saw blades snap in two, axes
bounce right off it."

Naji stepped up on the pilot's seat, leaned out past
the forward edge of the delta wing, and grasped the
overhanging limb. It was about three inches thick, covered in corrugated black bark.

"You can't just break it off," Head protested. "It—"

Naji reached under his robe with his free hand and
slid his *yataghan* free of its scabbard. With great speed
and no apparent effort, he whirled it once and sliced
upward. There was a dull ringing sound as the long
blade bit into the branch. He wrenched it free and repeated the maneuver. A perfectly symmetrical wedge
of wood, about an inch and a half thick, dropped into
the water and bobbed beside the port pontoon.

As Head gaped at it, Naji chopped twice more,
downward this time. The leafy outer end of the branch
fell away.

"Excuse me," Naji said, stepping past Head.

Stretching up, he gripped the bend in the limb and swung the *yataghan* four more times. With each stroke, the same sound—*chunk-riiinngg*—carried through the misty air.

Naji sheathed his long knife and handed the twenty-four-inch section of branch to Head, its ends clipped as cleanly as if by hydraulic shears. The pilot was agog, but not speechless.

"Whooaa, dude. That was way cool. Like I said, I've seen axes bounce off this stuff."

"Doubtless they were not made of Damascus steel." Naji smiled, patting the hilt of the *yataghan* through his robe. "Now, there is your new strut. How will we attach it?"

Head studied the damaged area beneath the pilot's seat. "Well, lessee. The mounts on the fuselage and the pontoon aren't busted, so I can just unbolt the broken pieces and chuck 'em." He slapped abruptly at a mosquito feasting on his jugular vein. "Then, if you can trim the ends of the branch some so they'll fit into the clamps, I can torque the nuts back up and we'll be good to go, Naji-dude."

The Yemeni nodded. "Trimming them will be no problem."

"The only other thing is, we've gotta lift the cockpit away from the pontoon to fit the new strut in there. We're gonna have to lever it up, somehow."

Naji pointed at a small dead tree floating near the shore roots. "What about that? It is nearly fifteen feet long."

"Yeah, it could work." Head pulled a crescent wrench, ratchet, and socket from a vinyl pouch beneath the pilot's seat. "Just let me get these bolts outta here."

"Excellent," Naji said. He drew his *yataghan* again. "Hand me our new strut."

"You got it, dude." Head passed him the section of branch and bent over his work. "Oh, by the way, keep an eye out for anything that looks like a stream of bubbles or fast-moving ripples, okay?"

"Very well," Naji muttered, shaving a piece of wood from one end of the makeshift strut. "But why?"

"Because that's usually all you see," Head grunted, working the first nut off over stripped threads, "before a monster crocodile lunges out of the drink and kills you."

Naji glanced sharply at the dark, muddy water around them and reached back for his Lee-Enfield, setting it close at hand against the pilot's seat.

They worked in silence for the next five minutes, Head extracting the broken strut and Naji whittling away at the marblewood replacement. The night air sang with mosquitoes, a cloud of which had descended upon the two men. Naji's long robes afforded him some protection, but Head's sleeveless shirt and shorts left a generous amount of skin exposed. He slapped at himself continuously as he cranked on the mounting bolts, complaining under his breath.

The last piece of broken strut splashed into the water. Head looked up, a squadron of mosquitoes hovering around his face. "Okay, that's it. The clamps are ready. Now we gotta lift the fuselage so we can slip the new strut in."

"Fine," Naji said. He held up the section of marblewood, bark stripped and ends whittled down. "Go and get that floating tree trunk. We will slip it between the cockpit floor and the pontoon so you can lever them apart. Then I will install this replacement."

Head slapped at his cheek, crushing six or seven mosquitoes into a bloody pulp. "Uh—me, dude?"

"You."

"Why me?"

"Why not?"

The long-haired pilot looked around at the black, shimmering water as though it was an acid bath. "Because I really don't catch a good vibe from this lake, dude. Nasty shit lives in it, you know? Sharks, crocs, snakes . . . *Eueugh!*" He shuddered, hugging his knees.

"Regardless," Naji declared, "you are going in. You are going in because if something grabs you—a crocodile, for instance—there is a much better chance of me being able to save you with one quick shot"—he tapped a finger on the barrel of his Lee-Enfield—"than of you doing the same for me, should our positions be reversed. No doubt you can appreciate the logic of this."

Head looked forlorn. "No, I can't really, dude."

"But it must be done. Come now, man, into the water. It will not take long if you put your back into it." Naji's swarthy face was stern.

"Oh, wowwww," Head grumbled. "Total bummer." But he lifted his leg across the pontoon, swallowed hard, and let himself slip off. There was a light splash, and a secondary cloud of mosquitoes swarmed up from the surface. The pilot swatted at them, his arms upraised. The water was only chest deep.

"This bottom is creepy on the feet, dude," he reported. "Feels like snot."

Naji closed his eyes briefly, grateful that he had never heard the term "snot" before—whatever it meant.

Head walked gingerly over to the floating trunk, slapping at mosquitoes all the way, and took hold of it. Maneuvering it around, he pushed the thick end toward the ultralight. Naji bent down, seized one of the root remnants, and heaved it onto the pontoon.

"All right," he said. "Now, lift your end of the trunk and push. We must slide it under the cockpit floor."

"Okay." Head ducked under the surface and came up with the trunk on his shoulder. "Howzat, dude?"

"Not high enough," Naji said. "Lift it more."

"Dude, it's kinda heavy."

"*Lift it, man!*"

"Okay, okay. No need to get uptight."

Head ducked under again and came up more slowly this time, holding the trunk above him with his arms fully extended. They were shaking with the strain.

"*Aaargghh,*" he gurgled.

"Good, good!" Naji exclaimed, tugging away at his own end. He lifted a foot and kicked down on the trunk. It rotated slightly and slid beneath the fuselage. "Now keep lifting and push!"

"Easy for you to say," Head gasped. Nevertheless, he thrust his weight awkwardly forward. Under the combined exertions of the two men, the trunk slid another six inches beneath the cockpit floor.

"Excellent!" Naji said. "Now, put your weight on the end. Pull down."

Head let his body weight sag against his hands, panting. There was a loud creak of flexing aluminum.

"The bent rear strut is binding," Naji observed, standing ready near the pontoon's forward clamps. "More weight."

With a deep groan, Head heaved himself out of the water, wrapped his legs around the trunk, and hung there, suspended. The *creak-pop* of thin metal was continuous as he and the tree immediately began to sag back toward the surface.

Naji jammed one end of the wooden strut into place and worked it back and forth furiously. "Hold, hold," he called. "Just a little more . . ."

Head clung to the slippery wood with all his might, feeling his shoulder blades touch the water. His face was being gnawed raw by mosquitoes, and he turned his head sideways to rub them off against his upper arm. In doing so, he looked straight at the lumpy, tooth-studded head of the crocodile that had just surfaced beside him.

"*Urrk!*" the pilot declared—and fell off the trunk with a loud splash.

The ultralight bucked, and the top end of the wooden strut slipped into place. "That is it!" Naji shouted, jamming it home.

The croc's huge tail erupted from the water, lashed through the air like a scaly bullwhip, and smacked down on the rear of the port pontoon. Naji lost his balance and nearly went in, just managing to save himself by snatching one of the delta wing's guy wires. The crocodile thrashed violently and rolled, churning the dark water of the little inlet to foam.

Head popped up, mouth open and eyes like saucers, sitting backward astride the base of the reptile's tail. "Uh—*dude*," he sputtered, looking at Naji—and the crocodile launched him sideways into a tangle of marblewood roots.

He floundered to the surface, his long hair snarled in the scraggly branches of a dead sapling. The croc surged around, directly in front of him. Head could do nothing but stare. The great reptile paused, its gleaming saurian eyes locking onto him—and lunged.

There was a loud report—and simultaneously the crocodile's brain pan lifted off in a sticky explosion of scale and bone. The animal's forward momentum carried it into its intended victim, driving him back against the tree roots. Then, with barely a twitch, it sank.

Naji jacked another shell into the breech of his Lee-Enfield, breathing hard, and trained the smoking rifle on the water just in front of Head. The pilot was gulping, pop-eyed, trying to draw air into his lungs after having had the wind knocked out of him. His mouth and nose were barely above the surface; his hair still entangled in the dead branches.

"Beard of the Prophet!" Naji exclaimed, looking down the barrel of his rifle. "What a beast!" His eyes flicked over to Head. "Do you still possess your lower half, pilot? Are you hurt?"

There was no answer for a few seconds. Then Head's paralyzed diaphragm relaxed, allowing him to

suck in a long, screeching breath of air. Another followed, and another.

"Maj . . . *major* bummer, man," he wheezed.

The corner of Naji's mouth curled in a faint smile.
Head was still in one piece.

The pilot grabbed hold of his own hair and yanked,
tearing most of it free of the entangling branches.
"Oww! Shit!" He yanked again, coming away this time
and leaving a good-sized sample of his dirty blond
mop in the dead sapling. "Freak me out, dude—I'm
standing on that big bastard's skull. He's layin' on the
bottom right here."

Naji nodded. "I do not think he will trouble you
again."

"Maybe so, my man," Head replied hastily, "but
The Head's outta here, *mucho* fuckin' *pronto!*"

He floundered over to the ultralight and heaved
himself up on the port pontoon, wasting no time in
getting his legs clear of the water. Naji lent him a
steadying hand, still watching the spot where the crocodile had disappeared. Head sat for a moment, dripping, then nudged the marblewood strut with his bare
toe.

"Look at that," he said. "Worked like a charm."

"Indeed," Naji replied, shifting his gaze into the
dark labyrinth of encroaching trees. He frowned, listening.

Head picked up his wrenches. "Four bolts on these
two clamps, and she's ready to fly, dude. I'll get 'em
torqued down." He began tightening the first nut.

"Good, good," Naji muttered absently. There was

little he could make out in the nocturnal jungle but dripping foliage and curtains of mist.

"That's one," Head said. "Workin' on number two."

"Mm." Some kind of insect or amphibian set up a croaking screech off to the left. Naji's head jerked in that direction. Slowly, the barrel of the old Lee-Enfield came up. Holding the rifle one-handed against his hip, Naji reached over to the cockpit's central support framework and released the clamp that secured the GPS. He tucked the little navigational unit under his robes.

"Got number two snugged up," Head muttered. "Crankin' on number three."

"Mm," Naji grunted again. He stepped carefully around the pilot and moved out along the pontoon, watching the jungle. The croaking call died away.

Head paused, slapping at mosquitoes. "Last one," he said.

"Hurry."

Head looked at Naji—standing on the end of the pontoon with his rifle on his hip—shrugged, and bent over the final bolt. For the next few seconds, the only sound was the clicking of the ratchet.

Head sat up triumphantly and tossed the wrenches onto the pilot's seat. "She's done, dude!" he declared. "*El completo!*"

The first Leopard Soldier came out of the trees without a sound, lunging down on Naji like a great silent bat. The Arab wheeled and ducked, firing upward one-handed. The attacking silhouette wilted in midair before hitting the water with a tremendous splash.

With a howl, a second black shape exploded out of the foliage next to the starboard pontoon, machete swinging. Naji pivoted on the balls of his feet, robes flying, and ripped his *yataghan* clear of its scabbard. There was a ringing clash of metal against metal, a burst of sparks . . . Naji leaping to the opposite pontoon past the attacker, his arm a blur of motion . . . a hideous gurgling sound . . . and the Leopard Soldier seemed to pause in midturn beside the cockpit framework. Then his head drooped off his shoulders, his neck slashed three-quarters through, and he toppled slowly into the dark water beside the corpse of his comrade.

The sound of shouting echoed through the dank jungle. A light flashed between the trees, a hazy glare in the dense mist.

Naji leaped back across to the port pontoon and seized the stunned Head by the collar of his sleeveless shirt, pulling him to his feet.

"This has been a stressful stop, dude," the pilot croaked.

Naji propelled him along the pontoon and onto the heavy roots lining the shore. "There is no time to talk!" he hissed. "We must lead them away from the plane! Come now, quickly!"

CHAPTER 13

"Ben?" The voice was a weak rasp.

"Yeah, Nick. It's me."

Ben leaned forward on his arms and climbed out of the rocky pool, grunting under the weight of his twin air cylinders. The quiet jangle of equipment on D-rings, the slap of wet rubber, and the soft *plash-plash* of water cascading onto the stony floor seemed very loud in the tight confines of the prison pit. He stood there for a moment, his hands on his knees, panting and dripping.

The dark figure by the wall raised itself to a sitting position. "I must be dreamin'," said Nick's voice. "Yeah . . . just a goddamn dream . . ."

Ben straightened, covered the lens of the searchlight with his left hand, and flicked it on. Holding it close to his body to further prevent any glare from reaching the pit opening, he walked carefully toward the sitting figure, his wet gear creaking. A yard away he dropped to one knee and let more of the light seep through his fingers.

"It's no dream, buddy," he said softly. "It's Ben. I'm really here."

Slowly, stiffly, the figure leaned forward, and just like at the end of Ben's nightmare in Al-Mukkala, Nick

Fenzi's craggy face materialized out of the darkness, caught in the searchlight's muted glow. Out of reflex—relief—Ben started to smile . . . then stopped.

There was far more gray in Nick's tangled black hair and beard than Ben remembered, and the lines in his face were more deeply etched. He looked vaguely cadaverous, the skin drawn tight over his cheekbones, but loose around his mouth and jaw. Black bags hung under his eyes. There was an ugly welt running from the corner of his left eye, where the skin had been smashed open, down past his mouth. The wound was flecked with dried blood and looked puffy, as if sections of it had become infected.

"Ben?" Nick repeated. Then he coughed—a rattling, hoarse hack from deep in his chest—and sagged back a little. "Goddamn. Ben." His lips twisted into something resembling a smile. "You got a cigarette? I'm dyin' for a fuckin' cigarette, bro."

"Later for that," Ben whispered. "Look—can you move okay? You need to swim, buddy. It's the only way I can get you out of here."

Nick squinted at him. "How far?"

"Pretty far. Out through a cave system and then halfway across the lake."

"Shit. I'm a little beat up, bro." Before Ben could reply, Nick continued. "But fuck it. It'd rather drown than rot away in this hole."

Ben put a hand on his shoulder. "I thought so. Can you stand?"

"Yeah. Kinda shaky, though. No real food."

"You're one long swim and a three-hour floatplane

flight from a steak and a beer in the Hotel Excelsior in Krumake," Ben said. "That help?"

Nick rolled to his knees, grinned weakly, and stuck his thumb in his chest. "Tough guy," he said. "Let's go."

Ben put a finger on Nick's jaw and turned his head, examining the welt. "What's this?"

"One a' them black troops smacked me in the face with a rifle butt. Then some ugly-ass white guy pistol-whipped me."

"How're your brains?"

Nick shrugged. "Scrambled. But then, they always were, so what's the difference?"

"Hurt?"

"Like a motherfucker. But what the hell—so does a quart of tequila the mornin' after, and I lived through a few thousand of those." Nick grinned again. "Like I said: let's go."

"Okay. C'mon."

"*Hoy!*" The guttural bark of a native voice came down sharply from the pit opening above.

Flicking the searchlight off Ben dived onto his face along the rocky wall, the weight of his tanks crushing the breath out of his lungs, and lay as still as death.

Nick spread his hands, weaving unsteadily on his feet, and looked up. "What the hell d'you want?" he shouted.

A light flashed in his eyes. "No noise! You talk in sleep, white boy? No noise!"

"Ah, fuck you," Nick growled. "Go get me some food, sambo."

The light jerked around and there was an eruption

of native cursing. Ben caught something in broken English that sounded like "cut rude tongue out that white boy," followed by the distinctive *click-clack* of a gun bolt being pulled back.

There was a sudden short blast of machine-gun fire—*BRRRRP*—and a cluster of slugs hammered into the wall about ten feet over Nick's head. He dived onto his belly as powdered limestone and rock chips rained down on top of him. The sound of deep laughter reverberated through the prison pit.

"You done talkin' now?" the native voice inquired. "Good. *No noise!*" The light snapped off, and silence filled the night once again.

They lay motionless on the stony floor of the pit for what seemed like hours, but was in reality something less than five minutes. Ben spent most of that time picturing what would happen to his body if a machine-gun bullet were to hit one of the high-pressure air tanks on his back. The resulting explosion would certainly kill him, and, in the confined space of the prison pit, probably Nick as well. But the Leopard Soldiers did not return. How they'd missed spotting him, Ben couldn't imagine. Black suit, black gear, the darkness of night— but no cover, and they'd had a light . . .

Nick. Nick had drawn their attention away, focused it on himself. Slowly, Ben got to his hands and knees and looked over at the man lying facedown by the edge of the pool. Nick Fenzi was a pisscutter, and that was a fact. Always had been.

He glanced at his watch. Forty-two minutes before mid-lake rendezvous. He had an extra thirty, if Head didn't forget. No. Naji wouldn't let him. An hour and twelve minutes to get there, with Nick kicking awkwardly alongside him. *Air*. They'd make it out of the cave, but probably have to complete the swim on the surface with the buoyancy compensator fully inflated like a life vest.

Ben tried not to think about the two of them floundering across the midnight lake, legs kicking down in the black turbidity of the upper layer . . . the aggressive open-water sharks sensing the motion . . . starting to gather below, unseen . . . to home in . . .

No point in worrying about it now.

"Nick," he called softly.

There was a muffled hack, then the sound of spitting. "Yeah."

"You're okay, huh? Not hit?"

Nick propped himself up on his elbows, and Ben could almost see the flash of his teeth in the pitch-darkness. "That troop couldn't hit me even if he wanted to. I'm fine."

"Good." Ben crawled over beside the older diver and sat back on his haunches. "Time to go." He tapped his watch. "Rendezvous with our ride. Do you still have the satellite uplink e-mail unit you used to talk to Maggie?"

"Uh-uh," Nick replied. "Batteries finally gave out. Too bad. The first few days there, I could get a short message out to her every night." He reached into his boot and extracted a smooth, shiny silver rectangle with rounded edges and corners. Like Maggie's, it was only slightly larger than a Zippo lighter. Nick stuck a thumbnail into a barely visible seam and pried the two halves apart, opening it. "Ain't technology a helluva thing?" he said. "It worked long enough to bring you here, bro."

"Lucky me." Ben flicked his searchlight on, once again muting the glare with his free hand, and ran his eyes over the unit's miniaturized keypad and LCD screen. "Where's the antenna?"

"Here." Nick fingernailed out a small silver button and extended a thin, telescoping metal rod four inches long. "That's it. Point her at the sky on a clear night, you got comms. The keypad's so small you have to type in with a toothpick or pin. I used a wood splinter I found down here." He placed the unit on the back of Ben's hand.

"I'm amazed you managed to keep it. Didn't these guys search you the day you got grabbed?"

"Oh, yeah. Just not well enough."

"How'd you hide it?"

Nick grinned, "I swallowed it, bro."

Ben blinked at him. "You *swallowed* it?"

"Yeah. It was a tight fit. Kinda like that old drinkin' game where you swallow hard-boiled eggs whole. 'Cept it didn't slide down so good. And I had to drink a lot of water for three days before I saw it again. Had terrible bellyaches the whole time it was in my gut." He shook his head. "Hope I never have to do that again."

"So you . . . got it back." Ben glanced down the unit quivering on the back of his hand. "And it worked?"

Nick picked up the little device again. "Don't worry, I washed it *real* good. And yeah, it worked—it's water-resistant."

Ben had to smile. "You're one crazy bastard, you know it?"

"I know it."

There was a wet *snick* as Ben pulled his SOG diving knife from its scabbard. Reversing it, he held it out to Nick. "Stick the uplink unit in your pocket. Since it's waterproof, maybe it'll survive the swim. Now take this knife and cut loose the mask and fins that are duct-taped to my tanks. They're for you. And let's get the fuck out of here."

"Bro, you don't have to tell me twice." There was a soft ripping sound as Nick sliced through the tape and freed the diving gear. "Here," he said, handing the knife back.

Ben shut off the searchlight, crawled across the floor of the pit, and sat on the edge of the pool with his legs dangling into the water. Quickly, he shoved his feet back into his fins and repositioned his mask on his forehead. Nick sat down beside him, fins on, his boots tucked into his belt, rubbing spit onto the inner faceplate of his own mask.

"How'd that happen?" he asked, pointing at the semicircular bite divot in Ben's long fin, just barely visible in the starlight. He dipped up some water in his mask and rinsed it before slipping the strap behind his head.

"You don't want to know," Ben replied, "but you're gonna find out. Just stay cool and don't make any sudden moves, all right? Remember, we should be okay as long as we're in the caverns or near the island. If we have a problem, it'll be out in the middle of the lake. But we're just gonna have to do the best we can."

Nick shrugged. "Looks like a shark bite to me. There's a few in this lake; I saw them when we were drillin' up core samples, and once in a while one rolls in this here pool. Weird, ain't it? But what the fuck, it's a short life. Let's go."

Ben nodded and pulled his mask down over his face. "Come on, tough guy. Stay on my right—that's the octo-reg side—and don't let go of my harness. Oh, and don't forget to kick. I'm not towing your ass all the way to the plane."

He placed the Poseidon regulator's primary second stage in his mouth and slipped off into the black water, half-turning so his tanks would clear the pool's lip. Invisible bubbles whirled up around his face and head, and the cool, dark silence of immersion enveloped him once more. A second later he felt Nick drop in beside him, his friend's fingers groping for his right shoulder. Slipping the octopus second-stage regulator free of its retaining clip, he placed it in Nick's hand.

He let himself sink down the flooded chimney about five feet, pulling Nick with him, before turning on the searchlight again. Nick had the octo-reg clamped in his mouth, breathing easily, his torn, dirty denim shirt and khaki trousers billowing around him. He was on Ben's right, one hand firmly grasping the shoulder strap of the buoyancy compensator. Behind the untinted faceplate of the mask Ben had given him, his eyes were very calm.

If you have to rescue someone from a third-world prison by scuba-diving him out through a shark-infested cave system in the middle of the night, a good choice of rescuee— without question—is an experienced commercial diver like Nick Fenzi.

Ben gave Nick's upper arm a quick squeeze, then

vented a little more air from his buoyancy compensator and began to drift downward, toward the immense underwater cathedral at the chimney's lower end. Nick stayed with him, feeling his way down the tight passageway, his free hand on the limestone wall. Ben glanced at the air-pressure gauge: 2265 psi. There was still a lot of breathing medium in the big twin cylinders—but now two men were draining it. From this point on, the gauge's indicator needle would drop quickly.

They continued to descend, feetfirst, until the chimney widened and they emerged beneath the roof of the central cavern. Ben panned the searchlight around and down, and felt Nick stiffen as the beam caught the broad coppery side of a large bull shark cruising by less than ten feet away. The sense of being lost in empty space was acute, and Ben decided that for Nick's benefit a quick orientation was in order.

Neutralizing their buoyancy so that they were suspended just below the ceiling, he once again switched the searchlight from spot to diffuser, lighting up the entire cavern interior. Nick's eyes were the size of saucers as he took in the upswept limestone pillars; the fantastic array of ledges, arches, and crystalline formations; the sheer size of the domelike chamber; and the dozens—if not hundreds—of sharks undulating through the gin-clear water. Speech unavailable to him, he looked over at Ben and slowly shook his head in wonder.

And then, with a sizzling *snap* that Ben could feel through his glove, the searchlight burned out, leaving them in complete and utter darkness.

CHAPTER 14

What was that number? The compass bearing from the bottom of the chimney to the caving spool . . . to the Cyalume lightstick marking it . . .

Oh-eight-seven degrees. For certain . . . almost. And the compass bezel was set on that heading—if all the scraping around hadn't moved it.

Ben reached down by his side and groped for his air/depth-gauge module, to which the compass was attached. The darkness surrounding him was absolute, as if he was immersed in a vat of roofing tar. He felt Nick's other hand lock onto his harness. The older diver was there, only inches away, but Ben could not see him. Without even a fraction of a lumen of light available to them, his eyes were useless. The smothering blackness; the knowledge that they were hovering in an uncharted underwater cave with a dwindling air supply—surrounded by sharks—generated an onrush of claustrophobia almost nauseating in its intensity.

Gritting his teeth, Ben fought the horrible feeling down.

The lightstick. Where was it?

He could not even be sure he was facing the right direction.

His ears were not pressuring up, so he was not sinking. He had attained neutral buoyancy as they had dropped out of the chimney, so in all probability they were still floating just beneath the opening . . . or very close by. He brought the module up to his faceplate, praying that he would see . . .

The luminescent green faces of the air gauge, depth gauge, and compass.

They came up into his field of vision like a disembodied trio of miniature flying saucers, the plastic casing in which they were mounted totally invisible, as was the attached regulator hose. Relief at having something his eyes could fix upon surged through Ben like a warm wave. The gauges and compass had absorbed sufficient ambient light from the searchlight beam to retain a soft glow. They were readable.

The compass bezel was still set on a heading of 087 degrees. Holding the instrument level, at chest height, Ben slowly rotated his body until the compass needle lined up with the bezel's north axis. That was it, he had a direction. All he could do now was swim the heading, descend no more than another fifteen feet, and hope to hell the lightstick would appear out of the darkness.

Ben swallowed hard, his throat as dry as sandpaper. There would be only one chance to run down the bearing. If he didn't find the marker on the first try, he'd have lost his point of reference and the compass would be useless—he'd never find the chimney opening again. He and Nick would be reduced to groping around blindly until they ran out of air. *A pleasant thought.*

Giving Nick's arm another squeeze, he began to swim forward, keeping the compass needle exactly in line with the north axis of the bezel. His ears pressured up slightly, and he equalized them by cracking his jaw. It was difficult to maintain a constant depth while moving ahead, eÿeing the compass, and looking around for the lightstick.

Something bumped Ben's right calf, hard. His blood chilled momentarily as he recalled being jostled in the dark by the swarming mid-lake sharks during his approach. But then his leg was brushed again and he realized that it was only the edge of Nick's fin.

The unrelenting blackness seemed to distort everything—including his sense of time. How long had they been moving forward? Surely this was too far. Or was it not far enough? Perhaps they had missed the lightstick, or veered off behind some limestone arch or pillar that blocked their view of it . . . yes, this was definitely too far . . . they should stop . . . backtrack . . .

There.

A lone dot of cold, greenish white light appeared against the black void, slightly to the right and just below them. Almost choking with relief, Ben kicked hard for it, not daring to blink for fear it might vanish. Beside him, Nick labored along, invisible—both hands still clamped on the shoulder strap of the buoyancy compensator.

The little blot of light grew in intensity as they approached. Then—very suddenly—it disappeared. Ben's heart leaped into his throat. *Gone. It was gone. What the hell*—

The light reappeared.

Jesus. Thank you for—

It winked out again.

Certain he was on the verge of having a major heart attack, Ben paused and tried to even out his breathing. *What the fuck—*

The light was back.

All at once it came to him. Unseen in the pitch-black cavern, sharks were passing back and forth between the divers and their destination, their bulky, ten-foot-plus bodies completely blocking the lightstick's weak glow. When a shark moved on, the tiny greenish white dot reappeared.

Briefly, Ben wondered just how many large sharks were cruising through the darkness within arm's reach of him *right now . . .*

He kicked onward, half-dragging Nick with him, his eyes locked on the light. No more sharks interposed themselves in the rapidly narrowing gap, and at last—feeling as though he'd just sidestepped the hangman—Ben laid a hand firmly on the caving spool. Without hesitating, he snapped its short tether to one of the D-rings on his harness. Whatever else happened, the spool wasn't going to get accidentally dropped.

He examined the lightstick. The chemicals within it would continue to emit their luminescence for at least another hour before fading completely. Pulling his SOG knife from its scabbard, he cut the plastic tie-wrap that attached the Cyalume stick to the caving spool, drew a second tie-wrap from the pocket of his buoyancy compensator, and secured the glowing tube to his wrist. It wasn't a searchlight, but it was the only source of illumination they had, and it was better than nothing. Not much good for spotting sharks ten or fifteen feet away—but at least they wouldn't crack their skulls open on shelves of rock while trying to follow the caving line out to the lake.

Nick was hanging beside him, resting quietly. Ben held the lightstick up between them. The greenish glow it cast made the older diver appear almost spectral against the black background—a ghost of Nick Fenzi rather than the living, breathing man. The thought irritated Ben, and he chased it from his mind.

It took only a few seconds to free the spool from the rock column to which it had been secured. Ben raised the lightstick again so Nick could see him, motioned with his head in the direction they had to go, and began to reel in the thin cord. As it came tight, he began to follow it, conscious of the fact that any excessive pulling might cause the line to cut over a sharp edge somewhere in the crevice passageway. Which would most definitely mean the end of the trip.

They kicked slowly through the empty black water, surrounded by a little halo of green light. Every so often, out of the corner of his eye, Ben would catch the scythe shape of a shark's pectoral fin or tail as it glided past only a few feet away. Once, they had to pause, then veer cautiously to the side as they came up on a huge bull floating directly in their path, nearly immobile, its belly grazing the caving line. Its black-green eye followed them with baleful awareness as they detoured around and beneath it.

Ben didn't see the crevice until they were barely an arm's length from the limestone wall. The caving line was taut across an edge at one side of the opening, and as he continued to reel it in, he noted with alarm that it was frayed where it had been in contact with the rock. He began to reel even more gingerly . . . there had to be many more points between cavern and lake where the line was being abraded.

He glanced at the air gauge—1670 psi. They were sucking air like a pair of badly tuned diesels. And there was still a long way to go.

Get moving.

The narrowness of the crevice, at least near its cavern end, proved to be something of an advantage. The lightstick's weak green glow reflected off the pale limestone of both walls, giving them a better sense of orientation, and they made good time through the first two hundred feet of the winding passageway. On three separate occasions, Ben was forced to pause and extract the caving line from sharp-edged cracks into which it had somehow worked itself, the final time tying a sheepshank knot around a badly frayed section that was hanging by two threads.

Nick had a heart-stopping moment when one of the larger bull sharks, swimming more rapidly than the others, came grinning up at him out of the darkness and butted him on the forehead with its nose. There was a strangled underwater exclamation, a flailing of arms and legs, a whirl of bubbles . . . and the shark contorted its sinewy body past them and off into the gloom. Ben reached out quickly and seized Nick by the shirt, supporting him in the water column. The older diver had lost his grip on the buoyancy compensator.

The crevice was widening now, and Ben was conscious of the fact that he was getting cold. Nearly two hours in the seventy-something-degree springwater of the cavern had conducted away a significant portion of his body heat. But soon it wouldn't matter. After emerging from the passageway, they were going to have to swim away from the island on the lake's surface, bathed in the tepid murk of the uppermost layer. They would have little choice—the air gauge was reading 925 psi.

He felt Nick's hand lock onto the shoulder strap of his harness, and once more he began to reel, kicking forward as he did so. Gradually, the limestone walls widened outward, until at last the rock disappeared and they were following the all-but-invisible caving line through empty black space.

Not empty, Ben thought. There were sharks all around, cruising in and out, above and below. He began to consider their chances of making it to the rendezvous point by swimming across the surface of the lake, given the pack-hunting behavior of the bulls once they were clear of the island's strangely tranquilizing springwater. *Lousy, at best.*

And what about the soldiers above in the old fort? They could have discovered that their prisoner was missing by now, be scouring every inch of the island's rocky shoreline, searching the nearby waters for a swimmer. Even if he and Nick heard boats overhead when they exited the far end of the crevice, they would be unable to stay submerged without air.

Ben chewed the silicon rubber of his regulator mouthpiece.

680 psi.

He reeled faster.

The Cyalume stick was dying—the chemicals it contained losing their light-emitting potency. Ben pulled himself around a corner of rock, following the line, visibility now reduced to less than two feet. At his side, Nick labored on doggedly, clinging to him like a Siamese twin.

And then—suddenly—the long, claustrophobic swim was over. The caving line dead-ended at the spur of rock Ben had used as an anchoring point before proceeding into the inner reaches of the passageway. He took a quick look at his compass to get an approximate exit direction. Between that and keeping a hand on the relatively smooth right-side wall—if memory served—they'd make it the final fifteen feet to open water, even with no line to follow and a fading light.

455 psi.

Not only were they going to have to surface; they were going to have to do so right under the ramparts of the old fort . . . sentries or no sentries.

Hope the fog hasn't lifted.

Ben chewed his mouthpiece. The soldiers he could do little about. *But what about the sharks?* The possibility of coming under attack from below, floundering helplessly in the dark water while his legs were being chewed off, he found distinctly unappealing. Sharks were attracted to low-frequency vibrations, such as those generated by kicking and other swimming motions, particularly at the surface. They'd already targeted him once, and that was when he'd been submerged and swimming along smoothly. From below, Nick and he were going to look like two prime filets as they tried to swim away from the island.

But maybe there was something he could do about that. . . .

The caving line fully retrieved, he tapped Nick's shoulder and began to kick through the darkness toward the crevice opening, one hand on the wall. In less than ten seconds, the flat limestone made a sharp ninety-degree turn away from his fingers and he knew they were out.

390 psi. And going fast.

Wasting no time, Ben powered along the rock face, dragging Nick with him. On the same level as the mouth of the crevice, about twenty or thirty feet to the east, just around the first large column of limestone, there had been . . .

A large fishing net, complete with floats.

Ben's outstretched hand landed on top of the rotten mesh, his head bumping one of the Styrofoam spheres. Quickly, he surveyed the float arrangement by the dim light of the fading Cyalume stick, then pulled his SOG knife from its scabbard and dived down along the net's lower edge. Nick stayed with him, trying to keep out of his way.

Locating the small lead weights that were strung along the bottom of the net, Ben began to saw through the rotten manila line securing them. One by one, they fell away, vanishing into the black depths. The net began to lift, buoyed by its few remaining floats.

Suddenly, Ben's second stage began to breathe hard, squealing on each inhalation. He shot a glance downward at his air-pressure gauge. The needle was bouncing under 200 psi. They were on their last few cubic inches of air, still at a depth of forty feet or more.

Holding his breath, he sawed frantically at the manila. A half dozen more lead weights tumbled free. The net lifted again.

Air hunger began to gnaw at him, flashing hot, prickly spots before his eyes. He began to swallow convulsively, the large muscles of his shoulders and biceps burning precious metabolic oxygen as he hacked through the rope that supported the weights. He was on the verge of passing out. He had to breathe.

Three more weights dropped away, and Ben sucked hard on his mouthpiece. The nearly drained tanks gave up one more blessed lungful of air . . . enough to slash away for another thirty or forty seconds . . . or, more wisely, head for the surface before—

The net began to rise rapidly, gathering speed. Ben drove the SOG knife through the manila one last time, slicing away two more weights, then seized the ascending mesh and let it drag him upward, Nick clinging alongside.

He exhaled and tried to draw another breath. The regulator gave him two-thirds of what he needed and cut off dead. The air was gone. Out of the corner of his eye, Ben glanced at Nick. In the fluctuating green light of the Cyalume stick, his friend's face was corpselike, unnaturally composed. The useless second stage was no longer in his mouth.

But from between his lips, a small stream of bubbles trickled. Ben realized that the experienced older diver was consciously controlling the exhalation of his final breath—relaxing his muscles, making the oxygen last, venting his lungs as the decreasing water pressure associated with the ascent caused the air within them to expand.

Ben dug his fingers more deeply into the slimy mesh, hanging on. The air hunger intensified, becoming acute. The hot spots flashed before his closed eyes. He began to swallow hard, again and again. A black fog began to cloud his mind, shutting it down.

Where the hell's the surface?

All at once the water was warm on his face—*thermocline*—and the pressure on his arms, the sensation of motion, disappeared. Beside him, he felt Nick kick upward. Letting go of the mesh, he did the same . . . and just as he was about to slip into unconsciousness, his head broke the surface.

Air.

With great heaving gasps he sucked it in, his lungs feeling as if they were being penetrated by hot knives. Blinding pain throbbed in his temples, and he struggled feebly to stay afloat. A few feet away, Nick was also floundering, barely able to keep his mouth and nose above water.

Ben coughed and retched. *To feel this bad, you had to be—*

Alive.

They'd made it.

Groping for the exhaust hose of his buoyancy compensator, he pushed the vent button on its mouthpiece and managed to blow a couple of breaths into it, inflating the chambered vest to full capacity. As he bobbed higher in the water, he looked over at Nick.

The older diver was going down, only his weakly

clutching fingers and the top of his head visible. Ben flopped out an arm and caught him by the hair as he sank. Summoning his last reserves of strength, he hauled his friend up and got the nape of his neck across the shoulder pad of the buoyancy compensator, turning his face clear of the water. Locking his arms around Nick's torso, he laid his own head back and floated quietly, panting in great drafts of air, completely exhausted.

They hung there in the black water, surrounded by the gently bobbing floats and tangled mesh of the ruined fishing net, for nearly five minutes . . . the stark walls of the old French fort looming ominously above them. A loud hum permeated the air—the sound of electric generators. The dull glare of two small rampart lights burned down coldly through the thin mist, gleaming off the crumbling white Styrofoam of the net buoys. A single glance in the wrong direction by anyone manning the structure, and they would be spotted. But until their strength returned, they were beyond caring.

A shadow moved across a dimly lit window set high in the fort's stone wall, directly above the underwater crevice that had taken Ben into the island's inner cavern.

In his quarters, Amon Klegg, the White Colonel, was pacing.

CHAPTER 15

"How can a fully grown man be so clumsy?" Naji hissed. "Will you hurry up, fool?"

He glared back at Head as the bedraggled pilot attempted to negotiate a slime-covered fallen log that spanned ten feet of reeking black ooze. Behind him, through the trees, the flashlight beams of the pursuing Leopard Soldiers stabbed through the shadows, probing the darkness. The Africans were singing as they hunted, a low, droning chant of male voices that vibrated menacingly in the night air.

"Comin', dude, comin'," Head replied, waving his arms wildly for balance. "Whoaaa. Slippery-ass tree."

He tap-danced sideways, feet skidding and upper body contorting—and lost his balance just as he reached the end of the log. Naji grabbed the front of his shirt and yanked him upright, sparing him a nosedive into the muck.

"That way," the Yemeni whispered, shoving him onward, "between the two big trees."

As Head wobbled off across the tangled mat of wet roots, Naji dropped to one knee, leveled his rifle, and fired. The loud *CRACK* of the old Lee-Enfield was immediately followed by the faint tinkle of shattering glass, and one of the lights on the far-right flank went out. A series of high-pitched shrieks accompanied by deeper-voiced exclamations echoed through the dripping jungle. Naji smiled grimly, turned, and leaped after Head as a barrage of machine-gun fire commenced—orange-red tracer bullets streaming into the foliage well off to the right.

"I gotta tell ya, dude," Head wheezed, slumping against a tree trunk as Naji caught up with him, "this really sucks."

Naji scowled, eyeing the movement of the flashlights as the Leopard Soldiers resumed their pursuit—in the wrong direction. "Can you not, once in a great while, express yourself in formal English?" he muttered irritably. "I cannot comprehend half of what you say at any given moment. Lambs suck. Infant children suck. I do not understand how 'sucking' applies here."

Exasperated, Head waved his hands, disturbing the flight paths of two or three hundred mosquitoes. "The situation, okay? To put it formally, it *sucketh.* You dig?"

"May Allah the Compassionate and Merciful deliver me from the likes of you," Naji said, rolling his eyes up at the tree canopy. He grabbed Head by the shoulder and stepped past a tangle of thorny creepers. "Come. We are still too close to the plane. These are experienced skirmishers. They will soon realize that we have eluded them and double back. We must lead them off a little farther. And *no noise,* pilot—unless *I* make it."

Head shrugged. "Cool."

He set his hand down on the coiling body of an emerald tree viper, shrieked like a banshee, and tumbled backward over a large rotten stump into a pool of black slime. There was a metallic *shiinggg* as Naji's *yataghan* rang out of its scabbard, followed by a hollow *thunk* as the blade embedded itself in the low branch over which the snake was draped. The viper's diamond-shaped head, lopped off cleanly, fell between the gnarled roots at Naji's feet and disappeared.

"Shaitan's beard!" the Arab cursed, eyes darting out at the black jungle. The deep-voiced hunting chant of the Leopard Soldiers, which had been fading gradually, was interrupted by a chorus of shouts. Distant lights flashed back in their direction through the dark labyrinth of trees and foliage.

Naji dived onto his stomach on the matrix of twisted roots and reached down toward the stinking pool. *"Pilot!"* he whispered urgently. *"Pilot! Where are you?"* He wriggled forward and plunged an arm into the thick black ooze almost to the shoulder. *"Pilot!"* he hissed again, feeling around desperately.

Nothing.

Naji shifted his weight and tried to extend his reach, the sulphurous fumes bubbling up from the slime nearly choking him. The resonant sound of deep voices shouting back and forth became louder.

Then, in a great eruption of mud and motion, Head broke the surface—on the opposite side of the pool.

"Pilot!"

Head responded by noisily blowing out a spray of black ooze, floundering away from Naji's outstretched hand, and seizing a tangle of roots. He began to pull himself out of the pool, choking and wheezing—moving *toward* the oncoming soldiers.

"*Not that way!*" Naji hissed. "*Pilot!*"

The sound of Head's coughing reverberated through the trees. A powerful beam of light flashed across the rotten stump next to Naji. He froze, his black robes turning him into a shapeless lump on the jungle's root-matted floor. The light veered off in another direction. The voices of the Leopard Soldiers were very close now, mere yards away.

Just beyond Head's struggling form, dark shapes began to materialize out of the shadows. Moonlight glinted off a half dozen gently swinging machete blades.

Naji rose to his knees and picked up his Lee-Enfield, keeping low. "I am sorry, pilot," he whispered, looking across the glistening black surface of the pool. "Allah grant you luck. Perhaps I can draw them away."

He lifted the rifle to his shoulder, fired twice at the stalking shapes, then turned and fled across the slippery roots, moving from tree to tree as noiselessly as a wraith.

"What the bloody hell's going on over there?" Glowering at the window of his quarters—through which the faint but unmistakable sound of sustained automatic weapons' fire was percolating—Amon Klegg banged his tea mug down on the map table. The big sergeant to whom, earlier, he had tossed the savagely abused *Quori* girl, stood nearby, shifting nervously on his combat boots.

The White Colonel scowled at him. "The southeastern sector of the lakeshore was reported clean of organized resistance. Units in there are supposed to be conducting terror sweeps, patrolling for *Quoris* and eliminating them by machete—not engaging in full-scale military firefights." The way Klegg stared at him made the big sergeant feel as though *he* was personally responsible for the unexpected gunfire.

"Uh—yes, *sah*," he began. "You—"

"Keep your mouth shut, Sergeant; I didn't ask your opinion."

"Yes, *sah*!"

Klegg kicked his chair back from the map table, got up, and strode across the room to the window, his bush boots clumping loudly with every step. Throwing open the hinged iron grating with a bang, he put his hands on his hips and stared out across the misty black lake. There was yet another scattered *pop-pop-pop-pop-pop* of distant gunfire. The White Colonel squinted toward the southeast, scratching the mat of hair on his chest, but could see nothing. The lakeshore was too far off, the night too hazy for him to catch the winking of muzzle flashes or the orange threads of light that indicated tracer bullets.

"Give me that bloody transmitter," he barked.

Hurriedly, the sergeant retrieved the small hand-held field radio from the map table and trotted it over to Klegg, who snatched it and punched in a frequency.

"The *kaffir* bastard who's letting his unit shoot *Quoris* instead of cut them up, as I fucking ordered, is going to have a short life," he snarled, depressing the transmitter's *Call Alert* button.

* * *

The lieutenant of Leopard Soldiers in command of the fourteen-man platoon pursuing Naji was one of the best trackers and guerilla fighters in King Billy's entire army. A member of a legendary *Malmoq* hunter/warrior family, he had been raised in a tradition that prescribed certain rites of passage into manhood . . . including the slaying of a male lion using only a short thrusting spear, and the secret murder of a rival family's son, of the same generation as he. Both tasks he had accomplished on schedule, just prior to his thirteenth birthday.

Hunting was in his blood, something he enjoyed. Hunting men was what he enjoyed most of all. The initial firefights with the army of the previous regime had been exhilarating—a warrior's bread and butter—but they had not lasted long, The chopping up of *Quori* men, women, and children he considered merely routine—he had more respect for a lion or elephant or springbok than he did for members of that despised tribe. If any of them lived, after he and his comrades were through, they could live in terror—too traumatized by what they had seen, heard of, and barely escaped even to breed.

But this, now, was the circumstance for which he had often prayed—dangerous pursuit over difficult terrain of a lethally capable enemy, a man or men who were, without a doubt, nearly as skilled as he. *Gods of Wood and Water! To shoot a flashlight out of a soldier's hand in the pitch-blackness of night, in such a way that it sent the entire hunting platoon off in the wrong direction—and then to slip away almost without a sound! This was no terrified* Quori *woman or child . . .*

The lieutenant of Leopard Soldiers sucked his filed teeth. There was at least one great warrior in the fleeing party, a crack shot who moved through the dark jungle as he did, as silently and invisibly as a leopard. An opponent worthy of the hunt. It would be an honor to kill him, and satisfying—for it would be proof that, as good as the rival warrior was, the lieutenant of Leopard Soldiers was better.

He had split off from his platoon—they made too much noise moving over the swampy, root-matted terrain—and circled close to the lake in a wide flanking maneuver. Treacherous work, moving over slimy roots and bottomless sinkholes . . . but it was about to pay off. As he stood silently behind the coarse trunk of a thornwood tree, fingering his compact machine gun, his flickering eyes caught a movement in the misty darkness.

A mere fifteen feet ahead, a tall figure clad in a long black cloak detached itself from a huge, half-fallen cork tree and ghosted sideways into the shadows of an overhanging stingberry bush. The lieutenant ran his tongue over the sharp tips of his filed teeth. Impressive. Even with the poor footing, there had been absolutely no sound.

The man in the black cloak hunched slightly, his back to the lieutenant, a long rifle resting in the crook of his left elbow. He appeared to be scanning the jungle ahead and to both sides.

But not behind.

The lieutenant of Leopard Soldiers stepped out from behind the thornwood tree. No twig or root cracked beneath his combat boots. His battle gear, rigged for stalking, did not jingle or clatter. He made no noise whatsoever.

Slowly, he brought up his machine gun, holding it at hip height, and leveled it on the broad back of the black-cloaked man just ahead of him. And then he grinned, his filed teeth gleaming in the faint starlight, savoring the moment of the kill. It was good to be the best. He had always been the best.

Always.

As he began to squeeze the trigger of the machine gun, the tiny *Call Alert* light on the communications unit clipped to the left breast pocket of his battle jacket flashed twice. A second later, the accompanying audible alert sounded.

Beep-beep.

With almost unbelievable speed, the black-cloaked man whirled and threw himself sideways. Before the stunned lieutenant of Leopard Soldiers could depress the trigger of his weapon, something hit him in the left side of the chest with tremendous force, knocking him backward. His filed teeth bit through his lower lip as he landed spread-eagled on the soggy root-mat. The stars visible through the overhead jungle canopy spun before his eyes. He choked once, blood clogging the back of his throat, and died.

Naji disentangled himself from the stingberry bush, keeping his Lee-Enfield trained on the man he'd just shot, and stepped toward the still-quivering body. To his inland side, there was renewed shouting and the occasional dim flash of light. Having heard the single report of the Lee-Enfield, he knew, the Leopard Soldiers would be working their way back in his direction.

He stopped at the dead man's boots and peered down. This one had been good, had beaten him. If not for the strange, soft beep that had given him away at the last second, it would now be Naji stretched out upon the wet roots with a hole through his vitals.

The tall Arab leaned over and examined the body more closely. He had fired instinctively—one-handed—at the unnatural sound, not so much seeing as *sensing* his target. And it had been a good shot. The .303 caliber slug had smashed the beeping communications unit before tearing through the African's heart and out his back. His eyes were open, staring upward, his broad lips peeled back in an agonized grimace. Naji grunted in surprise as he noticed the man's abundant facial scarification and sharpened teeth.

There were more shouts off to the right, and lights shafting through the trees. Taking one last look at the lieutenant of Leopard Soldiers, Naji moved off toward the lakeshore, heading south.

As he did, he smiled to himself, remembering for the thousandth time something his father had once told him: *Should you ever find yourself caught in a game of life and death, my son, fret not about your performance. Be reassured that a man can finish no worse than second.*

"Bloody hell!" Klegg swore, punching the *Call Alert* button on his communications unit yet again. He waited a few seconds, but there was still no reply. "Bah!" He banged the transmitter down on the map table and screwed his face up at the big sergeant. "Put the lieutenant in charge of Unit Four on report. Field court-martial with summary execution of sentence . . . if and when I feel like it." He locked his hands behind his head and stretched. "Fucking *kaffirs*."

He looked over at the little brown pebble sitting on the end of the map table. The alluvial diamond really did look like a shrunken, rotten peanut, deceptively unimpressive in its raw state. He chewed his lip. Given its shape, and barring any major flaws or unsightly inclusions, this particular stone would probably yield two faceted and polished gems of well over three karats apiece. Even if it did contain significant flaws, it could still be cut into a half dozen smaller gems of close to a karat in size. Either way, it was worth a lot of money.

A briefcase full of them would be worth a fortune.

Klegg glanced at his watch. Nearly 3 A.M. He turned and looked out the window at the mist steaming off the surface of Shark Lake. The sky was a blue-black dome above the horizon, shot through with stars. It was really quite beautiful, in spite of the stiflingly thick air.

"Sergeant," the White Colonel said, "I'm going to sleep for a few hours. I want you to wake me up at seven o'clock, and at seven-fifteen I want the American in the pit brought to my quarters."

"*Sah!*" the big sergeant responded, saluting and clicking his heels.

"You're dismissed."

"*Sah!*"

The sergeant left the room, closing the door behind him. Klegg continued to gaze out the window, over the dark lake with its shifting banks of mist and fog . . . and further consider the possibility that the American named Fenzi might be on to a sizable source of diamonds such as the one resting on the map table. And that he might be persuaded to reveal the location of such a source—given the appropriate motivation.

Klegg smiled as he watched the mist drift and curl over the black water. It was amazing what a man could be encouraged to reveal using only a pair of truck batteries and a couple of six-foot lengths of medium-gauge wire. If that didn't work, there was always the straight razor.

He felt pleasantly tired now. Making the *Quori* girl scream had relaxed him, vented off his excess energy. Four hours of sleep would be plenty. Then—the new project.

He turned away from the window, not bothering to look down, and shut the iron grille with a clang. A night-flying stork that had alighted upon the rampart directly above Klegg's quarters jumped into the air with a harsh croak, startled, and dropped halfway to the water before getting its wings fully deployed. As it soared down and away from the old fort, it passed over the unusual activity that the White Colonel, by the remotest of chances, had missed seeing:

Within a stone's throw of the fort walls, surrounded by the hanging folds of the rotten fishing net and its half dozen Styrofoam floats, the American named Fenzi and his rescuer were kicking themselves away from the island heading eastward as rapidly as their tired legs would propel them.

CHAPTER 16

Sass knocked on the door to Maggie's hotel room and waited. There was no answer, and no sound from within. Glancing up at Olssen, who was standing in the hallway with her, she cleared her throat impatiently and knocked again, harder.

Nothing.

"*Fuck*," she said under her breath, and slammed the palm of her hand rapidly into the door a half dozen times. The noisy pounding triggered a muffled protest, some incoherent mumbling . . . and thirty seconds later the door opened. Maggie squinted out of the darkened room with half-drugged eyes, her face puffy with sleep and her hair askew. She was clad only in a rumpled white shirt and panties.

"Th' hell?" she muttered. "Whassup?"

She left the door open and wandered back toward the single large bed, unsteady on her feet. Sass followed her into the room, switching on the overhead light, with Olssen trailing close behind. Flopping onto the mattress on her back, Maggie draped the crook of her elbow across her eyes to block out the sudden glare.

"Hello, Berndt," she said, without looking at him.

"Maggie." Olssen's gaunt Nordic face was set, severe.

Sass folded her arms, standing with one hip cocked, and frowned down at her disheveled acquaintance. "Hey. Why don't you get yourself vertical and shake the pills out of your head. We need to talk."

"Mmm-mm-mffph." Maggie writhed a little on the sleep-tossed bedcovers. " 'Zit time to go pick the boys up?" Her voice was thick.

Sass looked over at Olssen, blinked, and took two steps forward. Reaching down, she grabbed Maggie by the upper arms and yanked her upright. The unkempt brunette head bobbled. Maggie gave a little shriek and wrenched herself away, slapping blindly. She rolled across to the far side of the bed, put her feet on the floor, and sat facing the wall with her head in her hands.

A few seconds later, she reached over to the night table beside her and retrieved a pack of cigarettes and a book of matches. Lighting a menthol slim, she crossed her bare legs and propped her elbow on her knee, the cigarette poised between her fingers at an upward angle. Her maroon-painted thumbnail snapped repeatedly across the filter. *Click. Click. Click.* She kept her back to Sass and Olssen.

"So whaddya wanna talk about," she muttered, exhaling a stream of smoke. It wasn't a question.

Sass walked around the bed so she could see her face. "I don't like talking to the back of someone's head—especially someone I've just done a considerable favor for."

"Oh, really?" Maggie shook back her mane of

brunette hair and coolly looked Sass up and down. "It's Ben Gannon who's doing me the favor. What exactly is it that *you've* done?" She smirked unpleasantly and drew on her cigarette. "Besides sleep with the guy when he's not offshore, spend his money, and tag along wherever he goes?"

Sass bit off the retort that sprang to her lips and managed—narrowly—to quell the impulse to throttle Maggie Fenzi with her bare hands. "What's this all about, Mag?" she asked instead.

The hard-faced brunette sitting on the bed stared at her, smoke curling up between them. "Me, for a change," she said finally. "It's about *me*."

Sass leaned back against the wall and let out a long, careful breath. "Okay. It's about you." She brushed a strand of blond hair out of her eyes. "Berndt here just filled me in on the shit Nick pulled during the jackup crew's escape from Bisotho last month. He told me he told *you* all about it by phone. Not that Nick had been captured by Leopard Soldiers on the way out, the way you described it to *us*, but that he'd stolen the goddamned truck the crew had commandeered and left them all stranded in the jungle." She paused. "That's not the story you gave Ben."

Maggie shrugged, chewing one of her maroon talons. She took a quick pull at her cigarette. "Doesn't make any difference. The Leopard Soldiers caught him anyway, and they stuck him in that pit. Before the satellite e-mails dried up he messaged the whole situation to me. I still needed Ben, one way or the other, to get him out."

"Why didn't you tell him the truth?"

"I thought he'd be less inclined to help Nick if he knew what he'd done." Maggie smiled without humor. "Thought he might think twice."

Sass's eyes flashed. "So you lied to him about it."

"Hey, honey." Maggie stabbed the cigarette at Sass. "Ben still *owed* my husband a life. He knew it, and you knew it. Whatever Nick may have done to get himself into this jam, it has nothing to do with whether or not Ben should have agreed to help him. I was just calling in a debt for my old man when he needed it paid, that's all."

Sass's expression darkened. "You're sure tight with Nick these days, huh? You two have been on the downslope of your marriage for five years now. Hell, you were separated for most of last year, weren't you? What'd you do—go to counseling and hold hands?"

"We worked it out." Maggie looked at the wall and drew deeply on her menthol slim. "If it's any of your fucking business."

"When the shit you and your husband churn up starts to bury Ben," Sass erupted, "you'd better *believe* it's my fucking business!" She took a step toward Maggie, but halted when she felt Olssen's big hand on her shoulder.

"Easy," he rumbled softly. "Easy. We must talk some more."

Sass balled her fists, struggling to regain her composure. "Ben came here to try to get an old friend out of a third-world prison. I went along with him because it was his choice, and because I didn't want to see a wife lose her husband. I was fool enough to feel sorry for you and give you the benefit of the doubt. You took advantage of us."

"No, I didn't." Maggie got to her feet and raked her fingers through her hair. "I love my husband. I want him back."

"Right. You love him so much that you're screwing some stoner pilot the day you get into Krumake."

"I told you," Maggie said, "I fucked that moron just to get the use of his plane. It's not as if I had a lot of time to pick and choose."

Sass snorted. "He's a decent sort of boob. Like I told you at the airstrip—he'd have done it if you'd asked him nicely and offered to pay him a fair price. Even rich people like to be paid for their time and trouble."

"Who wants to spend good American cash for something when you can get it for free?" Maggie retorted. "Besides, he was young enough to have decent stamina and I needed to work off a little tension. Most of Nick's pumping power disappeared along with his fiftieth birthday. Probably had something to do with the ten or twelve thousand gallons of tequila he consumed during the last thirty years. Although," she added bitterly, "it didn't seem to stop him from porking every barmaid in every oil-field roadhouse from Matamoros to Mobile. Guess I just got a little too familiar for the bastard, huh? A little too old. Boring old Maggie."

She drew a breath, seemingly unaware of how loud her voice had become—and of what she was saying. Sass and Olssen shot each other quick glances.

Maggie crushed out the butt of her cigarette, picked up a fresh pack from the night table, and began to pace the room. "Twenty-three years I've put in with Nick Fenzi. I was making nearly two grand a *week* dancing at those high-class men's clubs in Houston back in the late seventies, and I gave it all up for him. Get that good little girl's better life, be a decent wife. All that shit. Better life, my ass. Do you realize that in the first ten years we were together, that sonofabitch never made less than *ninety thousand* dollars a season—and never saved a single penny of it? No nice house, no new cars, no investment portfolio, no proper insurance . . . *nothing*. Nothing but a stream of wrecked secondhand Corvettes, bad loans to lowlife oil-field-trash buddies, thousands of dollars in bar bills, and *tens* of thousands of dollars in cocaine. By the time I figured out that nothing was ever going to change, I was too old to go back to dancing. Late thirties, an extra ten pounds, a little sag here and there—and you're washed up. Out of the big money in the good clubs."

"Mag," Sass cut in, "you *know* you partied away that money with him. You matched him drink for drink, toot for toot."

"Yeah, but I wouldn't have done it if he hadn't been leading the way!" Maggie blurted angrily. "And we *quit*, you know? More than seven years ago." She looked at the wall, her eyes haunted. "We just can't *stay* quit."

There was a pause, a little click as she lit a fresh cigarette with her gold Dunhill.

"I'm forty-nine," Maggie went on, her voice hollow. "I'll be fifty next month. I like nice things." She fingered the expensive lighter, gazing at it. "Things that cost money. I make twenty-one-five a year as an office manager for a tire distribution company. Four years in, I'm the only one in the entire place with half a brain, and that's my salary ceiling. No benefits. Talk about your dead-end job. God knows Nick earned and spent nearly two million over twenty years doing whatever the hell he felt like—even if it meant that at this point in our lives we wouldn't have a pot to piss in or a window to throw it out of."

She blew a stream of smoke. "But he was going to put it right, you know? Said he was going to clean up his act after he got fired from O.U.S. and keep it clean. Buckle down and get to work, make us some money, and do something smart with it this time." She batted her eyelashes at Olssen, suddenly looking waifish, like a lost little girl. Sass had to give her credit, she could turn it on in a split second. "And this job with you, Berndt, it meant a lot to him. He told me he felt lucky to have an old friend like you, someone who would give him good-paying work." Maggie's dark eyes brimmed, and her lower lip trembled.

But Olssen wasn't buying it. "If he was so grateful," he said, his voice metallic, "then why did he strand us all in the jungle? What kind of thanks was that?"

Abruptly, Maggie's demeanor changed. The hard-case ex-stripper was back. "Well, I don't know," she muttered, sticking the cigarette between her lips again. "He must have had his reasons, or he wouldn't have done it." A thought occurred to her. "Maybe he'd spotted some soldiers and was trying to decoy them away from you—ever think of that?"

Olssen's expression was glacial. "That was not what happened."

Maggie walked around Sass, her arms folded across her chest, and stood at the foot of the bed. "Beats me, then," she said, breathing out smoke. "But it doesn't really matter at this stage of the game, does it? The floatplane should be in the air pretty soon. I'm sure blond-and-bubbly here filled you in on the details of our little operation. You can ask him when he gets back."

Olssen stepped closer to her and drew something out of his trouser pocket. "Are you sure it doesn't have anything to do with this?" he rumbled softly. He held up the little brown pebble he'd shown to Sass earlier.

Maggie glanced at it and looked away. "What the hell's that? Cat turd?"

"No. A high-grade alluvial diamond. We drilled and retrieved over three hundred shallow core samples from the bottom of Shark Lake. Of all those, only two contained a thin upper sediment layer studded with these nodules. We weren't sure what they were at the time, if they had any value. We thought maybe they were manganese pellets or some such thing.

"There were no geologists aboard the jackup. We were just going to ship the core samples to an independent petroleum industry lab out of the country to test for the presence of oil, then report the findings to the Resource Development Ministry of the former Bisothoan government.

"I was curious. I kept one of the nodules, intending to have it analyzed once the job was done, for my own interest. It was in the bottom of the small rucksack I took with me when we fled to Kuballa—I'd forgotten about it. I found it after I'd returned to Europe and had a gemologist look at it. He said it was one of the finest uncut diamonds of its size he'd ever seen, and offered to buy it on the spot."

Olssen paused, running his eyes over Maggie's face. "Nick was curious, too, as I recall. *Very* curious." He reached down and lightly touched the expensive sapphire-and-emerald broach that lay on top of the bedside dresser. Beside it lay Maggie's amethyst necklace and diamond-stud earrings. "You know gemstones, I take it?"

Maggie tucked her bejeweled left hand under her arm. "I like them. They're a hobby. I have a few." The small diamonds on the multiple rings of her smoking hand glittered as she raised her cigarette to her lips.

"I take it Nick does as well." Olssen smiled thinly. "Know a diamond when he sees it, I mean. Even one as ugly and plain as this, *ya*?" He tossed the little pebble into the air and caught it. "Perhaps he was the only man on the jackup who knew what had come up in those two random core samples."

Maggie drew hard on her cigarette and blew a long cloud of mentholated smoke at the ceiling. "I have no idea what you're talking about," she said.

Olssen's sparse smile remained on his face as he stepped away from her and put the diamond back into his pocket. "Pity," he commented. "I thought maybe you would."

Maggie sat down on the bed and propped herself up against the headboard. "Still too early to drive to the airstrip," she muttered. "Maybe they'll e-mail or call on the VHF." She sucked on her menthol slim.

Very slowly, Sass moved around to the foot of the

bed, stopped, and looked Maggie Fenzi up and down. "Why is it," she asked, "that when I watch you, when I listen to what comes out of your mouth—I keep hearing that old song?"

Maggie smirked at her, feigning weary patience. "What song, honeybuns?"

" 'Diamonds Are a Girl's Best Friend.' "

Sass and Olssen left Maggie in her room and went back down to the hotel bar. As tired as they both were, there was little point in attempting to get any sleep. They ordered coffee, black, and took a table along the bar's trophy wall, beneath the plaque-mounted head of a rhinoceros.

"This is the longest night of my life," Sass remarked, placing the uplink unit and VHF radio on the table beside her coffee cup. "I'm so wired and tired I don't know whether I'm coming or going." She glanced at her watch with a sigh. "I feel like I should be doing something, but all I can do is wait until it's time to go meet the floatplane. That's still not for three hours."

Olssen stirred a teaspoon of sugar into his coffee. "I think it took me until I was nearly sixty to realize that, sometimes, doing nothing *is* doing something. You are waiting, which is what is required at present. Or, I should say, *we* are waiting." He smiled. "Consider me involved now. As a friend. We will do what we can to see that Ben returns safely to Kuballa."

Sass nodded gratefully, her own smile tight. "Thanks, Berndt. It means a lot to me. Things with Maggie just seemed to start off bad and get worse by the hour. It's nice to have someone . . . I don't know . . . on my side, I guess."

"Rest assured that you do," Olssen said. "I came here on business—such as it is—but when good people are in danger, business must wait. That's my philosophy anyway, which is probably why I'm not rich. But"—he smiled—"it's the least I can do for an old North Sea colleague."

Sass squeezed his big hand. "Again, thanks."

"Of course." Olssen sat back in his chair. "It's quite apparent that Maggie Fenzi's priorities differ from yours. Not a very happy or contented woman."

"I don't know what happened to her," Sass said, shrugging helplessly. "She *used* to be happy. I mean, she was always a bit wild, but then so was Nick. They seemed tailor-made for each other, you know?" She thought for a moment. "I really haven't seen much of her over the past four or five years—just heard from Ben that she and Nick were having a little trouble. I guess it was more serious than I thought. She's changed."

Olssen nodded slowly. "The woman is frightened. Of *everything*. It happens to people who spend their lives playing and indulging themselves and consuming—they never develop a personal philosophy on which to build enduring happiness . . . a calm spiritual center, if you like. They end up terrified because, eventually, they discover that no matter how much they feed their own selfish wants, they can't fill the void inside. That's the odd thing about self-indulgence—the more you consume, the more you take for yourself, the emptier you become. By fifty, the hole can get pretty big."

"Fair amateur psychology, Berndt," Sass declared. "So what's the cure?"

"You already know it," Olssen replied with a wry smile, "but you're well adjusted and happy, so you don't consciously think about it." He sipped his coffee. "The cure is simple. Give, instead of take. Oddly enough, it fills that void right up. What a contradiction, eh? It took me sixty years and two failed marriages to learn that."

"At least you did."

"*Ya*, in the long run." Olssen set down his coffee cup and scratched the gray stubble on his chin. "Look, I should fill you in on a few things that may turn out to be useful. As I mentioned, I came back to Krumake to see if there might be some way to salvage my disastrous business situation with regards to the leased jackup rig. Perhaps a break in the fighting or a shifting of hostilities to another part of Bisotho that could allow me to put a skeleton crew on the rig and take it back downriver to the Indian Ocean. At the very least, I thought I might be able to get some close aerial photographs of it sitting in Shark Lake—assuming the rebels haven't blown it up or sunk it—that might prove useful in court. Show that it is still in one piece, merely out of my hands, and not destroyed.

"And I have to admit—the thought of possibly getting back aboard, even for fifteen minutes, and collecting those two diamond-studded core samples . . . well, it's irresistibly tempting. I'm quite sure that even if rebel soldiers went through the rig—stole what they could and vandalized the rest—they wouldn't bother themselves with several hundred muddy cylinders wrapped in plastic. Only two out of the whole lot contain the rough diamonds—and I doubt if they'd know what they were looking at even if they found them."

Olssen gazed at Sass. "I tell you honestly. Picking up those core samples—even if they contain only a half dozen or so diamonds like the one I showed you—would enable me to keep my head above water long enough to force TransArctic Corporation into legal mediation regarding their rig. The lawyers could arrive at some kind of semireasonable settlement instead of this ridiculously high payout for an aging jackup. The insurance company would be on my side. They don't want to pay ten times what the thing's worth, even if I contribute my full two-million-dollar deductible.

"And as to the origin of the diamonds—as far as I'm concerned they belong to no one. The government that contracted me to drill core samples is defunct. The new 'government'—and I use the term loosely—is responsible for my losing the rig I leased from TransArctic. So I have no qualms whatsoever about retrieving the diamonds I drilled up—even if they do come from Bisotho without a mines-and-minerals permit—and using them to cover the losses I've incurred."

Olssen took another sip of coffee and smiled wearily at Sass. "All this is a long-winded way of telling you that I've contracted with a pilot of my own, here in Krumake, who flies a large seaplane and is willing to take a run over the rig in Shark Lake. He will even set down for a short time so I can board her, if there is no military activity nearby. My flight could be a second chance for Ben and his companions if something goes wrong with your initial plan. I hope not, of course, but there it is, if you need it."

"Thank you, Berndt," Sass responded. "For the moment, though, I'm still counting on seeing them touch down on the airstrip just outside town about two-and-a-half hours from now. Or getting a call saying they're back earlier than expected—maybe out of fuel and sitting upcountry somewhere in Kuballa waiting for me to come pick them up in the Land Rover."

Olssen nodded encouragingly. "I'm sure that will be the case," he said.

CHAPTER 17

Nick was wheezing badly, his face lined with strain.

"Sure . . . sure is hard to kick," he gasped, "with all this netting around us. Keeps hangin' up my . . . legs . . ."

"I know," Ben said. He looked back the way they had come. The island fort was almost completely obscured by the drifting mist. "Hang on a minute. Take five."

"I can . . . do that." Nick sagged on the tangled ropes that were supporting him between two of the fishing net's rotten Styrofoam floats. His breathing sounded almost tubercular—wet and ragged.

Ben rolled onto his back, his empty twin tanks and fully inflated buoyancy compensator bobbing him high in the water, and located the waterproof GPS. As Nick watched, too tired to speak, he brought the unit up in front of his eyes, the faint red light cast by its tiny screen reflecting off his wet face.

"Satellites lost me when I went into the cave," Ben muttered. He spat lakewater. "*Yuk*. Tastes like a Louisiana oil field in late August."

"Wou—wouldn't mind bein' in the Rathskeller in

Morgan City right now," Nick panted, "havin' me a beer and a smoke."

Ben smiled, punching buttons. "You'll get there. Hang tight." He squinted at the unit's little screen. "Okay. It's acquired again. Here comes the position . . . got it. We're about—lemme convert it . . . um . . . four hundred yards northeast of the island—which is the first waypoint I entered. To get to the primary rendezvous location, we'd need to swim north-northeast for at least another six hundred yards."

Nick blinked at him, still breathing heavily. "Piece a' cake. Let's . . . let's go."

"I'd like to, but I think we've got a problem."

"Yeah? Just wha . . . just what we need. We ain't got enough . . . of those . . ."

Ben craned his neck and gazed off into the shifting, intermittent curtains of fog to the north. "I've been watching the whole time we've been kicking away from the fort. The mist parts pretty regularly. Sometimes I can see clear across to the opposite shore. The thing is, I don't see the floatplane." He held up his wrist and looked at his dive watch. "And we're overdue. Late. The net's been slowing us down."

"Well, let's just ditch the fuckin' thing." Nick thrashed a fold of mesh off one arm. "The shit's drivin' me crazy, bro."

"Take my word for it," Ben said. "We want to keep it around us. And don't churn the water like that."

"Okay, okay." Nick settled down and hung quietly between the two rotting balls of Styrofoam. "You're sure bein' careful about these damn sharks. What's the big deal? They're just sharks. We work with them hangin' around us all the time. Back in the cave it didn't even look like they knew we were there."

"I think the springwater in the cave anaesthetizes them somehow," Ben said. "The sharks out here, in the middle of the lake, are different. They're big bulls— Zambezi sharks—hunting in packs. They've already rushed me once, when I was first approaching the island—scared the hell out of me. And I'm in no hurry to repeat the experience.

"Now look, I don't think we should waste any more energy trying to kick northward to the first rendezvous site. Like I said, I haven't seen any sign of the floatplane, and we're way late already. I think we should head toward the backup rendezvous location on the lakeshore, southeast of the island. Even if the plane isn't there, we'll be able to get out of the water. If something's happened, and my guys don't show, we can try to make our way overland toward Kuballa." Ben grinned wearily. "At least you're out of that hole."

"Amen to that, bro."

Ben rolled onto his stomach, lying beside Nick across a sheaf of netting buoyed by three more Styrofoam balls. "*Arrgh*. Tanks are damn heavy."

"Why don't you ditch 'em?"

"Nah. We need the buoyancy compensator, and there's no quick-release on the backpack. The cylinders are bolted on; we'd need a wrench to get them loose."

"Great."

Ben leveled the GPS unit in front of his eyes. "Okay. We need to swing to the right about ninety degrees. Can you kick some more?"

"Yeah, let's do it."

Side by side, they began to drive forward with their fins, Ben kicking wide to the left to turn them toward the southeast. "Okay," he said, watching the GPS screen, "that's good. Straight ahead now."

"Where's the island at?" Nick asked, already breathing heavily.

"Over there," Ben replied. "Off to the right. Look, you can just see the fort between the fogbanks." The outline of the dark structure was momentarily visible in the drifting mist.

"Huh." The older diver shifted a little on the tangle of lines and mesh supporting his chest. "Funny thing . . ."

"What's that?" Ben panted, working hard.

"If we keep swimming in this here direction"—Nick paused to gulp air—"we're gonna pass real close to the jackup."

Ben spat. "Yeah? That's nice. Maybe we can get hold of one of the legs and rest for a few minutes, if we need to. Is it jacked up high, low, or is it floating?"

"Ummm—it's jacked up about twenty feet, as I re-call." He looked over at Ben, his wet hair plastered across his forehead. "How about we stop there? We could signal your guys from the deck, maybe."

"Stop there?" Ben shook his head. "What for? We get that far, it's only about another three-quarters of a mile to shore. We can take a rest, but we don't want to miss the second rendezvous." He glanced over at his friend. "Why? Don't you think you can make it?"

"Well, yeah, probably . . ." Nick shrugged, coughed

up a wad of phlegm, and spat. "Just thought it might be easier, that's all. A little less . . . swimmin'."

"If we need to stop, we'll stop," Ben said. "But where we want to be is onshore to meet the floatplane, right?"

"Oh, yeah, bro," Nick rasped. "No argument there."

"All right. Let's cover some distance."

They kicked steadily through the lukewarm black water for the better part of fifteen minutes, the mist around them opening and closing like curtains of gauze, before they saw the first fin. It rose directly in front of them, a dark triangle nearly two feet in height, and cut across their path some ten feet ahead. Then, curving around to their right, just outside the folds of the fishing net, it sank slowly and disappeared.

"Big one," Ben muttered, feeling his legs and feet begin to tingle. "Two feet of dorsal fin, and I didn't even see his back."

"Yeah. Big . . . for . . . a bull shark." Nick gasped out the words, his breathing tortured. He sounded so bad that Ben glanced over at him. A thin rivulet of blood was running from the corner of his mouth down into his wet, matted beard.

"Hey," Ben exclaimed, "you're bleeding!" He grabbed the older diver's shoulder as he went into a fit of coughing. "Easy, easy. You okay?"

"*Acchh!*" Nick hawked and spat "Yeah, bro. Lungs're a little heavy, that's all. And I think I bit my lip."

Ben frowned at him, running his eyes over the pale, drawn face. "You sure you're not coughing up blood?"

Nick forced a smile. "Not me, buddy. Bit lip is all."

"Well, okay." Ben let go of his shoulder. "Do us both a favor and swallow it, will you? We don't need blood in the water at this particular moment."

"No . . . sweat."

"Keep kicking. We've still got to—"

There was a sudden eruption of splashing as a shark charged into the folds of the net to Ben's left and violently shook its entire body. The dark water was churned to foam as the animal thrashed back and forth, half-entangled in the mesh. Ben recoiled instinctively, tucking in his legs as the pale belly and one pectoral fin rolled clear of the surface.

"Jesus!" Nick panted, his eyes wide.

"Pull that netting in closer!" Ben said. "Make sure there's plenty of it around us on your side!" He reached behind him and raked in an armful of sodden mesh. "We keep the barrier thick enough and maybe they won't be able to get in close enough to bite."

"Maybe they'll even . . . lose interest," Nick wheezed, clawing in folds of netting. The rotting Styrofoam floats bobbed around his head, getting in the way.

Unseen beneath the surface, a second shark drove into the mesh near Nick's waist, pushing him sideways into Ben. "Shit!" the older diver exclaimed. "I can feel him snappin' at me down there!" He struggled for a few seconds, then relaxed. "He's gone."

"He get a piece of you?"

"Nah. But he was close. I could feel him chewin' on the net."

Ben managed a wan smile. "Probably didn't like rotten meat."

Nick coughed and spat. "Marinated is more like it,

in my case." He glanced around. "Look, there's a couple more of the bastards."

"Yeah. Just cruising, huh?"

"So far."

Tentatively, they began to kick again. Ben checked the GPS. "Bear left a little. Okay—that's good. Now straight."

"Aye, captain." Nick settled between the Styrofoam floats and labored away in silence for a moment. "This was a good idea, freein' up this fishing net."

Ben eyed a fin cruising by about six feet away. "Ever hear of the Johnson Shark Screen?"

"No."

"It's a gimmick I read about back in the late sixties, when I first started diving. A guy named Johnson developed it for protecting military pilots who had to bail out over the ocean. Basically, it was a big black plastic trash bag with an inflatable collar, attached to a standard inflatable life vest. When a pilot hit the drink, he aired up the vest and collar, unfolded the bag, and climbed inside."

Nick's brow furrowed. "The bag was . . . full of water?"

"Right. He was still in the water, floating, but now all the sharks saw was a shapeless six-foot sack—no legs kicking, no bare skin showing. And no blood spreading around if the guy was bleeding. The bag removed the stimuli that attract sharks and cause them to attack."

"How about that . . ."

Ben nodded, checking their heading on the GPS screen. "It was a pretty clever idea. Anyway, I thought this old net might do the same thing, if we could get enough of it around us."

"Well . . . I reckon it's . . . *sorta* workin'," Nick grunted. He watched another fin wiggle in close, then veer off. "They know we're . . . in here. They just . . . ain't figured a way . . . to get to us."

"Looks that way. I—" Ben broke off in mid-sentence. "What the hell's that?"

A dense fluttering sound, like leaves rustling in a stiff wind, began to grow rapidly in volume. It was accompanied by a staccato clucking noise—and a few seconds later a flock of water storks descended out of the fog, skidding onto the lake's surface all around them, white-feathered wings beating the air. A cluster of them gathered about fifteen feet to the right of the fishing net, squabbling and maneuvering.

As if triggered by a starting gun, the bull sharks attacked, their hurtling bodies rupturing the water beneath the storks. Great bronze heads stabbed upward, jaws snapping, dragging down bird after bird in a flapping, splashing melee of feathers, foam, and teeth.

"*Jesus*," Nick muttered. "Why don't they just take off?"

Incredibly, the storks appeared not to comprehend what was happening—to understand that the danger was coming from below. One after another they were yanked beneath the surface by unseen jaws, or smashed sideways and down by lunging bronze bodies that exploded from the water like onrushing torpedoes. Ben and Nick watched incredulously as a single stork backpedaled across the surface in front of the net, wings flogging the air, its bill snapping at the huge head and gaping maw of a bull shark that lunged and missed at least a dozen times before finally dragging it down. Not once did the bird try to take flight.

Then, as quickly as it had begun, the attack ceased. The flock was gone. All that remained of it was a scattering of white feathers on the oily black water. Then the fog closed in again, and that too disappeared.

"Holy shit," Nick said. He peered right and left. "See any more sharks?"

Ben shook his head, and began to kick with renewed vigor. "Nope. Not on the surface, anyway."

"Maybe they're fed."

"Could be." Ben thought a moment. "You know, I bet they target those birds all the time. Did you see how fast they hit? They probably recognize the sound of a flock landing. There are millions of birds around here. It's got to be a great food source."

"Makes sense," Nick said, coughing a little.

"Something similar happened when the sharks attacked me on the way in to the island. They had me pinned in a crevice, were going crazy trying to get at me. Then all of sudden they just up and left. Disappeared like somebody rang the dinner bell somewhere else."

"Yeah? Might have been a flock of birds landing, eh?"

"That'd be my guess."

They fell silent and kicked onward, legs aching and feet cramping in their long fins. Though the water was warm, the loss of body heat was beginning to tell. Fatigue was setting in, overwhelming the adrenaline that had kept them going so far. But the shore was barely three-quarters of a mile off. *One more effort*, Ben thought. *One more hard push, and we're there.*

And then a great black shape loomed up out of the mist, towering above them in the hazy night air. Ben paused in his kicking, and Nick raised his head. Water brimmed against the base of a huge vertical column that emerged from the surface of the lake not twenty feet away.

"The jackup rig," Ben said. "That's one of its legs. We'll be onshore in an hour."

Nick nodded, gasping in air, and started to say something.

But instead he reared back with a sharp groan, clutched his chest, and rolled over facedown in the black water.

CHAPTER 18

Naji paused to listen, cocking his head. The Leopard Soldiers pursuing him had just come upon the body of their fallen lieutenant—if the angry shouts echoing through the dripping jungle were anything to judge by. He reckoned them to be not more than 150 yards distant. They were sure to continue the hunt with renewed vigor after discovering one of their own lying dead upon the root-mat.

Making virtually no sound, he ran southward another seventy-five yards, parallel to the lakeshore, weaving between crooked tree trunks and ducking under low, vine-draped branches, unerringly sure-footed on the slimy roots and fallen logs. Overhead, through intermittent gaps in the tree canopy, the stars glittered hard and cold against the night sky, no longer blurred with haze. The mists were thinning as dawn approached.

Naji leaped over a jagged stump and sidestepped into the shadow of a large marblewood tree. Squatting, his rifle across his knees, he gazed back the way he had come. There was the faintest sound of deep voices, chanting once again—but no light. The Leopard Soldiers were well behind him—for the moment—feeling their way along, searching out his spoor.

He faced the direction he had been heading and leaned back against the tree trunk, breathing deeply. For the better part of an hour he had been dodging around in this miserable, gloomy swamp. It was time to think.

The plane. The plane was still there, but it was useless now. Almost certainly, the pilot had been killed—shot or hacked to death at the edge of the stinking muck pit into which he'd fallen, the imbecile. Along with extreme annoyance, Naji felt a pang of regret. The man who called himself "Head" had been a whiner, an incompetent, a terminal adolescent—but not a quitter. And not a coward, for all his fidgety nervousness. If only the mud pool had not been so deep, the Leopard Soldiers not so near . . .

It could not be helped now. And there were those still alive to consider. *Ben-Ya-Min.* Where was he? What was he doing at this moment? Had he managed to free his friend—what was his name—*Nick*? Were they swimming helplessly out in the middle of the lake, looking for a floatplane that wasn't there?

No. Naji glanced at his wristwatch. It was seventy minutes past rendezvous time. *Ben-Ya-Min* would not have waited longer than the agreed-upon interval, treading water in the dense mist, if there were no sign of the plane . . . if indeed he had returned to the drop-off point at all.

He would have proceeded to the secondary rendezvous location, on the southeastern shore. Where was it, exactly? Naji closed his eyes and tried to visualize the large, detailed map he had been shown in the guest room of the Hotel Excelsior only a day and a half—it seemed like an eternity—earlier. He could remember the general shape of the lake's southern end, a few of the shoreline details—but no one specific spot stood out in his memory. He could not even make an educated guess. At the time of the hotel room meeting, *Ben-Ya-Min* had not yet selected the backup rendezvous location.

The GPS. Naji pulled the unit from beneath his robes and looked at it. In the palm of his hand was the exact position of the secondary rendezvous. This device would even lead him there, if only he knew how to work it. Inwardly, he cursed his own ignorance. The ability to operate the GPS was the difference between continuing to stumble around in the dark, exchanging potshots with pursuing soldiers, and moving quickly and efficiently to the rendezvous location.

He glanced back around the tree trunk. There were no flashlight beams, and only the faintest echoing vibration of the ominous hunting chant. He had a little time.

He closed his eyes again, picturing, remembering. *Ben-Ya-Min*'s hands had moved with easy precision over an almost-identical GPS unit aboard the floatplane, just before he had disappeared over the side. There had been a power switch on the housing of his device. Naji's thumb searched, found a similar switch, pushed it.

The little screen flashed into life, backlit letters and numbers displaying and changing in rapid succession. The lean Yemeni blinked. Graphics began to appear—

circles within circles, a diagram of the planet Earth rotating, more circles, and a series of bar graphs showing . . . what?

This went on for several minutes. Naji watched, per-
plexed, and was about to try pressing a few buttons at
random when the screen suddenly flashed again and
the English words SATELLITES ACQUIRED came up
in bold capital letters. He waited. The screen changed
once more, this time bearing the title MENU. Beneath
this was a selection of what appeared to be choices.

ROUTES. STATUS. TRACK LOG SETUP. NAVIGA-
TION SETUP. DIS & SUN CALC. I/0 SETUP. CUE
REFERENCE. WAYPOINT LIST.

Waypoint List.

Naji concentrated, and Ben's words returned to him:
*"I can punch a waypoint into this thing and it'll tell me
which direction I have to move in—right or left—in order to
stay headed for the target. See this little screen? The floating
arrow tells me which way to turn. These numbers tell me
how far off course I am, how far it is to the target, and how
far I've already come."*

Waypoint. *Ben-Ya-Min* had referred to the location of
the secondary rendezvous as a waypoint. And here
was a category entitled "Waypoint List." But how to
look at the list? Naji examined the illuminated keypad.
Fourteen buttons, some with numbers, others with odd
symbols or words such as *Enter, GoTo, Quit,* and *Mark.*
He shook his head slowly. It was truly baffling.

There was an odd button set above the main keypad. It was twice the size of the others, and had four
tiny arrows set around its perimeter—pointing up,
down, and to either side. Perhaps one could—

A shout echoed through the trees, much louder than the background chanting generated by the main body of Leopard Soldiers, Naji shot a fast glance over his shoulder. A figure—perhaps forty yards back—darted between two trees, barely visible in the darkness.

Naji held his breath and pressed the center of the large button. *Nothing.* But the rubber pad felt odd, as though it was mounted on a central bearing. Maybe . . . he pushed on the arrow at its upper edge. The button tilted slightly under his fingertip, the screen flashed once, and the unit gave off a burst of rapid beeps.

The same kind of beeping that had alerted Naji to the presence of the recently departed lieutenant of Leopard Soldiers. He glanced quickly around the tree. No movement. He turned back to the GPS. Despite the flurry of tones, the information on the screen had not changed.

This time he pressed the lower arrow. The screen flashed, the unit beeped once, and a horizontal bar moved down the screen, highlighting the word ROUTES.

Aha.

He pressed the arrow again. A single beep, and the highlight bar dropped to the next word: STATUS. Hurriedly, he pressed the button six more times, until the words WAYPOINT LIST had been selected. Then, once again, he glanced around the tree.

He found himself looking straight at the belt buckle of the Leopard Soldier who had stalked up noiselessly behind him, machete raised. Naji caught a glimpse of filed teeth in a grimacing mouth and white eyes glaring out of a scarified ebony face as he jerked himself back around the tree trunk and lunged for its opposite side.

There was a grunt of effort followed by a *whisshh-KRANNGG* as the machete hissed through the air and impacted the marblewood where Naji's head had been a fraction of a second earlier. Wet bark flew, the Leopard Soldier stumbled to one knee with an undecipherable curse, and then Naji was fully around the tree—lying on one elbow with his rifle pointing directly at the African's face.

The Leopard Soldier froze, his machete half-raised, then opened his mouth to yell, his filed teeth flashing. Naji jerked the Lee-Enfield's muzzle in warning and raised a finger to his lips. The African snarled in frustration, but did not call out. Keeping the rifle trained on his opponent, Naji rolled gracefully to his feet.

The deep chanting was becoming louder, accented by the occasional shout. Slowly, the Leopard Soldier's sweaty visage twisted into a half smile. He could wait. The tall one in the strange black hood and cloak could not. And a shot would give him away.

Naji's hand went beneath his robes and came out gripping his *yataghan*. He raised it, tip pointing up, and waved the blade back and forth, holding the Leopard Soldier's eye. Then he nodded and shifted the Lee-Enfield's barrel to one side. The African's eyes widened in understanding. He nodded in response and let his short-barreled machine gun drop to the root-mat. Widening his stance and crouching, his face tensing into a sneer, he brought the machete up in front of him.

Very slowly, Naji stooped over to set down his rifle, his eyes never leaving his opponent's. He let it rest against a thick root, then—the seconds ticking by—removed his hand from the stock.

The Leopard Soldier grinned, immediately raising the machete high. In one blinding motion Naji snapped his knife arm forward. The *yataghan* whipped end over end between the two men—and then its haft was protruding from the vee of the African's throat, just above his sternum. The man blinked, looking down in astonishment at his new appendage. The machete slipped from his fingers. He emitted a strangling sound, his eyes bugging, and began to paw at his collar. Blood poured from around the embedded blade, soaking the front of his battle jacket.

Naji bent to retrieve his rifle as the Leopard Soldier sagged to his knees—mouth working, his lips shiny with blood. The lean Yemeni waited. The dying man stared up at him once more, made an odd bubbling noise, and fell forward onto his face. His hand clawed feebly at the wet roots . . . and then he lay still.

Naji listened for a few seconds, examining the black jungle behind him. The chanting was plainly audible, but unbroken and far enough away that it was unlikely the main body of soldiers had been alerted by the brief commotion. He scanned the foliage for signs of any flank scouts like the one he'd just introduced to the business end of his *yataghan*. But the immediate area seemed clear.

He stepped forward, got his toe under the Leopard Soldier's shoulder, and turned him over. The African's eyes were shut, his lips pulled back in a horrific leer, his filed teeth gleaming palely in the darkness. There was a lot of blood.

A thin smile crossed Naji's face. It had been a pass-able throw—accurate and hard enough to drive the blade of the *yataghan* through the soldier's body so that five inches of tip protruded from his upper back. Naji grasped the still-quivering haft of the weapon, put the sole of his foot on the dead man's chest, and wrenched upward. There was a sound like chicken bones split-ting under a cleaver, a fresh gout of blood, and the blade came free.

He wiped the long knife on a nearby leaf frond and slipped it into its scabbard. Then he stepped back be-hind the marblewood tree, bent down, and retrieved the dropped GPS. The unit, with its tough plastic cas-ing, appeared undamaged.

WAYPOINT LIST was still highlighted. Naji frowned as he ran his eyes over the buttons. One of them, hopefully, would reveal the list. The numbers? His intuition told him no. It had to be one of the worded keys. *Quit?* No. He did not want to quit any-thing. *Mark?* Possibly. To mark something was to take note of it, record it. *GoTo?* Also possible. He did want to "go to" the list. And finally, *Enter.* Another good choice: he wanted to "enter" the waypoint list.

Which one? He did not have forever to ponder the question. Taking a deep breath, he pressed *GoTo*.

The unit responded with multiple flashes and a se-ries of rapid beeps, as when he had pushed the upper-most arrow of the big key. Nothing on the screen changed.

He exhaled slowly, somewhat relieved. At least he had not confused or broken the infernal contraption. Closing his eyes momentarily, he directed a fervent request toward Allah: *Most Compassionate and Merciful Lord, once I pass from this life of troubles into Paradise, I will gladly give up half my rightful quota of dark-eyed heavenly houris if you will only guide your humble servant's finger to the correct button on this wretched machine.*

He pushed *Enter.*

The unit beeped and the screen flashed. The heading WAYPOINT LIST appeared, with only three entries beneath it: 1st RENDZV, 2nd RENDZV, and FORT.

He pushed the lower arrow on the large button twice. The highlight bar dropped to the entry 2nd RENDZV.

He pushed *Enter.*

Again, the unit beeped. The screen flashed. A graphic display, almost exactly like the one *Ben-Ya-Min* had demonstrated aboard the plane, appeared—complete with floating directional arrow. There were several associated subtitles: LAT/LONG . . . a latitude and longitude—that was obvious to an old sea hand; BEARING . . . a direction expressed in degrees and corresponding to the floating arrow; HEADING . . . this would most likely, his helmsman's experience told him, be his course traveled once he began to walk, also expressed in degrees. And finally, DIST TO WAYPT . . . *distance to waypoint,* given in miles, and tenths and hundredths of miles.

Naji leveled the GPS in front of him, as *Ben-Ya-Min* had done, and turned slowly to the right. The graphic display changed as he did so, the directional arrow slanting ever more to the south. He swung to the left. The arrow reversed itself, maintaining its southerly orientation. Smiling broadly, Naji turned until the arrow was pointing straight ahead.

With one last look at the crumpled body next to the tree, he nestled his rifle in the crook of his elbow and began to pick his way forward over the slippery roots, keeping the GPS arrow aligned with the screen's central axis. Behind him, the hunting chant of the Leopard Soldiers increased slightly in volume. They were veering back toward him. In all likelihood, as before, there would be advance scouts.

But now he knew where to go. And the secondary rendezvous was not far. DIST TO WAYPOINT read 0.52 miles. Just over half a mile. He stepped up his pace. The Leopard Soldiers would have to be moving quickly to catch him.

He smiled up at the stars glittering through the tree canopy. *Allah, Most Compassionate and Merciful, your humble servant thanks you and entreats you to consider withholding only the least attractive half of his rightful quota of dark-eyed houris upon his inevitable entry into Paradise.*

Fifteen minutes later, Naji stepped cautiously out of the dense foliage and onto the gravelly sand of a narrow, crescent-shaped beach. Barely twenty feet wide, it ran for approximately fifty yards before terminating in yet another expanse of jungle. Half a dozen small dugout canoes sat on the sand just above the waterline, fishing nets spread over them to dry. The area immediately behind the beach had been cleared, and in the clearing stood three thatched huts, their open entrances dark. The grass roof of one had been half-consumed by fire. Only a sudden rain squall, Naji surmised, could have prevented such a flammable structure from being burned into a pile of ashes once it had ignited. Or *been* ignited. The spectacle of the flaming *Quori* village they'd overflown in the ultralight only hours before flashed before his eyes.

He began to walk down the beach, the GPS in his left hand, his right flexing on the grip of his Lee-Enfield. An object that he had taken for a piece of driftwood changed shape in the dim starlight as he approached. He stopped. It was the body of a woman, huddled in a semifetal position, her intricately patterned native wrap torn in several places. Three feet away was the turban that matched the wrap—still bound around her head, which had been hacked from her shoulders.

Naji stepped over the dark streams of blood that had run all the way to the waterline, staining the hard sand. There were more bodies—perhaps ten—spread along the entire length of the beach. He wondered that the scent had not yet brought crocodiles slithering from the lake to scavenge the corpses. These unfortunate people—fishermen, by the look of them—had not been dead long.

Madness.

He checked the GPS. The directional arrow was pointing slightly to the right, at a jungled point of land some seventy-five yards past the far end of the beach. The DISTANCE TO WAYPOINT reading was 0.11 miles. Naji peered into the darkness. That was it. The point of land was the second rendezvous location.

Wavelets lapped gently at the shoreline as he gazed out over the lake, its black surface still partially obscured by curtains of mist. He could see the silhouette of the island, a hard dark blot against the softer gloom of the far horizon, and to the south, somewhat closer, another shape, oddly symmetrical, almost tablelike. Exactly what it was, he couldn't tell.

He looked to the east, over the ragged treetop canopy at the back of the clearing. The black sky was just taking on the slightest hint of blue. The second rendezvous location would be good until dawn, and that was still more than an hour away. *Ben-Ya-Min* might be there even now.

Once again, the hunting chant began to vibrate out of the surrounding jungle. They were coming. Naji tucked the GPS beneath his robes, shifted his rifle in the crook of his left elbow, and began to trot swiftly down the beach—keeping to the hard, stony patches of ground and leaving no tracks behind him.

Ten minutes later, the wall of foliage at the north end of the beach rustled and parted. First one . . . then another . . . and another and another Leopard Soldier emerged from the jungle, battle gear steaming with dampness and heat, machine gun at the ready. The singsong chanting had ceased. Gliding forward silently like a rank of dark ghosts, they spread out across the beach and clearing.

The Leopard Soldier nearest the waterline scanned the coarse sand before him. There were no fresh tracks; only the fading boot marks of his own squad and the barefoot prints of the *Quori* fishermen they'd killed the day before. He stepped over the body of the decapitated woman in the patterned wrap with barely a second glance. Possibly she was one of the *Quori* bitches he'd beheaded yesterday. It was difficult to remember. There'd been at least five.

He ran his tongue over the tips of his filed teeth. Whoever the elusive warrior just ahead of them was, he would not escape. Not after shooting three fingers off the flashlight hand of one of his comrades and killing four others outright. When they finally caught him, they would take him alive—whatever the cost—and remove the skin from his body in one piece, ensuring that he remained conscious the entire time. It would take several days, if they were careful. Then, in keeping with their warrior code, they would eat his heart and thereby gain his strength and power, for he had proven himself to be a formidable foe. Even in the modern world of electronic communications and automatic weapons, one had to respect tradition.

It took less than three minutes to traverse the beach. He looked over at his comrades, strung out in a ragged line from the water to the back edge of the clearing. They had found nothing. A hand signal from the corporal at mid-rank, and they advanced into the jungle once again.

The Leopard Soldier stalked the tangled shoreline for another fifty yards before pausing beneath an ancient thornwood tree. Squatting down, he leaned against one of its huge gnarled roots. Ripples lapped at the reeds and drowned brush to his right. Through the twisted trunks just ahead, he could see starlight shimmering off black water. He had arrived at some kind of narrow point jutting out into the lake. A dead end for a fleeing man.

His sharp eyes probed the shadows and hollows of

the little peninsula for a full two minutes before he was satisfied that his quarry had not gone to ground. He had known that the man would not be there. This one was too clever by half to allow himself to be cornered with his back to the water. Licking his filed teeth again, the African moved on.

The Leopard Soldier had advanced nearly fifty yards, entirely bypassing the little point of land, when a large droplet of dark fluid splatted onto the very root against which he'd just been leaning.

Thirty feet up in the ancient thornwood tree, sitting comfortably in the crotch of two immense limbs, Naji wiped his lips on the back of his hand and shifted the wad of *qat* he was chewing to his opposite cheek. Wrapped in his black robes and *burnoose*, his rifle across his lap, he was all but invisible from the ground—even if passing eyes had been attentive enough to look up.

Folding his arms across his chest, he watched as the skirmish line of Leopard Soldiers moved slowly southward through the overgrown swamp. A fine, dignified old tree, this—taller than most of the surrounding vegetation. From it he had a commanding view of the beach and clearing, the lake, and the entire point of land that comprised the second rendezvous location.

He scanned the nearby shoreline. As yet, there was no sign of *Ben-Ya-Min.* But there was still an hour until dawn.

He could wait.

CHAPTER 19

"Take it easy, Nick," Ben said, supporting the older diver's head on his shoulder and keeping his face clear of the water. He continued to kick hard, slowly driving the fishing net and its cluster of Styrofoam floats toward the cylindrical black leg of the jackup rig.

Nick groaned, still clutching his chest. Even in the darkness, his face looked sickly pale, creased with pain.

A few rags of mist drifted slowly beneath the hull of the vessel, which was jacked up a good twenty feet in the air, as the fishing net came to a halt against the three-foot-diameter metal leg. Ben rested, breathing hard, and took stock of the situation.

The leg—one of four—appeared to be unclimbable. Smooth-surfaced, utterly devoid of ready handholds, it was covered in a thick layer of black grease—lubrication for the massive deck-mounted gears that moved it up and down. On either side of it, 180 degrees opposite each other, were two vertical tracks of triangular gear teeth. Even without the accompanying grease, the sloping shape of each heavy tooth would have made it nearly impossible to grasp.

Ben chewed his lip. There was an outside chance

that he could cut a length of the heavier top-line from the fishing net, throw it around the leg, and try to shinny up one of the gear tracks like a lumberjack climbing a tree. But such an attempt would be exhausting and, because of the abundance of grease, quite possibly futile. He couldn't afford to waste what little strength he had left.

"Nick," he said hoarsely. "Wait here. Rest on the floats and keep your face out of the water, okay? I've gotta go for a little swim . . . look for a way up."

Nick nodded, his head low. "I'll be . . . here . . . bro," he whispered through gritted teeth.

Ben patted his shoulder and slipped over the folds of the net into open water. Immediately, the uncomfortable tingling sensation returned to his legs and feet. They hadn't seen any sharks since the flock of water storks had been attacked en masse, but that didn't mean anything. Perhaps they'd lost interest in the fishing net and the clumsily kicking men it shrouded, and chosen to hunt elsewhere.

Rolling onto his back, letting the buoyancy compensator and empty tanks support him, he swam quietly toward the next leg, some twenty-five feet away. As he did so, he inspected the bottom of the jackup's hull, rust-stained and encrusted with the remnants of marine growth—barnacles, limpets, tiny corals—that had been killed by the transition from salt to fresh water. Twin bronze propellers mounted on pivoting industrial outdrives indicated to him that he and Nick had arrived beneath the starboard stern and that the jackup—unlike some that had to be maneuvered around exclusively by tugs—was self-propelled.

Moisture dripped from the hull's chines, the light plopping sound reverberating beneath the suspended vessel as if in an echo chamber. The occasional metallic groan quivered through the night air. Ben became aware of the characteristic smell, so familiar to him, that was common to all oil rigs—a combination of diesel fuel, petroleum solvents, paint, burnt metal, engine exhaust, and sewage.

He arrived at the port stern leg and took a quick circuit around it. As he'd expected, it was identical to the other—no handholds, access ladders, or dangling cables. The bow legs were likely to be the same.

Of course, there was no alternative but to check them out. Rolling onto his back once more, he began to kick his way forward, following the port chine. Droplets of condensed mist slipped off the scarred metal of the hull, fell lazily toward him, and struck the water near his head. *Plop . . . plop-plop . . .*

Without warning, something draped itself over his right shoulder. Some kind of tentacle—thick, rubbery, covered in slime . . .

Recoiling violently, shrugging the thing off his body, Ben whirled to see the intake hose of a deck-mounted water pump, hanging from the port gunwale and extending all the way to the lake's surface.

Jesus.

He reached out and grasped the flexible tube, his nerves buzzing. The hose was about five inches in diameter, made of heavy black rubber reinforced with internal coils of wire. He felt around with his fins. Four feet below the surface, it terminated in a bulbous metal foot-valve—a device that helped to prevent a high-volume water pump from losing its prime.

Not exactly an elevator, but it was a way up.

After slipping off his fins and securing them to a harness D-ring, Ben unbuckled the waist belt of the buoyancy compensator and shrugged his way out of it. The inflated vest and twin tanks bobbed clear, the regulator hoses dangling free in the black water. He had just finished buckling one of the unit's accessory straps around the intake hose when he saw a shark fin rise out of the water not more than three feet away and surge toward him.

Setting his feet on top of the foot-valve, he lunged upward, hugging the slippery hose to his chest. The water was still at mid-thigh. A second lunge, squeezing with all his might, and his tucked-up legs cleared the water by two feet. The bull shark rolled onto its side, its mouth half-open, and lifted its massive head. Its nose bumped the neoprene sole of Ben's left dive boot . . . and then it cruised on past, sinking out of sight.

"Nick!" Ben called, hugging the hose like grim death. "Shark. Stay in the netting until I get to you. I found a way up."

"Great," came the muted reply, reverberating off the bottom of the jackup. "Ain't seen any, myself."

"How are you feeling?"

"I might live, unfortunately."

"Good. Hang tight."

Ben set his jaw and began to shinny upward. The twenty feet to the deck had looked like a long way, but tired though he was, he found himself climbing over the side railing in less than a minute.

The deck of the jackup looked like a thousand others he'd seen—an organized jumble of bottle racks, compressors, generators, pumps, pipes, hoses, and chains. The four-level superstructure that contained the bridge, galley, and crew's quarters occupied the aft third of 120-foot-by-70-foot work deck. Most of the bow was taken up by a mid-sized drilling tower that rose sixty feet into the night sky, and two hydraulic pedestal cranes with telescoping booms were mounted amidships on the port and starboard rail.

The vessel had clearly been ransacked. Storage boxes and deck lockers had been broken open and their contents either removed or vandalized. Even though much of the equipment commonly found on the deck of an oil rig was too heavy to steal and too durable to be easily destroyed, whoever had boarded the jackup after her crew's escape had managed to inflict a considerable amount of pointless damage. The radiators of two large compressors had been smashed in—apparently by sledgehammer—and a portable five-hundred-gallon reservoir of diesel fuel had been holed with a fire ax—the blade of which remained stuck in one of the gashes it had inflicted. Most of the amidships deck was slick with diesel fuel. The smell made Ben's eyes water and his sinuses sting. He wondered why the wrecking party—most likely marauding Leopard Soldiers—had not taken the opportunity to toss a torch or grenade aboard the jackup as they'd left, just for the novelty of watching it go *boom*.

He picked his way sternward over puddles of fuel and items of smaller equipment that had been upended or otherwise vandalized. The first priority was to get

Nick out of the water. He eyed the starboard crane. It was useless—without the engine or generator room's diesels running, the jackup's systems were essentially dead. No power to the hydraulic pump, no hydraulic pressure in the lines. No pressure in the lines, no power to the crane.

He didn't want to leave Nick floating in the fishing net while he went belowdecks to try to locate the power plant that ran the crane hydraulics. And he didn't want to risk having any of the rig lights come on and attract attention from the island or lakeshore, either—a very real possibility if he fired up a generator or engine without first tracking down and shutting off the main breakers. Hell, with all the fuel spilled everywhere, he might blow them both to kingdom come if he put electrical current through a starter switch.

That would make for a quick end to a long goddamn night.

There was a narrow walkway between the starboard railing and the side of the stern superstructure. As Ben moved past the gear housings of the starboard stern leg and onto the vessel's tiny back deck, he found himself looking at a davit—like a small gallows—not more than eight feet high, with a four-foot horizontal boom. A thin steel cable ran through a pulley at the end of the boom from a hand-cranked winch mounted on the davit's upright. Its free end had been spliced into a lifting eye, from which a shackle dangled.

Perfect.

Ben leaned over the stern railing. "Nick!" he called down through the drifting fog.

"Yeah."

The fog thinned and, twenty feet below, Ben was able to make out the top of his friend's head—the rest of his body was still swathed in fishing net—next to the rig's leg. The half dozen rotting white Styrofoam buoys supporting the mesh bobbed around him like a cluster of skulls. As Ben watched, the thick, torpedo-shaped back of a bull shark arced around Nick about six feet away, circling.

"There's a hoisting davit here. I'm going to lower the cable to you with a life ring on it. Get it under your arms and I'll crank you up to the deck, got it?"

"Sure, sounds good."

"It'll be there in a second."

"You might wanna hurry up. I got three bull sharks sniffing in close to me down here. They're *baa-a-ck . . .*"

"They like you. Hang on and don't move."

Ben lifted one of the stern life rings from its supporting hooks on the aft bulkhead of the superstructure and quickly shackled its short tethering strap to the end of the davit cable. Flipping up the release catch on the hand crank, he swung the davit boom outboard and began to pull wire off the spool, lowering the life ring. It clunked into the greasy leg once as it neared the surface, and then Nick caught it with an upraised hand. Pulling it down over his head, he got it under his arms and nodded upward.

Engaging the spool's catch, Ben began cranking rapidly. The davit creaked and gave a little under Nick's weight as he emerged from the water, finned feet dangling. At the moment he was lifted clear, one of the big bulls thrashed its tail across the surface, as if in frustration.

"Not this time, boys," Ben breathed, watching the predator's fusiform shape plane off into the black depths. He bore down on the crank handle, and a minute later Nick was hanging like a grappled corpse just below the end of the davit boom. Reaching out and seizing his belt, Ben swung him inboard and hauled him over the rail. The older diver released his grip on the life ring, slipped out of it, and collapsed in a sodden heap on the metal plates of the back deck.

"Some fuckin' rescue," he grumbled, giving Ben a weak grin.

Ben squatted on his haunches and set a hand on Nick's shoulder. "How're you feeling?"

"Like I been keel-hauled."

"How's the cut lip?"

"Cut lip?" Nick frowned.

"Yeah, the one you said you bit, remember?"

"Oh, that. Yeah, yeah . . . it's fine. Still bleedin' a little is all."

"Huh." Ben paused, his eyes moving over Nick's pallid face, over the wiry body—too thin for its large frame—beneath the clammy clothing. "You're right, buddy. They didn't feed you very well after they got hold of you."

"Nope."

"You're as skinny as a rake."

Nick coughed and smiled, wiping his mouth with the back of his hand. "Well, you know what they say. Bein' overweight ain't healthy." He sat up. "Whew. I'm feelin' better. A little cold, maybe. How about you? You've been swimmin' a lot more than me tonight."

Ben stood up. "I've got a bit of a chill. Not bad,

though. This suit helps a little, and the air's warm.
Come on." He extended his hand. "Let's have a look in
the quarters. Maybe we can find some dry clothes or
blankets and get you warmed up."

Nick clasped the hand and heaved himself to his
feet. "Okay."

Ben led the way forward around the starboard side
of the superstructure. "Unless there's a dinghy or
lifeboat on this rig," he said over his shoulder, "we're
going to have to go back in the water and swim for
shore. We can't stay here." He looked around the work
deck as they arrived at the front of the superstructure.
"And I've gotta tell you: I don't see a single damn boat
anywhere."

Nick hacked up a wad of phlegm and spat. "You
won't, neither. We took the dinghy and both lifeboats
when we abandoned the rig three weeks ago. If they're
still in one piece and not stolen, they're over there on
the shore." He pointed toward the east, where the
predawn sky was lightening noticeably above the trees.

"Great," Ben said. He looked around at the scattered
equipment. "Maybe we can cobble together some kind
of raft. Keep us clear of the sharks. Hell, it's only got to
hold together for half a mile."

"How 'bout a couple of planks lashed across a few
of these empty oil drums," Nick suggested. "That'd·
w-w-work, wouldn't it?"

Ben nodded. "Yeah . . . if we can't come up with
something better." He glanced at the older diver. "Hey.
You're shivering. Come on, let's go inside. There's got
to be some dry clothing in there."

"May—maybe some f-f-food, too." Nick clasped his

arms over his chest. "Maybe even a g-g-goddamn cigarette."

They crossed the deck and entered the superstructure through the main hatch. The watertight door was hanging open, the thick glass of its small porthole crazed by fractures radiating from a single bullet hole. The first cubicle to the right off the interior passageway was the toolpusher's office. It looked as if a tornado had gone through it.

Every filing drawer had been wrenched from its cabinet and dumped on the deck. All the wall maps and whiteboards had been torn down, along with a number of framed pictures. The office's two computer monitors had been ripped from their stations and smashed against the port bulkhead. Improbably, an electric single-cup coffeemaker sat on the back corner of one desk, untouched. It held a mug—full to the brim with black coffee—bearing the words "The Answer Is Still NO!" rendered boldly in red.

"That's a t-toolpusher's cup if I ever s-s-saw one," Nick said, his teeth chattering. He picked up the mug and sipped. "Fuckin' awful. Cold and bitter. Just the w-w-way I like it."

"I'll bet." Ben ran a hand over the wall-mounted VHF radio set. It looked as if a rifle butt had smashed in its front panel. On the deck beneath it were the remains of six portable battery-powered VHF handsets, commonly issued to deck personnel. All had been crushed into fragments. "Shit. Thought we might have a chance of calling my guys, wherever they are now. Maybe there's still a working radio up on the bridge."

"I was kinda wonderin' why you d-didn't have a radio with you on an operation like th-this," Nick said.

Ben shrugged. "I had to dive to come and get you, remember? I didn't have one that would stay waterproof under pressure. All the comm gear is on the floatplane. This was strictly a short-notice rescue, bud. I had to make do with what gear I had."

"L-like James Bond w-without Q."

"Yeah, something like that." Ben put a hand on Nick's upper arm. "Come on. Let's go to the crew's quarters. Get some dry blankets for you while I do a couple of things."

"W-wait." Nick pulled open the only drawer remaining in the toolpusher's desk. "I remember that drilling-chief bastard. He s-smoked like a f-furnace." He rummaged at the back of the drawer. "*Ahhh!*" Triumphant, he withdrew his hand, holding a crumpled pack of Dunhills. "Jackpot. There's even a b-book of matches."

"What more could a guy want?" Ben commented. "Coffin nails and caffeine. You're one happy camper. Now let's go, before you die of exposure right here."

Nick lit one of the British cigarettes with a shaking hand and followed Ben out of the office and down the passageway. The last door on the port side opened onto a six-bunk dormitory. Like the toolpusher's office, it had been ransacked, bunks overturned and metal lockers ripped from the walls. Mattresses and bed linens were piled haphazardly on the deck, and a variety of personal articles lay scattered around the room.

"Hey, look." Ben stooped and pulled a navy blue coverall from beneath one of the mattresses. "Strip off those wet clothes and put this on. It should be big enough."

"Okay," Nick said, puffing out a cloud of smoke and taking the garment.

Ben thought for a moment. "I'm going up to the bridge. If I can find a radio, I'll try to get hold of the guys on the floatplane. They're probably over there on shore, at the backup rendezvous location. If they could taxi out here and pick us up, it'd save us another swim—or a paddle, if we build a raft." He paused again, frowning at the bulkhead. "Hell. Maybe we should just get back in that fishing net and keep kicking. It's only a half mile to shore. We don't want to waste any more time getting out of here."

"Well—" Nick began. Then he doubled over and clutched his chest, the cigarette dropping from his lips. "*Aaagghh!*"

Ben caught him as he sagged to his knees, his head bowed. "Hey, hey. You all right?" He helped his friend lie back on a nearby mattress. Nick's teeth were clamped together, his face a mask of pain.

"Ch-chest hurts like a b-bitch," he managed to grunt. "Comes and . . . goes."

"Lie still," Ben pulled a blanket from a pile of bedding and drew it up over Nick's huddled body. Then he placed two fingers on the side of the older diver's neck just below the hinge of his jaw. "Huh. Pulse is pretty steady—that's good. No fluttering." He regarded Nick in puzzlement. "Still hurt?"

"Y-yeah, goddammit. Might ease up if I lie here a b-bit, though."

"Okay." Ben stood up and let out a long sigh. "Okay.

Let me see if I can find our ride. You just lie there until I get back, all right? I'll be up on the bridge for a few minutes."

Nick nodded, still grimacing. "Sounds g-good. I don't th-think I'm gonna be able to swim right now."

"Okay, buddy, take it easy. I'll get us out of here some other way."

Ben left Nick on the mattress and went out into the passageway. Jogging down it, he came to a set of stairs opposite the toolpusher's office. Mounting them two at a time, he climbed rapidly to the fourth level above the deck, which, as he'd expected, housed the jackup's bridge.

What he hadn't expected was that it would be riddled with bullet holes: the forward windscreen completely shot out; the interior panels, bulkheads, and much of the bridge console equipment—including the navigation and radio gear—utterly ruined. He touched the shattered dials and meters of both the shortwave and VHF units. They were useless.

Cursing under his breath, Ben sat down in the captain's chair and propped a foot up on the chromed ship's wheel. The damp air blew gently through the paneless frame of the forward window, cooling his face. All of a sudden he felt tired. Very, *very* tired. They were still a hell of a long way from getting clear of Shark Lake. A long way from getting out of Bisotho.

He looked out over the shifting, dissipating banks of fog and mist on the surface of the lake, at the bluing dawn sky to the east, at the black island fortress from which they'd made their escape. It looked much closer from the jackup's bridge than it had from the water—

stark and ominous. When he squinted hard and concentrated, Ben was almost certain he could see the tiny figure of a sentry passing beneath one of the two rampart lights. The dull hum of the fort's electric generators was just barely audible.

He glanced at his watch. Four-twenty. Naji and Head had to be waiting at the secondary rendezvous. They would stay there at least until the sun poked its upper rim above the tree canopy. Ben shifted in the captain's chair. They needed to get out of here *now*, while they could still rely upon the cover of darkness. But Nick couldn't swim anymore—not with what looked like a bad heart—and trying to put together and launch a raft that would hold them both seemed unrealistic at best. If there were just some way to contact Naji and Head . . . to tell them he and Nick were aboard the rig. Some way to let them know they could easily motor out, pick them up, and then fly the hell out of this godforsaken—

Ben gazed across the dark water at the rampart lights atop the island fortress. Naji, at least—if not Head—would be looking toward the lake, searching for any sign of him. Looking toward the island . . . past the blacked-out jackup . . .

There was a rechargeable flashlight mounted on the bulkhead next to the jamb of the starboard door. Out of the line of sight, it had escaped the machine-gun fire that had raked the rest of the bridge. Rising from the captain's chair, Ben plucked it from its holder and flicked the thumb switch. It came on instantly, throwing a powerful white light on the aft bulkhead.

He switched it off, then turned and began to climb the angled ladder that led to the bridge roof.

High in the thornwood tree, Naji had settled into a waking doze, his *burnoose* pulled around his face to foil the clouds of bloodthirsty mosquitoes. Although he was completely relaxed, his eyes still roved over the surface of the lake, alert for any disturbance that could indicate a swimmer. He was concerned. Still no sign, and it was less than two hours until dawn.

He dipped into the little bag of *qat* beneath his robes and pushed another fingerful of the aromatic leaf into his cheek. Chewing slowly, he stretched his sore neck. *Shaitan's beard*. Perhaps he was too old to—

A flash of light, where previously there had been only darkness, caught his eye. It came from the indistinct, table-shaped structure that stood in the lake less than a mile southeast of the fortified island. What new trouble was this? Leopard Soldiers, widening their search? What else could—

There it was again. A brief pinpoint of white light, small but clear, above the remaining night mists. Two quick flashes, then a long one. And now . . . only darkness once again. Slowly, Naji began to count, getting to fifteen before the light reappeared. *Flash-flash. Flash-flash. Flash.*

Darkness.

It was most definitely a signal. The hair on the back of his neck began to prickle, and he glanced down at the shadowy jungle below. Perhaps the soldiers hunting him had decided to concentrate their sweeps, go over old ground more thoroughly . . . coordinate their search from an observation post on the water . . .

Flash-flash. Flash-flash. Flash.

And again, the same five-flash pattern. It had to mean—

Naji blinked suddenly. *Five flashes?*

His own words to Ben echoed in his head: *"This episode has come to be known in the history of my tribe as The Affair of the Five Flashes . . ."*

It was all he could do not to shout for joy. Under the folds of the burnoose, his swarthy face split into a grin of delight.

Ben-Ya-Min!

There were fishing canoes lying on the beach not one hundred yards from where he sat. Slinging his rifle, over his shoulder, Naji spat a stream of *qat* juice and began to descend the ancient thornwood tree with all possible speed. Clearly, *Ben-Ya-Min* could not come to him, as planned. Therefore, he would go to *Ben-Ya-Min*.

Ben flashed the sequence eight more times over five minutes, then lowered the light and climbed back down into the bridge. If Naji was watching, he'd have seen the pattern, and he was too sharp not to recognize it. He'd have Head motor the ultralight out to the rig, pick them up, and they'd be on their way back to steak, beer, and bed in Krumake.

And if not . . . if something had happened to them . . .

Well . . .

Ben drew a deep breath and exhaled slowly.

Later for that.

CHAPTER 20

Maggie Fenzi stood apart from Sass and Olssen, staring down the empty dirt runway from which the ultralight carrying Head, Ben, and Naji had taken off only scant hours earlier. The VHF radio and miniature satellite uplink unit lay on the hood of the Land Rover, silent, as they had been all night. Though dawn was little more than an hour away, the sky to the west was still dark. And as empty as the runway.

"You son of a bitch, Nick," Maggie said aloud, her voice trembling. "You're never, *ever* going to come through for me, are you?" She turned and faced Sass and Olssen across the vehicle's hood. Her eyes were bloodshot, vacant. "I should have remembered. The only thing about Nick Fenzi you can count on is that you can't count on him for anything."

Sass felt heat flare in her cheekbones. "Excuse me, but there's more than one person to consider here. I *do* count on Ben Gannon, so if you don't mind, we'll wait a bit longer without making useless comments, O Great Voice of Doom. It's still early."

Maggie lit a cigarette and shook her head. "They're not coming back. I can feel it."

"Oh, shut *up*!" Sass exploded. "Jesus Christ, you

drag us all into this mess, and before it's even had half a chance to be over with you're throwing up your hands and writing everyone off! You don't have the faintest idea what's happened to Ben, Naji, Nick, or that—that—stoner pilot . . . Head! They're not even late yet. They might fly over those trees two minutes from now. Or maybe they won't get back into Kuballa until later in the day. Who knows? Even if they *are* late, it doesn't mean they won't make it."

"You don't know Nick like I do," Maggie said hollowly. She blew a stream of smoke.

"But I know Ben!" Sass replied. "And he doesn't get into things without having a pretty good idea of how to get out of them." She pointed a finger at Maggie. "So if you can't say anything helpful or hopeful, just *shut the fuck up*!"

Maggie snorted and turned away, her cigarette poised between her fingers, maroon thumb-talon snapping across the filter. *Click . . . click . . . click.* She walked off several yards across the runway.

Crossing her arms, Sass spun and leaned back against the Land Rover's front fender. She glanced up at Olssen, who was standing near the passenger door, and angrily knuckled a tear from the outside corner of one eye. "Damn."

The tall Norwegian frowned at her sympathetically. "Easy now."

Sass nodded and took several deep breaths. "I'm okay."

Olssen reached into his pocket, retrieved a stick of gum, and began to unwrap it carefully. "What we'll do is stay here, as we agreed, until an hour past sunrise. If

Ben has not returned by then, and we haven't heard anything on the VHF or by uplink, then you will accompany me to the harbor where my chartered seaplane is. If the pilot is still willing—and he looked like a can-do sort of fellow—we'll head over the border mountains to Shark Lake. If we should happen to spot Ben and company, and they are anywhere near the lake or river, there is nothing to prevent us from dropping down quickly and picking them up . . . as long as they are not being held captive."

Sass blinked at him. "Please don't even think that, Berndt."

The old Norwegian diver smiled. "All right."

She looked over her shoulder at Maggie, who was standing on the runway about thirty yards away, facing westward and smoking. "What about her?"

Olssen sighed, his brows knitting. "If she can control herself, she can come, too," he said. "After all, this is about her husband, isn't it? I don't suppose I can leave her out of the mix."

"That's decent of you," Sass remarked, "especially considering what you've been through with Nick . . . and her own warm and fuzzy attitude."

"*Ya*, well . . ." Olssen shrugged. "She may find herself tossed from the plane if she annoys me much further. I've already had to tolerate one Fenzi. Two is more than anyone should have to endure in the space of a single month."

"Huh." Sass looked up at the sky for a moment, then changed the subject. "How'd you find this seaplane for charter? The best Maggie could do was Jefferson Deadhead Jones and his Incredible Flying Jalopy."

Olssen chewed his gum slowly. "I suspect her choice had something to do with cost. Money—getting more of it—seems to be her major preoccupation. It's not cheap to charter a twin-engine seaplane nearly the size of a DC-3. I'm doing it as a company expense. What the hell, I'm already going down the tubes. What's one corporate aircraft charter more or less?"

Sass scowled at her feet. "I can't believe there was a perfectly good plane available and I let Ben take off on this wild-goose chase in that rattletrap kite. I really wasn't thinking."

"You were both thinking about an old friend who was in trouble," Olssen said. "The desire to help can blind us to reality sometimes. Affect our judgment."

Sass turned, put her hands on the hood of the Land Rover, and gazed at the lone figure of Maggie Fenzi standing out on the dark, deserted runway beneath the empty sky.

"*Ya*," she sighed.

After one last look around the ruined bridge, Ben descended the stairs to the main-deck level of the superstructure. His mind was whirling with "what-ifs." What if Naji and Head didn't show up with the ultralight? What if Nick's condition worsened? What if they found themselves stranded on the jackup in daylight? What if—no—what *would* happen when the soldiers manning the fort discovered that Nick was gone? How long before they decided to have a look at the rig, once they were satisfied that their escaped prisoner was no longer on the island? Ben paused near the tool-pusher's office and gazed out across the deck at the old fort, still nearly invisible in the darkness but for the glare of its two rampart lights. At night, he supposed, the jackup, with no lights at all, was virtually impossible to pick out from the island.

A thought occurred to him, another possible avenue of escape, but he dismissed it out of hand. He would give Naji and Head time to motor out with the ultralight. They *had* to have seen his five-flash signal.

He proceeded down the passageway to the room where he'd left Nick, wondering what he was going to do if the older diver actually suffered a major heart attack. Having Nick keel over dead would kind of make the point of the whole exercise moot—and he was most definitely looking *bad*.

Ben stepped through the door of the crew quarters and stopped. The mattress was empty; the blanket he'd pulled up around his friend tossed aside in a heap. Nick was nowhere to be seen. A crushed Dunhill lay beside the pile of wet, filthy clothes he'd shed, still smoldering.

Puzzled, Ben looked back out into the passageway. "Nick?"

There was no answer.

A dull boom echoed through the abandoned jackup.

The hair prickled on the back of Ben's neck. He bent down and picked up the broken-off arm of a wooden chair that had been thrown against the aft bulkhead of the crew quarters. Stepping through the doorway, he began to retrace his steps, as quietly as he could, back toward the toolpusher's office.

He stopped by the stairwell. "Nick?"

Silence.

Drawing a breath, he went to the main-deck hatch and looked out. There was no sign of movement, on the rig or on the surrounding water.

Another dull boom echoed through the vessel, vibrating the steel plate beneath the soles of Ben's neoprene boots. The sound came from below, from deep in the jackup's hull. He listened as it died away, then stepped past the opening's watertight door and walked across the work deck to a lower-level access hatch near the starboard rail.

The manhole-type hatchway was substantially narrower than his shoulders; he had to hunch and wriggle to make it through, his feet slipping on the rungs of the slender steel ladder. Expecting to drop into near-total darkness, Ben was surprised to see that the passageway directly beneath him was illuminated by a soft red glow. Of course: the last thing Olssen's crew had done before abandoning the jackup was shut down the power plants. In the absence of generator electricity, the emergency belowdecks battle lanterns had kicked on, each powered by its own individual battery. Even now, after several weeks, they were still giving off a fair amount of light.

Ben's neoprene boots touched down softly on the grating of the internal passageway. Narrow—barely three feet between bulkheads—and low, with pipes and electrical conduit running just overhead, it stretched off fore and aft along what appeared to be the entire length of the hull. Ben got his bearings. The engine room would be toward the stern, washout pumps and other drilling-operations support equipment in the bow compartments.

Clunk. BOOM.

The sounds came from the bow, as near as Ben could tell. Flexing his fingers on the broken chair arm, he began to pad noiselessly along the passageway. It was difficult to see detail very far ahead. Between each fading battle lantern was a large pocket of shadow. He had a fleeting impression of creeping through a torch-lit medieval dungeon in an old movie. All the scene lacked was Boris Karloff in an executioner's hood.

There was activity of some kind in the forward pump room. Ben glided up along the inboard bulkhead, paused, and peered cautiously through the entrance hatchway. The compartment was small, subdivided by racks of metal shelving. On the shelves were numerous plastic-wrapped core samples, numbered and tagged. There was a broad steel table in the center of the room, welded to the deck between the housings of two immense drill-water pumps. A large flashlight, switched on, had been hung from an overhead hook, pointing down. On the table was a single core sample—a cylindrical plug of mud three inches in diameter by about four feet long. The plastic wrap had been ripped back, and a section of the core sluiced away with water, leaving a scattering of gravel and stone chips. A mud-stained pillowcase lay on one end of the table next to a water bucket.

There was another loud boom, as if something heavy had fallen to the deckplates, accompanied by a round of cursing. A moment later, Nick came staggering around the end of the nearest bank of shelves, carrying a second core sample in his arms. Muttering to himself, he dropped it onto the tabletop and began tearing at the plastic.

Ben stepped into the pump room. Nick was too pre-occupied by what he was doing to notice him. As Ben watched, he examined the core, marked off a two-foot section by scraping out a couple of gouges with the tip of a screwdriver, and reached for the water bucket.

For several seconds, he stabbed repeatedly at the core sample with the screwdriver, breaking up the compacted sediments between the gouges, then sloshed water from the bucket over the chunks and began to paw through the resultant muck with both hands. More water. More pawing. Then a triumphant grunt. Nick held up a small pebble between his thumb and forefinger, squinted at it under the light, grinned, and slipped it into the pillowcase.

Ben watched him repeat the procedure three more times before stepping forward. "Hey."

Nick flinched as if jolted out of a dream. He stared at Ben for a moment, then licked his lips and bent back over the table.

"Almost done," he said breathlessly, rummaging through the wet mud.

Ben moved up opposite him and looked down at the sticky mess covering the tabletop. Nick slopped more water from the bucket over the remaining chunks and crumbled them with his fingers, feeling through the soup.

"*Yeahhh*," he intoned, raising a mud-slicked hand. Another pebble, half the size of a man's thumbnail. He grinned across the table at Ben, the glare of the suspended flashlight playing over his pale, dirt-streaked face.

"What are you doing?" Ben asked quietly.

Nick dropped the pebble into the pillowcase and began to rake his hands through the liquid mud again. "Playin' out the hand I was dealt," he rasped. "Game got interrupted about three weeks ago. Now I'm finishin' it."

"I don't follow."

"Well, it's like this, bro," Nick said. "You know how, maybe two or three times in your life, something good comes your way for no reason? Something tasty, a real score. As if capital-L Life—after shitting upon you repeatedly, day after day, week after week—suddenly decides to throw you a big, meaty bone?"

Ben stirred. "Mm."

"That don't ever happen to me," Nick went on. "I work like a fuckin' dog, do a good job for a company— and they fire me so they can bring five younger guys along to take my place. 'Thanks for bein' an ace employee, Nick, ol' buddy—now fuck off.' I make good money in diving for thirty years, but I just can't get a break when it comes to investin' it, lendin' it, or hangin' on to it. My old lady spends it like our last name was Rockefeller, not Fenzi. Plus, just for shits and giggles, I start havin' trouble with my right lung. Hurts like a bitch sometimes." He coughed, smiled, and spat a wad of phlegm onto the tabletop. Under the overhead light, it was foamy and bright red against the chocolate brown mud. "Ain't been to the doctors. Don't want to know. What're they gonna tell me, huh? Stop smoking? Too late. I'm in trouble? I already know that. So who needs the overpaid, holier-than-thou bastards, anyway?" Nick raised his hand, displaying a pebble. "Ha. Another one. Pretty big, too."

Ben looked him up and down. "I thought you were having a heart attack in the water," he said slowly.

Nick shook his head. "Nah. That was just to get you to stop. Sounded like you wanted to swim right by the jackup. I couldn't let you do that. Not when we were so close to it."

Ben was silent. Then he pushed a finger through the muck on the tabletop and nodded toward the pillowcase. "What are you looking for here?"

"Yee-haw," Nick said, coming up with another tiny stone. "These little beauties. Alluvial diamonds." He started to put it into the pillowcase, then hesitated and held it out toward Ben. "Here. This is for you."

"What?"

"I'm serious. Thanks for comin' and gettin' me out."

Ben ignored the diamond. Instead, he leaned over the table and looked Nick in the eye. "You're not out of here yet. And if you keep fucking around in the mud much longer, we may not get out at all." Anger showed on his face for the first time. "What kind of goddamn game do you think you're running on me?"

"I told you," Nick rasped, spitting again. "I'm just playin' out the hand I was dealt, that's all. You pass these chances by when they come your way, you wind up a lifelong loser. Not me, bro. I know a good thing when I see it." He raked another pebble out of the muck. "There ain't a lot of 'em here, but what's here is high quality.

"We were coring, and in one small area where we

sank the drill, we must have hit a pocket in the prehistoric river that used to run through here, where the lakebed is now. This one little pocket—one little two-foot layer—was packed with diamonds. They weren't anywhere else, and we drilled over three hundred cores. Just a fluke of nature that they were concentrated there. And two cores' worth ended up on the jackup. I was the only guy onboard who recognized what they were. I said to myself, 'Self, this is your lucky goddamn day—your once-in-a-lifetime royal flush at the million-dollar game. Don't fucking blow it.' And I ain't, for a change."

Ben backed away from the table, watching coldly as Nick raked his fingers through the mud again and again, breathing hard, his eyes glassy. "I'll be on deck," he said. "And when my guys get here with the float-plane, I'm leaving. If you want to leave with us, be there."

He turned and stepped out through the hatch into the narrow, red-lit passageway.

CHAPTER 21

Ben had returned to the bridge of the jackup and was studying charts of Shark Lake and northern Bisotho by flashlight when he spotted the dark shape of a dugout canoe emerging from the mist off the port forward quarter. Alarmed, he snapped off the light and ducked low behind the steering console. The canoe drew nearer, and as it did he was able to make out the distinctive shape of *burnoose*-style headgear in the silhouette of the lone paddler.

He trotted quickly down the four-flight staircase to the main deck, hurried forward past the clutter of wrecked equipment, his feet skidding on spilled diesel fuel, and reached the bow handrail just as the slender dugout slid up beside the port leg.

"Naji!" Ben called softly.

The paddler's shrouded head went back, and even in the darkness Ben could see the white-toothed grin. *"Ben-Ya-Min!"*

"Are you all right?"

"Yes, Allah be praised! And you, my brother?"

"Still in one piece."

"Inshallah! We are not so easy to kill, you and I, eh?"

"By a hair, I guess," Ben said. "I don't know what

happened to you, but I think maybe I'm just lucky." He looked around the deck. "There's a spool of heavy line up here. If I toss the end down to you, can you tie off the dugout and climb up?"

"Most assuredly, my brother."

"Okay. Wait a second."

Ben stepped away from the gunwale, tipped the nearby spool of three-quarter-inch manila up on its edge, and rolled it over to the handrail. A quick clove hitch secured the end of the line to the top rail. Then, stripping off a half dozen big loops, he glanced down, nodded to Naji, and let the coils of coarse rope drop into the Yemeni's outstretched arms.

Naji knotted the end of the rope around the canoe's forward thwart, slung his rifle over his shoulder, and began to climb toward the gunwale, hand over hand, his black robes flowing around him as he moved. Once again, Ben was impressed. The big man was as agile as a cat. In less than ten seconds, his hand slapped the top rail and he clambered over onto the main deck.

"Beard of the Prophet," Naji said, breathing hard, "I am not the youth I once was, I fear."

"You couldn't tell by watching," Ben remarked. He extended his hand. "Good to see you. Thanks for still being here."

Naji shook with him. "But where else would I be? Did I not give you my word that I would help?" He grinned again. "The perfect signal, by the Great Sands! There could be none other than you on this festering lake that would use the sequence of the Five Flashes." He chuckled deep in his throat.

"Glad it worked," Ben said. He looked over the rail

at the drifting mists, "Where's Head? Where's the plane?"

Naji's swarthy face fell. "Alas, my brother. The pilot, I fear, is lost. I did my best to keep him from harm after we were ambushed by a squad of those same soldiers we saw murdering villagers on our flight into this bog of a country. But he was clumsy as I have never seen clumsiness in another human being, and had no gift for covering ground silently. For some reason known only to himself, as we were evading our pursuers, he decided that it would be a good idea to seize a nearby venomous serpent with his bare hand, whereupon he shrieked like a Sanaa market woman, gave away our position, and fell into a disgusting mud pit. I could not save him, though I tried, as the black thug soldiers were not slow to pinpoint the source of his outburst, may Allah the Compassionate and Merciful carve the livers from their—"

"Head's dead?" Ben cut in. "Where's the plane?"

"We had to leave it at the point where we were ambushed, my brother," Naji explained. "On the shore, some distance north of here. It is quite possible that the soldiers, curse them, have found it." He turned his head and spat viciously. "Had we still the services of the idiot pilot, we might yet sneak past their incompetent patrols, see if the craft is still there, and make our escape by air." He raised an eyebrow. "Is it too much to hope, *Ben-Ya-Min*, that among your many skills you might also have knowledge of how to fly?"

Ben sighed. "It is. I don't have a clue. I'd just get us killed." He paused for a moment. "Damn. Poor guy. He's a Deadhead now, for sure."

"Eh?"

"Never mind." Ben looked at the lean Yemeni. "You're sure he's dead, right?"

"He was still alive when I left him, my brother," Naji said. "But judging from the proximity of the machete-wielding soldiers who were in the process of charging us, I do not think he remained that way for long. I tried to draw them after me as I fled, but there was little else I could do."

"Shit." Ben sat down on the spool of manila and stared at the deck. "No pilot, and no plane." He was suddenly engulfed by a wave of fatigue and rubbed a hand across his aching eyes.

Naji leaned against the handrail, unslinging his rifle and cradling it in its customary position in the crook of his left elbow. "What of you? It has been several hours since you departed from the floatplane. I take it you did not find your friend. And how come you to this place?"

Ben looked up. "Wrong. I found him."

"Dead?"

"No, alive. And I got him out. He's down in the bow-pump room right now."

Naji's dark face split into its familiar grin. "But that is wonderful news, my brother! Is he injured? Why is he not here with you?"

"He's okay for the time being," Ben said. He hesitated. "We've had a slight difference of opinion. Turns out he had his own agenda involving some alluvial diamonds."

Naji's blue eyes narrowed. "Eh?"

Without going into personal details, Ben quickly

outlined what Nick had told him about the diamond-studded core samples, and how the older diver had faked a heart problem to trick Ben into stopping at the rig instead of swimming on to the second rendezvous point. Naji listened, his face grave, and when Ben finished, he scowled.

"Your friend has a strange way of demonstrating his gratitude for your efforts on his behalf, my brother."

"*Our* efforts," Ben corrected. "You're in this mess, too, and a third man who risked his neck to fly us in here is dead. And Nick's down there in the pump room picking little fucking stones out of mud pies."

"I have seen it before," Naji said. "Diamonds, gold, money—they make some men forget what is truly valuable in this life."

Ben got to his feet, his face flushed, angry. "Fuck him. I told him when the floatplane arrived I was leaving. The dugout's what we have. Come on, we're getting out of here. We'll try to make the Kuballan border overland. Think we can do it?"

Naji shook his head slowly. "Not at this time. There is increasing patrol activity on the lakeshore. They are looking for me, I am sorry to say. Apparently, they have not taken kindly to having four of their number killed in a single night."

Ben blinked in surprise. "You killed *four* men?"

"Four murderous thugs who were trying to kill *me*," Naji said, remembering the decapitated *Quori* woman and the other slashed victims in the fishing village. "I will not dignify such bloodthirsty vermin by continuing to refer to them as soldiers. Oh, and one rather large crocodile."

"*Crocodile?*"

"Indeed, my brother. The creature had taken a liking to the pilot, Allah keep him."

"Christ."

Before Ben could think of anything else to say, Naji went on, "You are angry with your friend Nick, are you not?" He didn't wait for an answer. "You think you will walk away from him now, having freed him from his captivity and brought him this far. Tell me. This friend of yours—did he or did he not save your life at one time?"

"He did."

"Ah. Then, as we determined earlier, you owe him a life debt. Now, consider, even though this man who once saved your life has become distracted by thoughts of worldly riches, if you leave him here and we two escape, what is likely to happen to him?"

Ben looked at the blue glow of the dawn horizon. "He probably won't make it out alive if they catch him again."

"Then, my brother, the debt is not paid." Naji shook his dark head sympathetically. "You cannot leave him to die, no matter what he has done."

Ben drew a deep breath. "I know," he said.

There was a clattering sound from the far side of the deck, followed by a string of curses. Ben and Naji turned to see Nick emerging from the narrow access hatch amidships, the knotted pillowcase in one hand. He'd bumped into an empty oxyacetylene cart, knocking it over.

"Your friend, I presume," Naji muttered, observing him with interest. "The man we sought."

"Right," Ben said. He folded his arms and leaned back against the handrail.

Nick came shambling across the deck in his baggy, mud-stained coveralls, the pillowcase clasped tightly beneath one arm. "Hey! Told you I'd be up soon, bro." He looked Naji up and down briefly. "Hiya."

Naji nodded in response as Ben spoke. "This is Naji. He's one of the men who volunteered to come along with me to get you out of that old fort."

"That's great," Nick said, wiping his mouth on the back of his hand. "Appreciate it." He glanced around, then back at Ben. "Where's everyone else? You said there was more than one guy."

"There was one other man. He didn't make it. He's dead."

Nick's expression sobered slightly. "Oh."

"Yeah," Ben said, looking at him hard. " 'Oh.' And there's no floatplane. He was the pilot."

"Huh." Nick blew out a long breath. "That ain't real convenient." He dug in the breast pocket of his coveralls and extracted one of the battered Dunhill cigarettes. "Got a light?" he said to Naji.

The lean Yemeni regarded him impassively. "No."

"Too bad. Oh, hey—never mind. I got it." Nick stepped over to a cutting rig chained up to the handrail, turned on the gas to the torch head, and scratched a flint striker in front of the burning tip. A three-inch cone of blue flame appeared with a soft *snap*. Smiling, Nick raised the torch and lit his cigarette. "Ahhh," he said, shutting off the gas. "Tastes good."

He looked expectantly at Ben, smoke trickling from his nostrils, his eyes veined and puffy. "So how do we get out of here?" He took the small pillowcase from beneath his arm and shoved it into one of the deep side pockets of his coveralls. "I'm ready to go home," he said, forcing a thin smile.

A long moment passed in silence before Ben answered. "Aren't we all. Let's go up to the bridge. I've got an idea that might work, if we don't waste too much more time getting started, but I need charts and maps to explain it to you." He turned his eyes to the east. "We've got to have darkness to cover our movements, and it'll be dawn soon."

CHAPTER 22

It couldn't be.

It wasn't possible.

Aghast, the big sergeant of Leopard Soldiers once again shined his powerful flashlight down into the old well where the white American had been imprisoned for the past two weeks, probing the shadows with its beam. He could see every square inch of the dank, stony floor, the entire surface of the small pool of black water that occupied nearly a third of the pit's bottom.

The American was not there.

Sweating, he glanced at his watch. Seven-oh-six. In precisely nine minutes, he was supposed to be at the White Colonel's door with the prisoner in tow.

And unless the man suddenly popped to the surface of the pit's tiny pool, that was not going to happen. The sergeant of Leopard Soldiers licked his filed teeth. Good fortune tended not to follow those who disappointed the White Colonel.

In desperation, he shook the rusty black-iron bars of the grille that covered the pit opening. A hundred years old and corroded to half their original thickness, they were still solid enough to support the weight of a one-ton truck. The padlock that secured the grille was new. The walls beneath the lip of the pit were smooth, vertical limestone, with nary a finger- or toehold to be seen.

There had been soldiers in the fort's inner quadrangle all night, walking to and fro. The American could not have escaped unnoticed, even if he had somehow climbed the thirty feet to the top of the well, which was impossible, and gotten through the grille, which was even more impossible.

It was well-known to anyone familiar with Bisothoan history and military lore that the pool in the prison pit of the old French fort, for all practical purposes, led nowhere. During the previous century, many native captives, desperate to escape, had attempted to swim out, never to be seen again. A man needed gills to survive underwater for so long and the senses of a bat to find his way out in pitch-blackness—if indeed there was a passable route to the lake. And then there were the sharks. The old rumors about fins rolling up in the pit's pool had not been substantiated in recent years, but there were certainly roving packs of large *tiburi*—locally notorious for their ferocity— haunting the open waters of the lake.

The sergeant glanced again at his watch. Seven-twelve.

Slowly, he rose out of his crouch, glared at the surrounding Leopard Soldiers, and began to walk across the quadrangle toward the stone stairs that led up to the fort's second level. Those who had been on guard near the pit stepped hurriedly out of his way, avoiding his gaze. Whatever else happened, they could expect harsh disciplinary action in the near future.

Feeling like a condemned man, the sergeant began to climb the stairs, his mind racing to come up with the words he would use to tell the White Colonel that his prisoner was missing. It was still racing as he walked down the second-level corridor, and as he turned to face the door of the colonel's quarters.

Seven-fifteen.

The sergeant of Leopard Soldiers squared his shoulders and knocked.

"Come!"

He opened the door and stepped inside. Amon Klegg was fully dressed in bush boots, black jungle trousers, and black military fatigue shirt. The contrast with his crew-cut white hair and pale gray eyes gave him an icy Teutonic appearance, as if he had just walked off a Nazi recruiting poster. He was loading bullets into a small ammunition clip, his automatic pistol lying on the nearby tabletop, the flap of his hip holster open.

The sergeant came to attention, his eyes locked straight ahead. Klegg looked him up and down, his pinched face fusing into its usual scowl, and finished pushing the short shells into the clip. Then he picked up the automatic, inserted the clip into the bottom of the handgrip, and banged it home.

Smack.

The sergeant flinched visibly.

Klegg holstered the pistol and secured the flap. Then he placed his hands on his hips and walked forward until only a few inches separated him from the other man.

"You were ordered to bring the American to my quarters," he said softly.

"Yes, *sah*! I—"

"Shut up."

"*Sah!*"

The big sergeant swallowed hard, but remained rigidly at attention. Klegg sidestepped around him, gliding on his bush boots, staying close, staring at him with his pale viper's eyes.

"My order has not been carried out," the White Colonel said. "I do not care why." He moved around the sergeant, staring unblinkingly as he did, until he was directly in front of him again. For a few seconds, he stood motionless. Then, with the speed of the snake he resembled, he struck the sergeant a vicious blow on the side of the face with his hard open hand. The big man gasped and reeled slightly.

"Stay at attention, Sergeant," Klegg said, turning away. He picked up a towel off the end of his bunk and wiped his hands. "Now. You may report."

Trembling with both rage and fear, the sergeant drew several deep breaths, his chest heaving, before he spoke: "Sah! I mus' inform the Colonel that prisonuh has drowned himself, *sah*! Try to swim out well bottom. No chance, sah."

Klegg's eyes narrowed. "Where's the body? Eh? *Eh?*"

"Uh—no body, *sah*! Man try to swim deep underground. Get lost, die down in hole." The sergeant looked directly at Klegg for a split second. "No body, *sah!*" he repeated.

Abruptly, Klegg stalked forward and struck the

man on the opposite side of the face. *"That* is for boring me with such gross stupidity, eh?" he shouted. *"Eh?* How do you know the American drowned if you don't even have his body? *Eh?"* He hit the big man a third tremendous crack on the other side of his face.

Something inside the sergeant snapped. He was a warrior, and a warrior did not permit any man—*any man*—to slap him about like a fourth or fifth wife. He had endured months of such treatment from the White Colonel. With a strangled howl, he ripped the short machete he wore at his side free of its scabbard and raised it high.

Amon Klegg backpedaled on his feet like a welterweight, putting a couple of yards between himself and the enraged sergeant, drew his automatic in one smooth motion, and shot him rapidly six times in the chest. The big man who had been his aide for over two months stumbled backward, his machete clattering to the stone floor, and sprawled at full length on his back, dead.

Klegg stepped over the spreading pool of blood, ignoring the sergeant completely, and opened the door to the passageway. Several Leopard Soldiers were running toward his quarters, alerted by the shots. The White Colonel stopped them with a wave of his hand. "The mutineer on the floor in there attacked me. Get rid of him."

He proceeded past the bewildered soldiers without another word. Descending the external stairs that led down to the fort's inner quadrangle, he got the attention of the men around the rim of the prison pit by firing a single shot into the air. The Leopard Soldiers drew back as Klegg stomped off the last step and across the intervening space, the very image of suppressed fury.

"Come to attention, damn you!" he snarled. There was a simultaneous slapping of leather against rubber as the dozen soldiers near the pit got the heels of their jungle boots together fast.

Klegg snatched a flashlight from a nearby guard and beamed it down through the iron grille. The Leopard Soldiers stirred uneasily in the predawn darkness as the White Colonel circled the pit, checking it from every angle. When at last he snapped off the light and stalked back toward them, the expression on his narrow face would have frozen boiling water.

"Three men—you, you, and you—get down into that pit and check the pool. Take ropes, swim down as far as you can, eh? I want to know if there's a body in there, and if there are any bottom or side passages that might lead out."

The three soldiers he'd selected stood immobile, their eyes growing wide in their scarified ebony faces. The pool, every *Malmoq* warrior knew, was a place of dead men. Klegg's malevolent expression twisted even more. "*Now*, you black bastards, *now*!" he bellowed, spittle flying from his thin lips.

The trio broke ranks and sprinted toward the pit. One man ran for a large equipment container beside the fort wall and lifted out a coil of heavy rope. Another prepared to lower an old Jacob's ladder that was the pit's sole means of entry and exit. The third fumbled with the padlock on the iron grille.

Klegg wheeled and faced the remaining men, gesturing with his pistol. "The rest of you—search the fort and the entire shoreline of this bloody island. Check the shallows, eh? Two men—you and you—go up on the ramparts and spot for the others with searchlights." His voice degenerated into a reptilian hiss. *"I want the American found!"*

The Leopard Soldiers scattered in a cloud of dust, shouting to each other. As they swarmed through the fort and out the main gate onto the rocks, Klegg followed the two men he'd designated as spotters up one of the stone stairways to the ramparts. The island was small. The American would be located. Of that he was sure . . .

Unless, of course, the man actually *had* swum into some kind of black hole leading off from the pool, gotten lost, and drowned. In that event, it was unlikely his body would be recovered. Still, Fenzi hadn't seemed to be the suicidal type. He was too much of a hardscrabble Yank for that.

He could not have climbed out of the pit through the grille by himself. It was possible that he might have been able to bribe one or more of the guards with tales of diamond caches—Americans of Fenzi's cut, in Klegg's experience, were notoriously effective con men—but that was unlikely. You couldn't trust a *kaffir* as far as you could throw him, but Klegg had confidence in his soldiers' fear of him. It was early yet. They wouldn't be souring on him for another few weeks, when familiarity turned to hatred and then to open mutiny.

By that time, he'd be gone. His face twisted in amused disgust, He'd been through the same process as a contract mercenary for vile little fourth-rate African governments on nearly a dozen previous occasions. It was always the same. Flog the available black rabble into some kind of military competence, touch off their bloodbath revolution, and then take the money and run before they lost their fear of the dreaded "White Colonel" and tried to cut his throat. It would be no different this time in Bisotho. As usual, the remuneration had been far less than promised. But here was one Nick Fenzi, poking around the shores of Tiburi Kunga in the middle of a military terror campaign, with a valuable alluvial diamond in his pocket and a distinctly larcenous gleam in his eye.

Klegg walked slowly along the upper catwalk of the old fort, looking out across the misty black surface of the lake. Below, on the rocks outside the walls, the Leopard Soldiers were checking every crevice, every inch of shoreline—every possible hiding place. The two men operating the rampart spotlights shouted and pointed, swinging the powerful beams this way and that.

It would take the better part of two hours to complete a thorough search. The White Colonel paused at the end of the catwalk and gazed down at the scrambling soldiers below. It would be a shame if Fenzi could not be found. There was more than a single diamond connected to him. Klegg could feel it.

An hour and forty minutes later, Klegg was stalking slowly amongst the Leopard Soldiers reassembled in the quadrangle, his face screwed up in disgust. "Not a sign of him, eh? Not a single sign." He paused, turning on the heel of his boot. "*A man does not—just—disappear!*" he shouted.

The last soldier of the three who'd been ordered to check the prison pit and pool was just emerging at ground level, clinging to the top of the Jacob's ladder. Stripped to the waist, barefoot and soaking wet, he rose to his feet and came to attention beside his two companions. Klegg strode across the quadrangle and fixed him with his pale stare.

"What did you find, eh? *Eh?*"

The man shrugged, his muscular blue-black torso gleaming wetly in the first rays of the early-morning sun. "Could see nothin', sah. I swim way down, mebbe twenty—thirty feet . . . no man there, *sah*. An' walls of pool widen out, mebbe fifteen feet down." Anxiety registered on his dark face as he recounted what he'd just done. "A big empty there, *sah*. No light, can feel nothin'. Without rope tied to me, I don't get back out again." He shivered a little, even though the sun was already quite warm.

"Bloody hell!" For a moment, Klegg felt an uncontrollable urge to strike the swimmer as he had the big sergeant. You never knew about *kaffirs*. The miserable savage might have been too afraid to do a thorough search of the pool and spent the past hour and a half diving to a depth of five feet, just to keep himself out of trouble.

He did not hit the man, however, merely wheeled around and confronted the rest of the Leopard Soldiers. "You will search again!" he shouted. "And I want one of the boats to circle the island this time, checking the shoreline from the water! Go!"

He turned once more to the swimmer. "Get back down there," he snarled. "This time, make sure you do a complete check, eh? Don't come up without finding something."

It was useless to argue with the White Colonel, no matter how unreasonable his orders were. The swimmer and his two companions saluted and made ready to clamber back down into the prison pit.

Klegg watched as they disappeared into the dark hole for the second time, the muscles of his jaw working. His fingers closed around the hard diamond nugget in his pocket, rolling it back and forth. Analyze, analyze—go over every detail of the previous night, the last time Fenzi was known to be in the pit.

The American *might* have drowned trying to swim to freedom . . . but somehow Klegg didn't think so.

CHAPTER 23

"I told you," Maggie said, her voice dull. "I told you they weren't coming back."

The Land Rover jounced as it pulled away from the dirt airstrip, Sass at the wheel with Olssen beside her in the front passenger seat. The tires spun in the gravel as she accelerated the vehicle toward the whitewashed buildings of Krumake, bright under the warm light of the newly risen sun.

"Yeah, you did," Sass muttered through clenched teeth. "Now keep quiet about it." She steered the Land Rover through a tight turn, its rear wheels sliding out in a controlled drift. A plume of dust billowed up behind the vehicle as it roared toward the city, continuing to gain speed. From the backseat, Maggie blew a silent stream of cigarette smoke at the windshield, eyeing Sass blankly in the rearview mirror.

"Easy," Olssen rumbled, touching her elbow. "It's only a short ride to the harbor. We have time."

Sass eased up on the gas pedal slightly. "Right," she said. "Sorry."

The ultralight was nearly three hours overdue, with no communications coming through from Ben or Head on either the VHF or satellite uplink. Trying to make contact from the runway had been fruitless. The VHF, they already knew, would not transmit over the mountains into Bisotho, and the e-mail message they'd sent out via the uplink unit had generated no response.

Sass had felt her concern grow until it threatened to turn into panic—an emotional reaction she despised because her own experience told her it was worse than useless. It made one blunder around in an unproductive funk instead of thinking clearly and taking effective action. Thank God Berndt Olssen had turned up with an alternative to sitting and waiting. His controlled, reassuring presence was the antidote to Maggie's zombielike negativity. It was unbelievable. Overnight, she'd turned from a can-do woman with a purpose and a plan into a dazed, self-pitying child. Her initial confidence, Sass realized, had been an act— a thin veneer hiding someone coming apart at the seams.

"Turn here," Olssen said, pointing to the left. Sass braked and took the Land Rover down the side road he'd indicated—barely missing a ramshackle beverage cart loaded with large glass coolers of red, green, and purple drink. The startled vendor hopped about in the Rover's dust, shaking his fist.

The whitewashed buildings whipped by as they sped along the narrow, winding road through Krumake's oldest section. Pedestrians stepped rapidly aside as Sass laid on the horn, clearing a path. The foot traffic thickened as they wended their way farther into the city, forcing her to slow down. Near the harbor, they were reduced to a mere walking pace. An impenetrable mass of people, goats, chickens, and dogs crowded the Land Rover's front bumper.

"This gate," Olssen directed, waving a hand at the green-shirted guard. They entered a harbor compound that Sass recognized as a continuation of the same customs yard in which she, Ben, and Naji had moored the *Teresa Ann*. She looked eastward down the waterfront, past chain-link fences and rows of pallets stacked with goods and machinery. Only a couple hundred yards away, the familiar bluewater ketch lay quietly on her lines next to the dock pilings.

Sass parked the Land Rover near the main customs building. Several uniformed officials were crisscrossing the yard, but did not pay them any particular attention. Olssen got out, shut the door, and headed for the customs office. Sass glanced at Maggie in the rearview mirror—then took the keys out of the ignition, exited, and followed him.

The interior of the office was air-conditioned and well lit, with a distinctly modern feel—right down to the potted palms and imitation ficus trees. It was divided into two sections, a large waiting area near the entrance and, behind a half curtain of multicolored bead strands, an inner chamber containing a huge desk of dark, polished thornwood. Sass followed Olssen through the bead curtain, glancing around. Then she smiled. Behind the massive furnishing, looking as globose and jovial as ever, was Mr. Kikkononikakka.

At the sight of Olssen and Sass, he rose from his ornate wooden armchair and spread his arms wide, beaming all over his incredible black moon face. "Ahh,

Mr. Olssen!" he exclaimed. "Here exactly on time, and you bringing the pretty lady Miss Sasha Wojeck—delightful, delightful, by Jove!" His expression metamorphosed into one of sympathetic concern. "Not hearing yet from Mr. Ben Gannon, and Mr. Naji al-Tahl, and Mr. Jefferson Deadhead Jones, hmm?" His small, shrewd eyes flickered from Sass to Olssen and back again.

The Norwegian motioned Sass to sit down in one of the two hard-backed chairs at the front of the desk. In response to her questioning look, he smiled, and said: "Very little goes on in Krumake, and indeed the whole of Kuballa, that Mr. Kikkononikakka does not know about."

"Uh-huh," Sass replied, taking the seat. She scanned the wall behind the desk as Olssen and Mr. Kikkononikakka shook hands. It was covered by a multitude of framed photographs, most of them eight-by-ten blowups. In every one, Mr. Kikkononikakka was standing center stage with his arm around an exotic, absolutely gorgeous Kuballan woman dressed in flowing traditional raiment and turban, or with his hand on the shoulder of a long-legged, long-armed, ovoid-bodied native man nearly as tall as he. The pictures of the men usually included some kind of vehicle or heavy machinery—cranes, trucks, cargo boats, and aircraft—both military and civilian.

Mr. Kikkononikakka settled his prodigious upper body into the armchair and smiled. "Ah, lovely lady noticing great bunches of pictures behind me, yes?" He half turned in his seat and made a sweeping gesture with one arm. "The hugest joy of my life, don't

you know? Wives and sons of Kikkononikakka! An
abundance of sons, by the Lord Harry!"

"I'll say," Sass remarked. "How many are there?"

"Goodness gracious!" Mr. Kikkononikakka enthused, waving his hands and rolling his eyes toward
the ceiling. "Dutiful fertility of nine beautiful wives
producing fourteen sons, yes indeedy! All grown now,
tall and handsome like Papa!" He smacked both palms
into his chest and grinned like a happy jack-o'-lantern.

"Congratulations, Mr. Kikkononikakka," Sass said.
"They're all fine-looking people."

"Thanking you," the big customs official replied.
"Miss Wojeck as generous as is lovely, absolutely and
positively! Now," he said, directing his good-humored
gaze at Olssen, "gentleman from Norway still desiring
the charter of one seaplane with pilot?"

"*Ya*, correct," Olssen said, nodding. "You already
have my company check made out to Kikkononikakka
& Son Air Services, Limited. If possible, we'd like to
leave for our overfly of Shark Lake immediately."

Sass blinked at the rotund African. "You own an air-
charter service? I thought you were a government customs official."

Mr. Kikkononikakka beamed, opening one of a
dozen leather-bound ledgers piled neatly along the
edges of his desk. "Oh, yes, yes! Dedicated civil servant, me! Excellent pension in five more years, don't
you know? But—Great Jumping Jehosephat! So many
wives and sons needing money, money, money! So, by
thunderation—one son, one father-and-son company,
ha ha!"

Olssen leaned toward Sass. "Mr. Kikkononikakka is

something of an entrepreneurial wizard, *ya*? All of his
sons were trained in various capacities by the Kuballan military during their compulsory national service.
When they were discharged, he set them up in busi-
nesses of their own, based on their individual special-
ties. It's quite the local family empire, really."

Mr. Kikkononikakka clapped his hands. "Kikkononikakka & Son Air Services, Limited! Kikkononikakka &
Son Engine Repair, Limited! Kikkononikakka & Son
Dredging, Limited! Kikkononikakka & Son Roofing
and Aluminum Siding, Limited! Oh, so many more, I
say! Almost losing count myself, woe is me!" He threw
his fantastic head back and roared with laughter.

"Ah-*hoooooo*!" He sighed, settling down and wiping
tears from the corners of his eyes. "Now, business." He
flipped through the ledger he'd opened. "Yes, by thunder. Overnight electronic clearing of check just fine
and dandy, Mr. Olssen." Making a quick notation with
a gold pen, he slapped the booklet shut. "Seaplane is
serviced and ready," he announced, rising to his feet
once again. He smiled and indicated a small door in
the corner of the room. "My son Koko waiting to fly
you over Tiburi Kunga. Excellent pilot, Koko, by Jove!
Fighter pilot in Kuballan Air Force. Trained in French
Mirage jets, don't you know! But still"—his face became grave—"much trouble in Bisotho. I tell him, careful, careful! No unpleasantnesses or accidents with
valuable charter customers, blast and confound it!" He
grinned again suddenly. "You have nice ride, eh?
Right through there . . ."

"Thank you, Mr. Kikkononikakka," Olssen said,
getting up.

"I'll be right along," Sass said. "I need to find out what Maggie's going to do." She looked pointedly at the Norwegian.

The old diver shrugged and nodded. "It's best if you handle it, I think. I'll be waiting out on the dock, by the side gates."

"Okay." With a final smile at Mr. Kikkononikakka, Sass headed for the main door of the customs office.

Maggie was still sitting in the backseat of the Land Rover, a fresh menthol slim poised in her right hand. Sass opened the door and slid in behind the wheel. Turning, she put a forearm up on the driver's headrest and waited until Maggie met her eye.

"We're flying to Bisotho," Sass said evenly, "and we're leaving in the next few minutes. We're going to fly over Shark Lake and down the upper half of the Tiburi River to try and find the guys. Berndt says you're welcome to come if you want to."

She waited. Maggie averted her eyes and stared out the windshield. She looked terrible, closer to eighty than fifty. Her wavy brunette hair was limp and tangled, falling over her forehead. Her complexion was a pale gray, her cheeks hollow, and her eyes bloodshot with great black circles beneath them. Mascara had mixed with tears and run over her cheekbones, giving her the appearance of a sad mime. In an unconscious, habitual motion she brought the cigarette to her lips, drew deeply, and returned her smoking hand to its familiar cocked position. Her maroon thumbnail snapped across the menthol's filter as she exhaled. *Click . . . click . . . click . . .*

Simultaneously, as if squeezed out on cue, two immense, glistening tears welled from her eyes and ran down her haggard face. Her hands and lips trembled. When she spoke, her voice was a ravaged croak.

"I . . . *can't*," she whispered. "I just can't do it anymore." The maroon thumbnail clicked repeatedly. "I won't let him let me down again." She looked at Sass. "Have you ever come to realize that the man you threw your lot in with, whose back pocket you stuffed all your hopes and dreams into, whose every goddamned promise you believed in because you *wanted* to . . . was nothing but a useless, drunken, hustling, drugged-out bullshitter who was never going to amount to anything?"

Ben's face flashed before Sass's eyes. "No," she said.

Maggie failed to stifle a wracking sob. "Lucky you," she managed to choke out, her free hand going to her mouth. It took a moment for the spasm of despair to pass. "I'll be here," she said finally. "I'll wait for you right here . . . but I can't go."

Sass regarded her in silence, thinking. Then she pulled the ignition keys from the pocket of her jeans and put them on the seat beside Maggie. "Go back to the hotel. I'll come find you there." She turned to leave, putting a hand on the door handle, then paused and glanced back. "You love Nick, don't you," she said.

Maggie's dark eyes, wet and haunted, locked on to hers. Very slowly, trembling, she nodded twice. "No," she whispered.

Sass's face softened. For a long moment, she sat with Maggie in the Land Rover. Neither of them spoke. Then she opened the door, got out, and walked off toward the side gate of the customs dock without looking back.

Olssen and another man, who looked like a middle-weight double of Mr. Kikkononikakka, were standing at the edge of the dock, talking quietly. Ten feet below, tethered to the nearest piling by a long painter, floated a small rubber dinghy. Both men turned to acknowledge Sass's approach.

"This is our pilot," Olssen said. "Mr. Koko Kikkononikakka. He says 'Koko' will do just fine. He's the senior Kikkononikakka's eldest son."

"One of many," Koko added, beaming like the spitting image of his father, which he was—minus one hundred pounds. His English, although stilted, was better than that of his parent. "I have many brothers. Moko, Poko, Topo, Bopo, Dopo, Lopo, Foto, Hoto, Lomo, Somo, Julius, Erving, and Abe."

"Julius, Erving, and Abe?" Sass repeated.

Koko's grin went from ear to ear. "Obviously, you can tell that my father is a fan of American basketball," he said, "and, in particular, of the great Doctor J."

"Uh-huh," Sass replied, nodding. "And Abe?"

"Aha! My father is a great admirer of Abraham Lincoln."

"Right, right," Sass said. "Because he freed the slaves."

"Well, yes," Koko asserted. "But more so because he wore a nice hat. My father has always admired a man who can wear a formal top hat with panache. Yes, panache—I believe that is the word. He himself has a collection of over two hundred such hats."

Baffled by this information, Sass could only nod.

Olssen, amused, took the opportunity to cut in. "Well, now—perhaps we should be off, *ya?*"

Sass nodded again. "*Ya.* And Maggie isn't coming."

"Somehow, that doesn't surprise me."

The younger Kikkononikakka descended an iron ladder to the dinghy and assisted first Sass, then Olssen into it. Then he seated himself in the stern next to an ancient Seagull outboard, fired it up with one pull of the starter cord, and in a few seconds had the little boat skimming over rills and wavelets toward the center of the harbor.

Rapidly, the dinghy bore down on an elegant but rather dated-looking seaplane that was tethered by its nose to a large orange mooring buoy. Sass looked it over, intrigued. About forty feet in length, with broad, high-set wings that spanned perhaps fifty, it had a stubby, solid aspect that gave it an air of reliability, if not speed. Sass was reminded of the old DC-3s and Dakotas of World War II vintage, many of which were still flying after half a century.

Unlike Head's much smaller ultralight, this aircraft did not sit above the water on an arrangement of struts and pontoons, but directly on it, like a boat. In fact, she noticed, the forward portion of the fuselage was hull-shaped—as was, it seemed logical to assume, its entire underside. A small sponson-type float, supported by a light framework, hung beneath each wing about two-thirds of the way outboard; its obvious purpose to prevent a tip from burying while landing or taking off.

Two immense radial engines, with triple-bladed propellers spread like the open talons of a great bird, were mounted in the leading edges of the wings, port and starboard above the cockpit. The cockpit's forward windscreen was oddly shaped—split into two rounded panes that gave the aircraft a distinctive, arched-eyebrow appearance. The seaplane's aluminum skin was weather-beaten, half-silver and half-red, with the words "Kikkononikakka & Son Air Services, Ltd." painted along the side of the fuselage in bright blue letters.

"Nice plane," Sass called to Olssen over the buzzing whine of the Seagull. "It looks like a getaway car from one of those old gangster movies."

"*Ya*," Olssen replied, nodding. "Not far wrong. That's a Grumman Goose—one of the best small flying boats ever designed. They started building them in the thirties, and even now there are a considerable number of them still in the air."

"Can you tell how old that one is?"

"Sixty-three years!" cut in Koko from the stern. His toothy grin was nearly as wide as his father's. "Manufactured by the Grumman Aircraft Corporation of Bethpage, Long Island, New York, in 1938. U.S. Navy duty from 1940 to 1957. Transferred to the U.S. Department of Fish and Wildlife for domestic operations from 1958 to 1971. Acquired at auction and rebuilt by the Mormon Church of Salt Lake City, Utah, for use as an African missionary plane, 1972 to 1989. Abandoned in the Kalahari Desert from 1990 until 1994, when it was recovered by Kikkononikakka and various sons, reconditioned to proper specifications—including a complete rebuild of the twin 450-horsepower Pratt & Whitney Wasp R-985 radial engines—and placed in service with Kikkononikakka & Son Air Services, Limited of Krumake!"

"And there you have it," Olssen told Sass.

"I'm impressed," she replied, and meant it.

"*Ya.* A fine old plane with an honorable service record."

"And a knowledgeable pilot . . . which, after Jefferson Deadhead Jones, is a nice change."

Olssen readied the painter as Koko throttled back the outboard and the dinghy coasted up to the port side of the Goose. Sass grabbed the edge of one of the small passenger-cabin windows as the inflatable bumped the riveted aluminum fuselage. After killing the engine, the tall Kuballan pilot clambered forward, flipped back the latch of the plane's small side door, and pulled it open.

Sass climbed aboard, followed by Olssen. Koko secured the dinghy to a length of line floating off the mooring buoy before disembarking and kicking the little inflatable away from the aircraft's side. Stooping over to keep from hitting his head on the low ceiling of the small passenger cabin, he made his way forward to the cockpit.

Leaning against one of the seven aluminum-framed, leather-covered seats, Sass noted to her surprise that the cabin floor was made of mahogany, so brightly varnished that she could see her reflection in it. In fact, the entirety of the plane's interior, restored to its original condition, bespoke an era when brass, leather, and wood—not plastics and artificial fabrics— were the construction materials of choice in aircraft, automobiles, trains, and ships. It felt good—more human, somehow.

"Please come forward," Koko called back from the cockpit. "Mr. Olssen, you take the copilot's chair." He indicated the seat beside his. "Miss Wojeck, you sit in this auxiliary fold-down seat between us. Belts buckled, please."

He pumped a priming lever on the console several times and pushed an ignition button. A high-pitched whine began. Sass could see the blades of the starboard propeller, at the top edge of the pilot's side window, begin to turn. Then the engine coughed once and roared into life, the three blades whining into a single silvery disk.

"Shark Lake, one hour," Koko said, the ever-present Kikkononikakka grin creasing his wide face. He pumped a second priming lever and punched the ignition button for the port engine, watching his rpm and oil pressure gauges intently as the big Pratt & Whitney belched out a cloud of smoke and began to growl in unison with its twin.

Two minutes later the venerable old Grumman Goose was accelerating down the same shipping channel that had brought Sass, Ben, Naji, and the *Teresa Ann* into Krumake Harbor only days earlier. It plunged gently up and down over light Indian Ocean swells as it approached takeoff speed, then lifted into the air, engines at maximum rpm. Water streaming from its keeled underhull, the Goose banked hard, climbing steeply, and curved off toward the low border mountains to the southwest.

CHAPTER 24

Klegg was leaning against the northeast capstone of the old fort's ramparts, smoking one of the six Russian Sobrani cigarettes he permitted himself each day, when the two sergeants overseeing the second search for Nick Fenzi approached. Through narrowing eyes he watched them come, harsh smoke trickling out of his nostrils. He could tell by their body English that they had found no sign of the missing prisoner.

The pair of sergeants halted and came to attention, eyes shifting in every direction but his and looking extremely uncomfortable. Klegg removed the Sobrani from between his lips. He took his time, saying nothing, making them sweat. It was something he did very well.

"Report," he said finally.

The sergeants glanced at each other. The one on the right cleared his throat.

"Prisonuh not here, *sah*." He stared rigidly at a spot just above Klegg's head.

Amon Klegg did not move. Even the smoke from his black cigarette seemed to freeze in midair. And yet, despite his complete stillness, the malevolent energy he exuded was enough to turn the two strong men's knees to water. Both were picturing the corpse of the senior sergeant who had somehow displeased the White Colonel when, quietly, he spoke.

"Dismissed."

Saluting and turning, they practically ran back along the catwalk and down the rampart stairs to the quadrangle.

Klegg finished his Sobrani and crushed it under the heel of his bush boot. Fenzi, apparently, was well and truly gone. And whether he was dead or alive, his connection to a possible source of alluvial diamonds had gone with him. Annoying, to say the least.

Analyze, one more time. The American had been in the pit as recently as the early hours of this same morning, when two guards had heard him raving to himself and ordered him to keep quiet, emphasizing their command with a burst of machine-gun fire. They had not hit him, of that they were certain. They had seen him dive to the floor of the old well, then turn his head to look up at them.

Little else of note had occurred. There had been that irritating report from one of the rampart sentries, undoubtedly walking his patrol in a marijuana-induced state of lethargy, of lights in the water, but that was all. The fool had probably been gazing addlebrained at star reflections or some such—

Dive to the floor of the old well . . .

Dive.

Lights in the water.

Klegg's back teeth ground together as the idea formed in his mind.

Divers?

If there was a way out of the prison pit through some little-known underwater passage, it could only be negotiated successfully with the aid of diving gear. Fenzi had had nothing of the sort. But, possibly, someone could have accessed the pit from the outside. Someone highly skilled at diving and underwater navigation, armed with prior knowledge of a route beneath the island and a considerable amount of nerve. The British SAS had such skills, as did the American SEALs. Fenzi was an American, but not one of such consequence that he merited a SEAL operation.

Or did he? Klegg waved over one of the rampart sentries with a jerk of his arm. The man came running, his battle gear jangling on his harness.

"Get Sergeant Mapfumo. Tell him I want the American's passport. It's in my quarters on the top right corner of my desk."

The sentry knocked his heels together, saluted, and dashed off toward the staircase.

Uncharacteristically, Klegg removed his 10 A.M. Sobrani from its elephant-ivory cigarette case several hours earlier than usual and lit it with a wooden match. He gazed out across the lake, now mist-free in the midmorning light, and inhaled slowly. Who was this Nick Fenzi? Some important U.S. senator's derelict son? There was no shortage of those. Some kind of political operative—perhaps CIA—nosing around as field operatives tended to do? Unlikely. Fenzi didn't fit the mold, was too much of a fly-by-night soloist to be plugged into the Company. Still . . .

"Passport, *sah!*"

Klegg stirred and looked up. Sergeant Mapfumo

was standing at attention, holding out the little dark blue booklet.

"What took you so long?" the White Colonel snarled, snatching it. "Dismissed."

As Mapfumo whirled and disappeared, Klegg thumbed through the travel document. There was the man's picture, taken probably eight or nine years ago. He had resembled a lower-class bum even then, needing a haircut and a shave. Klegg shook his head slightly. Americans—most of them seemed to take pride in being ill-bred, like the collection of mongrels they were.

Birthdate: February 10, 1944. Birthplace: Baton Rouge, Louisiana.

Occupation: Commercial diver.

Klegg sat bolt upright. He had been looking at several commercial diving hardhats just recently . . . where had it been . . .

Of course. On the jackup boat that had been core sampling for the former Bisothoan government. He'd toured it briefly after the crew had fled, had allowed his Leopard Soldiers to take what they wanted, and had noted the expensive-looking fiberglass-and-stainless-steel helmets hanging in an alcove near the rig's drill floor. There'd been diving support aboard. And Nick Fenzi had been captured on the shore directly opposite the jackup boat's position, where it had been sitting abandoned since the first week of the military coup. . . .

Fenzi must have been one of the rig's commercial divers. Klegg flipped the pages of the passport. There was the most recent stamp: the unmistakable work-entry crest of the previous government. The American had been admitted to Bisotho on a temporary work visa. He'd escaped from the jackup with the rest of the crew, then attempted to return to it—in the heart of a bloody terror campaign. What for?

Slowly, a scar of a smile cut across Klegg's pinched face.

For *diamonds*.

The foreign drillers must have found diamonds during their core-sampling operation, but had been unable, for some reason, to take them along during their initial escape. Perhaps Fenzi had come back with accomplices, other divers, in an attempt to reboard the jackup boat. Yes—and other commercial divers would have had the skill, perhaps the geographic knowledge, to get into the prison pit via an underwater passage beneath the island and then make their way out again, taking their comrade with them. Klegg paused his rapid-fire thinking momentarily. If they'd come for diamonds on the jackup, why had they bothered with Fenzi? He hardly seemed worth the added risk. Perhaps the grubby-looking American had better friends than he deserved.

Or maybe he really was dead in the pool of the prison pit, the victim of a misguided attempt to swim to freedom—or simply driven to suicide by despair. It didn't matter. If there were any diamonds for the taking, they were almost certainly aboard the jackup—unless Fenzi's accomplices—if indeed he'd had any—had managed to get away with them. *Improbable.* They would have been intercepted by roving land-based Leopard Soldiers engaged in terror operations all along the shores of Shark Lake.

Klegg rested his mind again for a moment, drawing on his Sobrani. The sum total of the mental exercise was that the abandoned jackup boat was the most likely place to look for the brothers and sisters of Fenzi's single alluvial diamond. Beautiful. A possible fortune, sitting right under his nose for over two weeks, less than a mile away.

He turned to gaze at the familiar sight of the deserted rig standing in the middle distance to the south, experiencing something akin to inner glee—an emotion that rarely visited him.

The Sobrani fell from his parted lips.

The jackup, which he had casually observed only the previous evening, was gone.

Ben glanced at his watch and thumped the heel of his hand against the twin throttle levers on the jackup's control console, making sure they were all the way forward. The wind coming through the broken-out windscreen of the bridge ruffled his hair as he nudged the steering wheel slightly to port and tapped a finger on the dual tachometers. The diesels were redlining at 5500 rpm. He considered running down to the engine room and removing the governors that limited each power plant's rotation, but thought better of it. For the sake of another thousand rpm, it wasn't worth blowing the engines up through the main deck.

The Tiburi River was approximately four hundred yards wide in its upper reaches—twenty miles of fast-flowing water between Shark Lake and the old British locks bypassing the Tiburi Cataract. On either side of the jackup, thick walls of impenetrable green jungle slipped past at what Ben estimated to be—given the awkward vessel's maximum speed and the flow rate of the river—in excess of ten knots.

Three or four knots of that was current, which made it difficult to keep the barge-shaped jackup centered in deep water. Ben found himself additionally motivated to pay close attention to the helm by the sight of numerous jagged rocks protruding from the river's shallows—black-stone fangs waiting to bite through steel plate as if it were soft meat.

As he'd hoped, the sound of the island fortress's own diesel-powered electric generators had masked the noise of their escape. After locating and isolating the main circuit boxes so as not to inadvertently flash any lights in the predawn darkness, he and Nick had had no trouble firing up the main engines. The jackdown of the hull to the water and the gearing up of the four huge steel legs to their fully retracted positions had taken a bit longer to accomplish, but had gone off without a hitch. Fortunately, the bridge compass had not been smashed, and Ben had immediately gotten the jackup under way on a heading that would take them to the entrance of the Tiburi River.

Naji was leaning over the chart table, examining the map on which Ben had hurriedly sketched their escape route. "Umm. This secondary road that leads northward from the lock system to the Kuballan border. I make it forty-two miles through unsettled jungle, my brother. Why are you so certain that this is our best way out?"

Ben spun the wheel as a large eddy caught the jackup's hull and began to draw it off course. "Precisely because it's unsettled," he said. "Look—what's going on in Bisotho, right now? An ethnic war. A terror campaign. One tribal group is trying to kill or drive out the other. In order to conduct a terror campaign, you have to have someone to terrorize—so it doesn't make any sense that there'd be much military presence on this secondary supply road, at least not any we wouldn't be able to evade. There's a vehicle depot at the locks—a rebuild shop, you know? I remember someone mentioning it to me a few years ago when I was in Bisotho working for British Petroleum. Funny the things you remember."

"Thanks be to Allah that you did."

"Yeah, well—I figure there's a good chance we can find a useable truck or jeep at the depot, and scrounge enough fuel to make it forty-two miles. Even if it only gets us halfway up the road, twenty miles overland on foot is better than forty."

"Indeed," Naji responded. He looked back down at the map. "An excellent maneuver, *Ben-Ya-Min*. We use the river to move away from the area in which we— I—have stirred up the rebel sold—*executioners*, curse them. A twenty-mile lateral movement, and then an overland sprint to safety." His eyes flashed and he grinned, totally in his element. "It is good. It is good."

Ben glanced at the opposing shores anxiously. "I hope so. We need to make the locks before someone notices that the jackup isn't where it should be. I don't know how organized the soldiers in that old fort are, but between losing Nick and seeing the jackup missing, my bet is that there'll be somebody coming after us pretty quick. I just hope we don't run into any trouble right at the locks, and that nobody catches us on the river. This thing's pretty conspicuous. The sooner we're off it, the harder we'll be to find. But for the time being, it's our fastest way downstream."

"As to our chances," Naji said, "luck favors the bold and well-prepared, does it not?" He tossed back his swarthy head and laughed like the desert rogue he was. "Whatever the outcome—*inshallah*! Allah wills it."

Ben nodded. "I reckon he does."

There was a thump just outside the starboard bridge door and Nick staggered into view, clutching his mud-stained pillowcase. Propping himself up on the bridge wing handrail, he coughed viciously for a solid thirty seconds, spitting red, and then proceeded through the doorway.

"*Ugghh*," he groaned, holding a hand over his abdomen and sitting down on one of the bridge stools. The knotted pillowcase, which he'd cut down to size with a knife, dangled between his legs,

"What's wrong with you now?" Ben asked, glancing at him. "Lung?"

Nick shook his grizzled head, looking deathly pale. "Nah. No more than usual." He burped. "I got a stomachache."

"I told you to get something to eat."

The older diver shook his head again. "It don't sit well. I'm sippin' a little of that canned juice I found until my gut sorts itself out again."

Ben turned back to the wheel and gazed out the paneless bridge window. "Got what you came for, huh?"

Nick didn't look at him, but raised the little bundle, which was about the size of a small beanbag, tossed it and caught it once. "Yup. And there's a few in here for you, too, once you stop bein' pissed at me." He looked over at Naji. "And for your friend."

Ben rotated the wheel a couple of spokes to starboard, eyeing another swirling eddy in the river just ahead. "Keep 'em," he said shortly.

"Awww, bro," Nick muttered, letting his head droop.

The conversation ended, and the only sounds to be heard were the muted drone of the diesels, the swash of fast water along the hull, and the metallic rattle of loose equipment vibrating in resonance with the thrumming propellers. Though the sun was shining in a relatively clear sky, a light rain began to fall, blowing in through the broken forward windows. The drops glittered in the sunlight as they fell, millions of them— *like a shower of diamonds*, Ben thought. Naji came around the steering station and stood beside him, spreading his big hands on the console, inhaling the ozone-rich air.

"I have been dead-reckoning our progress, my brother," he said. "It cannot be more than five miles to the lock canal—thirty, forty minutes at most."

"Good," Ben replied. He glanced out the port and starboard wing doors. "Where'd Nick go?"

Naji scratched his beard. "Ah. He went outside to get some air, I think. Perhaps to be alone for a few minutes." He paused. "Your friend is unhappy that you are angry with him, *Ben-Ya-Min*."

"Tough shit," Ben said. But the blunt response left him feeling hollow.

Naji changed the subject. "The rain is passing, I believe." He leaned over the console and peered up at the sky.

The pounding sound began on the lower levels of the port-side stairway, growing rapidly in volume. Ben recognized it immediately as the thumping of booted feet on grid-metal steps. A few seconds later, Nick appeared at the port wing doorway, clutching the jamb and gasping for breath.

"We got company," he coughed out. "Boats, two of 'em . . . comin' up from behind. And it ain't the Swedish Bikini Team."

CHAPTER 25

Klegg was standing in the bow of the lead boat, one foot propped up on the stern post, tapping the barrel of his drawn pistol against his thigh. The six Leopard Soldiers sitting behind him readied their weapons, growling to each other as they eyed the fleeing jackup some five hundred yards ahead. With its four tall steel legs fully retracted and towering over the hull and superstructure, it resembled nothing so much as a giant inverted table, floating down the river on its top.

He slapped the pistol against his leg impatiently, looking over his shoulder at the second boat plowing along, twenty yards off to the right and slightly behind. One of the problems associated with running a cut-rate revolution in a third-world country was that nearly all of the available money went for guns and ammunition. What little was left for vehicles usually went into trucks and personnel carriers for transporting soldiers over land. Aircraft—planes and helicopters—were unheard-of. Too expensive by far. As for watercraft—well the campaign in Bisotho was hardly a naval conflict. Boats, even for the White Colonel's use, had to be seized from those locally available.

Amon Klegg and his twelve Leopard Soldiers were forced to motor sluggishly down the fast-flowing upper Tiburi in two dilapidated twenty-foot fishing boats, their ancient gasoline engines grinding away noisily and spitting out clouds of sickly black smoke. The clumsy wooden hulls, which looked like poor imitations of a lifeboat design, did not handle well in the swirling, eddying water—particularly in the inexperienced hands of the two soldiers who'd been dragooned into manning the tillers. Both boats veered wildly all over the river's turbulent surface, badly oversteered by their underskilled helmsmen.

It was costing them time in the pursuit. "Bloody hell, keep these boats *straight*, damn you!" Klegg yelled, grabbing the gunwale as his vessel yawed hard to port, nearly dumping out several of the soldiers huddled amidships. The man at the tiller grimaced in despair, eyes popping white in his jet-black face.

Klegg had barely recovered his balance when a sudden violent impact, accompanied by a sickening crunch, nearly threw him over the port-bow rail. Flailing for a handhold, toppling, he instinctively squeezed the grip of his automatic, which went off—*pow*—shooting the Leopard Soldier immediately behind him through the breastbone. The man gasped, looked up at the White Colonel in stunned dismay, and sagged off his seat into the boat's centerline bilge.

Enraged, Klegg clawed his way to a sitting position on the tiny foredeck. His mood did not improve when he saw what had happened. The helmsman of the second boat had lost what little control he had as a result of entering a particularly nasty vortex, and allowed his vessel to careen into Klegg's. The heavy bow had bucked down on top of the lead boat's starboard gunwale, just aft of amidships, shattering hull planks and one stout rib. Bouncing free, the offending boat veered off across the river again, its passengers shrieking and engaging in a variety of spasmodic contortions.

Water poured in through the flexing crack in the lead boat with every right-hand roll. Yammering with panic, the Leopard Soldiers clambered over top of one another to get to the port rail—which brought the unstable vessel close to capsizing on that side. It did, however, have the effect of raising the damaged area of the starboard hull above the waterline—more or less.

Klegg was apoplectic. Whipping up his pistol, he fired repeatedly at the helmsman of the second boat until the nine-round magazine was empty. Fortunately for his target, crouching petrified at the tiller, every shot went high or wide as the boats pitched and wallowed on the churning water. But the soldier had had enough. With an appalled look on his face, he threw the rudder hard over and turned his boat back upstream, taking half the pursuit force with him.

"Come back here, you damned kaffir!*"* Klegg screamed, still pointing his empty automatic at the mutinous helmsman. But the retreating vessel disappeared from view as the lead boat swung around a bend in the river. Listing hard to port under the combined weight of the remaining Leopard Soldiers, it roared on after the jackup, white water spurting through the split in its side.

*   *   *

Ben was out on the starboard bridge wing, looking astern. "One boat just peeled off and headed back up-river!" he shouted through the open door. "The other one's still coming!" He stepped back inside, shaking his head and almost laughing. "Jesus Christ—they just ran into each other back there. Then I swear I heard shots being fired. I couldn't quite see what was going on. They're still too far back."

"Too bad they didn't sink each other," Nick growled, spinning the wheel. "Bastards." He clutched his gut and winced. "*Ugghh.*"

Ben took over the steering. "Stomach still bothering you?"

Nick nodded and spat into a wadded paper towel. "You try living on African cornmeal mush and water for two weeks and see what it does to you."

Naji entered through the port bridge door, cradling his Lee-Enfield. He was pushing shells from the criss-crossed ammunition bandoliers he wore into two spare rifle clips. "How many do you make it, my brother?" he asked.

"Hard to say," Ben replied "One boatload, at least. Maybe six, eight men? Maybe more."

"They are nicely bunched together." Naji's eyes had a predatory gleam. "I will let them get a little closer." He grinned. "It will be difficult to miss."

Ben's brow furrowed. It was several seconds before he spoke: "Are you going to kill them all?"

"If I am able," Naji said happily.

"Do you think that's necessary?"

The Yemeni looked at Ben in surprise. "Does it bother you, my brother?"

"Yes. Especially if we don't need to." Ben spun the wheel to port, steering through a strong eddy. "If you knock down one, won't the others back off—take the boat out of range?"

Naji sighed. "You are softhearted. We will reach the locks soon. Those I do not disable or kill will pursue us overland. They will likely call for reinforcements, if they have not done so already. I may never have this chance again, to eliminate them while they are collected together in one small boat."

"He's got a point," Nick muttered, leaning on the console and rubbing his stomach.

"Yeah, I know." Ben looked at Naji. "There's no other way, is there?"

The Yemeni shook his head. "I do not think so, my brother."

He paused, then turned and stepped out the port door, heading aft along the bridge catwalk. Ben's mouth tightened at the corners. "Dammit," he said under his breath.

Nick scowled. "Hey. Don't worry about those fuckin' niggers. You've seen what they do to their own people in this goddamn country. You want that to happen to us? Nearly happened to me already."

Ben glared at him. "Do me a favor, all right? Come over here and steer the fucking boat. And keep your mouth shut." He stepped toward the port door.

Nick took the wheel. "Where you goin'?"

"Out with Naji. Watch for that lock canal. It'll be coming up soon on the port side."

Ben walked aft along the bridge-level catwalk to the point where it hung over the stern like a little balcony, twenty-five feet above the jackup's churning wake. Naji was sighting down the barrel of his rifle as he arrived, tracking the pursuing boat as it veered this way and that on the murky, coiling waters of the river. The smaller vessel had closed to within two hundred yards, despite its erratic course and smoking, overworked engine.

"Huh," Ben muttered. "There's a white guy in the bow of that boat."

Naji's rifle cracked. The black-clad figure in the bow flinched. One of the Leopard Soldiers behind him threw up his hands with a barely audible scream and fell back into his comrades. The Caucasian gestured violently at the helmsman, shouting something, and the boat immediately began to lose way.

Naji jacked the bolt of his rifle back and forth, ejecting the spent shell. "I should take them all, my brother," he declared softly. But he did not fire again.

Ben watched intently as the fishing boat dropped farther and farther behind. "Looks like you backed them off some," he said.

"For the time being."

Ben blew out a deep breath. "Good shot." He was silent for a moment. "Maybe that'll do the trick. Spook 'em back upriver like the other boat."

"I do not think so," Naji replied. "Look. They are holding their distance just outside rifle range." He brought the Lee-Enfield up to his shoulder and squinted through the sights. "Perhaps six hundred yards. Too far for some riflemen. I am capable of dropping a shot into the boat from here, but not of picking a single target."

They continued to watch in silence for another two minutes. Then Ben swore softly. "Looks like you won't have to worry about it. Here they come again."

"Full speed, damn you!" Klegg bellowed at the helmsman in the stern. "Overtake this time! The rest of you stay as low as possible. The sniper has a longer reach with his rifle than we do with our automatic weapons. Sergeant Mapfumo!"

"*Sah!* " The big man crouching below the foredeck next to Klegg's legs looked up.

"Stay out of sight until I give the signal, understood?"

"Yes, *sah*! "

"Remember, the upper left-hand corner of the superstructure. That's where he is."

Mapfumo nodded, sweat and spray glistening on his scarified blue-black face. He shifted his weight to his right knee and coiled into a loose tuck, keeping low.

Squatting down beside the sergeant, Klegg fixed his viperous stare on the stern of the jackup as it began to power into another bend in the river.

"Now then, you bastard," he snarled.

"Hey!"

Ben and Naji turned to see Nick looking astern at them, one foot out of the port bridge doorway.

"There's a channel marker comin' up, about a half mile ahead!"

"That'll be the entrance to the lock canal," Ben shouted. "Head into it once we're past the rocks!"

Nick disappeared back into the bridge. Ben touched Naji's shoulder just as the lean Arab was raising his rifle to his shoulder once again. "I'm going to help Nick. We don't want to miss that canal."

Naji nodded. Then he settled himself, took a deep, even breath, and began to track the oncoming boat with his Lee-Enfield. With one final glance astern, Ben hurried forward along the catwalk to the bridge door.

He had just stepped inside when he heard the sharp crack of Naji's rifle.

Klegg leaped to his feet as a second Leopard Soldier let out a strangled cry and spun out of his seat, blood spurting from his throat. *"Now, Mapfumo!"*

The big sergeant uncoiled like a spring, aimed, and hit the trigger of the Russian-made RPG-7 he held over his right shoulder. There was a whoosh of compressed gases and the rocket-propelled grenade launcher jumped. Its small, cone-shaped missile shot upward at a low angle, trailing a thin boil of white smoke.

The forty-millimeter rocket hit the back of the jackup's superstructure dead center, two levels below the bridge catwalk. It penetrated the unarmored bulkhead instantly and detonated. There was a tremendous *CRUMP* as the entire second level blew out, smoke and sheets of flame bursting from shattered windows and torn steel plate. The jackup rig vibrated as if struck by a giant sledgehammer, its four upright legs wobbling violently.

The after sections of the bridge and third levels collapsed into the ruins of the second—sheet metal buckling, beams cracking; chunks of burnt steel and ruined equipment splashing into the water at the vessel's stern. Klegg saw the black-robed man high on the bridge catwalk reel, his rifle spinning out of his hands, and vanish in a smudge of ugly yellow-brown smoke.

"Now, now, now!" Klegg screamed at his helmsman, gesturing wildly with his pistol. *"Get this bloody boat up alongside, damn your eyes!"*

Ben and Nick were hurled into the bridge console as the bulkhead behind them blew forward like a fifteen-foot-wide battering ram. The deck bulged and split under their feet. The compartment filled with blinding smoke and metallic dust. A wave of searing heat enveloped them, accompanied by the stench of charred steel, plastic, and paint.

Frantically, Ben pushed aside a torn section of bulkhead that was pinning him across the navigation console and looked astern. Where a sturdy steel wall had stood just seconds before, there was now only blue sky, partly obscured by whirling black smoke and tendrils of flame. Just below that he could see the river stretching back to the last bend, the jackup's white wake marking the deep center channel like a highway line.

In the turbulent water close behind the damaged stern, the pursuing boat was gaining steadily, the soldiers in it raising their machine guns, looking for movement.

Nick groped for the edge of the console, shedding dust and broken glass, and pulled himself to his feet. He looked around in bewilderment, hacking like a tubercular and blinking soot out of his eyes.

"See if this thing still steers!" Ben shouted, climbing over hot metal toward what remained of the port bridge wing. "Try to get into the canal!"

He clawed and kicked his way through the ruined compartment and out onto the twisted catwalk. The section of grating on which he'd left Naji was gone, as if a giant cleaver had sliced it away five feet aft of the bridge door. Ben froze momentarily, stunned, as the realization of what must have happened to his Arab friend began to sink in. *Not Naji . . . nothing could kill him . . .*

The blast of machine guns sent him lunging back against the wreckage of the port bulkhead, but the fire was not directed at him. Looking down through the catwalk grating, twenty feet below, he saw a fleet, black-robed figure dodging forward along the port side of the main deck, bullet strikes chasing him as he went. Nearly alongside at the extreme stern of the jackup, the damaged fishing boat veered in closer, the Leopard Soldiers clutching for balance as they tried to fire one-handed at their elusive target.

Naji dived behind a large air compressor welded to the deck near the port rail. A hail of slugs hammered into its cover, pocking the thin sheet steel with holes in a riot of sparks and paint dust. Then the fishing boat's starboard gunwale slammed hard into the side of the jackup, splintering wooden planks and throwing the Leopard Soldiers off-balance. It bounced away, the helmsman wrenching frantically on the tiller, and came in again.

Ben's mind was working so fast he hardly felt in charge of his own actions. Grabbing the twisted grating at his feet, he swung off the catwalk, hung at arm's length, and dropped the remaining twelve feet to the main deck. The occupants of the fishing boat did not notice him, intent as they were upon both killing Naji and not being tossed into the wild water.

Keeping low, Ben hurried forward and ducked behind a canvas-wrapped piece of equipment—about four feet high and mounted on a single deck-pedestal—next to the rail. *Engines both running*, the high-speed autopilot that had taken over his brain told him, *all pumps on, pressure to all water systems . . .*

Ten feet ahead of him, the fishing boat slammed once more into the side of the jackup. The pale-skinned imitation Nazi in the bow yelled something, waving his pistol. Ben ripped the canvas cover off the pedestal unit as two of the Leopard Soldiers poised themselves on the edge of their sinking boat, and lunged . . .

They sprawled on the deck of the jackup, scrambled to their feet . . . and Ben hit the trigger of the firefighting water cannon he'd just unwrapped. A horizontal stream two inches in diameter and driven by 700 psi of head pressure shot out of the cannon's brass nozzle. It struck the two Leopard Soldiers at chest level—battering them backward off the port rail, arms and legs flailing, and into the river. Their screams were cut off as the turbid water closed over their heads.

The fishing boat surged in again, its old engine roaring and spewing clouds of black smoke and white steam. The crack in its starboard side had widened—Ben could see it working, opening and closing like a ragged mouth—and the vessel was beginning to founder, losing speed. The black-clad white man in the bow was shouting again, looking astern at Ben and raising his automatic pistol.

Ben swung the water cannon outboard and pressed the discharge trigger, hosing down the fishing boat from stern to stern. The helmsman howled as the 700 psi of jet stream water took him full in the face, knocking him away from the tiller and over the side. Klegg got off one shot at Ben, missing, before there was a sound like a coconut being smashed on a rock and the fishing boat split completely in two.

Klegg and Sergeant Mapfumo flung themselves toward the jackup. Seconds after they hit the deckplates, the blatting roar of the old engine became a sickly hiss as water closed over the sinking stern section. And then there was nothing but a pall of steam and smoke over a disturbed spot in the river, with only a few pieces of broken wood bobbing along in the torrent beside the jackup boat.

Naji was on Mapfumo before the sergeant could fully get his bearings, yanking him backward over a Lincoln welding machine with a forearm locked across his windpipe, keeping him between Klegg and himself. The *yataghan* flashed as the Leopard Soldier scrabbled frantically for his sidearm, his machine gun having fallen into the river during the wild leap from the ruined fishing boat.

Ben tried to swing the water cannon around on Klegg, but the White Colonel was too fast. Leaping inboard and astern, he flattened himself against the forward bulkhead of the superstructure, whipped up his automatic, and drew a perfect bead on Ben's forehead. Out of options, Ben froze.

"Don't move!" Klegg shouted. He glanced at Mapfumo, bent backward over the welding machine, strangely placid. Then he saw the long knife; its point tucked snugly up beneath the sergeant's jaw. The black-robed man wielding it reached with his free hand for Mapfumo's pistol, which was still in its holster.

Klegg fired at Ben. The shot rang off the barrel of the water cannon, making him wince. "If you touch that pistol, your friend is dead!" the White Colonel bellowed at Naji, having correctly sized up the situation. "Let that man go!"

Naji retracted the hand reaching for the pistol, but did not shift his knife. Nor did he emerge from behind the sergeant or let him up. Rather, he locked his arm back around the man's throat, continuing to use him as a shield.

Ben took a step sideways. Klegg fired a shot that grazed the top of his right ear. "I told you not to move!" he shouted. He glanced back toward Mapfumo and his captor. It was a standoff, he decided—of a kind. Mapfumo was nothing, but the Arab-looking bastard was fast and capable, and here was a chance to ask a key question before the shooting resumed.

Klegg put the sight pin of his automatic on Ben's right eye and stared at him along the top of the barrel. "I want Fenzi!" he snarled. "Where is he? *Where are the diamonds?"*

What the fuck has Nick cooked up with this guy? Ben thought. "I don't know what you're talking about!" he shot back. "You—"

"Klegg!"

The shout came from overhead. All eyes shifted upward, Klegg backpedaling along the bulkhead, holding his pistol in both hands, trying to look everywhere at once. Nick was standing on the ruined port bridge wing, his arm extended out over the twisted handrail. He was holding the cut-down pillowcase, open, over the rushing water.

"You told me two weeks ago that we were gonna talk about the diamond you found on me!" Nick grinned down at Klegg like a gargoyle. "About how they usually come in batches—not one at a time. Okay. Except that I'm gonna talk, and you listen, asshole."

The White Colonel's eyes shifted continuously among Nick, Ben, and Naji and the helpless Mapfumo, as did the muzzle of his automatic.

"These are the diamonds, Klegg. All of them." Nick shook the cloth bag; a faint rattling sound was audible over the thrum of the engines. "Gotta be two, three hundred in here." He reached out with his other hand and extracted a nugget, keeping the pillowcase over the water. "Have a look." He tossed the pebble off the catwalk. Deftly, Klegg caught it and held it up. The look of pure avarice that passed over the man's face, Ben thought, told the whole story.

Klegg pocketed the stone in one quick motion and shifted his aim to Nick. The diver looked incredulous and began to laugh. "What are you gonna do?" he cackled. "Shoot me? I'll drop the stash, dickhead. *You'll get nothing.*"

Klegg wavered, looking confused. He swung the pistol back on to Ben.

"Oh, good idea!" Nick called. He jostled the bag. Four or five stones tumbled out and fell into the rushing river. "Oops! Jeez—those looked like good ones, too! Lotta money!" He tipped the bag up sharply. A stream of diamonds ran out and dropped through the air as if in slow motion—like ten pounds of lead shot-ballast being dumped from an old diving bell, Ben thought.

"*Stop!*" Klegg shrieked, his voice cracking. He raised the pistol to a neutral position by his shoulder. "Don't drop any more of them!" He looked around wildly. "Each one is worth thousands! There are enough for all of us . . . *if you don't drop any more!*"

"Yeah?" Nick exclaimed, his hair flying and his eyes half-crazed. "Think so?"

All of a sudden, for no reason other than being seized by a terrible impulse to do so, Ben whirled and stared astern. He caught a glimpse of the red-and-white channel marker at the mouth of the lock canal just as it disappeared behind the trees lining the last bend.

The last bend before the river's two-hundred-and-fifty-foot plunge over the Tiburi Cataract.

CHAPTER 26

"*Nick!*" Ben yelled. "*We missed the canal entrance! Turn this thing around or we're going over the falls!*" He pointed downriver. Above the jungle canopy just ahead, clouds of mist billowed upward, tumbling white like cotton batting against the eye-burning blue of the sky. For the first time, another sound became audible along with the thrum of the jackup's engines and the swash of the river—a deep, thunderous roar that seemed to shake the air itself.

Ben started forward. Klegg snapped the automatic down and put a shot into the deck at his feet, kicking up sparks. The ricochet went between his legs and, again, he froze.

"Stay there!" the White Colonel shouted, looking less sure of himself than ever.

Frantically, Ben glanced up at the bridge. "*Nick!*"

The older diver appeared to come back to earth, the crazed grin ebbing from his face. "The steering don't work," he called down. "She won't turn!"

"Then use the engines!" Ben yelled. Again he started forward, and once again he found himself staring into the muzzle of the black-clad man's automatic. Exasperated, he stopped. "Klegg! That's your name, isn't it? Klegg, listen to me. We've got about six minutes to get this jackup turned around and headed back upstream, or we're taking a one-way trip over the Tiburi Cataract! That means *all* of us, Klegg!"

The White Colonel blinked, lowering the automatic slightly. His pale face twitched as he glanced from Ben, to Naji, to Nick, and back at Ben again.

"I've got to get to the engine controls!" Ben shouted. "Get her reversed or grounded on the bank!" He took a deep breath and began to walk forward. "Shoot if you have to—we're all dead unless I try! You understand, Klegg?"

Abruptly, the White Colonel stepped back, out of Ben's way, and trained his weapon on Naji and the half-strangled Mapfumo. Naji's hand went to the sergeant's sidearm, still holstered at his right hip. His blue eyes were fixed hawklike on Klegg's.

"Nobody shoots anybody!" Ben yelled as he ran up the outer stairs to the bridge three at a time. "We're going to need every hand we've got!"

Naji had Mapfumo's pistol half-drawn, his *yataghan* still pressed under the sergeant's jaw. Very slowly, taking the sidearm with him, the lean Yemeni rose from his crouch behind the welding machine, partially exposing his torso. His eyes remained locked on Klegg's. Standing up straight, he tucked the pistol into his sash, moved his hand away from the butt, and lightened the pressure of the knife on Mapfumo's throat.

Klegg nodded imperceptibly, lowered his own weapon, and holstered it. He left the flap unsnapped.

"*Hey!*" Ben shouted through the broken windows of the half-demolished bridge. "Get forward, up by the anchor winch! Pull the lynchpins securing the hook! We're going to drop it if I can't turn this thing or make enough way to get upstream!"

Releasing Mapfumo, Naji wheeled and ran toward the bow, casting frequent glances over his shoulder at Klegg. But the White Colonel had made his peace for the moment. As Mapfumo struggled to a sitting position on the welding machine, weakly rubbing his throat, Klegg followed the Arab tribesman forward, taking up a position in front of the anchor-winch control panel.

Seizing a small sledgehammer racked nearby for the purpose, Naji knocked out the two large steel pins that secured the anchor in its drop slot when the vessel was under way. Then he and Klegg stood there on the bow—mutual necessity keeping them from flying at each other's throats—alternately staring up at the shattered bridge and out toward the billowing mist that seemed to approach with ever-increasing speed. The tons of water going over the Tiburi Cataract roared mightily.

"Oh, my God!" Sass breathed, her face pressed against the glass of the flying boat's forward starboard cabin window. "The jackup's going to go over!"

At the next window back, Olssen stared down in helpless dismay. "They've gotten her into the fast rapids just above the falls!" he exclaimed. "They'll never make way against that much current. Look— they're trying to turn her!"

The Grumman Goose continued to bank to starboard at a steep angle, circling at an altitude of two thousand feet. Directly below, the Tiburi Cataract was a steaming white clot on the serpentine artery of the river, a breathtaking collage of tumbling water, broken black rock, and drifting mist. Barely fifty boat lengths from the lip, the jackup rig was rotating slowly among long shreds of foam torn into the river's surface by exposed rocks.

"It's Ben, it's Ben!" Sass blurted, her face stricken. "I know it's him, Berndt!"

"*Ya*. Who else could it be?" the Norwegian replied. Frustrated, he banged his fist on the window's thick glass. "Koko! Take us lower! Much lower, if you can!"

"No problem!" The pilot's cheerful reply came through the open door between passenger cabin and cockpit.

The drone of the Goose's big radial engines dropped in pitch as it nosed down, still banking, and began to spiral lower over the vapor-shrouded falls like a great silver vulture.

Up on the bridge, Ben had both hands locked over the engine throttle levers, the starboard diesel full ahead, the port full reverse. The counterthrusting propellers set up a fearful vibration in the jackup's steel bones, rattling it like metal maracas. Ben gritted his teeth. The vessel was turning too slowly. Under his palms, the chrome T-handles of the levers were slippery with sweat.

"We aren't going to make it," he said to Nick. "The river's turned into rapids. We couldn't hold our own even if I got this barge headed directly upstream. I'm surprised we haven't—"

There was a tremendous bang and the jackup slewed sideways, opposite the direction in which it had been rotating. Ben and Nick lurched along the wrecked console, almost losing their footing. On the bow, Naji, Klegg, and Mapfumo were bowled across the deckplates, clawing for purchase.

"Hit bottom yet!" Ben finished, panting. "That's it! We can't get back upstream! All we can do is try to stop!" He waved furiously at Naji. *"Drop the hook! Drop the hook!"*

Staggering to his feet, the Yemeni leaped past Klegg and hit the brake-release button on the anchor-winch control panel. The big navy hook slipped from its cradle and dropped into the water with a foaming splash, its heavy cable freewheeling after it.

Nick stared out over the collapsed starboard bridge wing as the jackup continued to slide sideways toward the boiling clouds of mist that marked the lip of the cataract. "We're runnin' out of room, here, bro," he warned. "Maybe five hundred yards."

"Gotta let some scope run out," Ben said hoarsely, watching the winch unspool. He kept his hands on the diesel throttles, doing all he could to slow the jackup's inexorable drift toward the falls. "Hook won't catch if we don't let it have some scope."

There was a second wracking bang on the underside of the hull as the jackup collided with another submerged rock. "Maybe we'll go hard aground before we go over," Nick said, his voice tight.

Ben glanced at him. "Yeah. And maybe we won't." He licked his lips. "Don't bet your life on it."

He stared at the spool for another few seconds, then

waved a clenched fist and yelled, *"Hold it! Hold it there!"*

Down on the bow, Naji hit the brake button. There was a screech of asbestos linings and a puff of heat-generated smoke as the friction pads clamped down on the winch drums. The cable stopped unspooling, then went taut, vibrating like a huge guitar string. With a groan of stressed metal, the jackup canted over ten degrees and began to swing bow first into the current.

Klegg's hand strayed toward his automatic. As soon as he was certain that the jackup would hold its position in the rapids, the black-robed Arab would be the first to die. He was the most dangerous of the three. The others—Fenzi and the second American—would be much easier to handle.

A thin smile played across the White Colonel's face. He had a built-in advantage. He could afford to wait for rescue, if necessary. The fugitives could not. Once they had the boat secure . . .

The big Arab was watching the anchor cable, his back turned. The ground tackle seemed to be holding. Klegg's fingertips brushed the butt of his pistol. Too easy . . .

Without warning, the jackup lurched, throwing everyone off-balance. The anchor cable leaped in its hawsehole, suddenly slack. The vessel began to work its way downstream once more—drifting, jerking to halt, sideslipping, drifting again . . .

The anchor was dragging over the hard rock bottom. For the first time, with the Tiburi Cataract roaring only a few hundred yards away, Klegg felt real fear. Diamonds were useless to a dead man.

"She's dragging!" Ben shouted. He looked astern through the bridge wreckage at the lip of the cataract. It seemed close enough to spit over.

Nick grimaced, clutching his stomach. "*Urp*. We gonna try that last thing we talked about?"

"Now or never," Ben replied. He stepped around the ship's wheel to a set of controls on the far side of the console. Then he paused. "If she breaks up when we do this, Nick," he said, "it was nice knowing you— warts and all."

The older diver managed a smile. "Likewise, bro."

"Hang on." With a firm shove, Ben engaged the hydraulic motors that extended and retracted the jackup's movable legs. There was a squealing of gears, and the four immense steel pillars began to descend. The vessel bucked and wobbled as the current caught the large horizontal mud-mats affixed to the bottom of each leg.

"Full reverse that port engine again!" Ben said. "Try to keep her pointed upstream!"

"Man," Nick growled, manipulating the throttle levers, "moving like this, we're gonna bust them legs off when they hit bottom, sure as shit."

"Think positive, can't you?" Ben replied. "If they hold long enough for the hull to lift clear of the water, we've got it made. Once the weight's on the legs and the current's running underneath us, we're stable."

Nick shot a quick glance astern. "It better work. We've only got a couple hundred yards to go."

*   *   *

Naji, Klegg, and Mapfumo backed away from the bow as the legs descended, trying to keep their feet on the bucking deck. No sooner had they reached amidships and taken hold of handrails and equipment frames than the port bow leg hit the river bottom—*BANG*. The impact bounced the jackup so hard that twenty inches of daylight suddenly appeared between the soles of every man's feet and the deckplates. There was a horrific screeching sound as the gears bound, the leg started to bend, surely to snap, and then—*BANG*—the starboard bow leg hit.

BANG. BANG. The two stern legs crashed into the rocky bottom. The screeching sound quadrupled as the jackup vibrated to a halt, the swift current piling up water at its bow. The pressure on the wide hull, stalled in midstream, was enormous. The four steel legs sagged, their mud-mats scraping and rumbling on the riverbed, bending to the breaking point. There were ominous moans of tortured metal, the legs bending even more . . .

Then, with a great washing sound, the hull lifted clear of the onrushing water. One foot. Three feet. Six feet. The legs straightened, wobbling, the incredible strain gone, the weight of the vessel now pushing down vertically, as designed. The hydraulic motors ground on, lifting the body of the jackup ever higher.

Lying on his side, half-dazed from being thrown around the deck, Klegg struggled to clear his head and assess the situation. *Bloody hell—they'd done it! The jackup had jacked up! They were secure!*

In the next instant, mindful of whom he had to kill,

his hand went groping for his automatic. Simultaneously, he rolled to his knees, scanning the deck for—

The black-robed Arab was already on his feet, his blue eyes glittering over the barrel of the pistol he'd yanked from his sash and trained on Klegg's forehead. With a thrill of horror, the White Colonel saw the finger whiten on the handgun's trigger . . .

Mapfumo hit the Arab from the side at a dead run, driving him toward the bow. Simultaneously, the pistol cracked. Diverted from its intended path by less than two inches, the slug plowed a deep furrow in Klegg's left temple, knocking him unconscious.

Locked together, grappling for the pistol, the two powerful men stumbled up the deck in a bizarre dance, off-balance but not off their feet, driven by Mapfumo's body weight.

"Watch out!" Ben yelled from the bridge, powerless to intervene.

As they wrestled, tearing at each other like two wild animals, their momentum carried them off the end of the bow. For a split second they seemed to hang in midair, somersaulting—a blur of black cloth, camouflage fatigues, arms, and legs—and then they hit the murky water with a geyserlike splash.

"No!" Ben shouted. *"Naji!"* He bolted for the port bridge wing, heading toward the half-destroyed outer staircase, Nick on his heels.

Leaping down the stairs four at a time, he tore a life ring and line coil off the main-deck bulkhead and sprinted to the port rail. By the time he got there, though, it was only a matter of seconds, the powerful currents had whirled Naji and Mapfumo—still clawing at each other—well out from the jackup's side. Ben yelled the Arab's name again and heaved the life ring for all he was worth. It spun out like an oversize discus, trailing its yellow nylon line, and dropped into the water less than halfway to the thrashing men.

Ben gripped the rail, feeling as if he'd just been kicked in the stomach. All he could do was watch as the surging waters swept the pair toward the lip of the falls, less than 150 yards away. He saw a black-robed arm rise out of the foam, strike downward twice . . . and then Naji was stroking upstream, the limp body of the Leopard Soldier bobbing away from him.

It was futile. For every frantic stroke the Yemeni took, weighed down by his heavy robes, he was swept another fifteen feet toward the cataract. It could end only one way, and very soon. In desperation, Ben searched the deck for something . . . anything . . .

"What the hell is that?" Nick shouted, his voice hoarse, incredulous.

Ben jerked his head up in time to see the ultralight flash by, its push-prop whirling silver beneath the dirty white fabric of its wing, less than thirty feet from the jackup's side and five feet off the surging water.

"*Keep on strokin', Naji-dude!*" Head yelled above the whine of his engine. "*I'm comiiiiiiin'!*"

"What the hell is that?" Olssen exclaimed, blinking down through his window as the Goose circled. Five hundred feet below, just above the river, the pale triangle of the ultralight's delta wing floated past the jackup like a giant moth.

"The ultralight!" Sass cried. "That's the ultralight! It's going after the men in the water!"

Allah, Most Compassionate and Merciful, Naji prayed, swimming with every ounce of strength left in his exhausted body, *I have done my best—but this time, I know, it is not enough. Father, Grandfather, Uncles, I am overjoyed that I will see you once again in Paradise. We have much to talk about—perhaps the loan of a few extra houris, should you have any to spare.*

Head cut down the rpm and skidded the ultralight's pontoons onto the water, lining up on the desperately stroking figure just ahead. Half-flying, half-hydroplaning, he tweaked the aircraft to the right, traveling not much faster than the current.

"*Heyyyy, dude!*" he bawled. "*Look up! Look up!*"

For some reason, ten feet before the tip of the port pontoon would have split his head open, Naji did. Being run down by an onrushing aircraft notwithstanding, the Yemeni knew a gift from Allah when he saw it. Nearly blinded by spray, he threw his arms over the aluminum skin of the float as it scraped past. There was a tearing sensation, a sharp pain in his right elbow, and then he was clinging to the wooden strut he'd fashioned with his *yataghan*, half-sprawled on top of the pontoon—one leg hooked up and over, the other dragging.

Whooping like an insane cowboy, Head gunned the engine, building speed, and accelerated off the lip of the Tiburi Cataract into the wall of boiling mist . . . just as Mapfumo's body went over the edge and began its slow tumble toward the jagged rocks and vortices below.

The ultralight dropped sharply, whirling into a left-hand spin—too slow to fly and too heavy on its port side. All Naji heard, blinded by the whiteout and clinging like grim death to the pontoon and strut, was "*Shiiiiiiiiiiiiiiiiiiiiiiiit!*"

And then, in a brilliant flash of sunshine, the ultralight wheeled out of the mist cloud and arced over the foam-flecked waters of the Lower Tiburi—with barely twenty feet of altitude to spare.

Head was laughing like a madman, his long, lank hair flapping around his flying goggles in the slipstream. He reached down with his left hand and grabbed a fold of Naji's robe, leveling the ultralight as he did so.

"C'mon, dude!" he shouted. "Climb up into the back, man!"

Naji stared up at the pilot in astonishment. Slowly, his spent muscles shaking, he dragged himself up off the pontoon and into the rear passenger seats, remembering to shift all the way to the starboard side and balance the ultralight's payload. When at last he got the seat belt buckled across his waist, he slumped back in total exhaustion and raised a finger toward the lip of the Tiburi Cataract. Head looked over his shoulder at him, grinning—as ever—with his mouth open.

"*Ben-Ya-Min,*" Naji gasped. "*Ben-Ya-Min* is up there. And his friend Nick."

Head turned his attention back to the controls and gunned the engine, trying to pick up altitude as the ultralight soared down the river, flanked on either side by thick green jungle. "I saw them as I flew by," he shouted. "Once I get above the falls again, I'll come in and land next to the rig, headin' upstream! I'll keep the engine cookin'—taxi in as close as I can! Then they'll have to jump!" He glanced back at Naji once more and shrugged. "Best I can do, dude."

Drained, all Naji could do was nod.

"Now what?" Nick said.

Ben was still staring at the wall of mist that had just swallowed up the ultralight. The aircraft had never lifted clear of the water. Head had simply hydro-planed it off the edge of the cataract, whereupon it had dropped instantly and disappeared. There was no way of knowing if the miraculously resurrected pilot and his passenger were, at that moment, soaring off over the jungle canopy, or tumbling dead and broken in the rocky whirlpools at the base of the falls.

He turned away from the handrail and looked at Nick. "Now we figure out how to get off this damn thing," he said.

They made their way to the center of the work deck, which was strewn with loose drilling gear, gas cylinders from a rack that had snapped its retaining chains and overturned, and shards of glass, plastic, and steel from the RPG explosion. Under their feet, the deck still vibrated with the pulse of the idling diesels. The engines' steady mutter was inaudible, completely drowned out by the roar of the falls. A slight wind shift had begun to waft mist over the rig, wetting down every surface.

"Got any ideas?" Nick asked.

Ben looked around. "Not so far. We need to get a line to the bank somehow. Rig something that we can use to traverse the rapids."

"Yeah." Nick spat, rubbing his stomach. "Breeches buoy?"

"Like that, maybe. But we need some way to shoot a grappling hook and line into the trees. I don't think we have anything."

"How about riggin' high-pressure air to a section of pipe?" Nick suggested.

"Possible," Ben said, thinking of Rolly Savard and the NAOC-X. "I did something like that once." He pointed up. "How about this pedestal crane? The boom telescopes out—what—four full sections? Get us close."

Nick squinted at the crane, then toward the bank. "Maybe to those first rocks. Not all the way, I don't figger."

"*Neither of you move!*" The voice was like a rip in the air.

Ben and Nick jerked their heads to the left. Amon Klegg was leaning on a compressor skid, his automatic held at arm's length. Blood from the ugly wound in his temple had soaked his shirt and turned his face into a slick red mask.

The gun shook in his hand. Slowly, his lips twisted into a death's-head grin. "I need to talk to you, Fenzi," he croaked. His staring eyes shifted to Ben. "*You* I don't need."

Ben threw himself to the side as Klegg fired, sprawling behind a deck winch. The slug rang off the funnel of a ventilator cowl. Staggering forward, Klegg fired again. The bullet smacked into the heavy wire cable on the winch spool as Ben tried desperately to roll away.

"Klegg!" Nick yelled, starting forward—and then, with two earsplitting cracks, the stern legs of the jackup broke off at deck level.

The hull collapsed into the water with a jarring splash. The remaining sections of leg, still towering thirty feet above the bridge, tore out of their gear housings and toppled like axed redwoods. The port section fell away from the hull, crashing into the water just behind the flooded stern. The starboard leg fell forward, cleaving through the damaged bridge and weakened superstructure as if they had been made of cardboard. Klegg and Nick scrambled in opposite directions as the huge steel tube smashed into the slanting deck with a sound like a giant kettledrum.

The jackup tilted, the unbroken bow legs driving the stern under. Water surged halfway up the deck, flooding the lower superstructure. The fore-and-aft list approached forty-five degrees. Incredibly, the engines were still running. Ben, hanging by his fingertips from a generator skid, could feel their steady vibration through the steel deckplates pressed against his ribs.

With an ominous rumbling, the stricken vessel began to drag over the hard rock bottom toward the edge of the cataract, pushed by tons of onrushing water. Heavy equipment broke welds and snapped chains, sliding down the deck to smash into the forward bulkhead of the inundated superstructure. Ben saw Nick, clinging to a pad-eye some fifteen feet away, twist his body frantically to the side as a compressor that must have weighed three tons smoked past him on its skid rails, trailing paint dust and friction sparks. It crashed through the wall of the toolpusher's office in an explosion of splinters and spray.

His hands burning from gripping the skid, his arms about to pull out of their sockets, Ben could only watch in horror as the jackup ground its way closer and closer to the edge of the falls. The roar of the water was brain-numbing, the ongoing vibration ferocious. He could see the drop—look down through the boiling mist at the Lower Tiburi snaking away through the jungle like a dark, muddy vein, with the maelstrom of foaming whirlpools and jagged black rocks far below, as the rig started to go over.

There was a colossal screech of tearing metal, a shock wave that nearly wrenched the skid from Ben's failing hands, and the jackup scraped to a halt, its stern dangling over the precipice. Looking down between his feet, through torrents of water and spray, Ben could see the Tiburi Cataract's chaotic base—tons upon tons of river pounding into a fractured crown of gigantic boulders.

No way to jump. Certain death.

The rig shifted violently. One of Ben's hands slipped off the skid.

No place to stay.

Kicking on the slippery, tilted deck, he lunged toward Nick, who was somehow still clinging to his pad-eye. His hand slapped onto a broken weld-tab, caught it, held on. Then he was past the older diver, reaching for a hydraulic hose dangling from the starboard crane pedestal. The vibration from the engines continued to thrum into his chest through the deck-plates.

Crazy, he thought. *Just crazy . . . can't work . . . Christ—what's the difference?*

"Come on!" he yelled over his shoulder at Nick, choking on spray. "This way! *This way!*"

Summoning his last reserves of strength, he began to haul himself up the hydraulic hose hand over hand, climbing toward the crane.

"Good Lord," Olssen muttered, shielding his eyes against the sun as the Goose continued its sharp bank above the falls. The shattered rig was perched on the very lip of the cataract, held only by its two unbroken bow legs. Even from an altitude of several hundred feet, Olssen could see them bending far beyond the limits of their design.

Sass's eyes were riveted on the agile figure in the black diving suit, scrambling up the starboard rail near the pedestal crane. *Ben.*

"What can we do?" she whispered, barely loud enough for Olssen to hear. "There must be something we can do . . ."

The old Norwegian diver shook his head, and did not answer.

The ultralight tacked back and forth across the lower river, gaining altitude with agonizing slowness. Naji had recovered sufficiently to lean forward and grip Head's shoulder.

"Look!" he shouted, pointing. "Up there! We must hurry!"

Through a break in the mist Head caught a glimpse of the ruined jackup rig, poised on the edge of the cataract like a crumpled can about to be kicked into a gully. His perpetually slack mouth sagged open even farther.

"Oh, wow, man," he exclaimed. "Total bummer. We can't do diddly-squat for them now."

Naji stared at him. "Diddly . . . *what*?" He slapped his hand on Head's shoulder. "Never mind. Just get us to the top of the falls, pilot! As quickly as you can!"

Head shrugged. "You got it, Naji-dude." He started to bank around for another altitude-gaining tack across the river. "Goin' up."

Ben grabbed Nick's collar and hauled him up bodily along the last two feet of hydraulic hose to the base of the crane. There was another rumble, and the jackup tilted again, the deck now slanting at close to sixty degrees. Somehow they managed to hang on, clinging like limpets to the pedestal's slick surface, expecting at any second to feel the rig begin its deadly final plunge.

The climb had all but done Nick in. Gasping for breath, his salt-and-pepper hair plastered across his pale forehead, he looked mutely at Ben as if to say, "*What's the point?*" A thin trickle of blood was running from the corner of his mouth.

His jaw set, Ben clapped a hand on the back of Nick's sodden coveralls and dragged him up to a more secure position across the crane pedestal. Then, reaching around to the control panel, he pulled back on the rotational lever.

With the engines and pumps running, the hydraulic lines were still pressured up. There was a heart-stopping lurch, and the crane boom swung outboard, the rams straining against the abnormal leverage caused by the extreme angle of the deck. The boom tracked around, the heavy ball-and-hook of the lifting cable dangling at its end, until it was pointing out over the precipice at right angles.

Struggling not to fall off the slippery pedestal, holding on with one hand and working the controls with the other, Ben pushed in the boom-extension and cable-spool levers simultaneously. The four-section boom began to telescope outward, the lifting cable slacking as it did so.

"How much cable's on this crane?" Ben yelled at Nick over the roar of the falls.

Nick squinted through the flying spray at the rotating drum beside him. "I ain't real sure!" he shouted, coughing reddish spittle. "I think I heard Olssen say somethin' like two hundred feet!"

"Shit."

"Ain't it enough?"

His face grim, Ben looked out at the end of the boom, now partially obscured by mist. "It's gonna have to do," he shouted back. "Chart says the falls are two hundred and fifty feet high. I'd rather drop fifty feet than two-fifty."

Nick blinked at him. "What if we hit a rock?"

"Then we're fucked," Ben replied simply.

There was a jolt as the crane boom hit the end of its last extension. Now fully telescoped, it bobbed out in the mist like a giant fishing pole. Ben released the extension lever but kept the spool lever depressed. The cable continued to pay out, pulled through its sheaves by the weight of the descending ball-and-hook.

"Start heading out there," Ben shouted.

"*Jeezus* . . ."

"Maybe he'll give us a hand. Get going. It's the only way."

"We slidin' down?"'

"That's the idea. As far as we can go."

Nick gulped. But he reached out and with painful effort began to pull himself up over the spool cage and out onto the boom.

A shot cracked above the cacophony of tumbling water and groaning metal. One of the hydraulic jumper hoses leaped and began to spout oily green fluid. The crane boom lurched again as the rams holding it in place sagged, losing pressure. Through the actuator lever in his hand, Ben could feel the cable's descent rate decrease.

"*Jeezus!*" he heard Nick say once more. "Not this fuckin' guy again."

CHAPTER 27

Klegg was lying against the steeply slanted deck, his feet braced on the framework of a water pump. The whirling spray had soaked him, the diluted blood from the wound in his temple tinting his entire upper body. He was shaking as if in the early throes of hypothermia, the automatic he brandished literally rattling in his hand. The eyes boggling out of his gore-plastered face were inhuman.

"*Fenziiiiiii!*" he screamed. "*I want those diamonds!*"

"Are you out of your fucking *mind*, Klegg?" Ben hollered. "Don't you see where you *are*?"

Gnashing his teeth like a rabid dog, the White Colonel snapped off a shot at him. The slug ricocheted off the thick steel of the pedestal and clipped the outer edge of Ben's right kneecap.

"*Aggh!*" he gasped, flinching violently and nearly falling. Despite the sudden pain, he kept pressure on the cable-spool lever.

Klegg raised the pistol again, trying to steady its trembling barrel for a kill shot. The jackup lurched and tilted, grinding its way farther over the edge of the precipice. Klegg barely reacted to the violent motion.

"*Klegg!*" Nick yelled, before the South African could

fire at Ben again. "You want the diamonds, you motherfucker? Here they are!" He twisted sideways, lying on the jouncing boom, and pulled the knotted pillowcase from inside his coveralls. Stretching out his arm, he dangled the little sack over the abyss. "Same deal as before, asshole! Shoot me—shoot my friend again—and they're gone! *Adios muchacho!*" He nodded his head at Ben before Klegg could respond. "Cable's almost all payed out—I can see the spool. Climb past me, Ben."

Ben didn't argue. Groaning with pain, he clambered up onto the boom, expecting at any moment to feel a bullet burn into his back, and slid past Nick. "Keep going," the older diver rasped. Ben did.

The boom, extended to its maximum length, had the stability of a wet noodle. It bobbed and bounced under Ben's weight, slippery with spray and cable grease. After shinning along about forty feet, he found himself completely surrounded by a blinding white fog of spray and mist. He looked back. Nick, Klegg—even the jackup—were invisible. He looked forward along the undulating steel beam. No end in sight. Only wet, swirling, blank *whiteness*.

He dragged himself forward, the relentless thunder of the falls battering his ears, trying not to think of the sickening drop beneath him.

Nick smiled at Klegg, swinging the sack of diamonds gently from two fingers. The South African's wild eyes went from the bag, to Nick, to the bag, to Nick . . . and then he began to scramble forward, trying to keep the gun aimed as he moved.

Nick glanced out along the boom. Ben had vanished into the mist.

He smiled down at Klegg again. "You've been workin' so hard for these rocks, Klegg," he shouted, "I figure you deserve 'em!" He raised the bag. "Here. Go fetch!"

An audible gasp—half inhalation and half shriek—burst from the White Colonel as Nick tossed the sack over his head in a gentle arc. The South African twisted around in time to see the little bundle land in the skid of a winch some ten feet behind him. He stared at it for a long moment—*so near and yet so far*—and when he turned back toward the crane, Nick Fenzi's feet were disappearing along the boom into the swirling fog.

Ben had ripped the sleeves from his Lycra diving suit, wrapped them around his hands, and begun to slide down the greasy crane cable toward the base of the falls.

Little fishhooks—broken strands of wire in the cable's frayed surface—tore into his palms and inner thighs, the thin Lycra offering almost no protection. All around was the blinding, smothering white haze, increasing in density with every foot he descended. He began to gasp. It was like trying to breathe underwater without gills.

Then, in a sudden puff of warm wind, the fog tattered away and he could see the foam-streaked Lower Tiburi coursing off to the east through a vast carpet of emerald green jungle. Directly below, past his locked, sliding feet, the cable stretched down another twenty yards—no more—terminating in the rust orange ball-and-hook. Below that, obscured by intermittent wreaths of mist, was a seething cauldron of white water, rimmed by fanglike black rocks.

A fifty-foot jump at least. And maybe you came up, and maybe, you didn't . . . depending on what you hit, how powerful the whirlpools were, how strong the downstream current was—

Crack. Crack. Crack-crack. The unmistakable sound of pistol shots punched through the cataract's omnipresent roar.

"They're going down the crane cable!" Sass exclaimed. "Why didn't they spool it out all the way to the water?"

Olssen gazed at the bobbing yellow spar that jutted out from the wrecked jackup, its vertical cable barely visible through the clouds of mist. One dark-clothed figure was just alighting on the ball-and-hook at the line's lower end, while farther up, perhaps twenty feet below the end of the boom, another was sliding down. A third man was draped across the big winch on the crane's pedestal, attempting to crawl forward.

"Not enough cable," Olssen said. "They're going to jump." Hurriedly, he dug into the small duffel on the seat beside him and extracted a pair of compact, high-powered binoculars. Raising them to his eyes, he manipulated the focus rings. "That's Ben on the ball-and-hook," he declared. "The man above him, sliding down the cable, is Nick Fenzi."

As the Goose banked around yet again, the ultra-light soared past in the opposite direction, several hundred feet below. It, too, went into a steep bank, and Sass could clearly see the flapping blond hair of Jefferson Deadhead Jones and Naji's wind-whipped black robes in the open framework beneath the big delta wing.

"Berndt," she asked, "if Head and Naji are in the ultralight, and Ben and Nick are on that cable . . . who's the fifth guy?"

Olssen braced the binoculars against the cabin window. He took a long look before answering. "I don't know," he said, "but whoever he is, he's covered in blood and has a pistol in his hand. And he's pointing it, or trying to"—he refocused the binoculars as the flying boat leveled its bank for another pass—"at Nick Fenzi."

He passed the binoculars over the back of the seat to Sass. "I don't know what the hell's going on down there," he said grimly, "but it looks like we can do something to help now."

Rising to his feet, he went forward to the open door between passenger cabin and cockpit. "Koko," he called over the engine noise, "can you circle downriver, then come back upstream for a landing close to the base of the cataract?"

The pilot nodded, half-turning in his seat and lifting a headset phone from one ear. "That I can do. I see no signs of military activity on either bank, and the water is deep along the approach." The expression on his jovial blue-black face became apologetic. "I cannot taxi closer than two hundred yards to the whirlpool basin, though," he said. "The currents are too treacherous, and there is not enough room to turn the plane around for takeoff."

Olssen clapped him on the shoulder. "Thank you," he said. "Just do the best you can. The men abandoning that rig will be in the water soon. We want to be in position to pick them up, you see? I'll need something to reach them with."

Koko grinned. "Absolutely, by Jove!" he replied, sounding exactly like his father. "You will find a long gaff with a sharpened hook at one end hanging in clamps along the overhead liner of the passenger cabin."

Olssen paused in mid-turn. "Well, I don't think we'll want anything sharp, " he said. "Exhausted men might injure themselves. Can I remove it and just use the pole?"

"If you prefer," the pilot responded. "But they will be dropping to the rocks, then passing through the whirlpools. You will find it harder to pull in their dead bodies without some kind of hooking attachment." He grinned again, looking indefatigably pleasant, and turned back to the controls.

Half-blinded by blood and mist, his body shaking with pain, fear, and rage, Amon Klegg inched out along the jouncing boom, clutching his automatic. The bundle of diamonds he'd recovered from the winch skid now dug into his sternum like a nubbly little fist—secure inside his fatigue shirt, crushed between his chest and the metal surface of the spar.

He could see Fenzi intermittently through the haze of spray and water vapor, the man's dark form gliding downward along the thin thread of the crane cable. He'd gotten off four—maybe five shots at the slippery bastard as he'd fled after tossing the diamonds. The American had been hit, Klegg was sure of it. But he hadn't lost his grip, hadn't fallen.

Klegg had the diamonds, but they were not enough. What he wanted now was the diamonds—and Nick Fenzi dead.

The wind shifted, blowing the mist away. Momentarily, blue sky surrounded him, above and on all sides. He looked down. The unlimited view of the awful drop below and the Tiburi River winding off through the jungle toward the abnormally low horizon sent a jolt of vertigo through him. He reeled, hugging the boom. Then, less than forty feet away, perhaps twenty below, he again spotted Nick Fenzi.

The American was hanging in open air on the thin cable, a vast panorama of sky and jungle behind him, struggling to jerk free a coverall sleeve that had become hooked on a broken strand of wire. He looked up at the boom and, seeing Klegg, renewed his efforts. But he was tired, near exhaustion, and the tough fabric of the work garment would not tear.

I have you now, you bloody Yank shit.

Klegg sat up on the boom, squeezing hard with his legs, and leveled the pistol in both hands.

Plenty of time.

Much too close to miss.

He began to squeeze the trigger for a chest shot, then paused. He wanted to see the American's face. He wanted to know that Fenzi could see it coming—see who was killing him. His target was looking down, wrenching again and again at his caught sleeve.

"Fenzi!" Klegg shrieked.

The American's eyes snapped up. The White Colonel smiled at him over the barrel of his pistol. *Live in fear for a second or two, Yank.*

Fenzi stopped struggling. As he stared at Klegg, the middle finger of the hand in the trapped sleeve straightened and turned upward.

"Fuck you!" he shouted, and spat.

Not a satisfying reaction at all, Klegg thought, taken aback. *Damnable Americans.*

He centered the sight on Fenzi's breastbone and pulled the trig—

With a shattering roar and a hurricane rush of wind, something huge burst out of the wall of mist to his right. It descended upon him like a giant pterodactyl, blotting out the sun, dragging a swirling curtain of water vapor in its wake. The world became a chaotic whiteout. Then, without touching him, the thing vanished as quickly as it had arrived.

Amon Klegg swayed, clutching at nothing, the automatic falling from his hands. Invisible vortices of disturbed air tore at him from every direction, lifting him off the boom, forcing his weight outward.

A spasm of terror seized him, and then he was falling, tumbling over and over through brilliant sunshine and dim white mist, kicking and clawing, a high-pitched sound resonating in his ears above the roar of the falls.

His long, drawn-out scream lasted all the way down to the central whirlpool basin of the cataract, where his head met a point of jagged rock, got the worst of the encounter, and came apart like a coconut smashing on a steel spike.

*   *   *

"Ahaaaa!" Naji bellowed, pounding Head on the shoulder. "You did it, pilot! You did it! All praises to Allah the Compassionate and Merciful that you were not entombed in that stinking mud pit or hacked to pieces—no thanks to my worthless self, of course, for not safeguarding you more effectively—"

"Dude," Head said, "be cool. Ain't nothin' but a thing." He glanced down, banking the ultralight over the falls. "Whoooaaaa. Sure hope that really was a bad guy. He took a seriously terminal swan dive, there."

Naji sat back, cackling. "I assure you that he was," he shouted. "An odious villain, whom I would gladly have sent to his reward with my bare hands, had I been able—may Allah the Compassionate and Merciful cause him to be impaled anus to mouth on a red-hot spit and roasted throughout Eternity."

"Eueugh," Head exclaimed, squirming in his seat and looking back over his shoulder. "You come up with some vivid imagery, dude. Hey, do me a favor, okay?"

"Of course," Naji responded. "Ask."

"Introduce me to this Al guy sometime, will ya? I want to get on his good side."

The wind had shifted. Again, the mist closed in, obscuring the jackup, boom, and upper section of the cable. Ben locked his elbows around the coarse wire and flexed his aching fingers, his feet on the ball of the lifting hook. His ears were still ringing with the hideous scream Klegg had emitted as he'd tumbled past, close enough for the nails of one flailing hand to rake over his shoulder.

The South African had missed plunging into what looked like a fairly deep basin of foaming white water by less than ten feet. Even now, as the visibility deteriorated, Ben could see his broken body lying twisted on the jutting rocks, a lump of red gore where his head had been.

For the tenth time in two minutes, he tipped his own head back and yelled

"Niiiiiiick!"

And like the other nine times, there was no answer.

Ben let his chin sag forward onto his chest. He could not climb back up the cable—his arms were done. He could not stay where he was, with his fingers and feet cramping horribly. If forced to let go without control, without picking his spot, he'd end up like Klegg. Even from the lesser height of fifty or sixty feet, jagged rock made for a lethal landing pad. The jackup rig would be going over any second—he could feel its ever-increasing movement through the cable. It was a miracle that it hadn't toppled already.

"Niiiiiiick!"

Nothing.

Then the cable quivered. Ben looked up, and Nick came slipping down the wire like a drugged fireman on a greased pole, barely hanging on. Somehow, Ben caught him before his momentum carried both of them off the ball-and-hook to the rocks below.

"Godammit, Nick!" Ben panted, getting a foot through the lifting hook. "Pull up . . . come on . . . come on . . . *aarrrghh*!"

With tremendous effort, the older diver managed to get himself vertical, hugging the cable with his feet on the ball. Ben wrapped an arm around him, standing up in the hook. Nick grimaced, looked at Ben, and smiled. He kept his mouth tightly closed, his lips pressed into a thin line.

Ben gazed back. They were slipping. They had seconds to get off the ball-and-hook together—with some chance of missing the rocks.

"You ready?" he said, feeling strangely calm. "Jump out, that way, with me. Push off the ball. It's heavy enough to give us a little momentum."

Nick nodded, an equal calm in his tired eyes.

Ben found his shoulder, squeezed it. "I'll hold you up," he said. "I'll hold you up, Nick."

He looked down. He could just see the pool through the haze, seething like a nest of white snakes. Klegg's body was gone, washed away. The cable was swinging. Very slightly, but it would help.

"On three," Ben called, squeezing Nick's shoulder again. "One . . ."

The cable pendulumed slowly away from the pool. "Two . . ."

It paused . . . then, gently, traveled back . . . out over the foaming basin . . .

"Three," Ben said, and opened his fingers.

They fell locked together, turning over once in mid-air before disappearing into a billow of mist just above the jagged black rocks. The wet *splat* that followed a split second later was barely audible above the thunderous roar of the falls.

CHAPTER 28

The Goose was coming in fast and low, less than twenty feet off the water, for its upstream landing on the Lower Tiburi. Koko had swung off to the southeast for three miles, banked around, and gone into a steep descent to the northwest, lining the aircraft up with the river. With the wingtips lower than the tree canopy on either bank, they'd followed the waterway for several minutes, banking through bend after bend, until at last the majestic face of the cataract had reappeared a half mile distant.

Sass and Olssen were once again up in the cockpit with Koko, leaning over his shoulder to see out through the forward windscreen. The Kuballan slapped the copilot's seat next to him. "Please sit and belt in for landing, Mr. Olssen. You too, Miss Wojeck. On your foldout seat again. Quickly, please."

They complied, fumbling with straps and buckles. No sooner had Sass secured herself on the tiny stool just behind Olssen than the hull of the flying boat hit the water with a sturdy bump. It hopped back into the air, glided for a few seconds, then bumped down again. Sheets of spray flew out on either side of the cockpit and whirled up into the propellers. Koko switched on the windscreen wipers as water dashed into the forward panels. Keeping the aircraft in the center of the river, he throttled up and began to taxi nose-first into the considerable current.

The cataract and the boiling maelstrom at its base were less than four hundred yards ahead. Motors roaring, the Goose crept forward. The lip of the falls, high above, had almost disappeared behind the windscreen's top edge when Sass cried, "Look!"

The jackup rig was going over. It moved slowly at first, seeming to pivot in place at the top of a 250-foot column of cascading water and mist, then began to tumble forward. The two bow legs rose out of the stream, still unbroken, their mud-mats still attached. The long yellow strut of the crane boom wobbled, swung, and broke back over the main deck.

One of the dragging legs cracked off as the rig cleared the lip, gathering speed. It turned over completely as it fell, plummeting through the haze beside the vertical torrents of water. The event seemed to unfold in slow motion, as if the massive steel structure were *floating* down the cataract's face.

Then it hit the rocks. The barge-shaped hull crumpled like a tin can, folding in two. What was left of the superstructure simply shattered—bulkheads bursting and internal construction materials flying outward. The top section of the remaining leg—nearly sixty feet of thick-walled, three-foot-diameter steel tubing—snapped upward, spinning end over end like a broken twig—and landed a hundred yards off to one side with a *crang-crang-crang* of metal on rock. Tons of water hammered into the ruined hulk from above, exploding into rainbow-tinted curtains of spray.

"Where are they?" Sass cried, nearly frantic, staring at the chaos of white water. "Did they get off the end of the crane cable?"

"I didn't see!" Olssen replied. The lines in his weatherworn face were taut with strain. "They were still on the lifting ball when the mist closed in!" He cursed fluently in Norwegian and leaned close to the pilot, who was fighting to keep the plane properly oriented in the powerful current. "We must get closer, Koko! Men may be coming—"

"There's someone!" Sass shouted, unbuckling her seat belt and jumping up. She pointed through the windscreen. "Black suit—it's *Ben!*"

"Wait!" Olssen exclaimed, reaching back to stop her. "That man looks—"

He was too late. Sass was back at the cabin door, pushing it open, and reaching for the gaff before he could climb out of his seat. He came up behind her as she got the hook over the body, which was floating facedown in the foam.

"*Ben,*" she panted, her voice choked, tears springing to her eyes, "*Ben . . .*"

Olssen rested a hand briefly on her back, then grabbed the handle of the gaff and helped her draw the body in. It bobbed against the fuselage, turned over . . .

Sass screamed and fell back into Olssen. The bloody stub sticking out of the black shirt-collar glistened red in the midday sun—an exploded tomato decorated with bulbous gray brain tissue and a single hanging eye. The Norwegian stared, horrified, then looked away, fighting down the urge to vomit.

"It's not Ben," he shouted, wrapping his arms around Sass. "It's not Ben." He repeated it like a mantra for nearly a minute, until she stopped shaking. "That man was older, too slender to be Ben or Nick. He had thick gray hair on his chest and arms. Black military clothing."

His voice trailed off as he watched the smashed body drift away in the current, spinning slowly. *That was the man with the pistol*, he thought. *Is it possible that Ben and Nick have fared any better?*

He let Sass sit back against the nearest passenger seat, her tear-streaked face white with shock, and secured the gaff. Spray whirled in through the open side door as Koko gunned the engines and maneuvered farther upstream, dangerously close to the rocky cascades near the base of the falls.

Olssen rose to his feet and stepped up to the cockpit door. "We'll have to let ourselves drift back downriver to a place where we can tie off to the bank," he said to Koko. "I'll hike up along the shore and search on foot. We can't leave without checking the rocks and pools right near the cataract."

"Roger, wilco," the pilot replied. "I will be coming with you. There are two carbines in the utility locker behind the second bulkhead."

"So will I," Sass said over Olssen's shoulder, wiping away tears with the back of her hand. The old diver turned, raising an eyebrow. With a tight smile, he nodded.

"By Jove!" Koko erupted suddenly. "Men in the water, dead ahead!"

As one, Olssen and Sass crouched and stared through the windscreen. Two heads were bobbing in the lowest terrace pool of the central cascade. A bare arm came up, waved—and then the pair were washed out of the pool and into a twenty-foot spillway of surging white water. Five long seconds later, the two heads reappeared, drifting through the turbulence toward the Goose.

Koko was already throttling up the engines and maneuvering the plane sideways as Sass and Olssen knelt at the open door and deployed the butt end of the gaff. The propeller turbulence sent spray sheeting into the side of the fuselage and through the doorway, temporarily blinding them. Then the gaff jerked and sagged downstream, pulled by a heavy weight. Working together, Sass and Olssen leaned back and hauled with all their strength.

Ben appeared out of the fog, buffeted by white water, one hand clamped on the end of the gaff. He was holding Nick with his other arm, trying to keep the older diver's head supported. The current twisted him, forcing his own head under the surface. When he bobbed up, sputtering, his eyes locked onto Sass's. *Drowning here*, they said calmly. *Help, please.*

Olssen caught his hand as it slipped off the gaff. "Grab him," he gasped, his sixty-year-old back cracking under the strain. Sass sprawled on her belly beside him, reached down, and wrapped the fingers of both hands around Nick's collar.

"I'll hold him," she panted. "Get Ben up."

"Let go of him, Ben!" Olssen shouted. "Let go!"

Only when he'd twisted sideways and seen that Nick was secure did Ben release him. Then, with a tremendous effort, and with Olssen's assistance, he clutched the edge of the doorway and heaved himself up.

Sliding onto the floor of the passenger cabin, looking considerably less healthy than a drowned rat, he rolled onto his back and went into a coughing fit. "Get—Nick," he managed to say. "Pull—Nick—in . . ."

"We have him," Olssen croaked, hauling for all he was worth. Sass hooked her heels beneath the passenger seat and heaved until her entire body trembled. Nick's head and torso came in on top of her, sodden, filling the doorway . . .

Then he was inside, stretched out on his back on the cabin sole, his eyes closed and his face the color of parchment paper.

Still coughing, Ben slid over to him, raised his head, and cradled it in one elbow. There was a loud bang as Olssen slammed the side door shut, dogged it, and turned toward the cockpit.

"Koko!" he shouted, fighting to regain his own breath. "We've got them! Take off!"

The ultralight had been circling two hundred feet above the Goose for several minutes, Naji and Head observing the rescue action. The Yemeni had climbed into the forward passenger seat to further balance the light plane. Now, as they watched, the flying boat made a sharp turn in the foam-streaked basin, gunned its engines, and accelerated downriver, leaving a brilliant white wake on the murky water.

The Goose lifted into the air and immediately banked off to the northeast over the tree canopy. Naji sat back and clapped his hands, "Success, by Shaitan! We have done it!" He beamed at Head. "They head toward the border, pilot! Shall we follow them home?" He paused, then renewed his smile. "What say you, my brother?"

Head looked at him, his characteristic loopy, open-mouthed grin spreading across his face. "*Dude*," he said, "I'm *touched*."

He banked the ultralight around and settled onto a course that trailed the faster Goose. "They'll beat us to Krumake," he called over the noise of the slipstream. "They've got the horsepower. But it ain't far—maybe two-and-a-half hours in this baby; forty minutes for them." He tapped a console dial. "At least we've got plenty of fuel, my man."

"By the way," Naji shouted, straightening his flying goggles, "what happened to you in that mud pool? And how did you make your way back to the plane without alerting the Leopard Soldiers?"

Head shrugged. "Grabbin' that snake really freaked me out, dude. I musta jumped ten feet in the air. When I hit the mud, I went waaaaayyyy down . . . I mean *deep*."

"I tried to reach you, my brother," Naji interjected, "but I could feel nothing. And then you surfaced on the opposite side of the pool."

The pilot grinned. "I was really down there—I dunno—maybe six feet or more? But thanks for tryin'." He shrugged again. "Anyway, there I was, buried in black ooze, and I thought to myself, 'Headman, dude—you can't fucking *breathe*! This must change *el pronto*!' Can you dig it?"

Naji nodded politely, indicating that he could indeed. He would work out exactly what digging had to do with anything later.

"Well, it took a little floundering around—that shit was *thick*, dude—but I got hold of a tree root and started haulin' my ass out of there." He rolled his eyes and puffed his cheeks. "Never knew my own ass was so heavy. And if there's one thing a person should know in this life, in my humble opinion, it's his own ass."

Naji nodded again, closing his eyes, and smiled with some difficulty. "Yes. Of course."

"Anyway—I came up under a big spread of mangrove roots. Thought I was dead meat—blind, ears plugged, nearly smothered. I musta been down nearly a minute. By that time, you'd booked outta there. These scary black soldier-dudes were running all over the place, so I just stayed put. They were so keen to run *you* down that they didn't notice me. I waited 'til they'd disappeared, then figured, hey—why not go back to the plane? Check out the situation from above, maybe be in a position to help, huh? Took me a while to locate the damn thing, though. I got freakin' lost. Found it just after dawn. When I finally got into the air and up high enough, I spotted the jackup headin' downriver and figured it must be you guys." He laughed. "You know the rest."

Naji shook his head. "Truly, you are a wonderment,

my brother. *Perplexing*, sometimes . . . but still a won-derment." He glanced down as the ultralight's flight path and the course of the river began to diverge. "Look," he shouted, pointing.

Head looked down past the port pontoon. In the center of the river, a body was drifting—a black-clad body without a head, and with only one arm and one leg. All around it in the muddy water were sinuous, wriggling shapes, some nearly twice its length. As Head and Naji watched, one of the shapes darted in, the body jerked—and then there were no arms at all.

The freshwater bull sharks of the Lower Tiburi were feeding.

Nick's eyes fluttered open and focused on Ben, who was still cradling his head. Sass and Olssen had cut back his coveralls and found the source of the blood spreading beneath him on the floor of the passenger cabin—two bullet holes in his right side, punched be-tween his ribs just below the armpit. Amon Klegg's aim had been good.

Sass was working rapidly as she could with gauze and bandages, Olssen trying to keep the blood flow staunched with towels and direct pressure. It was a losing battle.

Nick smiled, and when he parted his lips to speak, a thick gob of blood ran out of the corner of his mouth and down his cheek.

"Ugh," he muttered. "Tastes funny."

"Don't try to talk," Ben said. "We'll be on the ground in a few minutes. Get you to a hospital."

"Oh . . . sure," Nick rasped. "Thanks." His eyes

flickered over to Sass. "Hiya, kid. Lookin' good, as usual."

"Shut up, Nick," Sass said, her hands moving quickly. Her eyes were very bright.

Nick glanced up at Olssen. "Hey there, Berndt. Nice to see ya."

"Nick." Olssen's face was grave, concerned. "You should do as Ben suggested, *ya*? Don't waste your strength talking right now."

"Well, hell," Nick replied, "what's the difference? I never could keep my mouth shut anyway." He fixed his eyes back on Ben's. "Hey, bro."

"Hey," Ben said.

Nick coughed, and a cup of blood erupted over his chin and onto his chest. He gasped for a few seconds, convulsing, then got his breath back.

"You know what I always thought, Ben?" he whispered. "I always thought I'd get rich bein' a big, bad deep-sea diver. Remember what they used to pay us back in the seventies for saturation diving? One thousand dollars a day. In the *seventies*." He coughed again. "Man, that was some real money."

"Sure was," Ben said.

"You know what else I thought?"

"No. What?"

"I always thought that when I kicked the bucket, I wouldn't want to be buried at sea or stuck in a hole in the ground. Thinkin' about all them critters—crabs, worms, and such—gnawin' away at me makes my skin crawl. Thought I'd like to be cremated. Nice and clean—no fuss, no muss."

"Why don't you keep quiet?" Ben said, squeezing Nick's shoulder.

"No, listen. *Listen*. I looked into it. Seems fine, 'cept for one thing. They cremate you in a furnace, in a burning container, like a special steel coffin. Most of you ends up as ashes, but your teeth are left, maybe a few bits of bone. Those get ground up and put in the urn with the rest of you. But you know, I found out— in case you didn't know already—there are sons-abitches everywhere, bro. Some of these funeral parlor assistants—they steal the gold that melts out of your fillings. Can you believe that shit? Like stealing the pennies off a dead man's eyes."

Sass choked, dropped the gauze and bandages, and buried her face in her bloody hands.

Nick grinned, swallowing with difficulty. "I worked hard for my fuckin' fillings. I want every bit of me that goes *into* the burnin' coffin to come *out* of the god-damn burnin' coffin—and go into the urn with my ashes. See?" He coughed blood. "I ain't providin' no *tip* for no funeral assistant."

"Don't you think that's enough crazy talk for now?" Ben asked. It was hard to sound casual with a lump the size of a softball in his throat.

"*No. Listen.*" Nick's hand came up, closed around Ben's biceps. "You owe me, remember? One life. I'll call it even if you do a coupla things for me. *Listen*. I want to be cremated—I don't care where—and I want *all* of me put in an urn, and I don't want my bits and pieces ground up, either. Then I want you to give the urn to Maggie. Tell her I want to be taken to the old live oak on the East Point of Tableau Island—you know the place I mean, back in Louisiana—and sprinkled around the base of the tree. And if she don't want nothin' to do with me"—his rasping voice faltered, and a look of pain unrelated to his wounds came into his eyes—"then I want *you* to do it, bro." He paused, and his hand slipped from Ben's upper arm.

He smiled again, and closed his eyes. "That'd make me happy. East Point . . . where you can see the sun come up. I always liked . . . the start of a new day . . . the beginnin' of something . . . rather than the end . . ."

"Nick," Ben said.

"Feel like . . . I'm . . . drownin,' bro," Nick whispered. "Feel . . . like . . . I'm . . . drownin' . . ."

Ben pulled him closer. "I'll hold you up," he said. "I'll hold you up, Nick."

There was no reply.

"Nick," Ben said.

No reply.

"Nick," Ben said again.

The flying boat's powerful engines droned on.

"Nick . . ."

CHAPTER 29

Maggie Fenzi had been standing on the customs pier with Mr. Kikkononikakka and a host of ambulance attendants as the Goose set down on Krumake harbor. Koko had radioed ahead to his father that the flying boat was returning with injured parties aboard, and in turn the efficient Kuballan had telephoned her at the Hotel Excelsior after alerting the appropriate emergency medical services.

Now she stood alone in her gray business suit—jacket and skirt, freshly pressed—with her arms crossed over her chest, hugging herself. Her hair was perfect, a controlled brunette mane, as was her makeup—maroon lips and nails, and black eyeliner, precisely applied. Her face was expressionless, neutral, and as pale as the white sheet covering her husband's body. The stretcher-bearers had paused in front of her with their burden, waiting as Ben—his bullet-clipped kneecap wrapped in towels and gauze—was loaded into the ambulance first.

Olssen and Sass stood beside the emergency vehicle, watching her. She'd shunned every attempt at sympathy from both of them. When she walked forward on her high heels, her movements were stiff, wooden.

She stopped a few feet from the stretcher, staring down at the wind-ruffled sheet.

"Goddamn you, Nick Fenzi," she said, her voice very clear. "You just never . . . never . . . *ever*"—she paused—"came through for me . . . *did you*?"

She spun on her heel and began to walk away, toward the compound's exit gate.

"Wait, Maggie," Ben called. "Nick wanted you to—"

She whirled.

"*I don't—fucking—CARE!*" she screamed, her eyes blazing. "I'm done with him! Do you fucking *hear* me? *DONE!*"

Under the stunned eyes of Ben, Sass, Olssen, the two Kikkononikakkas, and a dozen medical personnel, she stalked on through the gate of the customs yard, got into a waiting taxi, and was driven off into the narrow streets of the old town.

Ben was released from the local hospital later that day, his lightly chipped kneecap shot full of local anaesthetic, stitched up, and bandaged. Pain pills made him feel a bit thick-brained, but deadened the burn in his knee enough that he could hobble around on a pair of crutches. Now he, Sass, Naji, and Olssen stood at the front door of the street address provided, as per Ben's request, by Mr. Kikkononikakka.

"Where's Head?" Ben asked. "He did a great job for all of us."

"Our brother is at his airstrip," Naji replied. "I believe he is digging something."

Ben started to ask, then decided against it. Instead, he nodded up at the sign over the door of the large, stone-block building. "This is the place. Five o'clock on the nose."

Kikkononikakka & Sons Funeral Services, Limited, the sign read.

Olssen walked up the small flight of stairs and pressed a buzzer. The door opened immediately, and another younger version of the senior Kikkononikakka beamed down at them.

"Good evening, good evening," the tall Kuballan said pleasantly, in excellent English. "I am Julius Kikkononikakka. I am glad that you are here, but am sorry that you *must* be here. My sympathies." He bowed slightly. "We are ready. My partner and brother Erving is in the crematorium, waiting, in accordance with my father's instructions, for you to arrive and witness the procedure."

He stepped aside and beckoned. "Please. Come this way."

CHAPTER 30

It was an odd collection of characters that assembled at Krumake International Airport the following morning—a lithe, blonde woman standing very close to an athletic-looking man on crutches, the leg of his jeans cut open to accommodate a football-sized bandage around his right knee; an impressive-looking Arab dressed in flowing black robes and a *burnoose*, his hawklike, goateed face right out of a tale by Scheherazade; a lanky, long-haired hippie/beach-boy type whose face bore a permanently vacant look, as if he'd just lost his surfboard; a very tall, lean, weather-worn Scandinavian, slightly stooped with age and suffering from what appeared to be a very sore back; and various and sundry ebony-skinned young Kuballans—all of whom bore a striking resemblance to a single older native man wearing a customs official's uniform with wide green epaulets on the shoulders.

"I feeling that I must be letting you know," Mr. Kikkononikakka said, in his customary mangled English, "that Mrs. Fenzi departed for Athens at midnight, en route to London and then New York." He shook his broad head. "Uncivilized time for traveling, by cracky! I being most sorry for that lady, losing husband so tragically. Terrible, terrible."

"Yes, it is," Sass said. "If not for you and your son Koko, there might have been more than one casualty in this little misadventure. Thank you."

"Ahhh!" Mr. Kikkononikakka waved a hand. "No problem, by thunder! No problem at all. Delighted to be of service, yes indeedy!" Beside him, Koko beamed, nodding.

"Well, gang," Head announced, "I'm on my way. Got elephants migrating on the upper plateau, and a French film crew comin' in soon that wants to shoot a wildlife documentary. Gotta go work on the plane."

"Fare well, my brother," Naji said, shaking his hand. "Try to avoid mud pools."

"I can dig it," Head replied. He clapped palms with Ben. "Can't say I enjoyed every minute of it, dude, but it was interesting."

"That it was," Ben said, grinning. "Take care of yourself, Head."

"Gonna try, my man, gonna try." He waved as he shambled away, grinning his openmouthed grin. "Peace and love, people."

They all lifted their hands in return, watching him go, and a moment later Jefferson Deadhead Jones walked out through the tinted glass doors of the terminal building, into the bright Kuballan sunshine, and disappeared.

"Your flight for Djibouti is leaving in ten minutes," Ben said to Naji. "You don't want to be late."

He and the lean desert tribesman locked forearms. "Allah carry you and Sasha safely home, *Ben-Ya-Min*,"

Naji said. "I will think of you often." He grinned. "And you will seek out your brother Naji will you not, when life becomes too comfortable to endure? We will have another adventure, perhaps, if Allah wills it!"

"I'll come before that, Naji," Ben replied. "You can count on it."

Naji took Sass's hand, kissed it, and turned to Ben once more. "I must pray soon. Which way is Mecca, my brother?"

Ben smiled, thought a moment, then extended his hand. "'Bout like that."

Naji smiled back. "Allah keep you." Then he turned and walked away, his black robes flowing around him.

"That man," Sass commented softly, "is one in a million."

Ben took her hand. "That he is," he said.

He turned to Olssen, with whom Sass and he would share a connecting flight as far as Amsterdam. "About twenty minutes before we board, huh, Berndt? We can talk some more on the plane. Catch up a bit since the North Sea days."

"*Ya*," the old Norwegian diver said. "It will be nice to talk." He looked a bit downcast.

"I'm sorry about the jackup," Ben said. "Sass told me about the money problems this whole Bisotho contract has caused you."

"Ah, well," Olssen said, smiling, "that's life, eh? You hardly intended for the rig to go over the falls. You were damned lucky to get out of there alive." He sighed. "It is a pity, though. Six diamonds like the one I still have would have saved my business. But at least

I have the one. I will sell it to my Swiss jeweler and get some living money."

Sass touched his hand. "I'm so sorry, Berndt. I mean it. You deserve better."

"Agh!" Olssen grinned at her. "Think what trouble most of us would be in if we all got what we *really* deserved, eh?" He laughed.

Ben held out his hand to Mr. Kikkononikakka. "My thanks to you and your sons for everything, sir. I don't know what we would have done without your help. If there's ever anything I can do for you . . ."

Again, the jovial Kuballan waved such talk away, pumping Ben's hand. "It was nothing, nothing! But perhaps, maybe in future, if Kikkononikakka and Sons decide to expand business enterprises into United States—perhaps—I might call for advice and names of best restaurants, by Jove and Jehosephat! Ha-ha!"

Ben couldn't help grinning—the man's good nature was irresistible. "I'll be back from the States in about eight weeks. Thank you for continuing to look after my boat until then. I'll be in touch."

"Very good, very good! My pleasure, don't you know?" Mr. Kikkononikakka raised his hand. "Goodbye for now! Goodbye!"

"Goodbye!" chorused his mob of sons, and he and they turned and moved off down the terminal toward the main exit.

Several P.A. announcements in Kuballan and English echoed through the building's airy interior. Ben, Sass, and Olssen stood listening for a few moments as travelers shuttled past them in both directions, coming and going.

"Well, that's us," Olssen said. "Our flight is boarding now. Shall we?" He looked from Ben to Sass.

"Let's go," Ben replied, shifting on his crutches and adjusting the carry-on bag that hung over his shoulder. "Got everything?"

"*Ya*, I believe so," Olssen said, nodding. "Sasha?"

"I've got my load," she puffed, lifting a couple of small suitcases. "They'll stow under the seats and in the overhead, if I shove hard."

As they moved off toward the departure gates, Sass turned to Ben, who was hobbling along on his crutches with only a little difficulty.

"Have you got Nick?" she asked quietly.

He glanced at her, smiled, and patted his carry-on bag.

"Yeah," he said. "Nick's with me."

EPILOGUE

In the three weeks since they'd returned to the United States, Ben's knee had improved rapidly. Sass had decreed that he would stay off his feet, period, until he was able to bear weight on the injured leg without crutches, and enforced her edict with disapproving stares, good humor, and an abundance of delectable home cooking. As a result, convalescing in the spacious second-story owner's apartment above the restaurant of Wojeck's Marina, the Florida Panhandle business that Sass had inherited from her father, Ben had put on five pounds. It felt more like twenty-five. In addition, over the past week, he had started to develop a bad case of cabin fever.

His restlessness had prompted the phone call he was making now. Sass was curled up on the far end of the sofa, sipping coffee, watching him gaze out through the apartment's big picture window—past the dangling needles of the long-leaf pines that stood near the restaurant, past the forest of masts that jutted up from the marina's numerous boat slips, and out over the sparkling blue waters of the Gulf of Mexico. He sat in silence, his expression solemn, listening to Maggie Fenzi talk.

It was not a long call. Nor was it a two-way conversation. In under two minutes, he took the cordless phone from his ear without saying goodbye, pushed the disconnect button, and set the unit down on the sofa beside him. Then he sighed, tipped his head back, and rubbed his eyes.

"What'd she say?" Sass inquired gently.

Ben gave her a resigned smile. "It went something like this: 'I don't want *anything* to do with Nick. I don't care about his last *wishes*, I don't care what he said to *you*'—meaning me—'and I sure as fucking hell don't want to scatter his goddamn *ashes* for him and risk ruining a perfectly good dress! The son of a bitch left me without a penny at age fifty—so *fuck him* and the horse he rode in on! Goodbye!'" Ben blew out a long, tired breath. "Then there was a loud click."

Sass was silent for a moment. "Did she even thank you for what you did?" she asked finally.

"No," Ben said.

He looked over at the coffee-can-sized brass urn—a beautifully etched container adorned with African lacquered designs—sitting on the mantel above the small fireplace.

"Guess we'll have to take care of Nick ourselves." He looked back at Sass. "Five hours to the coast south of New Orleans on I-10. It's a nice day. Feel like a drive?"

The traffic was light all the way, even on the 610 bypass through Metairie along the southern shore of Lake Ponchartrain. It was another hour from New Orleans, through tiny bayou oil-field towns with names like Theriot, Dulac, Chauvin, and Montegut, to the tiny coastal wilderness preserve known as Tableau Island. Linked to the mainland by a two-hundred-foot wooden bridge that spanned the intervening channel, it was rarely visited. The road dead-ended at the small gravel parking lot in the center of the island, which was less than two miles long from end to end. Theirs was the only vehicle.

"Came here with Nick once to shoot ducks," Ben said, getting out of the car gingerly. He steadied himself on the aluminum cane he had recently begun using as a walking aid. "The state used to open a short season in the fall, a few years back."

"Get any?" Sass asked, smiling, as she shut her door.

"Yeah. We slayed 'em. And a bottle of tequila, too." Ben shook his head and laughed. "Talk about a recipe for disaster. Two moron oil-field divers, a fifth of booze, and a rack of loaded firearms. Good thing we were the only hunters around that day—the worst we could have done was shoot each other." His expression saddened momentarily. "It was a fine time, though. A fine time."

"Yeah, babe," Sass said, taking his arm. "I bet it was."

They walked through the long-leaf pines, over the low gray dunes crowned with golden stands of wind-rippled sea oats, and out onto the flat, sandy beach. The Gulf waters that lapped the shore were not emerald-clear like those in the Florida Panhandle, nor was the sand the same quartzlike white. Here, the effluent of the Mississippi and Atchafalaya rivers stained the Gulf of

Mexico a pale, muddy brown, and imparted the same organic color to the sand and sediment of the beaches.

It was beautiful, though, in its own way. Ben had always thought so, from the moment he'd first set eyes on the coastal bayou country, years earlier, as a young diver new to Louisiana's offshore oil fields. It was a place of black mangroves, white egrets, brown pelicans, and redfish; silver mullet and verdant green cypress trees; fast-diving ospreys and high-flying gulls. A natural place.

It took only ten minutes, despite Ben's slow pace, for them to reach Tableau Island's East Point. Somehow, a live oak had taken root there and grown huge, surviving winter gales and summer hurricanes to become incredibly gnarled and thick-limbed—the last tree on that end of the islet.

They walked up to it and stood beneath its low, sprawling branches. "Right about here, I guess," Ben said. He turned and looked out over the water to the east. "He'll be able to see the sun come up."

Sass handed him the urn. "What do we say?" she asked, and suddenly there were two big tears sliding down her cheeks.

Ben reached out a finger and wiped them away. "I think we say 'Goodbye, Nick. Rest easy.'" He smiled. "And 'See you later.'"

He opened the urn, knelt carefully, and began to sprinkle Nick's ashes around the roots of the old tree. The wind seemed to cooperate, respectfully dying down to a gentle breeze. As the canister emptied, Ben tipped it all the way up.

The remaining contents fell out. Ben dropped the

urn and sat back on his heels. He and Sass stared down at the ash-strewn ground.

Before them lay thirty or so blackened human teeth. A few chunks of charred bone. Several small, irregular droplets of gold. Two other droplets that appeared to be lead. And thirteen large brown pebbles that looked like dried, rotten peanuts.

Slowly, Ben leaned over and began to separate the items with his forefinger.

"Nick's teeth," he said. "And some bone. He didn't want them ground up, remember? The gold from his fillings." He paused at the gray-colored droplets for a moment. "The lead from the bullets that killed him. And—if what Berndt told us is correct—thirteen large, high-grade alluvial diamonds."

Sass dropped to her knees beside him. "They're worth a small fortune. But how—"

Ben grinned, shaking his head. "He must have swallowed them, the same way he hid the satellite up-link unit from the Leopard Soldiers. The same way he used to swallow whole hard-boiled eggs in bars to win bets. When he realized he might not get off the jackup with a sack of them, he swallowed as many as he could. The whole time we were escaping down the river, he was complaining about his stomach—said it was the food they gave him in the prison pit." Ben chuckled. "It wasn't the food. He had a belly full of diamonds."

"He was trying to give them to Maggie," Sass whispered. "He did it for her."

"But he wanted her to stand by him one more time," Ben said. "To do what we're doing right now."

They fell silent, kneeling beside each other, certain of Nick's intentions, but unsure of how to proceed. Above them, the twisted branches of the ancient oak tree creaked as the wind picked up, whirling some of the ashes into the air. There was a smell of rain; a squall was moving in off the Gulf.

Ben closed his eyes, feeling the breeze. After a minute or so, he opened them. "Okay, Nick," he said, and bent back over the little pile of diamonds.

"One for you," he said to Sass, separating a pebble. "One for me. One for Naji. One for Head. One, two, three, four, five for Berndt. One for Koko. One for Mr. Kikkononikakka . . ."

He sat up. There were two left in the original pile.

"Maggie?" Sass asked.

Ben looked at her. From offshore, there came a faint rumbling of thunder.

"It's not raining yet," he said. "Let me think about it."

ACKNOWLEDGMENTS

Many thanks to my agent and friend, Jimmy Vines
And
My editor, Doug Grad.

Additional thanks to Joe Pittman
And
Larry Bragg, Rick Ford, and Mike Smith.

ONYX

Realistic deep-sea diving adventure
written by an experienced commercial diver.

JOHN McKINNA

❑ ***TIGER REEF*** 0-451-40919-1 / $6.99
Ben Gannon and his girlfriend have sailed across the
Pacific for a restful vacation before he reports to work
at his next deep-sea diving job. But when they witness a
freighter under attack from machine-gun-toting pirates,
they find their lives in peril.

❑ ***CRASH DIVE*** 0-451-40885-3 / $6.99
Commercial deep-sea diver Ben Gannon has been
assigned to retrieve the bodies from a helicopter crash
in the Gulf of Mexico. Instead he discovers the bullet-
ridden bodies of the 'crash' victims, but someone
doesn't want the public to find out.... And very soon
he is forced to take matters into his own hands.